Books by Alyssa Maxwell

Gilded Newport Mysteries
MURDER AT THE BREAKERS
MURDER AT MARBLE HOUSE
MURDER AT BEECHWOOD
MURDER AT ROUGH POINT
MURDER AT CHATEAU SUR MER
MURDER AT OCHRE COURT
MURDER AT CROSSWAYS

Lady and Lady's Maid Mysteries
MURDER MOST MALICIOUS
A PINCH OF POISON
A DEVIOUS DEATH
A MURDEROUS MARRIAGE
A SILENT STABBING

Published by Kensington Publishing Corporation

A MURDEROUS MARRIAGE

ALYSSA MAXWELL

KENSINGTON BOOKS
http://www.kensingtonbooks.com

*To Joan Hammond, friend and mentor,
who shared my love of tea, history, and all things British.
Your encouragement through the years meant
the world to me.
You are sorely missed, my friend!*

ACKNOWLEDGMENTS

Many thanks to everyone at Kensington, most especially my editor, John Scognamiglio, for their continued support of this series!

I'm also very grateful to my fellow Sleuths in Time authors: Anna Loan-Wilsey, Meg Mims, Sharon Pisacreta, Victoria Thompson, Nancy Herriman, Ashley Weaver, Susanna Calkins, Jessie Crockett, and Radha Vatsal for their support, their generosity, and most of all their friendship!

A Murderous Marriage

CHAPTER 1

Cowes, Isle of Wight, April 1920

Phoebe Renshaw pressed a hand to her stomach in a futile attempt to ease the incessant gnawing inside. At a stern look from the countess, her grandmother, she remembered she shouldn't set so much as a finger against her frock, lest she wrinkle the ivory silk organza and ruin the effect of the folds and tucks and artful draping. Despite Phoebe turning twenty-one on her next birthday, her grandmother still had the ability to command her behavior with a twitch of a silvery crescent eyebrow.

Her sister, sixteen-year-old Amelia, wore the same frock, and they sported matching cloche hats covered in organza, lace, and coral silk roses, which seemed rather much for Phoebe's plain features but on Amelia looked a picture of springtime beauty, as if she had stepped off the cover of the latest edition of *La Mode*. Yet Amelia's features mirrored Phoebe's own ominous sentiments, which continued to tie her stomach into impossible knots.

Phoebe braved a glance at Eva, hoping Grams didn't notice. The lady's maid who had served the Renshaw sisters these past eight years had eschewed her dependable black today in favor of a deep blue, neatly tailored suit that accented her trim figure and whose pleated skirt swayed smartly just below her calves. Eva's gaze collided with Phoebe's for the barest instant, but that instant told all. Eva's expression loomed as overcast as the sky outside, as steely as the choppy waters of the Solent, that wide waterway between the Isle of Wight and the mainland, spread out before the Royal Yacht Squadron clubhouse. They had borrowed a room on the upper floor, in which to ready themselves for the coming ordeal. . . .

The irony that the original tower of this building had been commissioned by Henry VIII was not lost on Phoebe. Cowes Castle hadn't been a home to kings, but rather a fortress commanding the Solent and the entrance to the river Medina to keep out invaders from France and the Holy Roman Empire. This had been intended as a place of war, and its connection to that particular monarch seemed terribly ill omened. Six wives, two of whom met horrible ends . . .

Phoebe tried to shake the morbid thoughts away. What right had she to judge Julia's actions, much less whether those actions would bring her beautiful eldest sister happiness?

"Phoebe, come here and help with this." Grams flicked a slender, long-fingered hand impatiently. Unlike Eva, Grams had adhered to basic black, her wardrobe having varied little since Papa died, though today her mourning was softened by the sheen of silk trimmed with deep lavender velvet.

Grams was determined that the next few hours would take place with smooth precision, and for a moment resentment rose up in Phoebe. Julia wouldn't be doing this if not for Grams. An ember burned against Phoebe's heart, and the words she'd tamped down last night and all morning threatened to leap, flaming, from her tongue.

It felt awful to be so angry with someone you loved so much.

Grams beckoned again with a jerky motion of her hand. Yes, even she was feeling her nerves today, though for entirely different reasons than the rest of them. And Julia?

Phoebe didn't know what she was feeling. They had enjoyed a brief few months last year of getting along as sisters should. Then everything had changed, and Julia's manner had returned to the cool disregard of previously. And her admitting—*finally*—the reason for her derision hadn't helped. If anything, it had made matters worse, for Julia seemed to go out of her way to avoid Phoebe, or at least avoid being alone with her.

She crossed the room to the small circle gathered around her sister and gingerly grasped the edges of the lace veil while Eva and Hetta, Julia's new maid, secured it to the platinum-and-diamond circlet that embraced her golden, upswept hair. While the circlet had been in the Renshaw family for many generations, the veil had been Grams's mother's, the Honiton lace made in Devon and designed by the same William Dyce who designed the lace for Queen Victoria's wedding gown. But that was the only harkening back to a bygone age. Julia's dress, a sleek garment of ivory satin with an overlay of beaded lace, a drop waist, and whisper-sheer sleeves, represented the very latest in bridal fashion. Phoebe's and Amelia's frocks had been designed to complement, but not overshadow, Julia's.

Julia didn't speak as they fussed around her, but gazed placidly out the wide window overlooking the Solent. In the middle of the harbor, a steamer yacht weathered the tossing waters with barely a wobble. Even from here, it appeared a small ocean liner, with its stacks and masts and tiered decks. And yet how grim a scene it made, Phoebe thought. Though newly refurbished after its service during the war, the vessel took on the dismal pallor of the sky and the waterway surrounding it and made no promise of happy sailing. Another omen? Phoebe wondered how Julia felt about spending her honeymoon on the twelve-hundred-ton, three-masted steamer named *Georgiana*, after her soon-to-be husband's first wife.

"There now." Grams smoothed her fingertips down Julia's sleeves and stepped back with a satisfied, if slightly cunning, smile. "Let's have a look at you. Oh, Julia, you're stunning."

"You are, Julia, truly," Amelia agreed. Phoebe heard her frail attempt to infuse the comment with enthusiasm. "Just beautiful."

Eva nodded her concurrence. "Indeed, my lady. There can never have been a lovelier bride."

"Oh, *ja*." Hetta Brauer had been Julia's personal maid for several months now, but her English remained barely existent. Julia preferred it that way after discovering her last lady's maid eavesdropping and selling secrets to the scandal sheets. A sturdy, good-natured girl with a hearty flush to her cheeks and thick blond braids she wore looped about her ears, she looked as though she might have been plucked only that morning from a flower-carpeted mountainside in her native Switzerland. "*Lieblich.*"

While the others gushed their approval, Phoebe struggled for words but found none she could, in good conscience, speak. Yes, Julia looked beautiful, but then with her golden hair, deep blue eyes, and classic features, she always did. That wasn't the point.

Phoebe merely smiled and hoped the gesture appeared sincere.

"Thank you," Julia said simply.

Grams made another adjustment to the veil. "A shame he's

only a viscount. I had hoped for an earl at the least, perhaps a marquess. But, of course, Gil is a very *wealthy* viscount. You'll have a good life, my dear."

While the fortunes of many of the landed families had dwindled in recent years, Gil's had burgeoned, thanks to early investments in motorcar engines. During the war his factories had produced munitions and aeroplane engines, and he continued with the latter in peacetime. No one could accuse Gil Townsend of not taking advantage of opportunities when he saw them.

"Yes." A little tick contracted the skin around Julia's right eye. "And, after all, I had my chance at a marquess, Grams, and look how that turned out."

Grams pursed her lips tightly and said nothing. True, Julia had very nearly become engaged to Henry Leighton, Marquess of Allerton, the Christmas before last. That is, everyone had *believed* they were about to become engaged—all except Julia, who'd had other ideas. It turned out Julia had been right, but it was all a moot point now, anyway. Henry was no longer Marquess of Allerton. Henry was simply . . . no longer.

"What time is it?" Julia averted her face when Grams tried to adjust a pin curl framing her cheek. "Is it time to go yet?"

Eva consulted a porcelain clock ticking pleasantly on a nearby table. "Not just yet, my lady."

Julia frowned. "Then I'm ready too early. I can't very well sit and make myself comfortable until we leave."

"Don't you *dare* sit." Grams darted a scandalized glance at each sister. "None of you may sit, not even for a moment. I won't have you looking like wilted washerwomen. Eva, would you please watch for the cars and let us know when they arrive?"

Eva nodded and slipped out of the room.

"Oh, dear, how are you all going to ride in your grandfather's motorcar without wrinkling? I hadn't thought about that." Grams's expression registered something approaching horror. "What shall we do? Good *heavens* . . . Oh, I know. We could all walk up to the church."

"Arrive at my wedding on foot? Are we peasants now?" Julia aped Grams's scandalized look of a moment ago. "Shall I take off my shoes and stockings and go barefoot?"

"Oh, Julia, don't be ridiculous. I simply don't want you to wrinkle."

Julia tossed her head, but only slightly so as not to dislodge her headpiece and veil. "What would people think? No, I'm going in the Rolls-Royce, and there's an end to it."

A storm gathered between Grams's brows, and she looked about to retort. She wasn't used to being spoken to in such adamant terms by her granddaughters. By anyone, for that matter. But in this instance, she obviously agreed with Julia. An earl's granddaughter surely could not arrive at her wedding on foot. "Yes, yes, well, I suppose your grandfather mustn't walk even a short distance these days. You girls will go in his motor, and he and I, along with Fox, will ride in Gil's sedan."

This reminder of Grampapa's health sent a cold fear through Phoebe. He had suffered chest pains last summer, a symptom of his ongoing heart condition. He seemed thinner of late, paler, his zest for life on the wane. . . .

"You must try not to sit too . . ." Grams was saying. She paused, searching for words. "Rigidly."

"Perhaps you should lay us out on the seat and stack us one on the other," Julia muttered under her breath. Luckily, Grams appeared not to have heard.

Amelia went to her and sweetly said, "We'll try our best, Grams."

Grams nodded and looked about her, as if searching for something. "I'm going down to telephone the church and make sure everything there is ready. And then I'm going to make sure Fox hasn't gotten up to any of his usual nonsense." Grams left Phoebe and Amelia alone with their sister, except for Hetta, of course, but she apparently understood little of what they said.

Julia strolled to the window, her short train swishing across the area rug. A sigh came from deep within her. "Well. It won't be long now."

Phoebe had promised herself she wouldn't do this, but at the eleventh hour, she simply couldn't help herself. She practically launched herself at her sister, knowing she might have only moments before Grams returned. "Julia, are you certain—quite certain about this?"

Julia didn't bother looking around. "What are you talking about?"

"It's not too late to change your mind."

Julia chuckled. "Tell that to the church full of people and the caterer who is even now setting up the buffet on Gil's steamer."

"Never mind that. Gil is almost forty years older than you. Julia, *think*. What you do today will affect the rest of your life."

"The rest of Gil's life, perhaps."

"And what about Theo? You know you—"

Julia turned to Phoebe, her dark blue eyes sparking. "Forget about Theo. I have. A marriage between us would never work. Grams would never . . ." She let the thought go unfinished.

"No, perhaps Grams wouldn't, but isn't it time you stopped worrying about what Grams wants and do what *you* want?" The words stung of betrayal to her grandmother, for all they were justified. "This is your life, Julia. Your *life*."

"I'm marrying Gil, and there's an end to it." The same words she'd spoken to Grams about riding to church in the Rolls-Royce.

Unlike Grams, Phoebe wouldn't be put off so easily, not about this.

Light footsteps brought Amelia to Julia's other side. "Theo loves you, Julia, and you love him," she said. "Isn't that what marriage is? Gilbert Townsend is a good enough man, I suppose, but can you truly say you love him, enough to tie yourself to him for the rest of your life?"

The door opened, and Phoebe spun around, expecting to see her grandmother. But it was only a waitress, come to deliver more refreshments. Didn't she know Grams would have an apoplexy if she caught them eating in these clothes before the wedding?

"The rest of *Gil's* life," Julia said yet again in reply to Amelia's question. "He's much older than I, as you've both already pointed out countless times. He'll be gone soon enough, and then I may do as I please."

Phoebe whispered a caution. "Julia." With a flick of her gaze, she indicated the waitress setting down her tray on the low table near the sofa.

Julia remained oblivious to their audience. "If I can present him with a son before he goes, so much the better for me. Our child will inherit, and my place as Viscountess Annondale will be firmly established, and my fortune fixed for life."

"Julia!" Amelia whisked a hand to her mouth, her eyes round and filled with the same dismay that raised the gorge in Phoebe's throat.

"You don't mean this," Phoebe said, almost pleading. "You don't have to do this. You—"

The door opened again, this time marking Eva's return. She stopped short and stared across the room at them, no doubt sensing the strangling tension. Julia seemed not to notice her arrival as she spun fully around to face both Phoebe and Amelia. She reached out and seized Phoebe's wrist.

"You listen to me and listen well. Grams didn't want me to tell you this. She said you'd each learn in your own good time. But it's high time you both knew the truth. Our family is no longer what it was. The money is dwindling. If each of us doesn't marry well, Fox won't be able to support us. He won't be able to maintain the estate. We'll lose everything."

Julia spoke of their youngest sibling, fifteen-year-old Fletcher, whom everyone referred to as Fox or Foxwood—the estate he would one day inherit from their grandfather. Reminding Fox of his future inheritance and responsibilities had been a way to help him cope with losing his father in the war and having to grow up too quickly, and to prompt him to a better understanding of the role he'd one day assume—not that it had done much good. Fox remained an impertinent child who reveled in tormenting his sisters behind their grandparents' backs.

But the thought of Fox inheriting an empty title, a bankrupt estate . . . Surely Julia couldn't mean things were *that* bad. Phoebe understood that no family had emerged from the war quite as wealthy as they had been, and she knew Grams worried about that, but . . . She shook her head, unable to absorb Julia's claim. "I know the war and the death duties—"

"It's not just the war. It's everything. Most especially how far agricultural prices have fallen in the past couple of decades. Foxwood Hall doesn't support itself any longer and hasn't for some time now. We're slowly losing it. We certainly will if we girls don't do our duty."

"I know why you're doing this," Amelia whispered. Her eyes misted, and her shoulders shook beneath her ruched cap sleeves. "It's *because* you love Theo, isn't it? You think Gil will die soon, and then you can marry Theo and be happy. But, Julia, what if it doesn't work out that way?"

Julia pressed her face close to Amelia's and said in a voice she never used with her youngest sister, "Don't you dare ever say that again, to anyone. You don't know what you're talking about."

The door opened again, and this time Grams called out to them. "What are you lot doing huddled by the window? Come along. The motorcars are here. It's time to go. Amelia, are you crying? My dear, sweet child, I know you're over-joyed for your sister, but you don't wish to arrive at the church all blotchy-faced."

Phoebe and her sisters grabbed their wraps and filed from the room. Eva leveled a look of sympathetic support on Phoebe and touched her arm as she passed by. The waitress, still standing by the sofa table, also watched them go. Good heavens, Phoebe had forgotten about her, while the woman had simply stood there eavesdropping and enjoying a good bit of family drama. Well, no matter. She could gossip with her fellow servants all she liked. The Renshaws would never see her again.

Outside, she, Julia, and Amelia accepted a footman's help and slid carefully into the backseat of Grampapa's Rolls-Royce. Her grandparents were driven to the church in Gil's Mercedes-Knight tourer. The short ride along the Esplanade and up the hill to Holy Trinity Church seemed to take forever but was over all too soon.

Eva caught Phoebe's surprise as her gaze lit on the wait-ress. Eva had passed the waitress minutes earlier on the stairs, and the tray she had been carrying now sat on the sofa table. Had she been here all this time? When Eva her-self had returned only moments ago, the looks on her ladies' faces had told her all had not been well in her ab-sence. Words had been spoken, and wills tested. Obvi-ously, Phoebe had felt compelled to try one last time . . . and obviously, she must not have realized they had an audience. Or perhaps Julia, in defending her decision to marry the viscount, would not be silenced.

The waitress, about Phoebe's or Julia's age, wouldn't return Eva's gaze but leaned over to retrieve the tray. On the far side of the room, where two screens had provided privacy for the sisters to change into their wedding finery, Hetta hummed a vague tune as she gathered up their discarded clothing.

Eva's stride swallowed the distance between her and the waitress. "What are you doing?"

The woman assumed a moue of false innocence. "I brought the family tea and cakes, not that they made time for them."

"Yes, I see the tray. And I know when you delivered it, as I had to make way for you on the stairs. My question is, Why are you still here?"

"Oh, I . . . I remained to see if I could be of service."

Eva sized her up, from the top of her linen cap to her starched apron and the tips of her sturdy black boots. The woman's brown eyes darted nervously, and her hands tightened on the handles of the tray. "I think not," Eva concluded. "Heed me well. If you value your position here or anywhere, you'll not go telling tales. Whatever you might have heard here today is none of your business. Understand me? None."

Indeed not, and one might argue it was none of Eva's business, either. But her ladies, her *girls*, mattered more to her than anything else—more than her own affairs, at least for the present. They needed her, even Julia, the eldest. Sometimes *especially* Julia. And Eva needed them . . . to be happy.

"Remember," she whispered fiercely, "if the slightest breath of scandal arises in this town, I'll know where it originated, and I will not hesitate to speak to your employer."

The woman eyed Eva up and down in return, obviously perplexed by her warning and confused by her appearance. In her "Sunday best," Eva looked neither like one of the family nor one of their servants. In the end, the woman curtsied and scurried away with her burden of unconsumed tea and cakes.

Hetta, her arms draped with various items of clothing, came to stand beside Eva and watched as the waitress disappeared into the hallway. "A problem, *ja?*"

"Nothing we can't handle. Are you coming to the church?"

Hetta grinned and shrugged, reminding Eva of her limited command of English. Quickly, they packed away the clothing, and then the two of them made their way downstairs and outside through a service door. Arm in arm— for, despite their inability to communicate, Eva quite liked Hetta, and she believed Hetta returned her regard—they made the short climb up the hill and across Queen's Road to Holy Trinity Church, to arrive before the bridal party began their walk down the aisle.

Eva regarded Holy Trinity's tall Gothic windows, pinnacled buttresses, and crenellated tower. The buff coloring of the stonework reminded her of home, of the creamy Cotswold stone visible everywhere in the village of Little Barlow and the surrounding region. Had she not been so troubled by the event about to take place, she would have been amused at how taken aback Lady Julia had been at the idea of arriving to her wedding on foot. The trek from the Royal Yacht Squadron took no more than a few minutes, although admittedly, the blustery winds trundling off the Solent would have ruined her ladies' hair and possibly snatched Lady Julia's veil away.

Like the Royal Yacht Squadron clubhouse, the church overlooked the Solent, but from a higher vantage point, from where the New Forest on the mainland was often visible. Not today, though. Heavy, lumbering clouds afforded only a limited view of the harbor. Lord Annondale's *Georgiana* rocked sullenly on the waves, while smaller moored vessels, and even a few hearty souls willing to risk sailing through the currents, tipped and bobbed.

The church door stood open, and Eva and Hetta slipped into the very last pew. A relatively small number of guests filled the first several pews in the front. This soon after the war, a large and elaborate wedding would have been frowned upon. Millions of lives had been lost; millions more were still displaced, struggling and rebuilding. England hadn't fully healed, might never fully heal.

Besides, the groom had wanted a small wedding. Actually, according to Lady Julia, he had wished to elope, but her grandmother, the Countess of Wroxly, wouldn't hear of it. Eva had gotten the distinct impression Lady Julia hadn't wanted anything extravagant, either. She had seemed, these past weeks of her engagement, intent on getting on with it as simply and efficiently as possible. The normally demanding young woman had been all too complacent with her grandmother's wishes, from the guest list to the menu and everything in between. As if this wedding weren't really Lady Julia's, as if she were only an observer, and an indifferent one at that.

Eva studied the pale flowers festooning the altar and the chancel railing, and the netted ivory bunting strewn from pew to pew down both sides of the center aisle. Though these colors were meant to complement Lady Julia's wedding gown, Eva found them washed out, devoid of life. Her heart ached. A year from now, would Lady Julia resemble those faded blossoms?

The sounds of arriving motorcars set the church in motion. The vicar strolled out to his place on the altar, while, through a door opposite, an elderly man hobbled with the use of a cane, his right leg dragging with a telltale squeak from the prosthetic he wore. A dove-gray morning coat and black trousers spoke of a once-trim figure gone slack. Indeed, the Viscount Annondale's features still showed traces of a once-square chin, a strong nose, and a broad brow, but they had faded beneath age lines and sagging skin.

Julia, *beautiful*, young, vibrant Julia, would soon be this man's wife, would spend untold years in his bleak shadow. Oh, Eva knew people married for many reasons, and physical appearance, even physical condition, shouldn't matter . . . but . . .

This was *her* Julia, and it hurt to consider the future she faced.

Behind the viscount came another gentleman of a similar age and similarly dressed, but who walked without aid and with a still-youthful bounce in his step. A man of considerable height, especially beside his friend, he sported a tightly trimmed goatee and a clean-shaven head, which gleamed in the candlelight of the altar. She knew him to be Sir Hugh Fitzallen, the viscount's closest friend and best man. Once he took up his position beside his friend, they exchanged a few words. Viscount Annondale tapped his cane against the flagstones, as if impatient to get on with it.

Several chords were struck upon the organ, and a small commotion could be heard from the vestibule. Eva turned her head as young Fox entered with Lady Wroxly on his arm. Despite having turned fifteen not long ago, he stood a few inches shorter than she, though not with as marked a difference in height as a year ago.

The organ swelled in volume, and Eva's heart swelled in kind. Her throat throbbed and her eyes stung so badly, she only vaguely acknowledged the small procession coming down the aisle. That was, until Julia, on her grandfather's arm, stopped as though she had suddenly come up against a barrier. Her head turned, and she stared. Eva followed her gaze to the back of a dark head about halfway down the nave. The gentleman sat alone, having the entire pew to himself. He did not return Julia's glance, though by the stiffening of his shoulders, Eva believed he was very much aware of her.

No more than a second or two passed. Had the others noticed? Perhaps not, or perhaps they thought Julia's hem had caught beneath her shoe. But Eva didn't have to be told why she had stopped or at whom she had stared. Theo Leighton, the new Marquess of Allerton, had apparently decided to attend the wedding.

When the ceremony ended and the Renshaws and the Townsends formed their receiving line outside the church, Eva remained inside to say a little prayer for the couple's future. Soon Hetta stood to squeeze past her in the pew, holding her hands up in front of her face and saying, "Snap-snap."

"Oh, yes. The photographs."

She and Hetta hurried outside through a side door in the vestibule in time to watch the photographer herd the bridal party beneath a cherry tree's pale green leaves and pink blossoms. A hawthorn hedge was also in bloom and spread its branches behind them. A camera sat mounted on a tripod, ready to capture the images. Eva nodded in appreciation; the soft colors would make a beautiful back-drop for the photographs. A pity the sun showed no signs of making an appearance.

Hetta went to work straightening Lady Julia's gown and train and making sure her veil flowed just so over her shoulders. Eva patted curls into place and straightened sashes for Ladies Phoebe and Amelia, while Lady Wroxly's maid, the often dour-faced Miss Shea, applied a bit of powder to the countess's nose.

"All right, ladies, that's quite enough. Let's get on with it." Viscount Annondale thumped his cane against the grass. When the countess shot him a reproving look, he softened his stance with a grin and jokingly appealed to Lord Wroxly. "I say, Archibald, they're already as lovely as any four women have a right to be. Wouldn't you agree?" "Er . . . yes, quite right. Quite right indeed." Lord Wroxly's hesitation was not because he disagreed with the viscount's assessment; Eva was quite sure he concurred wholeheartedly.

His lordship had lost weight in recent months. More than that, he had shed pounds like rainwater off a peaked roof. Someone meeting him for the first time might think him fit and trim, if only the transformation had been accompanied by a robust complexion and energy to match. His heart had caused him grief last summer, and despite the countess ensuring he followed his doctor's orders to the letter, he had not been quite the same since. And now this wedding. He had yet to smile fully today, and his eyes were filled with worry and weariness.

The photographer, a good-looking young man with curly black hair who towered above the others in his ill-fitting suit, stepped up to his Seneca Competitor folding camera and peered through the viewfinder. He made several adjustments to the lens. Then he glanced up, frowning, and studied the group gathered beneath the hanging cherry blossoms. He walked to them and gently nudged some to the right and others to the left of Julia and her new husband. He took extra time positioning Julia at just the right angle, briefly touching her shoulder, her waist, her chin, to capture, he said, the right light.

He took several group shots, rearranging the party several times. Then he took only Julia, her sisters, and the countess. Each time, Eva noted, he took his time positioning Julia just so, experimenting with the shadows cast by the branches. Finally, after a few pictures of Julia and Gil alone, the photographer shooed everyone away, except for Julia herself.

He took photos of her with her bouquet and without, with her left hand raised to show off the platinum wedding ring with its large solitaire surrounded by diamond-studded filigree. He tilted her face to the right and to the left, raised her chin and then lowered it, snapped pictures of her smiling and then looking pensive. Each time, to achieve the pose he sought, he consulted with her in low tones and positioned her with the lightest touch of his fingertips. Lady Julia cooperated fully, warming to each direction with the ease of a Paris fashion model. Even so, Eva finally found herself looking away, as if she had been spying on an encounter of the most intimate sort.

She shook her head at the scandalous notion. The man merely wished to do the best job possible. Apparently, however, not everyone appreciated his efforts. Once again, the viscount thudded his cane against the ground, tugged his watch from his vest pocket, consulted the time, and shoved it back in. He sighed and coughed and let out a groan. None of this, however, had the least effect in hurrying the photographer along. It wasn't until Julia yawned and touched a hand to her forehead that the young man declared an end to the session. He would take more pictures once they reached the *Georgiana*.

"Well, it's done." The gusts shuddering off the water raised goose bumps on Phoebe's arms and legs, but inside, she felt even colder. Bleaker. She, her family, and about half the guests were being shuttled to Gil Townsend's steamer for the wedding reception. The motor launch would return for the rest in short order. Gil had rejected a wedding breakfast as terribly old-fashioned, and Julia hadn't cared one way or the other, so a shipboard, midday affair it was to be. Secretly, Phoebe suspected Gil hadn't wanted a wedding that reminded him in any way of his first one, or his first wife, for whom the yacht had been named. Though they never had children, word had it they had loved each other deeply, something that had not been required of aristocratic weddings a generation ago.

Apparently, it was not a requirement of modern weddings, either. A pang struck her conscience. Perhaps Gil did love Julia. Perhaps Julia would learn to love him in return.

Beside her on the built-in seat along the starboard rail, Owen Seabright nodded solemnly. "I hope they'll prove us wrong. I hope they'll be happy."

A longtime friend of the Renshaw family, the former major and decorated war hero had become so much more to them in the past year, and for Phoebe, he held a place infinitely more important than mere friend. She huddled against his side as much as was proper, seeking warmth. Silk organza presented no match for the early spring breezes racing across the Solent. Thank goodness Grams had settled on cashmere wraps for her and Amelia, though a coat would have been a great deal more practical. She and Owen might have joined her family and most of the rest of the guests who had crowded into the launch's cabin, *crowded* being the operative word. And stuffy to the point of making her a smidgen queasy. No, she'd rather be out suffering the cold beneath a dreary sky than crammed inside and unable to draw a fresh breath. As for Owen, he seemed impervious to the cold and other discomforts. She supposed war did that to a man.

The launch hit a rolling swell, and the stout woman just now picking her way from stern to bow stumbled. Gil's sister, Veronica Townsend, reached out to catch her balance on the outer wall of the cabin and—to Phoebe's astonishment— swore like a sailor. Owen chuckled silently, evidenced by the rise and fall of his shoulder against hers. The woman caught Phoebe staring at her, rather wide-eyed, she must admit, and changed course to join them on the bench seat.

"It's positively stifling inside that cabin." Tugging at her coat collar, she settled heavily onto the oiled canvas cushion on Phoebe's other side. Despite her complaint about the heat inside the cabin, she shivered beneath her velvet, fox-trimmed coat. Her next words proved that, like Phoebe, it wasn't so much the cold that produced her quiver, but the circumstances. "I cannot for the life of me understand why my brother ever entertained the foolish notion to ship us all out to that ridiculous yacht of his."

Phoebe's gaze drifted to the *Georgiana*, still some several hundred yards away. *Ridiculous* was hardly the term she'd use to describe it. Commissioned by the Royal Navy during the war, the yacht had seen service—and damage— patrolling the channel and the southern coastline. She had since been refitted and now boasted the most modern of conveniences, along with a gleaming hull and highly polished woodwork. Had this been summertime, the vessel would have presented a splendid prospect for a wedding reception, followed by a honeymoon voyage. But Phoebe did wonder, as did her grandparents, why the bride and groom would choose the inconvenience of having to ferry food and drink and guests out into the middle of a harbor weeks before the warm weather arrived.

"Why didn't your sister object? *I* certainly would have." Miss Townsend turned to face front and mumbled, "Not that *I've* ever *been* a bride. Or ever *will* be, for that matter."

Phoebe heard the resentment, plain as day. About the wedding? Or the fact that she'd never had one of her own? She glanced at Owen, who returned her gaze with raised eyebrows that said, *Don't ask me.*

"It was Gil's idea, from what I understand," she replied diplomatically, "and I suppose Julia didn't like to begin their marriage with a disagreement."

"Bah. She'll need to learn how to handle my brother if she's to have a moment's peace."

At somewhere around fifty-five years of age, Miss Townsend was indeed what most people would term a spinster. With a bulge around her middle, along with obdurate features in a square face that blended into her neck with barely a contour, her prospects at this point would be considered extremely slim, at least in society's view.

"Did you enjoy the ceremony, Miss Townsend?" Owen asked in an obvious bid to steer the conversation into more congenial waters.

"It was akin to any other, I suppose. Proper. Correctly small and tasteful." She shrugged and spared Phoebe a downward glance. "You and your sister did make a very pretty picture in your matching dresses and hats. Julia, *of course*, looked lovely."

Resentment once again, and Phoebe traded another glance with Owen. The slant of his mouth told her he had heard it, too. Would Julia find difficulty in the person of Miss Townsend? In marrying Gil today, had she also attached herself to someone intent on making her life troublesome?

"Phoebe, my dear, you're shivering." Owen came to his feet and extended his hand. "Miss Townsend, would you care to join us inside for the rest of the ride?"

She waved them on. "No, you go ahead."

With a hand at the small of Phoebe's back, Owen hurried her along the deck, but when they reached the door to the cabin, they passed it by and ducked around to the port side. They were by no means alone here, either. Several others, wrapped in overcoats, with their hats pulled low, drifted along the railing or sat in small groups here and there. Owen led Phoebe to an empty corner near the stern, where they could speak in semiprivacy if they kept their voices down.

"Phew," he said with a shake of his head. "Thank goodness for a brisk wind, or we wouldn't have had an excuse to escape. I didn't think she'd care to follow us. A bit of a shrew, isn't she?"

"I couldn't say. I've hardly got to know her at all. Perhaps it's only the strain of the day and this wretched wind." She tucked her chin and raised her shawl.

"It won't be as bad once we reach the yacht. It's the forward motion of the launch that's raising much of the breeze."

Phoebe smiled, regarding his dark eyes and firm features. "I'm glad you're here."

"Of course I'm here. I wouldn't miss your sister's wedding. Or the chance to see you so prettily turned out." He looked down at her in a way that sent fresh chills racing up and down her length, ones that certainly had nothing to do with the weather and that left her slightly discombobulated.

A brisk laugh and a shake of her head restored her equilibrium. "Another comment like that and you'll go overboard, Owen Seabright."

Another laugh skittered along the deck. Two men and a woman had gathered near the port cabin door. It had been the woman who laughed. Phoebe had met Mildred Blair briefly last night, when the Renshaws had arrived in Cowes and met Gil and his sister for dinner. From what she had gathered, Miss Blair worked for Gil, yet her manner toward him had struck Phoebe as being rather more familiar than a typical employee's. Her grandmother had certainly noticed, too, if her disapproving frowns were any indication.

The young woman excused herself to her companions and made her way over to Phoebe and Owen.

"Lady Phoebe." Without waiting for Phoebe to greet her in return, she directed her attention to Owen. "I don't believe we've met." She extended a hand clad in kidskin, black to match the trim on her coat, which draped from her shoulders and fell to her calves in the latest fashion. With raven's dark hair cut into blunt bangs and a clear, translucent complexion, she rivaled Julia in film star beauty. "I'm Mildred Blair, the viscount's personal secretary. So good of you to attend the wedding. Do let me know if you need anything. Are you staying at the Mariner Hotel with the rest of the guests?"

"Owen Seabright," he said. "And no, I won't be staying the night."

"Such a shame." Miss Blair spoke briskly. "The viscount has a lovely brunch planned tomorrow at the hotel. He and his bride won't be there, of course, as they'll have sailed away by then. Such a pity you'll miss it."

"I'll be there," Phoebe said. "My family and I are staying to see Julia and Gil off tomorrow. And then we'll be going over to East Cowes to tour Osborne House."

"Yes." Miss Blair curled her reddened lips tightly. "I meant Mr. Seabright."

"It's Lord Owen Seabright," Phoebe corrected her and, from the corner of her eye, saw his poor attempt to hide a grin. She realized Miss Blair reminded her of someone: her cousin Regina. Poor Regina. She had been larger than life, a vital force that swept others along for a breathless ride. The two women resembled each other, with their black hair, pale skin, and sense of style. There, however, the resemblance ended. Regina had never been intentionally rude—not to Phoebe, at any rate.

Yet she would not have accused Miss Blair of flirting. She saw no seductive pursing of her lips, no invitation in her gaze. What did she want, then?

Miss Blair sized up Owen with a raised eyebrow, looking neither intimidated nor impressed by his rank. "I see. Then, if there is anything *Lord* Owen needs, he has only to ask."

He drew Phoebe's arm through his. "Thank you, Miss Blair. We'll let you know if we require anything. If you'll excuse us." Once again, he hurried Phoebe along the deck, murmuring in her ear, "Should we meet one more charmer like the last two, I'll be obliged to you for throwing me overboard."

"And I'll gladly jump in after you."

CHAPTER 2

Eva stood on the main pier of the Royal Yacht Squadron, her arm linked with Hetta's. The launch would be back for the rest of the guests, but she and Hetta and a few other servants might not make it on until a third crossing. Nor had they been invited to wait inside the building after the ceremony. Thank goodness both women had worn their sturdy woolen coats and close-fitting hats.

Footsteps echoed on the boards behind her, and Eva glanced over her shoulder. What she saw made her slide her arm free of Hetta's and turn full around.

"My lord, good morning. Are you . . . going to the reception?"

Theo Leighton, Marquess of Allerton, smiled grimly and shook his head. "Good morning, Miss Huntford. No, I'm not going. Bad enough I attended the wedding. Although, I *am* an invited guest."

This produced a shock. "You are? That is . . . I mean . . ."

"It's all right. I was surprised, too. I suppose the countess invited me to impress upon me the fact that Lady Julia is taken now." He nodded to Hetta, who offered a shy smile and nodded back, though Eva caught the faintest hint of pity in her bright azure eyes. Hetta had not known him before the war, but its ravages were plain to see. His lordship had once been a handsome man—before the mustard gases of the Battle of the Somme. From the corner of his mouth to the left side of his chin and beneath, the chemical burns had left the skin pitted and stretched, a permanent sneer whether he willed or not. And his hands . . . It pained Eva to see him struggle to perform the simplest tasks, yet perform them he did, without assistance, with minimal fuss.

His last words sank in and took her aback. There had never been open acknowledgment of his affections for Lady Julia—at least not in Eva's hearing. The intimacy of his admission, so at odds with their disparate stations, sent a heat of confusion to her cheeks.

And yet he had ventured onto the dock to speak with her. She owed him her attention, and any solace she could offer.

"Miss Huntford, is she, do you think, happy?"

Her heart dropped. Of course he would ask this—the one question she felt incapable of answering truthfully. She prided herself on her honesty; speaking lies was abhorrent to her. She narrowed her eyes in the glare cast by the steely waters and studied the Marquess of Allerton. What did he seek? An assurance of Julia's happiness, or the knowledge that she had sacrificed her true desires for the good of the family? Which would put his mind more at ease, knowing she loved him still or believing her heart had switched its allegiance?

Desperation flitted at the corners of his eyes. His hands were balled in the pockets of his overcoat. He loved her; Eva believed that fully. And she realized, given the totality of the circumstances, what she must say.

"I believe my lady will be happy."

A breath whooshed out of him, causing his shoulders to sag, his eyes to momentarily close. "I'm glad. It's what I want. I watched her back at the church, listened to her take her vows, but I couldn't be sure. You know her better than anyone. If you say she is happy, then I can go away believing it and get on with my life."

Eva's throat clogged, and she couldn't trust her voice not to betray her. She forced a smile, a small one, which the marquess returned briefly. Then he thanked her, bade her and Hetta good day, and made his way back to the clubhouse. Moments later, a motorcar pulled away from the building—a gleaming Silver Ghost that had once belonged to Theo Leighton's deceased brother, who had been the Marquess of Allerton before him. He would make his way to the ferry landing and leave Cowes—and Lady Julia— behind him.

"All right, *ja?*"

Eva turned away from the retreating motorcar. "Everything is fine," she lied, because she could not have made Hetta understand, not with the language barrier between them. But she hadn't exactly lied to the marquess. She hadn't said, as he believed, that Lady Julia *was* happy. She had said she believed Lady Julia *would* be happy. Someday. Eva clung to the notion. But whether that happiness would someday include Theo Leighton, who could say?

The launch, having deposited its first round of passengers onto the decks of the *Georgiana*, had turned around and was once more approaching the pier. The doors of the clubhouse opened, and wedding guests began filing out. Judging by the number of them, Eva and Hetta would be waiting for a third crossing. She drew Hetta off to the side so they wouldn't be in the way.

If Phoebe had had any doubts about Mildred Blair's position in Gil's household, the woman briskly dispelled them now. As soon as they stepped onto the *Georgiana*, she shed her fashionable coat and began issuing orders to the crew and checking to see that everything had been laid out according to plan. Flowers and bunting adorned the main saloon and the dining room offered a buffet of choices from canapés and foie gras to seafood and fine cuts of beef, to the sweets and pastries surrounding the tiered wedding cake. Miss Blair inspected all, her face a mask of seriousness, her eyes keen and missing no detail, her hands quick and deft when rearranging was warranted. Upon completing her circuit of the yacht's public rooms, she disappeared once more into the dining room. Phoebe assumed she was on her way down to the galley to ensure all was running smoothly there.

Unfortunately, the boat itself was anything but smooth. Although from the Royal Yacht Squadron the vessel had appeared more or less stable, now that Phoebe had boarded, she could feel the deck swaying beneath her feet. So could the other guests, judging by their tight expressions. Phoebe rarely suffered from motion sickness, but she worried about Eva, whose insides became unsettled from bumpy motorcar rides, never mind boats on choppy waters.

Julia and Gil had boarded but had slipped away, following the photographer out to the top deck for more pictures. Phoebe was grateful her presence didn't seem to be required this time. Amelia and Fox had set about exploring. Phoebe had left them to it and instead strolled through each of the public rooms, exchanging light conversation with friends and relatives. She and Owen had gone in separate directions upon reaching the *Georgiana*, but every so often she felt his gaze upon her, a soft caress of his regard, and would look up to find his eyes smiling over heads at her.

She wandered beyond the saloon, where a conservatory lay enclosed in glass and furnished in bright colors. Had the sun burned its way through the clouds, she could well imagine the resulting cozy warmth, but today's overcast sky neither warmed the space nor invited the observer to stay. As a result, no guests had gathered here. With a shiver, she turned to retrace her steps, but in the small, connecting passageway she went still when voices made their way through a door that led outside, onto the starboard deck.

"I agree with you, Veronica," a woman's husky voice said. "She can be marrying him only for his money."

Phoebe didn't recognize the voice but guessed *Veronica* must be Gil's sister. The reply confirmed it.

"My brother's a fool. A man of his age . . . Good heavens, he'd better not come crying to me when she cuckolds him."

Phoebe dragged in an indignant breath, and it was all she could do to stop herself from bursting through the door and issuing a thorough dressing-down. But the two hadn't finished yet.

"She is a beauty, though. Even you must admit that, Veronica."

"*Humph.* Mark my words, she'll bring him nothing but trouble, Antonia. Trouble he well deserves."

The one named Antonia spoke more gently. "You've never forgiven him, have you, my dear?"

"Forgive? Why on earth should I? I'd have been happily married to Harold until he perished in the war, God rest him, and now I'd have children to comfort me and a home and an income of my own. Instead, look at me. I'm a lonely old spinster with no prospects and entirely dependent on my brother's generosity, or lack thereof. He hates me. He blames me for Georgiana's accident and has been taking his revenge ever since."

"But . . . I thought Georgiana died of the influenza. Surely you could not be blamed for that."

"I'm not talking about her death, Antonia. I'm talking about the accident that killed their unborn child and left her unable to have more. The carriage accident twenty years ago."

"But how can *that* have been your fault? Didn't a dray come barreling into the vehicle you and she were riding in?"

"Indeed it did. But going out that day was my idea. You see, I intended to meet Harold, and I asked Georgiana to come along to, well . . . you know . . . keep things respectable. Harold would not have compromised my reputation for anything."

"A true gentleman."

"That he was. But after the accident, Gil blamed us both and threatened to ruin Harold both socially and financially if he ever came near me again."

"He didn't."

"Oh, yes, he did. And he'd have done it, too. Vindictive to the last, my brother. And now he married this chit of a schoolgirl to get himself an heir, but also to rub my face in the fact that he can move on with his life just as he pleases, while I continue to languish in the obscurity of middle-aged spinsterhood. A woman of my age certainly can't expect suitors to come knocking at her door."

"I wish there was something I could do for you, my dear."

A dramatic sigh rumbled its way through the closed door. "I do appreciate that, Antonia. There is little to be done, at least for now. But someday, my friend, oh, yes, *someday* I shall have the last word and the last laugh. And then my brother will be sorry for the way he's treated me all these years. In the meantime . . ." Another sigh, although this one bordered on a groan. "I'd best make my appearance on the top deck. Gil wants a photograph of the two of us with the sea as a backdrop. I cannot imagine why."

Footsteps indicated the pair was moving on, and further conversation eluded Phoebe's hearing. It had become a bad habit, eavesdropping, but one for which she had learned to feel remorseful after the fact. As it was, she had learned her sister would find no friend in Veronica Townsend and indeed had better watch her back around the woman. Would Miss Townsend seek to redress her brother's wrongs through Julia? Phoebe must find a moment to warn her sister.

Julia and Gil didn't reappear until after the last of the guests had arrived. Then they took center stage in the saloon. Miss Blair also returned and coordinated with the waiters to make certain every guest held a glass of champagne. Many of her directions were pantomimed rather than spoken, while the staff moved with the precision of a choreographed dance. She directed the photographer, as well, showing him where to set up his tripod and equipment.

Phoebe couldn't help admiring the secretary's skill in managing such an event in these relatively cramped quarters. Having the wedding at Foxwood Hall would have been infinitely easier and would have pleased Grams infinitely more. But Gil had insisted. . . .

His best man, Sir Hugh Fitzallen, moved beside the bridal couple and raised his glass. Before he spoke, all three looked in the direction of the camera and smiled. Phoebe detected little sincerity in those smiles, but then, it wasn't easy to look carefree and at ease in picture after picture.

Besides, a steady stream of frigid air poured in through the yacht's open windows. Gil had insisted they be open, claiming that to close them would defeat the purpose of holding the reception out on the water. Phoebe tightened her wrap around her. Likewise, many of the guests had chosen to keep their overcoats around their shoulders.

At a nod from the photographer, Sir Hugh launched into his toast. "Julia, Gil, love 'beareth all things, believeth all things, hopeth all things, endureth all things.' "

Phoebe recognized the quote, from 1 Corinthians 13:7. Apt and lovely. He went on, but her attention wandered.

There hadn't been many guests on Gil's side of the aisle earlier, hardly more than a handful, and mostly all his age. Had he no young relatives, or elderly ones, for that matter? *How sad*, she thought, *to be so alone in the world.* Or had he simply not invited them?

Sir Hugh's baritone caught her attention again. "And as Socrates said, 'By all means marry. If you get a good wife, you'll be happy. If you get a bad one, you'll become a philosopher.' " He paused at the resulting chuckles. Gil laughed outright. Julia looked wary. The photographer captured the moment as Sir Hugh again raised his glass. "Here's hoping, Gil, that you never become a philosopher."

More laughter, but again, not shared by Julia. Instead, her gaze wandered to Mildred Blair, who hovered in the doorway of the dining room with an expression that reminded Phoebe of the doting approval of a governess. Which struck her as exceedingly odd.

"Thank God that's done." The voice startled her and, flinching, she turned to find her brother at her shoulder. "I was afraid it would go on forever."

"Keep your voice down, please." Phoebe glanced around to see if anyone had overheard. "I take it you didn't enjoy Sir Hugh's speech?"

Fox tossed his head, flinging a shock of fair hair out of his eyes. "I didn't mean the speech, goose. I meant Julia's stubbornness about marriage. I thought we'd never get her out of the house and off the dole."

"Off the—" Phoebe fought the urge to box her brother's ear. "You never grow up, do you?"

He smirked. "Granted, it'll be a while yet for Amelia, but you . . . you had better start thinking about your own nuptials, sister. Owen isn't going to wait around forever. Or is it that you haven't quite hooked him yet?"

"You really are insufferable, Fox."

"I'm a realist, which is more than I can say for you."

She shook her head at him. "Do you know how long it's been since you and I had a real conversation?"

"Funny, I thought we were having one now."

"No, we are not. This is you attempting to bully me with outmoded ideas."

"You won't think it's outmoded when I cut you off without a penny."

"You're an arrogant, obnoxious little boy." Without another word, Phoebe strode away, but she felt his smirk following her. She dearly would have liked to stay and say more, explain to him that, money or no, he would hold no sway over her life, now or ever. She also would have liked to make him understand—to drill it into that dull brain of his—that all of them would have to learn to earn their keep, because it wasn't enough to simply preserve Foxwood Hall for future generations. Their legacy needed to be more than that, needed to contribute in some way to the world, and to the good of England, if the Renshaw family were to maintain any standing or dignity within society.

"Everything all right?" Owen came up beside her and touched his fingertips to her shoulder—briefly. They had agreed ahead of time not to give anyone, especially Grams, reason to speculate about another impending wedding. But his timing couldn't have been better, almost as if he had read her mind and knew Fox had upset her. Or perhaps he had recognized the menacing expression on Fox's young face.

"Nothing I can't handle," she replied, looking up at his strong features. They steadied her, those features, however much they used to confuse her and make her blush in the most exasperating way. No more, for she had learned in the past year that she was his equal and, more importantly, that he saw her as such.

"Let me guess." He grinned. "Now that Fox has Julia married off, you're next."

"If he has his way. He's convinced it's the only viable option."

"You, of course, have other ideas."

"As a matter of fact, yes." She hadn't told anyone what she had in mind, not even Eva. She wished to attend university and perhaps study law. The very notion of what her future might hold made her heart pump faster.

"Then I've no reason to hope?" His expression told her he only half jested; hope did indeed glimmer in his eyes, but it was tempered by prudence and, most important of all, patience. She silently thanked him for that.

"Now is not the time to speak of the future, but I do have plans that must be set into motion before I make any permanent decisions."

His grin returned. "How mysterious."

"Not really. But as I said, now is not the time."

"I suppose I'll have to wait around indefinitely, then." He let out a long-suffering, rather melodramatic sigh, which made her laugh. Then she sobered.

"Do you mind very much?"

He shook his head, his lips curling ever so subtly. "Aren't the best things worth waiting for?" He raised her hand to his lips. "If you'll excuse me, I see your grandfather finally has less of a crowd around him."

She watched him go, half smiling, and marveling that not once had they discussed marriage. There had been no proposal, no plans voiced, yet somehow it had become understood that their futures were linked. She had been told on more than one occasion not to let a man like Owen slip through her fingers. There were so few eligible bachelors in England nowadays; so few had come home from the war that odds were women Phoebe's age might never marry if they didn't already have someone. But marriage driven by a sense of desperation?

Not for her. And if Owen felt content to wait, why should she rush things?

In a corner of the saloon, a gramophone trilled out a lively tune, and Phoebe recognized the light jazz of the Paul Whiteman Orchestra from America. There wasn't room on the *Georgiana* for a live ensemble, and besides, there would be no dancing, at least nothing more than a token swaying back and forth of the happy couple at some point. A few guests were tapping their feet, nonetheless, obviously tempted. But Gil—and Julia, for that matter— had made this stipulation perfectly clear, for Gil could not dance. Could not walk without the aid of his cane and the prosthetic appendage that had replaced his real leg from the knee down some twenty years ago.

She drifted into the dining room and found Amelia patiently awaiting her turn at the buffet. Phoebe lifted a plate of creamy white porcelain emblazoned with Gil's family crest in blue, green, and gold enamel. "Watch out for Fox," she whispered with a chuckle. "He's got one sister married off and is coming for us now."

Amelia apparently didn't find this amusing. "I know. He's already been round to taunt me. You're lucky. You have Owen. Do you suppose I'll have to marry someone I don't love for the sake of the family?"

They had moved up in line, and Phoebe had been about to reach for a serving fork. Her hand dropped to her side. "Dearest Amellie," she said, using Amelia's childhood name, "don't listen to anything Fox says. He's a spoiled child who thinks more of himself than he should."

"It isn't Fox. It's what Julia said earlier. About Foxwood Hall no longer supporting itself. Oh, Phoebe, we can't lose it. We simply can't. It's home. It's *been* home to the Renshaws for generations. I won't be the cause of it slipping away, bit by bit, until it's all gone."

"It won't."

"How can you be so sure, if we're already losing money?"

"Well, then, we must find ways to support ourselves. We must put ourselves to work and put Foxwood to work."

Amelia shook her head, her forehead puckering. "How?"

Phoebe sighed. "I'm not sure yet, but there has to be ways to make the running of the place more efficient while at the same time helping it make its own self-sustaining income."

"Good heavens. You're starting to sound like Olive."

Amelia referred to Olive Asquith, an unlikely friend of the family who unabashedly spouted socialistic ideals, despite her hailing from a wealthy and steadfastly Tory family. "I wouldn't go that far," Phoebe replied. She herself was no radical. But practical, yes; and she was becoming more so with each passing year, as she became more acquainted with the world beyond Foxwood Hall. "But we surely can't go on doing things as they have been done for the past several hundred years. The world is changing, and we must change with it."

"What is this? I do hope I heard you wrong." A matronly woman stepped around them and reached for the serving fork Phoebe had abandoned at the outset of her conversation with Amelia.

"Oh, hello, Aunt Wilma," Phoebe and her sister said in unison. Wilma Bancroft was their mother's uncle's wife, and a widow since before the war. Like many a wealthy woman her age, she was plump, direct, and made no apologies for her opinions and convictions. She tended to voice them often, and loudly.

Her graying auburn hair was pulled up into a pile of

curls on top of her head and secured with a befeathered bow and a bit of jeweled netting that draped over her forehead. She plunged the serving fork into a silver chafing dish. "You must remember, my girls, that tradition is everything. Abandon tradition, and you abandon civilization. And then where would we be?"

"Phoebe and I are only discussing the need to make Foxwood Hall more profitable, Aunt." Amelia looked to Phoebe for consensus, but Phoebe already knew their aunt's opinion about that.

"Yes, well, that is certainly no matter for feminine minds." The woman cleared her throat and sniffed decisively. "Really, girls. I fear I shall have to have a word with your grandmother." Aunt Wilma shifted her bulk away and continued on along the buffet, piling her plate high.

"Do you suppose she will?" Amelia frowned with worry. "Speak to Grams, I mean."

"Don't fret over it. Come, let's have something to eat. I'm suddenly famished."

They made their selections and searched for room at the long dining table or at one of the smaller tables set up along the sides of the room. Most seats were taken, though many of the diners only picked at their food while darting looks out the windows to the undulating horizon. Once again, Phoebe spared a thought for Eva and wondered how she was getting along below, whether seasickness had rendered her prostrate. She would have to sneak away soon to check on her.

She finally spotted a young man sitting alone at one of the tables, apparently undisturbed by the movement of the yacht as he tucked into his food with enthusiasm. Did he mind sitting alone? Why had no one joined him?

Phoebe gestured to Amelia. "Look, there's Gil's cousin Ernest. Let's sit with him."

As they approached the table, Ernest Shelton glanced up from his solitary meal. His eyebrows jerked upward as if with alarm, and his fork slipped through his fingers to clank against his plate. In his attempt to retrieve the implement, he knocked over his wineglass, sending a splatter of red droplets across the linen tablecloth and the sleeve of his coat. Conversations hushed as those nearby paused to see what the matter was. The poor man blushed nearly as scarlet as the wine. He started to rise, bumped the table with his thighs, and nearly fell over onto it. His attempt to right himself resulted in the table being lifted up onto two legs, wobbling once, twice, and crashing over onto its side. His plate of food went flying. The dining room fell into shocked silence.

"Oh dear," Amelia whispered with a gasp. "I fear we are to blame for this small disaster."

Eva and Hetta finally made it onto the yacht. Chilled through, they were only too happy to go directly below, where the staterooms, service cabins, and galley were located. Miss Blair met them, and Eva asked her to let Lady Julia know they had arrived and were available to perform any function the Renshaws required.

"I'm quite sure everything is being taken care of in a satisfactory manner, Miss Huntford. I truly don't see why you and this young woman here"—she spared a skeptical glance for Hetta—"were required to come aboard. We're crowded enough as it is."

"We only know what we were told, Miss Blair." Eva regarded the severe line of the woman's bangs and the preponderance of makeup emphasizing her large eyes. Miss Blair seemed to her a haughty package of conceit and control. Yet for all that, she had done an unassailable job of organizing the day, and Eva couldn't help but be grateful.

"Lady Julia wished us to be here," she said calmly. "If there is any way we might be of service to you, please let us know."

"There is. Please do your best to stay out of the way. You may use the small sitting room that adjoins the viscount and viscountess's stateroom." Miss Blair turned on the heel of her pump and strode away. Eva sighed and then noticed the sensation that had been slowly building inside her since boarding the yacht.

"Where is that sitting room?" She pressed her fingertips to her lips.

Hetta eyed her warily. "*Was ist falsch?*"

Eva wasn't sure what she had just been asked, but she elaborated, "I'm not feeling altogether well."

Hetta studied her, her brows knitting. Then she began peering into doorways, until she apparently found what she sought. "Fraulein Eva." She pronounced Eva's name the German way: Ava. She pointed through a doorway. "*Das Wohnzimmer.*"

Then she scurried back to Eva and, taking her arm, walked her to the sitting room Miss Blair had mentioned, for another open doorway looked onto a spacious bedroom. Hetta patted her shoulder before hurrying from the room. Eva barely had time to wonder where she had gone when Hetta returned, holding a glass of fizzing bicarbonate of soda and fresh mint leaves. As Eva sipped, her stomach gradually settled.

"Better, *ja?*"

"Yes. Thank you, Hetta." She blew out a breath. "You're a treasure."

It wasn't long before Lady Julia came to find them. "I'm so glad you're finally here," she said as she sailed—literally, her veil flowing behind her—through the sitting room and into the bedroom. "I've been longing to change out of this gown. And this dratted veil must go, as well. Good heavens, all those photographs. And mind you, it isn't over yet. I don't know how much more of it I can endure, especially out on deck. My teeth will be clacking from the cold."

Eva and Hetta followed her, Hetta quickly and Eva more slowly, testing the effects walking had on her stomach. All seemed well, for the moment. Lady Julia was already tugging at the pins that held her veil in place. Hetta, looking alarmed, closed the distance at nearly a run, and rightly so, for a tear in that precious lace would utterly destroy its value. With her combination of broken English and pantomime, Hetta bade her mistress sit at the dressing table, and she set to work removing the headpiece without making a shambles of Lady Julia's artfully arranged hair, though some minor repairs would be needed. Hetta's English might be lacking, but her skills certainly were not.

"Eva, come sit near me." Lady Julia moved over on the bench seat and patted the cushion. Puzzled, Eva squeezed in next to her, half perching and trying not to take up too much space. "Good. I don't wish to be overheard." She glanced in the mirror at Hetta's reflection and seemed satisfied when the Swiss woman met her gaze briefly and continued with her task.

Lady Julia's manner raised Eva's concerns. Could there be a problem in the marriage already? "Is everything all right, my lady?"

Lady Julia blew out a breath. "I'm horribly frustrated. I learned only minutes ago that Gil—that is, the viscount—and I are to be accompanied on our honeymoon voyage, and not merely by the crew, mind you."

"Who else is going with you?"

"Who isn't?" Lady Julia made a face. "Veronica Townsend, to begin with. Gil claims he hasn't the heart to leave her home all alone, that he dotes on her and she would be horribly lonely without him."

"I suppose that's the sign of a good brother, my lady."

"Oh, pish. Then that friend of his, Sir Hugh, is coming along, as well."

"That does seem irregular."

"Yes, Eva, it certainly does. My husband says Sir Hugh has been experiencing some personal difficulties and needs to get away to 'ease his mind.'" Lady Julia spoke with sarcasm. "Can you imagine that he needs to do so on *my* honeymoon?"

"Perhaps if the viscount speaks to his friend—"

"That's just the thing. He won't. He refuses to say a word to Sir Hugh about it. He says they've been friends a long time, and if Sir Hugh needs a favor, Gil is only too happy to oblige. 'What about me?' I asked him. And do you know what he said?" Lady Julia folded her arms indignantly.

"I cannot imagine, my lady."

"He told me I shouldn't make a fuss. Sir Hugh would keep to himself, and I'd hardly know he was on board."

"Well, it seems a diplomatic answer, my lady. He does seem solicitous of your feelings."

"Does he? Accusing me of making a fuss? When do I ever?"

Eva pursed her lips as she mulled over how to answer that question with tact.

Julia pursed hers, as well. "Never mind. But that isn't all."

Hetta finished with Julia's hair and gestured for her to stand. When she did, the maid began on the lengthy column of tiny buttons down the back of her gown. Just as Julia had docilely accepted the photographer's rather tactile directions earlier, she now stood patiently while Hetta worked. The only hint of her simmering irritation was the little ridge growing beside her inner right eyebrow.

"Gil finds it necessary to bring his secretary."

"Miss Blair?"

Julia's mouth tightened. "The very same. Why on earth should we have need of a secretary on our honeymoon?"

"Perhaps in case your husband finds he must attend to business matters?"

"Bah."

Hetta finished with the buttons, and Julia held out her arms while the sleeves were slid free, Hetta being careful not to catch the delicate fabric on the beautiful diamond-and-platinum wedding ring. Eva stepped closer to help hold the dress to prevent it dragging on the floor. Julia stepped out of it and, in her lacy underthings, crossed to the dressing room, where she flung open the door of a built-in armoire. The ensemble she had chosen for the re-ception consisted of a sleeveless, drop-waist frock that in-corporated ivory lace and satin in a way that complemented her wedding gown while being much lighter and easier to move in. A matching coat of the same fabric and length would drape over it to provide a bit of warmth.

Hetta joined them in the dressing room and raised the frock above Julia's head. As the garment fell into place with a swish, Julia once more confided in Eva.

"I do not like Miss Blair, Eva. I don't trust her."

Eva didn't, either, but she didn't feel it was her place to say so. "She's done a splendid job supervising the wed-ding."

"I'm not saying she isn't good at her job, but she is alto-gether too familiar with Gil. It worries me . . ." She glanced once more at Hetta, who showed no sign of following the conversation. "Eva," she said, lowering her voice, "I want you to watch her. Follow where she goes today, and tell me if you see anything unusual. Anything at all."

"My lady, do you really think . . ." Eva didn't know how to phrase it. The very idea that the viscount might be bringing his mistress along on his honeymoon was too repugnant for words. Luckily, she was saved from having to complete the question.

"I don't know what I think," Lady Julia declared. "Gil hasn't given me any reason to suspect anything, at least not really. But there is something in that woman's manner that leaves me uneasy."

Eva barely heard those last words; the ones that preceded them rang in her ears. Though she typically employed a strict policy of not questioning her employers unless invited to do so, she nonetheless blurted, "What do you mean by 'not really'?"

Her frock hooked and buttoned, Julia once again held out her arms, this time for the matching coat, which fell open in front to show the dress beneath. "I've seen him kiss her cheek. What kind of employer kisses his staff? Has my grandfather ever kissed your cheek, Eva?"

"Indeed not, my lady." Lord Wroxly had never done more than shake her hand at Christmas. But she had certainly heard of employers taking liberties, and she very much wished she could remain on board as part of the honeymoon staff. Hetta would be going along, but Hetta couldn't very well keep her ears open for clandestine conversations that might explain the connection between the viscount and Miss Blair.

"And yet, with all these tagalongs, Gil had the audacity to suggest the photographer stay behind."

Eva froze. "The photographer, my lady? He's coming, as well?"

"Why, yes, of course he is. He's to keep a record of our

trip, of all the sights we see. And Gil was completely for it until we were taking the last of the pictures out on deck. Then he started mumbling about wishing he could replace the man. Mr. Mowbry is his name. I think he's quite accomplished. Professional, patient . . . Did you see the care he took in making certain each photograph was perfectly staged?"

Indeed, Eva *had* noticed how the man had taken particular pains to make sure Julia stood just so, held her face in just such a position. Perhaps the viscount had noticed, as well, and hadn't appreciated the man's familiarity with his bride. Looking at Julia's expression now, at her utter bemusement with her husband's objections to the photographer, Eva believed she hadn't noticed anything unusual during the picture taking. But then, Julia often missed subtleties in favor of the larger picture, the larger picture in this case being her desire to look her best in her wedding album.

"There doesn't seem enough time to employ another photographer," Eva ventured, though she, too, found prudence in the notion of doing so.

"No, indeed there is not. Not if we are to set sail tomorrow morning, as Gil wishes. I asked him, 'Why all the hurry to be away?' and 'Wouldn't it be nicer to wait another day and visit with the relatives who are lingering in Cowes?' But no, he wishes to be off at the earliest opportunity, so barring deplorable weather, we sail at first light." After checking her appearance in the full-length mirror, she passed back into the sitting room. Eva and Hetta trotted after her. "Don't forget what I said, Eva. Find excuses to watch Mildred Blair. If she protests, tell her I asked you to keep an eye on things."

"She won't like that. She's already asked us to keep out of the way."

"I don't care what she likes. If she has a problem, she may come and see me. My husband has allowed her far too much license. It's time for her to learn that the Viscountess Annondale isn't nearly as tolerant of her antics, not by half."

CHAPTER 3

"What the devil is going on in here?" Gil Townsend tapped his way into the dining room, only to stop and scowl at the toppled table and the culinary chaos surrounding it. He slowly and deliberately raised his gaze to his cousin, assessing every inch of the mortified young man. "Ernie. I might have known you'd be the cause."

"Oh, no," Amelia began, "it was actually—"

Balancing her plate in one hand, Phoebe cut her sister off with a nudge to her wrist and a shake of her head. Judging from Gil's forbidding expression, she didn't think explaining how she and Amelia had brought on such a bout of jitters would help poor Ernest. She didn't understand it herself. They had merely wished to sit with the young man and become better acquainted. They were family now, after all.

Miss Blair appeared from a passageway at the far side of the dining room and walked quickly over. "Oh, dear. We'll have this cleaned up in a trice." Three waiters had followed her into the room, and she made a hand motion that set them to work. "Is the table defective? If so, I shall have it replaced."

"Hardly." Gil sniggered rather meanly. "The only defective here is . . . well."

"Oh, Gil, do stop tormenting poor Ernie." Veronica Townsend squeezed through the onlookers, some of whom had jumped to their feet at the sound of the crash. She stopped beside her brother and surveyed the damage. "Poor Ernie, you managed to really do it this time. Ah, no matter." She slid a sideways glance at Miss Blair. "Gil's trusty secretary will make it appear as if nothing ever happened."

Phoebe wondered at both Miss Townsend's shadowed glance and those last words, or, rather the tone in which she had spoken them, which hadn't sounded at all complimentary. Meanwhile, Ernest Shelton's face had turned fiery—not that it hadn't been scarlet previously. The poor man, lanky, angular, rather too thin, stood wringing his hands and mumbling apologies. Phoebe's heart went out to him. The waiters began clearing away the mess, but Ernest remained where he was, watching them sweep up food only inches from his feet. Murmurs rose like crickets at nightfall as the guests' attention remained on him.

Phoebe decided it was time to go to his rescue. "Mr. Shelton, we met earlier. I'm Phoebe, and this is my sister Amelia. Won't you join us . . ." She glanced around the room. There didn't appear to be three unoccupied seats together anywhere. With her plate, she gestured toward the doorway. "Perhaps outside? Would you care to fill another plate first?"

"Er, n-no . . . that is, I'd be happy to, er, escort you . . ."

"If I were you girls, I'd be careful he doesn't accidentally knock you overboard. Eh, Ernie?" Gil let out a laugh. Several others joined in, some heartily, others tentatively. His sister, however, grasped his shoulder and turned him almost roughly to face her.

"You really are insufferable," she whispered. "Why must you insist on lording it over those who can't fight back?"

"It was a joke, Veronica," he replied in a low rumble. "Why must you insist on taking everything so seriously?"

"Well, then," Phoebe said with an attempt to sound as though the past few moments hadn't been painfully uncomfortable, "why don't we proceed up to the top deck and enjoy this . . . em . . . glorious weather?"

She and Amelia stepped around Gil and his sister, and Ernie Shelton moved to follow. Gil slapped him on the back as he passed by. Rather than a friendly thud, the blow made a sharp thwack, which caught Phoebe's concern, but not just for Ernest Shelton.

No, her concerns were for Julia. Was Gil given to bursts of temper? Would he turn that temper on his wife?

Mr. Shelton accompanied her and Amelia up to the top deck, where more tables had been set up. The numbers here were thin at best, and those few burrowed into their coats and tucked their chins into their collars. Not the most comfortable position in which to consume a meal. Amelia immediately began to shiver, and while Phoebe wouldn't have blamed her sister for excusing herself and returning inside, she herself had no intention of doing so.

Instead, she pulled her cashmere wrap tighter around her and huddled lower in her chair. "Mr. Shelton, I believe you are Gil's cousin?"

"Once removed, yes. My father was his first cousin."

"I see. Why, that makes you his . . ."

"Heir, yes. For now. Until your sister, uh . . ." Another wave of color engulfed his face.

Phoebe nodded her understanding, making it unnecessary for him to continue. Besides, she had already known of Ernest Shelton's place in the family hierarchy. She had merely wished to start the conversation somewhere. While her initial reason for suggesting he join them had been to provide the man with an escape from the scene of his embarrassment, now she desired to learn more about her brother-in-law. She had the distinct feeling Mr. Shelton could provide her with details no one else would, assuming she could entice him to speak at all.

"Are you a close neighbor of Gil's?" She lifted her fork and knife and sliced off a piece of her chateaubriand.

"I live on the estate, actually." He didn't seem to derive any pleasure from the fact.

Phoebe ignored his downcast features and went on brightly. "Do you? Then you and Julia must know each other quite well."

He shook his head. "Not well, not yet. I . . . er . . . don't live at the main house. I've a cottage on the edge of the home farm. With a surgery."

"You're a doctor," Amelia said with no little amount of surprise. It surprised Phoebe, too, exceedingly much. She could hardly imagine this timid bundle of nerves having the presence of mind and steady enough hands to treat patients.

"Not exactly." He smiled, a self-conscious and apologetic gesture that revealed how one front tooth overlapped the other. "I'm the estate veterinarian."

"How splendid!" Amelia put down her fork and clapped her hands together. Her shawl slipped from her shoulders, but for the moment, it appeared she had forgotten the cold. "What kind of animals do you tend to, Mr. Shelton?"

"All kinds. Large and small. Farm animals, horses, dogs, and cats. Whatever needs tending."

"If I were a man, I'd certainly become a veterinarian. I do love animals." Amelia remembered her wrap and tugged it back over her goose-pimply arms.

"You can be a veterinarian if you wish to be," Phoebe was quick to tell her. "Isn't that right, Mr. Shelton?"

"Er . . . well, it'll take a bit of schooling first . . ."

"I'll be graduating this year. I've done quite well in the

sciences, actually. Our curriculum was changed a couple of years ago to include more academics. Our grandmother wasn't too keen on it at first, but she's come round. She and Phoebe ran the Haverleigh School for a bit after poor Miss Finch . . . Ah, well . . . I don't suppose you'll wish to hear about that. Not now, at any rate. I'm afraid it's not a very happy story."

Mr. Shelton gave Amelia his undivided attention, though Phoebe had the distinct impression he hadn't the faintest idea what to make of her ramblings. That he would indulge a child, and not make her feel as though she were talking out of turn, raised him quite high in her estimate.

"I suppose Gil's horses and dogs were taken for the war effort, the way ours were." Amelia traded a sad glance with Phoebe. "Only my pony, Blossom, didn't go. She was too small."

Horses from all over England had been commandeered by the army during the early years of the war. Grampapa had sent them willingly enough, but he had mourned their loss, along with that of his foxhounds and pointers. Well-trained dogs had become an asset on the battlefields, allowing messages to be delivered from trench to trench without risking soldiers' lives. Grampapa still hadn't found the heart to bring new dogs to Foxwood Hall, using the excuse that he had grown too old for the hunt, and would leave it to Fox to someday revive the old tradition, if he chose to.

"Actually, no," Mr. Shelton was saying in reply to Amelia's observation. "My cousin's horses were not sent to war."

Amelia's brow creased. "How can that be? I thought everyone had to make sacrifices, terrible though they might be."

"He did send this boat," Ernest said.

Amelia waved this notion away as being of little consequence. "That's no sacrifice. Who cares about an old boat? Horses and dogs have *feelings*. And we have feelings for them."

"I completely agree." Ernest sat a little forward in his chair. "It's not as if the animals had any choice in the matter."

"No, indeed," Amelia said indignantly.

"Did you fight in the war, sir?" Phoebe asked him.

"I served in my capacity as a veterinarian." He frowned. "You wouldn't think that would put me in much personal danger, but at times I found myself at the front lines, treating everything from scratches to thrush to bullet wounds."

"Bullet wounds?" Amelia looked about to cry. "Oh, how beastly we were to send them. We never should have allowed it, should we, Phoebe?"

"I'm afraid we had little choice, dearest. Our soldiers needed them."

"Well, I, for one, can't fault Gil for not sending his."

Phoebe didn't reply to this, especially since Amelia's position on the matter seemed to have suddenly shifted. But she silently wondered about her brother-in-law's failure to support the war effort as fully as he might have. And one detail about his refusing to send his horses puzzled her. "Is Gil able to ride?"

Ernest shook his head. "He hasn't ridden since . . . well, you know."

"His leg," Amelia whispered, and Ernest nodded. She screwed up her features. "Then why keep horses?"

"He breeds them," the man said succinctly.

Money. The realization that Gil hadn't sent his horses to France for purely financial reasons struck Phoebe with an almost physical impact. All over England, people had sacrificed and suffered privations, while their men had gone off to fight. Many had returned home maimed or never returned at all. But Gil Townsend had put his monetary investments above all that. Above his country.

"Phoebe, are you all right?"

"I'm fine," she replied to Amelia, but it was all she could do not to burst out about what she considered Gil's treason . . . his selfishness . . . his greed. Was she judging him too harshly? No. Sending Foxwood Hall's animals to help with the war effort had nearly broken dear Grampapa's heart and had aged him a good several years. Papa's death had certainly taken even more years off his life. Money had never been a consideration in his sacrifice or his grief.

What kind of man had her sister married?

Leaving Hetta in the stateroom, Eva made her way to the galley. Most of the food had been prepared in Cowes, at the Royal Yacht Squadron, and brought on board, so the activity here consisted mainly of ensuring there were enough plates, glasses, and cutlery available for the guests, along with opening bottles of wine and champagne. No one paid her any mind as she walked through the bustle, careful not to get in anyone's way but alert for Mildred Blair's presence. The woman was nowhere to be seen.

That would not deter her. Lady Julia had set her the task of keeping an eye on the woman, and she intended to do just that. In fact, if Miss Blair had gone upstairs, it might provide Eva with the perfect opportunity to observe her with the viscount. Perhaps her behavior was nothing more than that of a devoted, fiercely loyal employee. Or perhaps there was something more at play.

At the far end of the galley, a doorway led into a short, narrow hallway that ended with a spiral staircase leading up. At the top she discovered another door, which she guessed led into a service pantry, but just as she was about to swing the door open, familiar voices, speaking low but urgently, stopped her.

"You're overreacting, Hugh. Being ridiculous."

"And you're not taking this seriously enough."

She recognized the first speaker as Viscount Annondale, and the man he addressed as Hugh must be Sir Hugh Fitzallen, his best man. They sounded upset, contentious. Fully aware that whatever they discussed was none of her business, except where it might concern Lady Julia, she pushed the door slightly open with her fingertips, ready to simply walk through, as if on an errand, should they spot her.

But they didn't.

Sir Hugh thrust an unfolded card under the viscount's nose. Eva recognized the Annondale crest included in the design of the wedding invitations. "How can I be overreacting to *this?*"

The two men stood facing each other. Sir Hugh's back was to her, but over his shoulder, she had a clear view of the viscount. He curled his upper lip as he replied, "It means nothing. Merely a prank."

"A rather nasty prank. And what if it isn't? What if—"

"That's why we're pushing out to sea tomorrow, where we'll be safe."

"We can't stay on this tub of yours forever."

"We won't need to. I've got my people tracing this."

"I don't see how."

"Take my word for it, we'll soon know who our nuisance is. Probably a disgruntled worker at one of my factories, thinking he'll make my life uncomfortable. Which he hasn't."

"You'd better be right."

"I am." The viscount spoke with conviction, but uncertainty peeked out from his eyes and raised Eva's apprehensions. Usually light blue, those eyes had become dark and glassy. Dilated. A sign of fear.

Her nape prickled, and she longed to confront the men. Could Lady Julia be in some kind of danger? Not for the first time, Eva wished she had remained the sole lady's maid in the Renshaw household. Then she would be accompanying Lady Julia on this honeymoon voyage and would be on hand if needed. Would Hetta be able to identify a threat to her mistress?

"We should get back." The viscount spoke gruffly. "That damned photographer wants a few more family pictures, and I can't think of a reason to put him off without inviting questions from my wife."

Her mind whirling, Eva watched the two men return to the dining room. She counted off twenty seconds; then she, too, pushed through both doors and entered the dining room. She came upon Miss Blair immediately. Or, rather, Miss Blair blocked her from taking another step.

"Where do you think you're going? You can't come in here."

"I have a message for Lady Julia."

Miss Blair raised a sable-black eyebrow. "Lady Annondale, you mean."

Eva pretended not to notice the woman's hauteur. "I have a message for her."

"Tell it to me, then, and I'll see she gets it."

Impossible woman. "It's of a personal nature."

"I'm sorry, Miss . . ."

"Huntford."

"Yes. I cannot allow this. I myself am here only because there was a bit of a mishap earlier, and I was needed to supervise." Her face set, Miss Blair held out an arm to shoo Eva back into the pantry, at the same time advancing on Eva to force her retreat. Eva had no choice but to comply or create a scene, and she would not do the latter. As they descended the spiral stairs, she spoke over her shoulder.

"Then please let Lady Julia know I must speak to her."

"*Must* speak to her?" Miss Blair chuckled. "Really, Miss Huntsman—"

"Huntford."

"Yes, well, who is the employer here, and who the maid?"

Eva clenched her teeth rather than speak her mind to this woman. They reached the bottom of the stairs, and she turned to look Miss Blair up and down. She had dealt with arrogant women before, and not always ones born to the aristocracy. She remembered one in particular who had believed she'd been born to better things than what fate had delivered to her. That woman had dressed above her means and had lorded over whomever she could. Eva quickly assessed Miss Blair's wardrobe. While her taste could not be faulted—her attire not only suited her but also complemented her physical attributes perfectly—she had clearly not spent a fortune on her ensemble. No, her frock and matching jacket had been store bought, the fabrics good but certainly not the best.

"Whatever are you staring at, Miss Huntford?"

"Eva, is there something you wanted?"

With a burst of relief, Eva glanced up to see Lady Phoebe peering down at her from the top of the stairs. "There is, my lady."

She couldn't help a little grin of triumph as she eased past Miss Blair to retrace her steps.

As she reached the top of the stairs, Lady Phoebe whispered, "I saw you trying to enter the dining room, much to Miss Blair's disapproval."

"To put it mildly. She is the most difficult individual I've come across since I had the pleasure of Myra Stanley's acquaintance last summer."

Lady Phoebe gave a dramatic shudder, then sobered. "What is it? Is something wrong?"

That her lady would immediately assume Eva's errand involved something unpleasant said much about the nature of their relationship and their shared experiences in the past year.

"There *is* something wrong, my lady. I overheard the

viscount and Sir Hugh Fitzallen talking only minutes ago, here in this very pantry. Obviously, they slipped in here so as not to be overheard."

Any other mistress might have scolded Eva for eavesdropping, but not Lady Phoebe. "What were they saying?"

"They were very cryptic, and I only heard a snippet of their conversation. They were both clearly uneasy, but the viscount said Sir Hugh was overreacting."

"About what?"

"I don't know, but Sir Hugh said the viscount wasn't taking whatever it is seriously enough. And then he thrust out a wedding invitation and asked how he could be overreacting about *this*. There was quite a bit of urgency in his voice."

"A wedding invitation? How strange. What could have been written on it, other than whether or not the person invited planned to come?"

"I wish I could say. The viscount called it a prank. And then he said he was expected for more photographs with the family, and added something most curious."

"More curious than what you've already told me?"

Eva nodded. "The viscount said he couldn't think of any reason to put the photographer off without his wife asking questions."

Lady Phoebe's mouth dropped open in a show of indignation. "Do you think he's hiding something from Julia? What could it be?"

"I wish I knew. Although . . . he might simply resent the photographer out of jealousy. It seems the viscount wasn't happy about the attentions Mr. Mowbry paid your sister during the photography sessions."

"I noticed that, too. A cheeky sort, that photographer, albeit in a quiet way. But then, men typically do trip over their feet when it comes to Julia."

Eva heard the slight resentment in Phoebe's tone and

understood. She had been living in her elder sister's shadow for years now, and while Lady Phoebe had her own achievements to be proud of, it sometimes rankled her to see how effortlessly her elder sister moved through society, and among young men in particular. Eva moved on quickly. "They left the pantry soon after, and that's when I tried to come in to speak with your sister. I thought perhaps I should warn her, but in all honesty, I don't know what I would have said if Miss Blair hadn't blocked my way."

"I wonder if Miss Blair is aware of whatever the men were talking about."

"I hadn't thought of that. I assumed she was merely exercising her authority."

"*Humph.*" Phoebe tapped her forefinger against her chin. "I know you mean well, but it might be best to say nothing to Julia about this just yet."

"But those men were clearly uneasy about something. It might affect her."

"And it might have nothing to do with her. Eva, my sister always knows exactly what she's doing."

Eva doubted that—in fact, she knew Lady Julia to be a lot less assured than people often believed—but she kept that thought to herself.

"She's Gil's wife now, and that was entirely her choice. Yes, I know Grams has been after her to marry, but no one threw Gil into her path. It was her doing, and any matters that arise between them from here on in are none of our business."

With a sigh, Eva found herself reluctantly agreeing. "I suppose you're right. She probably wouldn't appreciate my interfering."

"That's right. You know Julia. Once her mind is made up, there is no changing it. We owe it to her, if not to trust her judgment, then at least to let her make her own mistakes." She ended with a grim lift of her mouth, which assured Eva that she, too, worried for her sister's future.

Below them, the galley door opened, and heels clacked their way up the spiral steps. Eva leaned over the railing to see Miss Blair framed in the circle of the stairwell.

"It's time to cut the cake," the woman said with a tap at her wristwatch.

"Already?" Phoebe frowned. "We haven't been here two hours yet."

"True enough, Lady Phoebe, but the bride and groom are anxious to begin their honeymoon, and they can't very well do that with all these people on board."

Eva gasped at the implied meaning. "Miss Blair, you will not speak to Lady Phoebe in that impertinent way."

"Oh dear, I do apologize." The woman didn't look one bit sorry. "Lady Phoebe, you strike me as a thoroughly modern woman. If I have offended you, please forgive me."

Eva narrowed her eyes at the secretary's obvious amusement.

"You are not mistaken in your impression, Miss Blair," Lady Phoebe replied evenly. "You have not offended me at all." Miss Blair showed Eva a satisfied smile. But Lady Phoebe hadn't finished. "However, should you ever dare take such a liberty with my sister, she'll see you out on your ear within the hour."

"Julia doesn't look very happy, does she?"

Phoebe agreed with Amelia. The cake having been cut, the bridal couple stood to one side of the tiered confection while a team of waiters passed around slices on small plates. While most brides at this point looked on with an air of happy satisfaction, delighting in their guests' enjoyment, such was not the case here. "She looks . . . puzzled."

"Yes, she does." Owen came to stand at Phoebe's other

shoulder. His hand briefly touched hers before easing away to his side.

"As well she should." Grams stood nearby, her arm linked through Grampapa's. Speaking just above a whisper, she added, "I fail to see what all the rush is about."

"Nor do I." Owen's eyes narrowed on the bridal couple, and he shook his head almost imperceptibly.

Grampapa issued a rumbling sigh. In the next moment his mouth stretched into a smile that didn't fool Phoebe for a moment. He hadn't been in favor of this marriage, but after asking Julia once if this was what she truly wanted, he had kept his opinions to himself. Gripped by a sudden welling of affection coupled with nagging worry for her aging grandfather, Phoebe went to his other side and slipped her hand into his. When a waiter offered him a serving of cake, he shook his head with a mumbled "My doctor forbids me."

"I don't wish any, either." Phoebe waved the waiter on. No, all things considered, she thought she might choke on it. *Oh, Julia.*

The groom was speaking, thanking everyone for coming, but Phoebe barely heard a word. Fox ambled over to her, his plate piled high with yellow cake, French cream, and berries.

"No cake? Are you mad? This is stupendous." He scooped a forkful and held it out to Phoebe. "Taste. Go on, taste it." When she shook her head, he persisted. "If I were you, sister, I'd develop a fondness for wedding cake. Isn't that right, sir?"

"Young man, watch yourself," their grandfather replied sternly. "You'll behave like a gentleman, or this is the last social occasion you will attend whilst I breathe."

Fox opened his mouth, then wisely compressed his lips and turned to listen to Gil, who was still addressing the guests.

"And we look forward to seeing you all when we re-turn." His words poured out in a hurry. "The launch is here, and you may begin boarding."

Julia placed a hand on his forearm. "Gil, most of our guests haven't finished their cake yet."

He paid her no mind. With his arm outstretched, he took several steps forward, as if to herd people from the room. The gesture succeeded. Almost as one, the company set down their plates on the nearest surface and began shuffling through the doorway into the main saloon. Miss Blair appeared among them, her arms piled high with overcoats, and added her voice to the effort of ushering people out to the deck.

More than a few curious glances were exchanged, but everyone kept moving. Except for Phoebe and the rest of the family. They remained in the dining room, and once the crowd had thinned, they surrounded Julia. With a glance over her shoulder, Phoebe saw that Owen had gone only as far as the saloon. His gaze met hers warmly, his concern evident. His slight nod seemed to say he would wait for her while she bade her sister good-bye, and that made her feel less bereft.

"My dearest granddaughter, you were beautiful today. We're so proud of you." Grams clasped Julia's shoulders and kissed her cheeks. Grams remained dry-eyed as they parted, and Phoebe didn't wonder. Life to Grams was a stoic progression of performing one's duty. It wasn't that she wouldn't miss Julia or worry about her. She would. But she wouldn't dwell on it or allow it to disturb her outward composure. To do so would be disturbingly un-Grams-like. Raising her silver eyebrows, she smiled at the groom. "Gil, take good care of her. Or you'll find yourself dealing with me."

Gil chuckled, a sound he cut off short with a look of uncertainty. Grams stepped back to allow Grampapa his turn to wish Julia well. Phoebe's throat constricted and her heart ached at the sight of the tears gathering in his faded blue eyes as he stepped up to Julia and wrapped his arms around her. He held her close for a long moment, started to release her, then held her more tightly. Phoebe heard the breath leave her sister, but Julia spoke no word of complaint.

"Be well, my darling, and call on me if you ever need anything."

"I shall, Grampapa. Thank you."

Amelia's turn was next, her eyes no drier than Grampapa's. "Julia . . . oh, Julia!" The rest was lost in sobs. She pulled away from her sister and retreated into Grampapa's embrace. That left Fox and Phoebe. The former, apparently still smarting from the chastisement issued by Grampapa, merely stood on tiptoe to press a clumsy kiss to Julia's cheek.

Phoebe's and Julia's gazes met then, a furtive, almost wary look veiling Julia's sentiments. Phoebe reached out to hug her, and Julia leaned toward her and touched Phoebe's shoulders, but barely. Her cheek skimmed Phoebe's briefly. Then she pulled away and straightened, and slipped her hand into the crook of her husband's arm.

"There now, the good-byes are said." Gil's tone was dismissive.

"Lord Annondale, are you detaining your guests?" Miss Blair strolled into the dining room as if she owned it, as if this were her celebration. Phoebe noted with no small amount of annoyance that she had the look of an exasperated schoolmistress admonishing a student. "I saved seats for the Renshaws on the launch so they won't have to wait for the next trip."

"We wouldn't mind waiting," Grampapa said.

"Good heavens, we wouldn't keep you waiting for the world. No, no, you must come now. I've reserved the best

seats in the launch cabin for you, so you'll keep warm."
Miss Blair had continued her advance into the room and
now stopped in front of Gil. "Shame on you, sir, for keeping them so long. I cannot take my eyes off you for a moment, can I?"

Gil's already florid face deepened yet more with a flush,
yet when Phoebe expected him to censure his secretary, he
merely gazed at her fondly.

"Gil didn't detain anyone, Miss Blair," Julia said tartly.
"They are my family, and they wished to say good-bye privately."

"Splendid," Miss Blair responded. "And now they have."

Julia spoke again without any further acknowledgment
of Miss Blair. "I'll see you all again in the morning, before
we sail." With that, she quickly kissed Grams again, hugged
Grampapa, patted Amelia's cheek, and turned away.

CHAPTER 4

Phoebe and Owen strolled along the Egypt Esplanade, which hugged the waterline along the Isle of Wight, beyond the Royal Yacht Squadron precincts. When Phoebe had first come here as a child, she had expected to find small-scale pyramids and statues of the Egyptian rulers and gods. Her letdown had nearly wrought tears. But then her father had patiently explained that the name of the esplanade had nothing to do with Egypt, but rather with the gypsies who had inhabited the area some three hundred years ago. Her disappointment had been short-lived as the wonders of ancient Alexandria faded before images of bright-colored tents and the vivid-hued clothing of lively dancing gypsies.

Now, however, there were neither pyramids nor gypsies along the esplanade, but merely trees and shrubbery on one side and the wide-open water on the other. The winds off the Solent hadn't ceased, and a light drizzle put a sheen on overcoats and on the green to their left. They walked on the landward side of the roadway, and Owen held an umbrella over their heads, attempting to angle it against the breeze. Phoebe had traded her cashmere shawl for a velvet coat that wrapped her in warmth. They might have remained at the hotel, but the only privacy to be had from family and the other guests was to be found out of doors.

"You mean to say you've never asked Gil how he lost his leg?" Owen turned to Phoebe with an incredulous look.

"Of course not. We all know it happened in the Second Boer War, but the details certainly aren't any of our business, unless he offers up the information, which so far he hasn't. I suppose he doesn't like to talk about it."

Owen chuckled. "How very British of you, my dear."

She swatted his arm. "So tell me how it happened."

"They were at the Battle of Bergendal, which should have ended the war then and there with a British victory, except it didn't. About five days in, apparently, their column was surrounded, and the two of them and about a dozen other men were cut off from their fellows. In an all-or-nothing bid, they decided to fight their way through, and Hugh came face-to-face with an enemy soldier, who fired at point-blank range." He shifted the angle of the umbrella as the wind changed directions. "By some miracle born of instinct, Gil shoved Hugh out of the way, and the shot went awry. They thought they were in the clear, but then someone behind them opened fire with a machine gun."

"Oh! I didn't know they had those back then."

"They weren't quite as deadly as nowadays, but yes, they existed. Sir Hugh was wounded in the arm. Nothing overly serious. Gil's leg, however, was destroyed. Several of the men died. Hugh and Gil and some of the others barely made it out. Hugh carried Gil across his shoulders."

"Good heavens, Hugh was a hero."

"They both were. Hugh would have died if not for Gil."

"Hmm . . . I wonder, though . . . Would Gil have lost his leg if not for Hugh?"

"What do you mean?"

"Saving Hugh distracted him—it must have. If not for that, would he have detected the presence of the machine guns behind them? Would he have gotten out of the way sooner?"

Owen tipped his head as he considered. "It's possible, I suppose. But how could Gil have done differently? He couldn't have let his friend die if there was something he could do to stop it."

"No, of course not. I just wonder if he ever thinks about how things might have turned out differently. They've been friends a very long time, haven't they?"

"They met at Eton and attended Oxford together. Their experiences in South Africa cemented their bond, and their activities coincided quite a bit after that. During the Great War, Gil and Hugh were part of the Dublin Castle administration in Ireland, both serving in the office of the chief secretary."

"Fitzallen. That's an Irish name, isn't it?"

"Anglo-Irish, with an emphasis on the Anglo. Hugh's family have been landowners outside of Dublin for generations. Still are, but most of his immediate family left their cousins to mind the flocks, so to speak, and brought the bulk of their money back to Britain. Hugh was an MP for a while, years ago. Stood for Brampton."

"And Gil served in the House of Lords. It's almost as if they've lived parallel lives, isn't it?" She thought of the conversation Eva had overheard on the *Georgiana*. "Did anything unusual happen in Ireland?"

"Lots of unusual things. Those were not easy times in Ireland. Still aren't."

"What do you mean?"

"You might not have heard much about it at the time, because the war in Europe was raging, but there was an uprising in Dublin four years ago. Members of the Irish Republican Brotherhood occupied the main post office and a few other public buildings in the city. They wished to bring attention to the cause of Irish independence. They made demands for a voice in their own governing and refused to back down."

"What happened?"

"They were finally overpowered, charged with treason, and most of the leaders were executed in short order. About forty of them."

Her hand flew to her lips. "Owen, that's horrible."

He nodded. "It's not something most British diplomats are proud of, but it happened all the same."

"Did Gil have anything to do with it?"

"Not directly, as far as I know. They continued in the administration until a year ago and retired, as is their due at their age."

"Eva overheard something earlier that makes me worry for Julia's safety." She related what Eva had told her. "Could these stem from Gil's time in Ireland?"

"Perhaps. Or it could be any number of things. Gil is a businessman and an industrialist, and such men make enemies, unfortunately."

Phoebe darted a look at Owen's fine features. "Have you?"

He smiled. "Don't worry. There's been nothing I can't handle."

"Owen . . ."

He put a finger to her lips. "Remember, I'm a fair man, and I neither take advantage of those who work for me nor renege on my financial obligations to those I do business with."

Admiration filled her, and gratitude that such a man had entered her life. Someday, she thought, she and Owen might marry and build a life together. Most women would call her a fool for postponing that day, but before she became any man's wife, she wanted to become self-sufficient in her own right. Would Julia ever aspire to a similar goal? She didn't think so. "I just wish . . ." She shook her head. Wishing would change nothing. Just as pleading with Julia to reconsider her decision to marry Gil had changed nothing.

Owen brought them to a halt, and they stood facing each other beneath the umbrella. His fingertips grazed her cheek. "I wish I didn't have to leave tonight."

"You need to get back to Yorkshire. You have a business to oversee and your own problems to contend with. Labor union demands can't simply be dismissed. You'll have to deal with them. Our family matters will work themselves out."

"I know they will. It's just that . . . I don't know . . . Something doesn't feel quite right."

She smiled ruefully. "Is it any wonder? This marriage isn't right. But what's done is done. Besides, despite recent history, we have no reason to think the past will repeat itself. Surely no one can be *that* unlucky."

She spoke of the three incidents in the past year that had involved murder—one at Foxwood Hall, another at the Haverleigh School for Young Ladies, and, finally, at her cousin Regina's home of High Head Lodge. With an ironic smile, Owen held her hand with his free one and drew her closer to him beneath the umbrella. Phoebe darted a glance around the park and the esplanade, hoping they would not be observed, then realized she didn't care. She raised her lips to his and parted them for his kiss. A sense of calm and contentment flowed through her, and when he lifted his face away, she smiled.

"Despite what I just said, I wish you didn't have to go, too."

He bowed his head again, this time to press his brow to hers. He sighed. "Please don't go looking for trouble while you're here."

She frowned. "Why do you say that?"

"Ha." He straightened. "As if I needed to explain."

"I'll have you know I never go *looking* for trouble." Her attempt to look indignant was halfhearted at best. "For some reason, trouble has a habit of looking for me."

"Indeed." He swung the umbrella to the ground and reached for her again, pulling her close. His lips nudged her chin upward and then covered her mouth, deeply and filled with promise, just as the rain misting their faces and the park around them promised to bring the fresh life of springtime to the island. It wasn't until the breath left her entirely that he eased away. "We'd best get back to the hotel before someone comes looking for you."

A muffled knocking yanked Eva from sleep. For a sluggish moment, she forgot where she was, then recognized the lumpy cot beneath her, placed in the dressing room of the hotel room shared by Ladies Phoebe and Amelia. She sat up, rubbing her eyes, and reached for the alarm clock she had brought from home. A scrap of moonlight illuminated the dial, which read a quarter to two.

The knocking continued. With a sense of trepidation and racing speculations, Eva came to her feet, grabbed her wrapper, and swung it about her shoulders as she hurried into the main room. Phoebe and Amelia were awake, as well; Amelia huddled in her bed while Phoebe padded to the door. They had switched on the table lamp between their beds.

Another pounding was followed by, "Phoebe, let me in."

"It's Julia." Phoebe reached the door and quickly unlocked it. When she swung it open, Lady Julia rushed inside, brushing past her sister almost as if she didn't see her.

Eva crossed the room to her. "My lady, what is it?"

"Oh, Eva!" Without a word of explanation, Lady Julia fell into Eva's arms and sobbed against her shoulder.

"My lady . . ."

"Julia, what is it?" Lady Phoebe moved behind her sister and stroked her back. "What's happened?"

Lady Amelia tossed her covers aside and padded barefoot to them. "Julia, you're scaring me."

Lady Julia trembled against Eva, frightening her, too. She had never seen her like this, had rarely ever seen her as anything but fully in control of her emotions. Which made this all the more alarming.

"Come, my lady. Let's sit down and talk about what's troubling you." Eva started to guide the others to the sitting area but decided all three of her ladies were so distraught, it might be better to sit where they might offer physical comfort to each other. With her arm around Julia's shoulders, she walked her to one of the beds, and the other two sisters followed. They surrounded Julia. Amelia reached to hold her hand but pulled back with a gasp.

"What happened to your hand?"

A silk scarf encircled Lady Julia's right palm. Eva lifted her hand to inspect it and saw flecks of blood that had come through the pale yellow fabric. Fury rose up in her, directed at whoever had done this. If that individual, whether the viscount or someone else, had entered the room at that moment, she would have flown at him and most likely clamped her hands around his throat.

Hysterics would achieve nothing. She drew a breath to contain her ire and spoke as calmly as she could. "My lady, what happened? How did you hurt your hand, and how did you get here?"

Lady Julia wiped her tears with the back of her uninjured hand, but to little purpose, for they continued to fall, albeit more slowly. "I made the deck steward row me over. He didn't wonder why. The entire crew knows what happened."

"But we don't, Julia," Amelia said soothingly. "Please tell us."

Lady Julia bowed her head and shook it slowly. "He's horrid. I cannot live with him."

"Gil?" Phoebe ventured.

"Of course Gil. Who else? We . . . we . . ." She shook her head again. "We argued terribly. He accused me of flirting with the photographer, said that I encouraged him to make advances."

Eva's insides turned cold. Blasted man, that photographer. She had seen his familiarity. Everyone must have seen it—obviously, the viscount had. But to accuse Lady Julia of instigating the man's behavior . . . and on their wedding night? It was unconscionable.

"Did you tell him you have no control over another person's actions?" she asked gently.

"What *do* you mean? What actions? The photographer, Mr. Mowbry, merely took pictures. He told me how to stand, where to look—" She broke off, sobbing once more. She buried her face in her palms.

Phoebe patted her sister's shoulder. "After Gil accused you, what happened next?"

"We argued over it for quite some time, with Gil becoming more and more angry. He called me some frightful things—gold digger, for one." A heavy silence fell as Eva, and no doubt Phoebe and Amelia, remembered Julia's words that morning at the Royal Yacht Squadron. Julia blew out a breath. "Yes, all right. Perhaps it's true. Perhaps I did marry him for his money. So what? Am I the first woman to do such a thing? It would not have been an empty arrangement. I have—or had—every intention of being a good wife to Gil, of making him happy for as long as . . . well, for the rest of his life." She treated them all to a defiant look. "I would have given him no cause for complaint."

"Of course you wouldn't." Amelia reached over to give Julia a hug.

"What happened next, my lady? How did you hurt your hand?" Eva held her breath.

"Gil finally became so fed up, he stormed from the room, and as he did, he stumbled. His shoulder hit a small mirror hanging near the door, and it fell." Julia paused to dab at her damp cheeks with the back of the scarf around her hand. Phoebe belatedly went to the bed table and brought back a handkerchief. "It shattered, and I cut my hand trying to pick up the pieces. You see, I knew the crew must have heard us. I didn't want one of the maids coming in and thinking my husband had become violent with me." She shuddered. "I couldn't bear the humiliation of anyone thinking he'd begun throwing things or threatening me."

Eva wavered between feeling as though her heart were about to break for her lady and wanting to throttle Lord Annondale. She needed the answer to one question. "Did he, my lady? Did he become violent or threaten you?"

Her relief came in a great wave as Lady Julia shook her head. "He did not, at least not physically. But he made his anger and his distrust perfectly clear to me. So clear, I don't know how I can ever bear to be in the same room with him again."

Phoebe caught Eva's gaze, and Eva saw her own anger mirrored in her eyes, and a sobering lack of surprise. They had both known that Lady Julia and the viscount were not compatible, that they would never suit each other once the initial glow of the wedding had faded. But surely neither of them had expected reality to sink in this soon.

"Then end it, Julia," Phoebe said quietly. "You can have the marriage annulled."

"And come *home*," Amelia put in longingly.

But Julia was already shaking her head. "There can't be an annulment. You see, we argued after we . . ."

"After you what?" Amelia asked and then contracted her mouth into a little ball of understanding.

Eva's heart sank to her very toes. The marriage had been consummated, which meant if Lady Julia chose to leave him, there must be a divorce. And the Renshaw name would be dragged through the gossip rags. Not to mention that, even though there had been only the one time, there could be a child.

What a disaster.

Judging by her grim expression, Phoebe thought so, too. "Perhaps Grampapa can intervene in some way."

"How?" Julia gave one adamant shake of her head, which quashed that notion. "No, Grampapa must not be involved in my mistake. His health . . ." She trailed off, and Phoebe and Amelia nodded sadly in agreement.

"Then what will you do, my lady?" Eva purposely kept her dismay and heartache from revealing themselves in her voice. Without the possibility of an annulment, and with Julia's refusal to allow her grandfather to become involved, her choices were few. What she needed now was support in making her decisions, not a display of emotion.

"What will I do?" Julia repeated in a murmur. With the handkerchief, she wiped the last of her tears away and let out a long, shuddering sigh. "There is only one thing to do. I made my bed. I must return and lie in it."

"No, Julia," Amelia said urgently. "You can't."

Julia slid off the bed and straightened to full height. "I don't know why I came here. A moment of cowardice, I suppose."

"Julia, don't," Amelia continued to plead.

Phoebe remained silent, her head bowed, her brows knit.

Eva came to her feet. "Shall I go with you, my lady?"

Amelia let loose a sob, and Julia bent to give her a hug. "I'm sorry I've upset you, darling. You mustn't worry about me. Married people argue all the time. Not usually on their wedding night, mind you." She made an attempt at laughter, which came out brittle and stilted. "But it will be all right. We'll sack Mr. Mowbry, though I'll be happy to give him a good reference for his next engagement, as long as I can manage to do so on the sly, without Gil knowing." She kissed Amelia before releasing her and straightening. Turning to Eva, she shook her head. "No, I'll go back alone. I . . . actually told the steward to wait." She studied her feet. "I knew all along I had no choice but to return. I just needed to . . ."

She surprised Eva by tossing her arms around her and burying her face in Eva's neck. Eva embraced her in return, patted her back, and whispered assurances that if anyone could make a success of even the darkest of circumstances, Lady Julia could. She only wished she could believe her own words.

Lady Julia dabbed her eyes a final time. All the while, Phoebe had looked on silently, her face nearly expressionless. Now she said, "Men get over their jealousies. Gil will get over this, and everything will be all right."

"Indeed. Thank you, Phoebe."

But as Julia and Phoebe exchanged glances, Eva saw the pain on Phoebe's features, the hurt in her eyes. And on Julia's features, she witnessed a flash of guilt, which vanished with a final, audible breath and a squaring of her shoulders. Not for the first time, Eva silently begged to know why these two young women couldn't breach the barriers between them and simply be sisters, and enjoy the comfort and strength and love that sisters should be able to afford each other. The answer had always eluded her, and she shook her head at her own inability to help them.

"Not a word of this to Grams and Grampapa," Lady Julia admonished her sisters, who nodded.

After exchanging her wrapper for an overcoat, Eva walked her out of the hotel and to the water's edge, where the skiff waited beside a short pier. The seas had calmed since that afternoon, and Eva needn't worry about Lady Julia's safety on the return trip. The man at the oars, the deck steward, seemed inordinately relieved to see her. He handed her into the boat, untied the small craft, and dipped the oars quietly into the blackened waters of the Solent.

CHAPTER 5

Phoebe tiptoed across the hotel room, being careful not to wake Amelia as she opened the door into the dressing room. She found Eva already up and dressed.

Eva regarded her with evident surprise. "Why are you up so early, especially after such a late night?"

"Quickly, help me dress, Eva, and then you and I are going out to the *Georgiana*. I can't let Julia set sail without checking on her this morning. She and Gil should already be up, since they're planning to leave early. If we hurry, we can go and be back before Amelia and everyone else is awake."

Not a quarter hour later, she and Eva squeezed into the rear seat of the small runabout she was able to hire at the Royal Yacht Squadron. The sleek, open boat with its glossy finish and outboard motor made short work of the distance to the *Georgiana*. When they arrived, a member of the crew met them and helped them board. Phoebe immediately realized something was wrong by the man's brisk manner and refusal to meet her eye.

He led them into the saloon and left them. All traces of

the wedding had been cleared away. The aroma of coffee drifted from the dining room. Moments later, Julia hurried in to greet them, yet she dispensed entirely with civilities.

"Gil is missing," she said. Phoebe noticed at once that the silk scarf Julia had worn around her hand last night had been replaced with a proper bandage.

She exchanged a puzzled glance with Eva. "What do you mean, missing?"

"He never came to bed last night, and we've searched the boat for him." Julia gestured wildly with her bandaged hand. "I thought he merely chose to spend the night elsewhere than with me, but this morning he's nowhere to be found."

"Maybe he went ashore," Phoebe ventured, "as you did."

"That's not possible, unless he summoned a boat from shore to come and get him. No one here brought him, and none of the small boats are missing. We wired the yacht club just in case, and he hasn't been seen there. I can't imagine where else he would go."

"He was angry last night," Phoebe said. "Perhaps he did arrange to be picked up and doesn't wish to be found yet."

Julia let out an impatient sigh, but rather than comment on Phoebe's suggestion, she motioned for them to follow her into the dining room. "Have you eaten?"

The smaller tables were gone, leaving only the dining table and chairs. Phoebe's stomach rumbled in response to Julia's question. A light repast of scones and fruit had been laid out on a sideboard. Phoebe and Eva helped themselves, poured coffee, and joined Julia at the table. At least Phoebe did. Eva remained standing, holding her cup and plate.

"Shall I go below, my lady? Perhaps see if I can assist Hetta with anything?"

"Don't be silly, Eva." Julia waved a hand dismissively.

"Sit. Eat. I'm glad you both came. I've . . . Well . . . there's no one here I can talk to. Hetta's a dear, of course, but you know how her English is."

Julia's admission warmed Phoebe as nothing else had during her time in Cowes—except, perhaps, Owen's parting kiss last night.

"My lady," Eva said after a sip of coffee, "is the crew sure the viscount didn't fall overboard?"

A look of alarm entered Julia's eyes, but then she shook her head. "Gil is too experienced a yachtsman to have fallen overboard from an anchored vessel in relatively calm waters. Even with his prosthetic leg," she added, as if either Eva or Phoebe was going to suggest otherwise.

"That's quite right, my lady. The viscount could not have gone overboard. Not without being pushed." Miss Blair, in a sleek-fitting velvet ensemble of midnight black and scarlet red, pushed through the pantry door. "Ah, I'd heard we had visitors." She offered a differential nod to Phoebe, then frowned as she noticed Eva sitting at the table. Phoebe tensed to defend Eva's presence in the dining room, but Miss Blair gave an infinitesimal shrug.

"How dare you say such a thing, even in jest?" Julia chided her.

"It was no jest. Merely a statement of fact. Since I've been in Viscount Annondale's employ, he has had no mishaps on board the *Georgiana*. Not even minor ones. One mustn't make the mistake of believing Gil's infirmity has rendered him vulnerable. He understands the sea and what it's capable of. He respects it and knows exactly how to handle himself when out in the middle of it."

"Excuse me." Julia's dark eyes narrowed. "Did you just call my husband by his first name?"

Miss Blair's full lips, bright red and glistening, briefly pouted. "Forgive me, my lady. The viscount doesn't always stand on ceremony with his employees."

"Doesn't he?" Anger emanated off Julia in waves; Phoebe sensed a storm waiting to break.

"No, he doesn't." Miss Blair smiled.

"Well, I do, and you'd do best to remember it."

Miss Blair's gaze drifted to Eva, and an ironic light came into her eyes. But she said only, "Yes, ma'am. Now, is there anything I can do for you?"

"The moment my husband is found, I want to be told."

"Of course." Voices could be heard from the saloon. Miss Blair unnecessarily announced, "Your guests are up, my lady. Do you wish me to ask the galley to send up a hot breakfast now, or will the scones and fruit do?"

Sir Hugh Fitzallen and Veronica Townsend strolled in together. Their chatter ceased when they beheld everyone else in the room.

"Well, then, good morning." Miss Townsend crossed to the buffet and poured coffee. "I didn't expect company this morning. Didn't Gil say we were to sail at first light?"

"My sister came to see me off," Julia replied in an indifferent manner.

"Isn't that spiffing of her? Good morning, Phoebe." Sir Hugh spoke brightly and flashed a broad smile. "And who is this lovely lady, might I ask? I'm sorry, I don't remember you from yesterday. Did we meet?"

Poor Eva flushed at this attention paid her, and peeked up at Sir Hugh in some confusion, especially when he offered to shake her hand. Phoebe was about to explain when Miss Blair did it for her.

"It seems the viscount isn't the only lenient employer. This is Lady Phoebe's maid."

Sir Hugh's hand drifted back to his side. The way Miss Blair said *maid*, as if it were code for some catching disease, made Eva blush more furiously. Phoebe wanted to throttle the woman. But Miss Blair's attention had already shifted.

"So then, my lady, hot breakfast or fruit and scones?"

Julia shook her head, frowning. "I don't know. Ask them."

"This is fine for me," Sir Hugh said, using two fingers to brush at his neatly trimmed goatee. "Is Gil up yet?"

"I don't require anything more," Miss Townsend said in her grim manner and plopped a spoonful of fruit onto a plate. "But yes, where is Gil, and why on earth haven't we sailed yet? The sooner we get on with this, the sooner I can return home and to life as usual."

When Julia allowed their questions to go unanswered, Sir Hugh appealed to Miss Townsend. "I don't remember Gil as a man who lies abed all morning. Indeed, during our army days, he was typically the first up in the camp. In Ireland, too. Have his habits changed as much as all that?"

Miss Townsend made a little *hmm* sound and rolled her eyes heavenward. "I suppose his wedding night has left him uncommonly weary."

"Veronica, really. Manners, my dear." Sir Hugh darted a glance at Julia, who remained intent on stirring her coffee and pretended not to have heard.

Miss Townsend shrugged, obviously indifferent to the consequences of her remarks.

Clearly, she was not happy to be on this voyage. But yesterday, when Eva had mentioned Julia's grievance that both Sir Hugh and Miss Townsend were going along on the honeymoon voyage—odd enough, indeed—the reason for Miss Townsend being included was that Gil hadn't the heart to leave her all alone at the family estate. By all appearances, however, Gil was doing his sister no favors.

As the pair seated themselves, Curtis Mowbry came into the room, a small box camera in hand. "Good morning, my lady. I'm surprised we haven't sailed yet." He set the camera on the table, before an empty chair, and went to the sideboard. He stared down at the offerings, selected a scone, and turned around. "I don't suppose a body could get some eggs with perhaps a rasher of bacon?"

"I'll go inform the galley." Miss Blair retraced her steps to the pantry.

After pouring a cup of coffee, Mr. Mowbry returned to the table, where he noticed Eva. "Hello. I don't believe we've met."

"My lady, I should go below. Surely there is something I can help Hetta with," Eva whispered beseechingly in Phoebe's ear.

Phoebe nodded and mouthed, "Go." Eva couldn't seem to leave the room quickly enough.

The photographer folded his considerable length into his seat at the table and consumed half a scone in one bite. Chewing, he said, "Something about the salt air works up one's appetite. I shall try not to eat you out of house and home when we hit the open waters, Lady Annondale." He glanced around. "Is the viscount awake? He said he wished to speak with me this morning. He was rather terse about it last night. Done in from his long day, no doubt. I suppose he wishes to lay out the parameters for when and where on the vessel he'll allow me to set up my camera." He washed down the scone with a generous sip of coffee. "You needn't worry, my lady. I'm the soul of discretion. You'll hardly know I'm here, yet when we return home, I'll present you with a record of your travels to treasure the rest of your life."

Julia's lips twitched into a tight smile. "I'm confident of that, Mr. Mowbry." Again, Phoebe noted that she didn't answer the question about whether Gil was awake. While Sir Hugh and Miss Townsend discussed the weather and the odds of smooth or choppy seas, Julia appeared to be studying Curtis Mowbry intently. Her brow furrowed. Suddenly, she said, "I meant to ask you yesterday, but in all the activity I simply forgot. You seem rather familiar. Have we met previously?"

"I don't believe so, Lady Annondale. Although I've little doubt I might have photographed an event you attended."

"Yes, yes . . ." Julia's scrutiny lasted another moment before she looked away. "That must be it."

She abruptly rose from the table and went to stare out one of the windows facing over the port side. Sky and water blended into a single tone of silvery blue, with a slightly darker line marking the horizon. When she lingered there, Phoebe went to join her. "Why don't you come back to the hotel with me?"

"Why would I do that?" Julia replied absently.

"Because one could cut the tension here with a knife. Stay with the family until Gil turns up." She moved closer and lowered her voice even more. "Let him come to you and make amends."

"How do you know any of this is Gil's fault?" Julia spoke in a monotone, thoroughly devoid of emotion. "Perhaps it's mine."

The pantry door swung open, and an elderly man in a dark suit, whom Phoebe recognized as Gil's valet, came into the room. His face was pale and waxy, as if he had just suffered a fright. "My lady," he said with a tremor in his voice, "there is cause for concern."

Julia turned away from the window. "What is it, Collins?" She gasped, and her hand flew to her bosom.

Phoebe's heart jolted as she realized what the valet carried—Gil's prosthetic leg, its leather straps and buckles dangling.

"It was in the viscount's dressing room. His crutches are missing. He would not have left the *Georgiana* in such a state. It is quite time to summon the police."

"Did I understand you correctly, Lady Annondale? You said your husband left the vessel without his leg?" Police Sergeant Davis, as he had introduced himself, looked as though he were about to break into laughter; at least Eva judged as much by the bulging of his cheeks and the compression of his lips.

"You heard what her ladyship said," she admonished him. "The viscount wears a prosthetic from the knee down. He lost his leg two decades ago, serving in the Boer Wars. It is no laughing matter, sir."

They were in the small sitting room off the main saloon, where Viscount Annondale displayed his service medals and commendations as well as his yachting trophies. Eva hadn't previously been here, and now her surroundings reinforced Miss Blair's assertion that the viscount could not have simply fallen overboard—not if these awards and recognitions were worth the gilt gleaming proudly from within their frames.

The sergeant cleared his throat. "Forgive me, my lady. Your statement took me unawares, is all. No disrespect intended. Now, you say you last saw the viscount around 1:00 this morning?"

"Yes."

"And where precisely was that?"

"Here, on the *Georgiana*. In our stateroom."

"I see." He jotted a note in his tablet. "What happened after that? Did you retire for the evening?"

"Gil—that is, my husband—left the stateroom."

"And went where?"

Lady Julia sighed impatiently. "That's just it. I don't know."

"Did he say anything when he left?"

Eva could see Lady Julia's composure being chipped away with each question. Her color rose, and she fidgeted with the embroidered edge of her Chanel tunic. Eva also noticed she kept her wounded palm facing downward at all times. She set her own hand over Lady Julia's jittery one, and it immediately stilled.

"He didn't tell me where he was going, if that's what you mean," she said. "I assumed he was going out on deck for some air."

"I see."

"But perhaps he went into Cowes," Lady Julia suggested.

"We're looking into the possibility." Sergeant Davis shifted his sights to Eva. "Do you have anything to add to Lady Annondale's statement?"

"I'm here only at Lady Annondale's request, for support."

"I take it you're her maid?"

"No, I serve her sisters. I was in Cowes last night."

"So then you've nothing to add?" The man eyed her expectantly.

Eva's insides froze. To say no would be a lie; to say yes and have to explain Lady Julia's pounding on the hotel room door last night . . . Why, it might lead to the wrong impression. That perhaps Lady Julia somehow was to blame for her husband's disappearance.

But that was ridiculous. No one had cried foul play. Eva was allowing her imagination to run away with her, basing present circumstances on past occurrences. . . .

"What Eva isn't telling you, Sergeant, is that last night my husband and I argued before he left our stateroom.

And afterward, I had the deck steward row me ashore, where I went to speak with my sisters. Eva was there."

"You and the viscount argued?" Sergeant Davis acquired a sudden interest that hadn't appeared nearly so acute moments ago. "About what?"

Lady Julia's fingers tightened around Eva's hand. "It seems my husband was under the mistaken impression that our wedding photographer had been flirting with me."

The policeman's eyebrows surged. "And *had* he been?"

"Not to my knowledge." Lady Julia pulled up indignantly.

"And to yours?" He shot this question at Eva.

"I . . . em . . . that is to say, it's not my place to judge. I'm merely on hand to serve my ladies."

"That didn't answer the question, Miss . . . ?"

"Huntford," she supplied and hoped he would end this line of questioning. Her hopes were dashed.

"Did you detect any flirtations between the photographer and Lady Annondale?"

"Certainly not on Lady Annondale's part," she replied truthfully. Beside her, Lady Julia stiffened. When the sergeant tapped his pencil and continued staring Eva down, she realized he would not relent until she answered the question. "As for the photographer, he did seem a bit preoccupied with posing her ladyship just so. He perhaps spent a bit more time with her than the others. But isn't that natural, sir? She *was* the bride, after all."

"Hmmm . . ."

After a knock on the door, another policeman poked his head in. "Sergeant, I think you'd better come and see this."

Sergeant Davis looked annoyed. "I'll be there presently." He addressed Lady Julia again. "I have one more question, for now. Lady Annondale, what happened to your hand?"

*   *   *

The moment the sitting room door opened, Phoebe jumped up from the sofa in the saloon. The sergeant came out first and spoke to the constable who had just gone in to tell him something. She had tried to hear what it was, but their murmurs had been too quiet. They strode past her, and then Eva and Julia came out, looking grim. She jumped up and hurried over to them.

"What happened?"

"He asked me a lot of questions," Julia said unhelpfully. She kept walking, and so did Eva.

"Where are you going?" Phoebe fell into step with them. "Where are *they* going?"

Julia sped her steps to keep up with the officers, who were now out on deck. "We'll find out when we get there."

They had not stopped to retrieve their coats, and a rigid wind hit them full on their faces and penetrated Phoebe's wool and velvet-trimmed suit as they made their way outside. The door opened again behind them, and Miss Blair followed them out. Julia looked as though she were about to protest but gave a slight shake of her head and kept going. They rounded the main cabin to the port side. Far ahead now, the two men proceeded toward the stern. Another constable awaited them there, in the shadow of a lifeboat suspended from its hooks and cables.

Phoebe's sense of foreboding grew with each step she took. The three policemen grouped themselves into a semi-circle, seeming fascinated by something on the gunwale.

"Well, Sergeant, what have your men found?" Julia spoke with impatient authority, but Phoebe recognized bravado when she heard it.

Sergeant Davis's mouth formed a severe line. "It looks like blood, my lady. Here." He pointed to the railing. "And here." He gestured at the deck.

"What on earth?" Julia rushed forward, only to stop short. At her feet, a dark stain marred the teak decking. Likewise, the same color splattered the railing. "It can't be blood."

Sergeant Davis tugged his cap lower over his brow. "Can't it, my lady?"

Her head snapped up. "I . . . don't know. Are you saying my husband might have met with an accident?"

"I'm saying any number of things, my lady. It could be your husband's blood. It could be from a member of the crew." He stared at Julia a moment, until his gaze dropped to her injured hand. Phoebe's stomach gathered into a ball of misgiving, and she guessed at his next words. She was not incorrect. "What happened to your ladyship's hand? I asked you inside, but you never answered me."

Phoebe stepped up beside Julia and slipped her arm through hers. She derived comfort from Eva's presence behind them and hoped Julia did, too. But it was Miss Blair who spoke next.

"I shall inquire, but I'm not aware of any member of the crew having injured him or herself since we boarded yesterday."

"Yes, please do inquire, Miss Blair," the man said, but rather perfunctorily, as if he didn't expect results from that quarter. He returned his scrutiny to Julia.

"I cut my hand on a piece of broken mirror," she said with a lift of her chin.

"And how did this mirror come to be broken, my lady?"

"It . . . fell from the wall. In our stateroom."

The sergeant let a moment pass as he weighed this answer, then asked, "And how did this happen?"

Julia let out a huff, and Phoebe pressed a cautioning hand on her forearm. Julia said, "From the vibration of the door closing. Obviously, it hadn't been hung very securely."

"Oh, I doubt that very much, my lady," Miss Blair said. "I personally supervised the refurbishing of the *Georgiana* when she was decommissioned after the war. I assure you, everything was—and is—tip-top."

Julia whirled to face her. "Haven't you some inquiring to do with the crew?"

The corners of Miss Blair's lips tilted upward. She gave a nod and turned on her heel.

"Can you show me this mirror, my lady?"

Julia hesitated, then nodded. "This way, Sergeant."

Inside, Phoebe, Eva, and several members of the crew, including the yacht's captain, were ushered into the dining room to await the sergeant's and Julia's return. No one spoke much, and not at all about what might have happened to Gil. The sergeant and Julia came in some ten minutes later, Julia looking pale and he looking bleak. Without a word, Julia took a seat across from Phoebe but didn't meet her gaze.

Sir Hugh, Veronica Townsend, and Miss Blair also came in, followed by Curtis Mowbry, who had left his camera behind this time. He wore a puzzled expression but, without a word, crossed to lean against the sideboard.

The sergeant cleared his throat. "Did any one of you see Viscount Annondale without his prosthetic leg last night?"

Around the table, heads shook.

"My lady," he continued, "the very last time you saw your husband, he was walking on two legs?"

She answered without hesitation. "Most assuredly."

"Have any of you ever known the viscount to leave the vessel on his crutches?"

Again, heads shook.

The captain, his face covered in a heavy growth of

beard, spoke up. "Lord Annondale is particular about not being seen without his leg. A matter of pride, it is. Only a most urgent matter would get him out from below deck on his crutches."

The sergeant digested this information. "I've heard he's an accomplished seaman, despite his disadvantage."

"That's right," the captain agreed. "Never need to waste a moment's worry about the viscount. If he thinks the seas are too rough for him, he stays within. Otherwise, he's as sure of his footing as you or I."

"He hasn't been as well as usual, though." This came from Sir Hugh. "Isn't that so, Veronica?"

"A bit of a chest cold." She compressed her lips, then said, "Another reason I thought this yachting honeymoon a daft idea. Sea air might be beneficial to the lungs, but really, dirty weather of this sort doesn't do anyone a lick of good."

The sergeant frowned. "This is the first I'm hearing about the viscount being unwell." He focused on Julia again. "My lady?"

"Yes, well, that's true. My husband has been a bit under the weather of late. As his sister says, his lungs have been plaguing him. But it's nothing serious. Not consumption or anything like that. His physician would have said."

Phoebe had a moment of doubt as to the truth of Julia's claim. Just yesterday she had referred to the fact that she would long outlive him. Given the near forty years' difference in their ages, that seemed given, but Phoebe had gotten the impression that Julia believed Gil wouldn't live many more years. *Had* his doctor issued a warning no one else knew about?

But even if that were true, Gil's health could have nothing to do with his disappearance today—unless he'd gone into Cowes, without informing anyone, to see a doctor. And that seemed unlikely.

A constable came to stand in the doorway, gesturing for the sergeant's attention. "We just had a shore-to-ship communication, Sergeant. Lord Annondale's been found."

"Thank heavens for that." Julia came eagerly to her feet. "Where is he?"

"He was found drifting against the pilings of the main pier at the Royal Yacht Squadron, my lady. Drowned."

CHAPTER 6

"Eva, I'm frightened." Phoebe sat with Eva on the hotel terrace overlooking Queen's Road and the strip of beach on the other side. Amelia and Grams had gone indoors, and only a scattering of people inhabited the other tables. Phoebe felt able to speak freely again.

"We don't know that there is anything to be frightened of," Eva reminded her, not for the first time since their trip to the *Georgiana* that morning.

The breeze off the water stirred the brim of Phoebe's sun hat and ruffled the hem of her frock. The sun had warmed since earlier, but Phoebe shivered nonetheless. "Julia is practically under house arrest here, and Sergeant Davis has turned the investigation over to his superior, Detective Inspector Lewis."

"Surely that's a good thing, my lady. He's more experienced in these matters than the sergeant. He'll get to the bottom of what happened, and all suspicion will be lifted from your sister."

"That's just it, Eva. Had they called in Scotland Yard, I'd be feeling a good deal more optimistic. The fact that they didn't tells me they're fairly certain of their suspect."

"Oh dear. I hadn't thought of it like that." Her finger traced the pattern in the wrought-iron table. "I could try ringing Miles." Eva spoke of her gentleman friend, Constable Miles Brannock, who kept the peace at home in Little Barlow. Phoebe shook her head.

"I don't see how he could help. Cowes is far out of his jurisdiction."

"He might be able to advise us."

"What we need is a good solicitor."

"I hope not, my lady. Besides, despite the viscount's sailing experience, it's still possible he fell overboard accidentally." She seemed about to add something more, but her mouth closed suddenly.

Arm in arm, Julia and Grampapa stepped out onto the terrace. Julia had changed into a black frock, visible beneath her open overcoat, and a black felt hat with a narrow brim. She wore a glove over her uninjured hand. The other she hid in her coat pocket but just then slid it free to swipe at a strand of hair that had blown across her face. That hand was as white as the bandage encircling it. Her eyes were puffy and red-rimmed, not from crying, Phoebe discerned, but from fatigue. No wonder, considering how little sleep she had gotten last night.

Phoebe stole the opportunity to study her grandfather's features. He had come to Cowes already looking strained. Now he seemed downright exhausted. Phoebe's heart ached with worry for him.

He spotted her sitting at the table, and she immediately schooled her features. With a small smile, she beckoned them over.

Eva came to her feet. "Lord Wroxly, Lady Annondale."

"Never mind the formalities, Eva," Julia said with a wave.

Still, Eva remained on her feet until Grampapa said,

"Please do sit, Eva. My girls need you here. Where is Amelia?"

"She's inside with Grams," Phoebe told him. "Didn't you see them?"

"We came from upstairs." Julia shrugged and sat down across from Phoebe. "Perhaps they went into the restaurant."

Grampapa sank heavily into the chair Eva held for him before she resumed her own seat. "Amelia is too young for all of this," he said with a sad shake of his head. "Yes, I quite well remember what happened at Haverleigh last year, and how well she held up. That doesn't mean the child should relive that kind of dreadful event all over again."

Amelia currently attended the Haverleigh School for Young Ladies. Phoebe, Julia, and even Grams had attended. Eva, too, had been admitted on scholarship but hadn't been able to complete her studies. They were all Haverleigh girls, which made a death—a murder—there last spring especially distressing for them.

"And certainly your brother must be shielded from the unpleasantness," Grampapa went on. "I left him with Sir Hugh in the library. They were pouring over a couple of atlases."

Phoebe thought to question whether this was a good idea, seeing that anyone on board the *Georgiana* last night could have been responsible for Gil's death, including Hugh Fitzallen. Then again, anyone might have rowed out to the vessel from Cowes, under cover of darkness, and confronted Gil on deck. She decided to hold her tongue. After all, Fox and Sir Hugh were in a public place.

"Is the detective inspector still here?" she asked instead.

"He has set up here for questioning," Julia explained. "Said it would be easier to conduct this part of his investigation here, where most of our wedding guests are staying. The crew is still aboard the *Georgiana*. Apparently, Sergeant Davis is still there questioning them." She stared down at the table, then raised her head with a mirthless laugh. "*Our wedding guests*. Married and widowed in less than twenty-four hours. Who'd have thought it possible?"

"Julia . . . ," Phoebe whispered but had no words to add.

Grampapa slid his arm around Julia and pulled her toward him to press a kiss to her cheek. "I'm very sorry, my dear."

"I know you are, darling Grampapa. I am, too. I'm sorry for Gil." She lowered her gaze, and when she looked up again, Phoebe was shocked to see tears glittering on her lashes. "It's my fault."

"You mustn't say that, my dear." Grampapa was quick to chide her, albeit gently.

"Why not? Because someone might hear me and think I'm confessing to sending him to a watery grave?" When she paused, Phoebe feared she might attest to the fact that Detective Inspector Lewis thought exactly that. It would only upset their grandfather and put further strain on his heart. She nearly breathed an audible sigh of relief when Julia took a different tack. "If I hadn't come to Cowes last night, after we argued, he would most likely be alive right now."

"You argued? You came to Cowes last night?" This news obviously perplexed Grampapa.

Julia patted his forearm. "We had a spat, and yes, I came to see Eva and my sisters. I needed someone to tell me everything would be all right. And it worked. I went back to the *Georgiana*, but Gil wasn't in our stateroom. It's such a large boat, though, that I didn't go looking for him. I assumed he'd return soon enough and was determined to stay awake until he did, but I fell asleep. When I awoke this morning . . . well."

Grampapa looked satisfied. "Then I don't see how you could possibly be to blame, Julia."

She drew a breath, evidently steeling herself to go on. "Gil obviously did return to our stateroom while I was here last night. He readied himself for bed but, for some reason, went back out on deck. Don't you see? If I hadn't left the *Georgiana*, I'd have been where I was supposed to be, in our stateroom, and Gil and I would have made up and gone to sleep. He'd still be . . ."

Grampapa was shaking his head, his expression stern. "You cannot know that. Gil might have gone out on deck again no matter where you were. His going overboard had nothing to do with you. Nothing whatsoever."

He ended on a loud, emphatic note, and Phoebe became aware of a sudden silence around them. Conversations had ceased, and the occupants of the other tables craned their necks for a view of Julia. Then the whispers began.

"Isn't that her?"

"It is. That's Julia Renshaw."

Julia turned her head at the sound of her name. Her color rose; her nose became pinched with tension.

"Julia Townsend, you mean," someone else said.

Phoebe pushed to her feet. "Let's go inside."

The whispers cut short as Julia, Grampapa, and Eva came to their feet. Grampapa returned their gazes with one of rebuke and put his arm around Julia again. "Never mind them, dearest. They've nothing else to occupy their small minds."

They were on their way inside when an individual came out, saw them, and halted abruptly. Dressed in a plain brown wool coat and matching hat, the young woman looked familiar to Phoebe, yet she couldn't recall where she had encountered her previously. She noticed Julia frowning at the woman, too, perhaps also with a sense of recognition.

Grampapa started them walking again and stepped around the woman, but Eva pulled up sharp.

"I'll come in presently," she said, and Phoebe nodded, trusting Eva to deal with whatever the matter might be and report back to her. Before the door into the hotel closed behind her, she heard Eva's angry murmur.

"What are you doing here?"

Before the waitress had a chance to answer the question, Eva grasped her by the forearm and drew her to the edge of the terrace, away from the occupied tables.

"How dare you?" the young woman protested. "You can't just tug me along like this. Who do you think you are?"

Eva came to a halt and dropped the woman's arm. "I am Lady Annondale's former maid and her friend. I asked you a question. What are you doing here?"

"I was asked to come by that detective fellow."

"Detective Inspector Lewis?"

"That's the one. He telephoned over to the Yacht Squadron, and my supervisor said I had to come talk to him here."

Eva studied her features and didn't like what she saw. This young woman seemed all too happy to be included in a police investigation, just as she had been all too happy to hover upstairs at the clubhouse yesterday and listen in on the Renshaw sisters' conversation.

"And have you spoken to him yet?"

"For a few minutes, yeah. Then someone came in and whispered in his ear, and he told me to wait out here, that he might have a few more questions."

Eva darted a gaze at the other hotel guests, some of whom stared outright, while others pretended not to be listening in but nonetheless darted looks in her direction. She once more guided the waitress away, this time down the steps that led to the road below.

"I was told to wait on the terrace," she objected.

"We won't go far." With a hand at her elbow, Eva started them walking along the pavement. A motorcar whizzed by. Beyond, waves shattered on the beach into glittering droplets. "What is your name?"

"Marie. Marie Tansley. Why?"

"Because I like to know whom I'm speaking to, that's why, Miss Tansley." If Eva borrowed a bit of her authoritative tone from the Countess of Wroxly herself, she could hardly be faulted. It was the countess's granddaughter she sought to protect. "Now, what have you told Mr. Lewis so far?"

A frown flickered across the woman's brow. "I don't think I should say. This is official police business, after all."

"Anything that concerns the Renshaw sisters is very much my business, Miss Tansley, and I take it quite seriously, not to mention personally. You deliberately eavesdropped on my ladies yesterday—"

"I did no such thing. I delivered refreshments—"

"And after setting down the tray, you lingered to hear their personal conversation." Eva didn't have to be in the room at the time to infer this correctly. She had seen the details in the sisters' faces: Phoebe's frustrations, Amelia's tears, Julia's stubborn resolve. They had argued about Gil, about Julia's reasons for agreeing to marry him. And all the while there had been Miss Tansley, her eyes lit by the excitement of having stumbled upon something beyond her mundane routine.

"Can I help it if those ladies yapped in my presence?"

"My guess is they didn't know you were there."

"They might have glanced behind them. It's not like I was hiding."

Eva stepped closer, practically toe to toe. "What did you tell the inspector?"

"I told him the truth." Her chin came up defiantly. "I told him just what I overheard."

"Which is?"

Miss Tansley's chin remained tilted as a veil of shrewdness descended over her features. She smiled in a way that made Eva want to smack the expression from her face. " 'He'll be gone soon enough,' Lady Annondale said to her sisters, 'and then I may do as I please.' " She leaned closer to Eva, like one gossip imparting a particularly tasty morsel to another. "And then her sister, the younger, prettier one, said, 'You think Gil will die soon and then you can marry Theo and be happy.' "

With that, Marie Tansley turned about and climbed the steps to the terrace. The blood drained from Eva's face, leaving her feeling faint.

CHAPTER 7

Amelia clung to Phoebe's hand as they followed Detective Inspector Lewis into a small office at the rear of the hotel. Phoebe guessed the detective to be somewhere in his late thirties, with dark hair silvering at the temples, cool gray eyes, and features one might call chiseled. He might have been handsome, she thought, if not for his habit of narrowing his steely eyes, as if boring his scrutiny clean through his quarry.

Phoebe felt like quarry at the moment, and she knew Amelia would give her favorite Kestner bisque doll, her prized childhood possession, to be anywhere else in the world. But obediently they entered the room after the inspector, and after Amelia reluctantly released Phoebe's hand, each took one of the seats toward which he gestured. He sat in the chair behind the desk, leaned forward, and tented his hands beneath the square line of his chin.

"Now then, my ladies, I'd like you to tell me about a certain conversation you had with your sister, Lady Annondale, just prior to her wedding to Lord Annondale."

Phoebe and Amelia exchanged a glance before staring back at him.

"Well?" His features remained steady; his expression implacable.

Phoebe cleared her throat, though she immediately wished she hadn't, for it only produced a tickle that made her cough. There being no water handy, the inspector waited for her to recover. Then he repeated his prompt of "Well?"

"Which conversation would that be?" Phoebe knew very well which one he referred to but wouldn't divulge a single detail until—unless—specifically pressed.

"We had many conversations, sir," Amelia said with such wide-eyed innocence, Phoebe couldn't tell if she was serious or deliberately playing ignorant.

Detective Inspector Lewis drew in a breath and let it out slowly, a sound that put Phoebe's nerves on edge. This was not the first time she had been questioned by an officer of the law. Last summer at Cousin Regina's house, High Head Lodge, Chief Inspector Isaac Perkins had treated her like a prime suspect. She had felt the room closing in around her, like a noose cutting off her oxygen. She felt that way now, except she didn't fear for herself. She feared for Julia, her grandparents, and the future of their family.

She realized Amelia had gone on speaking. "Most of what we said had to do with how beautiful Julia looked in her wedding gown. Oh, she was splendid, and the lace in her veil rivaled the lace in Queen Victoria's wedding gown, designed by the very same man, actually. William Dyce. Have you heard of him? The veil had been our great-grandmother's, and I must say it matched the ivory of her gown perfectly. Of course, Julia always looks wonderful. She's the prettiest of us Renshaw girls. Phoebe, of course, is the smartest, and . . ."

"*Ahem.*" Detective Inspector Lewis looked not only un-impressed but also utterly annoyed. "That's not what I'm talking about. Apparently, the three of you were left alone in the room, except for a waitress who came to bring tea or some such."

Phoebe's stomach sank to her toes. "Was there a waitress? I don't remember."

"Nor do I." Amelia folded her hands primly in her lap.

"I see neither of you is in a mood to cooperate, and that makes me ponder the reason why." The inspector rubbed his chin slowly with the back of his hand. "I would have preferred to speak to you separately. It was only out of deference to your grandparents' wishes that I agreed to see you together. Your grandmother in particular insisted. I don't mind admitting she rather frightens me a little, the countess does."

"Grams can have that effect on people," Amelia supplied eagerly, as if to commiserate with the man.

"Yes, well, let me tell you, if you don't start answering my questions right now and with a modicum of candor, I'll separate the two of you, and then we'll see what you each have to say."

Amelia stiffened against the back of her chair and reached out for Phoebe's hand. She even inched her chair sideways, the scraping of its legs loud on the hardwood floor. Phoebe grasped her sister's hand and returned the inspector's adamant gaze with one of her own.

"You needn't threaten us, Inspector Lewis. What do you wish to know?"

His nostrils flared, and his lips pursed. "What did you discuss with your sister after your maid and your grandmother left the three of you alone in the room on the second floor of the Royal Yacht Squadron clubhouse? Is that specific enough for you to be able to form a reply, Lady Phoebe?" A dark eyebrow went up in question.

"Yes, it is." She gave a sniff and squared her shoulders to let this man know she didn't appreciate his sarcasm, and neither would she allow him to intimidate her. "I asked my sister, Lady Annondale, if she was certain of her choice in marrying Lord Annondale. And she assured me she was."

The man's scrutiny shifted to Amelia. "Did you share your sister's concerns for Lady Annondale's decision?"

Amelia raised her chin and peered down her nose at him, looking much like Grams when she wished to put some impertinent individual in his or her place. "Of course I did. What loving sister wouldn't be concerned? One wants to be assured that one's elder sister is going to be happy, and once the marriage has taken place, well, what's done is done. We wished for Julia to have one last chance to change her mind, if she so wished." The detective inspector opened his mouth to comment, but Amelia interrupted him. "As it happened, she did not wish to call off the wedding."

Admiration swelled in Phoebe. However delicate Amelia often seemed, she could summon the pluck of a lioness when she needed to.

Detective Inspector Lewis hadn't finished with them. "Didn't your sister make a reference to her new husband not living much longer?"

Amelia's hand tightened until Phoebe's fingers throbbed. Phoebe replied, "Julia is much younger than Gil—Lord Annondale. Of course she would anticipate outliving him."

"Yes, but did she not seem to imply the viscount would not live much longer?"

"She implied no such thing." Amelia's voice rose in anger and left off on a wavering note. She swallowed and continued more quietly. "It was exactly as Phoebe just said. Julia simply knew she would likely outlive her husband. It's a perfectly rational conclusion to draw, under the circumstances."

"Is it?" He compressed his lips, his eyes once more going narrow and shrewd. "And what exactly did you say to your sister, Lady Amelia? What realization did you make con-

cerning your sister's motive for marrying the Viscount Annondale?"

"I . . . I don't understand."

"Oh, I think you do, Lady Amelia."

Amelia's trembling passed into Phoebe through their
clasped hands. Phoebe firmed her grip, hoping to steady
her younger sister, wishing she could reply for her. Even
lie, if she must. But she knew the man sitting before them
wouldn't allow it. Every aspect of his being forbade anything but the truth, because he already knew the answer.
He had heard it from the waitress.

Blast and damn.

"I . . . I . . ." Amelia continued to sputter, perplexity
turning her face feverishly red.

Phoebe couldn't endure it another moment. "Tell him,
Amellie. Just tell him the truth. It's no good trying to hide
anything, and indeed, there is nothing worth hiding. Julia
is innocent of all blame in Gil's death, as the police will
soon discover."

Amelia turned to her, her face filled with such wretchedness Phoebe's heart turned over. Amelia nodded and turned
back to the detective inspector. "I realized, and I said, that
Julia was marrying Gil for his money, so that after he passed
away, she might marry as she chose."

Detective Inspector Lewis appeared to weigh this for an
interminable moment, then asked, "And whom would she
choose?"

"Theo Leighton, Marquess of Allerton," Amelia whispered miserably, and Phoebe felt as if a door had just
slammed shut upon her family, trapping them in darkness.

The sight that greeted Eva in the hotel lobby heightened
her sense of impending disaster. Besides Miss Tansley, who
now occupied a settee, along with another woman in a ser-

vice uniform, Eva recognized several of the yacht crew and staff, each of whom looked grim and avoided meeting her gaze. Apparently, Sergeant Davis had sent them over from the *Georgiana* for further questioning. Mildred Blair was among them, not sitting but standing at attention near the front desk, scanning the room at intervals and obviously missing no detail. As if someone had put her in charge and bade her make sure no one made their escape. She wondered if everyone present, Miss Blair especially, had already been questioned. No doubt they had. And no doubt Miss Blair had had plenty to say.

With a sinking stomach, she also wondered what Miss Blair might have overheard between Lord and Lady Annondale last night. The woman seemed to have a knack for being in the right place at the wrong time, as if she had a sixth sense for trouble.

She thought to approach Miss Blair and try to discover what kinds of questions the police had asked her, but then the photographer, too, caught her eye. Though she had exchanged few words with him thus far, she surmised she would find out more from him than she ever would from Mildred Blair. With a breath to steel her and banish the last of the light-headedness that had nearly overtaken her outside, she strolled as casually as her slightly trembling legs would convey her.

Curtis Mowbry sat alone at the corner of a settee near a potted plant, smoking a cigarette. At Eva's approach, he flicked the ash into the ashtray on the table beside him, stood, and greeted her politely.

Eva gestured to the unoccupied side of the sofa. "May I, Mr. Mowbry?"

"Please do." He sat and then shifted slightly to make more room for her. "Are you waiting to be questioned, too?"

"No, actually. No one has sent for me." She settled beside him. Even sitting, he towered over her. "I suppose it's because I wasn't on the yacht when the—" She hesitated for a fraction of an instant and hoped he hadn't noticed. "Accident occurred."

"Nor were some of the others here." He gestured across the lobby with his chin. "That woman there—I'm told she's on the waitstaff at the Squadron. And those over there . . ." He used the same method to point out four individuals, three men and a woman, whom Eva vaguely recognized. "They're also from the Squadron. They were part of the catering team that supplied and served the food on the yacht."

Of course. She had passed them when she trekked through the galley yesterday. She felt a rising sense of alarm. "I wonder why they were called. They weren't on board last night, were they?"

Mr. Mowbry leaned to stub out his cigarette. "No, they'd all left by then. Apparently, the police wish to hear from everyone who came in contact at all with Lord and Lady Annondale. That's why I was questioned."

"Oh, you already were." Eva's pulse raced with eagerness. "What did they want to know?"

"I don't know." He shrugged one substantial shoulder. "Something about how the couple seemed to me. How they were behaving toward each other." He gave a light laugh. "I told them quite frankly that when I'm working, I don't notice such things. I see only through my camera lens—light and shadow, form, angles, and how they meld to form the whole. It's all that matters to me."

"I see. And they asked nothing about last night, after the guests left?"

"Actually, they did. Took me aback, really. How on earth am I supposed to know what Lord and Lady Annondale were doing after the guests left? As if it's any of my business. It was their honeymoon night, for goodness' sake. Besides, my quarters are a deck below theirs."

"So what did you do once the *Georgiana* quieted down?"

He hesitated, taking her measure. "You ask a lot of questions, Miss Huntford."

"Sorry. It's just all so distressing. Poor Lady Annondale, married and widowed in the same day. It seems so outlandish, like a dreadful novel."

"You're Lady Annondale's maid, yes?"

"No, at least not anymore. I serve her younger sisters now. Her new maid is called Hetta."

He nodded and said dreamily, "She's very beautiful, Lady Annondale."

"Yes, she is." Her reply came out harsher than she'd intended, but his observation had brought back those queer sensations from yesterday, when Eva felt as though she were intruding on an illicit intimacy. And Lord Annondale had wished to fire Mr. Mowbry. He'd been jealous. . . .

"I'm sorry. I didn't mean that to be impertinent," he said, as if having read her mind. "I spoke purely as a professional. Lady Annondale possesses a singular symmetry to her face that begs to be photographed. I'm quite sure it's nothing the average person would see, but when you deal with so many faces on a daily basis, you become aware of the subtleties of perfection, and how rare it is. I've experienced the same wonder photographing nature, as well. Have you ever heard of Lake Louise in Canada?"

Puzzled, Eva shook her head.

"It's a magnificent spot in the Rocky Mountains. The lake itself is a startling emerald green, but it's the mountains behind the lake, two massive peaks that form an almost perfectly symmetrical frame for the setting, that leave me in awe. It's quite astounding. Miraculous, really."

Eva found she could do nothing but stare at him as his zeal filled her as though it were catching.

He grinned broadly. "You think I'm balmy, don't you?"

"Not at all." Whatever anger she had felt toward him melted away. She saw his attentions toward Lady Julia yesterday in a whole new light, not the reverence of a man beguiled by a woman, but by his subject, his art. "I think you're enthusiastic in a way most people wish they could be. I think you love your work. And that makes you very lucky."

"Sometimes, very much so. Other times, I tear my hair out trying to get a decent shot. Like most of us, I work for a living, Miss Huntford, and if that means struggling to find the good side of a group of dour, prune-faced aristocrats at an event none of them wish to be attending, so be it."

Eva laughed. "I'm sure it can't be that bad."

"You'd be surprised." He fished in his coat pocket for his cigarette case and offered her a cigarette. When she shook her head no, he took one for himself and lit it. "You're concerned about Lady Annondale, aren't you?"

"Concerned is putting it lightly."

He turned away to blow out a puff of smoke. "You don't think she could have anything to do with her husband's death, do you?"

"Certainly not." Again, she spoke more sharply than she'd intended, but he had struck an ominous chord. Lady Julia had come banging at her sisters' door in the middle of the night, claiming she had seen a side to Gilbert Townsend she didn't believe she could live with. Eva had never seen her so distraught, her self-assurance more shattered. Yet, within minutes, Lady Annondale had rediscovered her resolve and her determination to make her marriage work. By the time she had left to return to the yacht, the old Julia had reasserted herself, and though Eva had continued to worry about her, she had trusted that Lady Julia would, indeed, find a way to repair the damage with her husband.

Had she been wrong? Deceived? Had Lady Julia's calm façade hidden a desperation that led to . . . to . . .

No. Violence could never be Lady Julia's way. She was too civilized, too decent. Many people saw her as Lord Wroxly's spoiled, selfish granddaughter, but Eva knew her better. The face she showed the world consisted of bravado and self-preservation. Deep at her core, where it mattered most, Julia Renshaw was a kind, compassionate individual.

She shook her head. More composedly, she said, "Lady Annondale made it quite clear she was committed to this marriage. If some malevolence befell Lord Annondale, it was by a hand other than hers. Of that I am certain, Mr. Mowbry."

He held her gaze. "I believe you. I believe hers is a beauty that goes deeper than the flesh, rendering her incapable of wrongdoing."

Eva's heart twisted. "You see that, too, Mr. Mowbry."

He seemed about to answer when a voice boomed through the lobby, silencing the quiet conversations.

"You may all leave the hotel now and return to your own lodgings. Those of you who work on the *Georgiana*, you may return there." The detective inspector stood at the entrance to the corridor that led to the hotel's private offices. "However, none of you may leave Cowes until you are instructed that you may do so."

"What's happening?" Eva murmured to no one in particular, gripped by a sense that something had changed, or was about to change, something both significant and horrible. Something in Mr. Lewis's voice had made her insides run hot and then icy cold. Those assembled rose to their feet amid renewed conversation, including speculation about what the police had concluded. Mr. Lewis strode to the nearest lift.

Mr. Mowbry crushed the butt of his cigarette in the ashtray. "I wonder if they've discovered something."

"Aren't you leaving along with the rest?" Eva asked him, surprised he hadn't followed the others outside.

"I'm staying here rather than on the yacht. Miss Blair was able to secure me a room."

"I see . . ." Her gaze remained riveted on the lift door through which Detective Inspector Lewis had disappeared. She felt frozen to the settee, dreading his return and afraid to allow a thought to form about where he went, though she believed she knew.

She noticed Miss Blair had also remained at her vantage point beside the main desk, and now she whispered a few words to the clerk, a man with small eyes and thin features, whose slicked hair gleamed excessively with tonic.

Eva's attention swerved sharply as Lady Phoebe and Lady Amelia emerged from the same corridor through which the detective inspector had entered the lobby. They looked pale, shaken. Phoebe spotted Eva and crossed the distance to her, Amelia at her heels. Eva stood as they approached her.

"You were questioned," she said rather than asked.

They nodded.

Phoebe said tightly, "He came at us relentlessly."

"If only I were capable of lying." Amelia dabbed at her eyes with the back of her hand.

Phoebe put an arm around her. "It would have done no good. Lying would only have made everything worse."

"Beastly man." Amelia sniffled. "What do you suppose he'll do next?"

Before Eva could comment, the lift dinged, and the attendant opened the door and stepped out. The detective inspector came next and paused, waiting. Her nerves stretched taut, Eva craned her neck to see who might exit the car next. A foot came into view.

A foot clad in buff kidskin, with a T-strap and a French heel. Lady Julia, her head high, her expression carefully indifferent, walked out of the lift with all the dignity of a queen. She was closely followed by Lord and Lady Wroxly and Viscount Foxwood.

After taking Amelia's hand, Phoebe hurried across the lobby to her family. A nightmarish quality took hold of her, and a little voice inside her insisted this could not be happening. And yet it quite clearly was, though, thank goodness, she saw no sign of handcuffs or other restraints. The indignity would have been too much to bear for all of them. The detective inspector was speaking to Grampapa, whose eyes swam with tears, while Grams protested quietly but nonetheless adamantly. Julia stood staring straight ahead, as if present circumstances had nothing to do with her. And Fox . . .

Fox looked as though he had been struck across the face. Not only had he broken out in an angry rash, his eyes glistened and his mouth hung open, as if he couldn't quite catch his breath. Phoebe had never seen him like this. At least not since . . . since they'd gotten word three years ago that Papa had died.

Amelia went straight to Grampapa's side and took hold of his arm. Her eyes filled with tears as she fixed her gaze on Detective Inspector Lewis.

Phoebe went to Julia. "What's happening?"

"Is it not obvious? The inspector here has drawn his conclusions, and I am to be charged."

Despite having already reached this conclusion, Phoebe felt as though a cement weight had been dropped on her heart. "He can't be serious."

Julia emitted a small laugh. "He believes that when Gil and I argued, I broke the mirror in a rage and then went after Gil to push him overboard." She fell silent, clutching the handle of her handbag with both hands, the bandage on one a glaring testament to her supposed guilt.

"But the blood on the deck railing could have been Gil's."

"They didn't find a stab wound on the body," Julia murmured between her clenched teeth.

"This is absurd," Grams was saying. She darted a glance around the lobby. Despite the absence of most of those who had been questioned, there were still a few hotel guests, not to mention wedding guests, lingering. Watching and listening. Grams flushed a color that rivaled Fox's rash. But she went on speaking, as though undaunted. "She is our granddaughter. Her father, our son, was a war hero. She has never run afoul of the law in her life. Surely you cannot mean to—"

"I'm sorry, Lady Wroxly, but I've no choice. Lady Annondale had plenty of motive, according to multiple sources, not to mention opportunity."

Plenty of motive. Phoebe wanted to scream her protests. Amelia fell to weeping against Grampapa's shoulder, no doubt blaming herself for what she had been forced to reveal.

"Release her into my recognizance, then." Grampapa patted one of Amelia's hands as he spoke, though Phoebe wasn't sure who needed comforting more. Watching her grandfather felt akin to watching a ticking bomb, for she feared that at any moment dismay might cause him to collapse.

Detective Inspector Lewis shook his dark head. "I can't do that, either, my lord. Not in a murder case."

Grams took hold of the detective inspector's upper arm and forcibly turned him to face her. "Do you hear yourself, young man? Murder? Lady Julia Renshaw—Viscountess Annondale? She married Gil Townsend of her own free will. She would not then turn around and . . . and . . . do what you're suggesting she did."

Married Gil of her own free will. If only that were true, Phoebe thought desperately. If only there hadn't been so many mitigating circumstances that drove Julia into this marriage. If only Grams had shown patience and put Julia's needs first.

No. Phoebe halted those thoughts. This wasn't Grams's fault, either. At least not deliberately. If Grams had pushed Julia toward marriage, it was because the changing world frightened her, because she saw her way of life slipping away and she herself didn't know how to adapt. In her way, Grams was just as vulnerable as Grampapa, with his vicarious health. And she was just as distraught.

"I'm terribly sorry," the detective inspector was saying.

Julia finally awakened from her trancelike state. "It's all right. Grams, Grampapa, you mustn't worry. Let the police do as they must. Eventually, they'll discover the truth." She hesitated, regarding her hand, and then tugged the glittering wedding ring from her finger. After pressing it into Grams's palm, she met Detective Inspector Lewis's gaze. "Shall we? There is no point in lingering any further."

"Julia, my darling girl." Easing away from Amelia, Grampapa caught Julia's shoulders and drew her to him. The overhead light flashed on the twin tracks of moisture scoring his cheeks, and a sob rose in Phoebe's throat. Julia leaned into his chest, her cheek against his collar, and allowed him to enfold her for several seconds. Then she pulled away and straightened, kissed his and Grams's cheeks, touched Amelia's hair and Fox's shoulder, traded a glance with Phoebe, and crossed the lobby to the street door.

CHAPTER 8

Phoebe watched, helpless, as her grandfather took several unsteady steps to follow Julia, his hand reaching out as if to stop her from leaving. Slowly, the arm descended to his side, and he simply stood, watching as the street door closed and blocked out the sight of Julia being assisted into the police vehicle.

Grams went to him. "She'll be all right, Archibald. The police will realize what a monstrous mistake they've made and will let her go."

"Good God, Maude, what if they don't? What if..." His hand rose to his heart. Alarmed, Phoebe went to flank his other side.

"You mustn't worry. We all know Julia isn't capable of—" She broke off before saying *murder*. They must not say it, especially not in Grampapa's hearing. Behind her, Amelia sobbed quietly. Fox was still uncharacteristically silent. The entire lobby, too, had gone quiet as looks of pity surrounded the family. She resisted the temptation to tell them all to mind their business. "Come. Why don't we all go upstairs?" she suggested, gently turning Grampapa away from the street door. She looked around until she found Eva. "Where is Hetta?"

"I've no idea." Like the rest of them, Eva was leached of color, and her voice was flat. "I'd have thought she was upstairs with your sister. I haven't seen her in quite a long while."

"We haven't seen her, either," Grams said with a puzzled frown, which deepened as she, too, glanced around the lobby. Several of their onlookers flinched at Grams's cold, blade-sharp gaze. "Phoebe's right. Let's go upstairs. Fox, Amelia, come along."

The five of them, along with Eva, piled back into the lift. The operator didn't ask for their floor; he already knew where they were staying. He merely worked the lever to set the lift in motion. When he steadied the car and opened the door for them, Phoebe didn't exit with her family.

Eva hovered uncertainly beside her. "My lady?"

From the corridor, four faces turned to her in confusion.

Grams spoke first. "Phoebe, what are you doing? Come out of the lift."

"I need to speak to Julia."

"You can't." Grams took a step toward her but stopped before reentering the car. "You cannot go there, to the . . ." She trailed off, looking alarmed.

"I have to, Grams." She turned to her grandfather. "You know I have to. We can't just leave this to the police, or you know what can happen. I don't mean to upset you, and—"

"Phoebe, come out of that car this instant," Grams commanded in the tone that brooked no argument. "Eva, you too."

Eva didn't move, but even without looking at her, Phoebe sensed her indecision.

It was Grampapa who settled the matter. He pressed a palm to Phoebe's cheek and said, "Go help your sister, and bring Eva with you."

It took some time for the desk clerk to summon a taxi-cab for them, and when it arrived, Phoebe gave the driver the address at Mill Hill and Birmingham Roads. The Cowes Police Station took up the entire corner, with entrances on both roads. She and Eva paused outside on the pavement, working up their courage, and then, with Phoebe leading, strode up the steps and in through the main entrance. There Phoebe's bluster dissipated, not because she lost her nerve, but because Julia was still being taken into custody and could not yet have visitors.

Taken into custody. The term made her feel ill. She and Eva took seats side by side on a wooden bench facing the main desk. She considered the irony of both their hotel and the police station having a front desk, of there being accommodations inside for those spending the night. She and her family and all the others at the hotel could leave anytime they liked. Not so Julia. There would be bars holding her in, and cement floors and walls and—

How would her sister bear it?

She slipped her hand into Eva's and held on tight.

The door leading into the station's main room opened, and a constable beckoned to them. "Lady Phoebe, you may come in now."

She and Eva stood, and the man held out the flat of his hand. "Only one of you at a time."

"But . . ." Phoebe knew no argument could change police policy. With a nod at Eva, she followed the bobby along a series of corridors until they reached a locked and gated door. The clank of the man's keys turning in the lock sent chills racing down her spine, and another shiver racked her as he locked the door behind them. She steeled herself for the sight of Julia—beautiful Julia—in a barred cell, but to her relief, the officer led her into a bare, utilitarian room that held a rectangular table and several hard wooden chairs.

"Your sister will be along shortly. Make yourself comfortable." With that, he left her. She sat, or rather perched, at the edge of one of the chairs. Making herself comfortable wasn't possible; the very notion was ludicrous.

She scanned the room, looking for ways in which she might be observed, but the walls appeared solid enough. She wondered whether Julia would be handcuffed or, worse, shackled. Did they do that to suspects within the police station? Would they do that to the Viscountess Annondale?

The door opened abruptly, and Julia came in. To Phoebe's vast relief, she bore no restraints of any kind and still wore the black ensemble of earlier today. The officer who brought her said, "Ten minutes," and left them alone.

"Phoebe, what on earth are you doing here?" Julia sat facing her. "Have you lost your mind, coming to a place like this? Supposing there had been reporters outside?" Her eyes widened. "Were there?"

"Not that I noticed. But of course I'm here, Julia. I want to help you."

"It isn't a good idea, not this time." She shrugged a shoulder in her habitual way. "You'll only be dragged down with me. Go home, Phoebe. And by home, I mean Little Barlow, not here. Take the rest of the family with you."

"Julia, we're not going anywhere. We're going to help you whether you like it or not." Phoebe rested her forearms on the table and leaned farther forward. "Now, when you left the *Georgiana* last night, do you remember seeing anyone on deck other than a crew member? One of your guests perhaps?"

"No, there was no one but the deck steward and his assistant, at least not that I saw. Who knows? Hugh might have been up somewhere or Veronica or even Miss Blair. Who can say? Phoebe, leave it alone. I'm innocent, and the police will confirm that."

"As the police would have confirmed that Vernon was

innocent of Henry's murder a year ago Christmas? What if I had left well enough alone then? An innocent man would have hanged." The moment the words left her lips, she wished to recall them. Julia stiffened as if she'd been struck across the cheek. "Julia, I'm sorry . . ."

She was treated to another shrug. "Do you think they would hang me? Just think of the scandal. The Earl of Wroxly's granddaughter. My, it would sell heaps of newspapers."

"Don't talk like that," Phoebe said with a growing sense of horror. "Don't make jokes."

Julia nonetheless laughed softly. "Isn't it the biggest joke of all? Good heavens, who'd have thought my wedding would lead me here? I should have seen disaster coming, I suppose."

Tears burned the backs of Phoebe's eyes, and she blinked furiously to prevent them falling. "What are you talking about?"

"I should never have married Gil. You were right. You and Eva and Amelia. I didn't love him. It all seemed so convenient and temporary, a way to have my cake and eventually eat it, too. It was wrong of me, and now I'm forced to pay the piper. There's rather a poetic elegance to it all, isn't there?" She sat back, looking infuriatingly calm, almost serene. Phoebe wanted to grab her by the shoulders and shake sense into her.

"Stop it, Julia. You're in serious trouble, and you must take it seriously."

"But I am, little sister. I cannot imagine anything more serious." Her voice wavered, and suddenly Julia's mask of composure slipped, revealing pure terror in her dark blue eyes—eyes that had typically held a practiced indifference since their father died. Now her beautiful features contorted.

"Then please let me help you," Phoebe pleaded. "Tell me everything about yesterday and last night. Gil's sister was angry with him about this wedding. More than angry. She was furious."

"Yes, Veronica's never taken a liking to me." Julia sighed, all signs of desperation gone as quickly as they had come.

"And Gil and Sir Hugh had some kind of argument, which Eva overheard, and—"

"Oh, Phoebe, you're always on the alert—you and Eva." She shook her head sadly. "I don't deserve your efforts. I've been positively swinish toward you these past several years."

"That doesn't matter."

"There's where you are wrong." Julia smiled as though they were having an ordinary conversation over tea. "It all matters. Everything I've done, said, thought. I haven't been the best of individuals. The universe has its ways of bringing things into balance."

Phoebe dropped her head between her hands and tugged at her hair. "What are you saying?"

"I'm saying, go home and leave this to fate. I'll be fine. You'll see." She came to her feet, signaling an end to Phoebe's visit.

Phoebe sprang out of her chair. "I'm not giving up on you."

She hurried around the table and caught Julia in her arms. For a long moment Julia's arms remained at her sides. Then, slowly, they rose to embrace Phoebe, but all too briefly. Julia went to the door and knocked twice. It opened, and the same police officer who had brought her now led her away.

Phoebe called after her, "I'll have Hetta bring some of your things. We'll have you out soon, I promise."

With tears in her eyes, she followed another man in uniform, whose image blurred as he brought her back out to Eva.

"So then, we begin with Veronica Townsend and Mildred Blair," Lady Phoebe said when she and Eva returned to the hotel.

After checking on Lord and Lady Wroxly, they'd gone to Lady Phoebe's room to make plans. Amelia had soon joined them, and while Phoebe had looked as though she wished to send her younger sister elsewhere, she had forgone doing so. Instead she had admonished Amelia to be quiet and had sworn her to secrecy. Eva doubted the former would last long, but she had every confidence Amelia would adhere to the latter.

"I'll never forgive Miss Blair for insinuating the mirror could not have fallen off the wall when Gil stormed from the stateroom," Lady Phoebe said. "The police believe Julia tore it down in a rage and threw it at Gil and then later pushed him overboard. And as for Veronica Townsend, she was clearly incensed by this wedding. At the time I overheard her conversation with her friend, I didn't know whom she resented more, Julia or Gil."

"Maybe Miss Blair said what she did because she's guilty," Amelia suggested, earning her a look of rebuke from her sister. Eva smiled inwardly. She had known it wouldn't be long before the youngest Renshaw sister decided to air her opinions. Still, she shook her head.

"What would Miss Blair stand to gain from Lord Annondale's death?" Any way Eva looked at it, she could find no benefit to Miss Blair from the viscount's death. "Even if she and Lord Annondale were—" She broke off, about to say, "Having an affair," as Lady Julia suspected, but not liking to in front of young Amelia. Lady Phoebe obviously caught her meaning, however, for she compressed her lips and nodded sagely.

Perhaps Miss Blair had become so angry about the marriage, she'd argued with the viscount and things had turned violent. But that wasn't something Eva cared to discuss in front of a sixteen-year-old girl. She went on, "Lord Annondale employed Miss Blair and, by all appearances, allowed her quite a lot of freedom in how she performed her duties. What will she do now?"

"Perhaps that's something we need to find out." Lady Phoebe unhooked the gold bracelet around her wrist and set it on the night table between the beds. "Just because something isn't obvious doesn't mean it's nonexistent. She might be entirely innocent, but I don't believe for a moment that things happen on that yacht without her knowing about them. Mark my words, she has information."

"But how to get it from her?" Eva was all too eager to clear Lady Julia's name. She and Lady Phoebe had worked well together in the past, with Lady Phoebe poking around among her set—the toffs, as Eva's father called them—and Eva probing belowstairs. Now she feared their plans would go awry without a modification or two. "My lady, I have an idea. For some reason, Miss Blair seems to detest me."

"That's rather a strong sentiment," Lady Amelia pointed out.

Eva explained, "Nonetheless, Miss Blair took an immediate dislike to both Hetta and me. She clearly considers us her inferiors, and I doubt very much she'll even speak to me, much less confide. On the other hand, my lady, you might encounter a similar problem with Miss Townsend, who expressed an aversion to your sister and might transfer those sentiments to you, as a family member. I believe we'll have better results if you approach Miss Blair and I ingratiate myself to Miss Townsend."

Phoebe grinned. "Eva, that's brilliant. You're right.

Veronica Townsend was so bitter toward Julia, it's quite possible she'd treat me in kind. But you . . . If you were to offer her both your services and your sympathetic ear, she might open up." She shook her head slowly, obviously deep in thought. "Miss Blair is puzzling. I don't so much mind her entertaining lofty ideas about herself. That speaks of ambition and self-esteem, both good things, in my opinion, though some of her behavior would give Grams the vapors. But I must say I do not like her looking down her nose at her peers and fellow service staff. It's arrogance at its worst, and it tells of a selfish nature. There is something about her . . ."

"Which makes her suspicious," Amelia concluded with a satisfied air. "I still say you should consider her."

"Let's not go jumping to conclusions and assigning blame randomly," Phoebe warned her. "That's what happened to Julia."

Amelia's expression fell, and she bent her head to study the counterpane on her bed.

"And let us not forget these ladies are merely a beginning." Eva stood and crossed to the bathroom, where she leaned over the tub to turn on the taps. Lady Phoebe had been inside a jailhouse—a *jailhouse*—for heaven's sake. She would want to cleanse away all traces of the experience and change into fresh clothing. Eva went back into the main room and opened the armoire. She took out an evening frock and laid it across the foot of Phoebe's bed. "There is also Sir Hugh and whatever matter he and Lord Annondale had argued over during the reception."

"And Ernest Shelton," Lady Phoebe reminded her. "Gil acted abominably toward him, and I believe it wasn't the first time. Ernest is Gil's cousin and heir, and a man with a respectable profession. Yet Gil treated him as if he were some sort of half-witted buffoon."

"It was horrid," Amelia agreed. "It embarrassed me no

end, so I can only imagine how Mr. Shelton felt. Though he did recover nicely and was quite charming with us afterward, wasn't he, Phoebe?"

Lady Phoebe nodded, but with a pensive look. "Still, he stood to lose a lot because of this marriage, namely, the inheritance he'd been counting on these many years. The prospect of Julia producing a new heir can't have been a welcome one."

Eva counted on her fingers. "That throws suspicion on three people who were on board the *Georgiana* last night. Miss Townsend, Sir Hugh Fitzallen, and Ernest Shelton. In my opinion, Miss Blair is most likely innocent, but she might know something that could help your sister. Who else need we consider?"

"What about the photographer?" Lady Phoebe cocked her head to the side. "He was on board last night. Though I can't imagine why he should wish to murder Gil."

"Curtis Mowbry." Eva perched beside Phoebe's evening frock and traced her fingertip along the beaded neckline. "If you had asked me this morning, I'd have said I *could* imagine a reason."

"His flirtation with Julia," Amelia said more sagely than her years should have allowed. "But surely he must know he could never be with a woman like Julia. Gil might have been jealous, but that doesn't mean anything more would have come of it."

"Yet his attentions did seem awfully excessive at times," Phoebe said.

Amelia shook her head. "He's probably that way with everyone. You know how artists are."

"You seem to have changed your mind about the man, Eva." Phoebe removed her earrings and placed them beside her bracelet.

"I sat with him in the lobby just before the police . . ."

Once again, Eva trailed off, not liking to speak of Lady Julia's arrest. "Anyway, he spoke of his work in artistic terms, about symmetry and perfection, and I realized it wasn't your sister who enthralled him, but rather her potential as a photographic subject. He compared her to some mountains behind a lake in Canada."

"Then again, perhaps Gil confronted Mr. Mowbry and they fought, and Mr. Mowbry pushed him overboard—even accidentally." Amelia's suggestion came with rather too much enthusiasm for Eva's liking, but then she turned serious. "You realize, there is one more person we haven't considered."

Lady Phoebe shot her a reproving look. "I don't know that *we* have to consider anyone, Amellie. But whom do you mean?"

Amelia compressed her lips, hesitated, and said, "Theo."

"That's crazy." Phoebe waved a dismissive hand.

"He was here, Phoebe. At the wedding."

"But then he left," Eva said, "before the reception even started."

"Did he? How do we know for certain?" Amelia appealed to them both. "I don't like to think it. I like Theo. Very much. But mustn't we consider him?"

Lady Phoebe went so entirely white, Eva became alarmed. She said, "No, we mustn't consider it. Lord Allerton might have been at the wedding, but I don't believe for a moment he had anything to do with Lord Annondale's demise. Nor did your sister."

"But . . ." Phoebe trailed off and reached for Amelia's hand. "You said it, Amellie. You said Julia was marrying Gil for Theo, so that when Gil died, Julia and Theo would be free to marry."

Lady Amelia's eyes misted. "I didn't mean it. I wish I hadn't brought up Theo's name. I wish to take it back."

"Both of you, calm down, please." Eva spoke with more authority than she normally dared with her employers. "I spoke to Lord Allerton after the wedding, and all he wanted was to be assured of your sister's happiness."

"How could you assure him of that when it was so obvious Julia *wasn't* happy?" Amelia demanded.

Eva decided on a different tack. "It should be easy enough to discover if Lord Allerton returned home yesterday. I'll simply ring Miles and ask him to check."

"What if he didn't go straight home?" Amelia's worries were etched across her youthful brow. "What if he went somewhere else, and we can't prove he didn't stay in Cowes?"

"Eva's right," Lady Phoebe said decisively and sat up taller. "Theo didn't do this, and Julia is innocent, too. We're letting our fears guide us. Circumstances call for logic and cool heads, and the assumption that both Julia and Theo are innocent. We must believe it and never waver from that belief. Now then, Eva, let's set our plans in motion."

Lady Amelia slid off her bed. "What do I do?"

"Behave yourself," her sister said, then relented. "All right. You can hang about the lobby, dining room, and terrace as much as possible, and keep your ears open."

"That's all?" Lady Amelia looked dejected, but Eva thought she knew how to remedy that.

"What your sister is asking is important," she said. "People say all kinds of things to each other when they believe those around them aren't paying attention. Besides, if your grandparents knew your sister and I had discussed such matters in your hearing, I'd be sacked immediately."

CHAPTER 9

Phoebe couldn't believe her good luck upon entering the lift. Miss Blair already occupied the car and was on her way down to the lobby. She held a coat, suggesting an intention to leave the hotel. They traded polite greetings, and Phoebe expressed her sympathy for the passing of Viscount Annondale. The woman accepted her condolences with a cold thank-you and a tilt of her head. They fell silent, and Phoebe's ire grew with each instant the woman failed to inquire after Julia, who was, technically, still her employer. She groped for a way to continue the conversation, and then an idea came to her.

In the lobby Miss Blair headed for the street door. Phoebe called her name. "I have something I'd like to discuss with you, unless you're in a hurry."

The raven-haired woman eyed her curiously. After an initial hesitation, she came back in Phoebe's direction. "Yes? I have a few moments I can spare."

Phoebe nearly chuckled at Miss Blair's haughty tone, one she was not accustomed to hearing from anyone but perhaps her grandmother. "Would you care to sit in the conservatory with me? I'd suggest the terrace, but I don't have a coat with me."

"Of course." Without another word, Gil's secretary led the way, another potential slight to Phoebe, were she the sort to put importance on the deference due her station. Julia, she could well imagine, would not have endured the woman's impertinence. When they reached the conservatory, a room of bright windows, tiled flooring, and airy furnishings, Miss Blair strode to an unoccupied corner and sat in a wicker chair without waiting for Phoebe to seat herself. She leaned slightly forward, as if impatient to hurry matters along. "What may I do for you, Lady Phoebe?"

Inwardly, Phoebe flinched yet again that Miss Blair expressed no concern for Julia, or for the Renshaw family. While the woman's arrogance didn't have the power to unsettle Phoebe, this lack of compassion and consideration took her aback and angered her. She swallowed the emotions and said, "In view of circumstances, I'm wondering what you plan to do once we are permitted to leave Cowes."

Furrows grew between the woman's bold black eyebrows. "I'm sorry. I don't understand why that should concern you."

Again, she suppressed the urge to either laugh or chastise the woman. "What I'm getting at is . . . Will you be seeking new employment? And if so, I might be able to help with that."

"I see." The woman's expression betrayed nothing of her thoughts.

"Although, with Mr. Shelton poised to inherit the title and the estate, I suppose you might stay on in his employ."

Miss Blair's gaze sharpened, and Phoebe knew she had guessed correctly. Judging by their brief encounter in the *Georgiana*'s dining room yesterday, after Mr. Shelton's accident, she had concluded Miss Blair and Mr. Shelton didn't share any particular regard for each other.

Miss Blair cleared her throat quietly. "You know of someone looking for a private secretary?"

"Indeed yes. My family. We might be interested in hiring your services."

"To what end?"

With a sigh, Phoebe sat back. Clearly, Miss Blair required frank speaking rather than the subtle inferences Phoebe was accustomed to employing in polite society. "Foxwood Hall could use a good secretary."

This much was true, actually. Mr. Giles, the butler who had been at the Hall for decades, used to run the estate like clockwork, with nary an activity off schedule or an item of linen out of place. In recent years, however, age had rendered the dear man somewhat less than efficient. The head footman, Vernon, helped fill the void, while still allowing Mr. Giles to retain his position, but in truth a capable steward would take the pressure off the staff in the day-to-day running of the household.

Whether Miss Blair would be the right person for the job, Phoebe didn't know, but she would make her interest appear as sincere as possible.

"Have you no estate manager?"

"We don't, actually, not since the war. Grampapa has a solicitor who oversees the family accounts and investments, and the home farm finances, of course, but there is no one presently in the position of steward."

"And your grandfather would accept a woman for the job?"

"I believe he would. I couldn't help noticing how well you organized the wedding and reception yesterday. You are a model of proficiency." Was that going too far? Apparently not, for Miss Blair basked in the praise.

"Thank you. When I accept a task, I take it very seriously."

"That is obvious. Which is why—"

Puzzled ridges appeared once more above Miss Blair's nose. "I cannot help but wonder why you'd concern yourself with my future with your sister currently residing at the Cowes Police Station."

Phoebe winced and for a moment couldn't gather her breath to reply. She forced herself to remain calm and not to react in anger. "Miss Blair, my sister is innocent and will soon be released. Of that I have no doubt." The woman before her had the audacity to raise a dubious eyebrow. Phoebe pretended not to notice. "You, however, have been left both without employment and homeless, have you not?"

Ah, that hit its mark. It was Miss Blair's turn to flinch, and her gaze darted to a couple sitting across the way, as if she feared they had overheard the talk of her sad plight. "Indeed I have," she murmured. "Although my circumstances are not as dire as all that. Lord Annondale paid me handsomely, and I've enough laid by to keep myself off the streets."

"For the time being," Phoebe said evenly. "But you're a young woman. Surely you haven't the means to simply retire to a life of leisure."

Miss Blair's red lips became pinched. "That is true."

"So then, if you would kindly supply me with a bit of information, I will pass it on to my grandfather. How long did you work for the viscount?"

"Nearly ten years now."

"Oh, I wouldn't have thought nearly so long. You must have been very young when the viscount hired you."

Miss Blair made no comment.

"And where are you from?" Phoebe asked.

"I wouldn't necessarily say I'm from anywhere in particular. My . . . family . . . moved around quite a bit when I was a child."

Phoebe heard the hesitation in her voice. She smiled. "Have you a large family, Miss Blair?"

"Does it matter?"

"Well . . . no. I only ask out of curiosity."

The woman's eyebrow twitched, and she waited for Phoebe to continue.

"Lord Annondale's primary home is outside of London. Would you mind living in our out-of-the-way Cotswold village? Have you any experience with country life?"

"It wouldn't matter to me, Lady Phoebe."

Phoebe was getting nowhere. Her questions had been meant to prompt conversation, and so far she had failed miserably. And then she remembered a question Miss Blair herself had asked, one that might prove useful. "You asked whether my grandfather would hire a woman for the steward's position. Why was Lord Annondale agreeable to having a woman as his secretary? He struck me as someone who believed in tradition. Who would insist upon it. Men in charge, women in the home. It does seem rather odd." She borrowed Miss Blair's custom of raising an eyebrow in expectation.

A subtle rush of color suffused the woman's cheeks. "I suppose it does seem a bit unusual," she said slowly. "A mutual acquaintance recommended me. I attended North London Collegiate School and later Girton College in Cambridge, so my qualifications were quite in order."

"Girton!" Phoebe's sudden enthusiasm was genuine, and her heart raced at the notion of attending university, for it was exactly what she hoped to do—someday. "How fortunate for you, Miss Blair. You must have enjoyed your time there immensely."

"Yes."

Perhaps, she thought, but that didn't explain the woman's blush when Phoebe first raised the question, or why hints of it continued to tint her cheeks. More and more, it appeared that Julia had been right, that Gil and Miss Blair had enjoyed more than a professional relationship. She needed to find out more, but Miss Blair proved a formidable subject.

A mutual acquaintance . . . such a vague reference. Phoebe was surprised Miss Blair hadn't cited family connections to Gil. That would have been the most likely scenario, but also easy to verify. As would a reference that had come from a schoolmistress. Miss Blair didn't wish Phoebe to know who had made the recommendation, and she wondered why.

The woman startled her by rising abruptly to her feet. "Is that all for now?"

Phoebe had the distinct impression that even if she wished to continue the interview, Miss Blair had other ideas. She stood. "For now, yes. Thank you, Miss Blair. So then, where are you off to?" Normally, she would not have pried in such a blatant way, but Miss Blair didn't seem attuned to subtleties.

"I have a couple of errands to attend to. Estate business. My employer might no longer be with us, but neither has my employment been terminated. Yet. Good day, Lady Phoebe."

"Good day." Phoebe waited until Miss Blair had disappeared through the conservatory doorway before hurrying out herself. She intended to follow the woman, but when a certain pair of individuals crossed her path, her plans suddenly changed.

Eva set the receiver on its cradle and sat contemplating the telephone for some moments. Her conversation continued to trouble her greatly. Theo Leighton, Marquess of Allerton, had yet to return home to his estate on the outskirts of Little Barlow. Miles Brannock, her beau of some months now and a constable with the Little Barlow branch of the Gloucestershire police force, knew this to be true because he had happened upon Lord Allerton's housekeeper purchasing supplies in the village only that morning. She had had no word from the marquess since he'd left for Cowes two days previously.

That didn't mean Theo Leighton hadn't decided to go up to London for a change of scenery, or to any number of other locales. It didn't mean he was still somewhere in Cowes.

Eva prayed not.

Another matter troubling her was that while talking to Curtis Mowbry earlier, she had neglected to ask him if he had ever met Lady Julia before. Lady Julia had indicated the photographer seemed familiar, and the notion niggled, especially considering his behavior toward her. Yes, he had given an explanation. His talk of artistic perfection had charmed Eva, but now she wondered if that had been intentional on his part. It was all too easy to trust someone when face-to-face, but time apart had reminded Eva to trust no one connected to yesterday's wedding. Well, it shouldn't be too difficult to track him down again and question him further. In the meantime, someone else warranted her attention.

She perused the dining room but saw no sign of her quarry. Neither the conservatory nor the library yielded any better results. But on the terrace, Eva spotted Veronica Townsend sitting with two other women, one of whom she recognized as Lady Wilma Bancroft, an aunt of the Renshaw siblings. Should she wait and approach Miss Townsend when she was alone?

Before she could decide, Lady Wilma saw her and waved her over. Eva well imagined what the woman would ask her, and she wasn't wrong. "Huntford, how is my niece? I assume you have information about her. Servants always know everything."

Eva bobbed a curtsy to the three women. The third was only vaguely familiar to her, and while she couldn't name her, she assumed her to be one of the Townsends' guests. "Lady Phoebe visited her sister earlier."

With a look of outrage, Lady Wilma drew herself up taller. "She went to the police station?"

"I accompanied her, although I was not permitted to go farther than the lobby. Lady Phoebe reports that her sister is upset—naturally—but remains calm. She says she is certain the police will discover the true culprit."

"Humph." Miss Townsend lifted her teacup for an audible sip. She obviously did not agree that any other culprit existed. Eva waited for Lady Wilma to correct Miss Townsend in no uncertain terms, but the chastisement never came.

"If you do see my niece"—Lady Wilma sniffed and adjusted the beribboned hat atop her pile of graying hair— "do tell her we are all praying for her."

Eva felt a frown spreading across her forehead for all she had spent years perfecting the art of masking her true feelings to anyone but her ladies. "Have you no other message for her? An assurance that you believe in her innocence, perhaps?"

"My dear girl," the third woman said to her briskly, "your loyalty is commendable. But the best thing you can do for the Renshaw family is be there to comfort the younger sisters—and their brother, too, I suppose—and prepare them for the worst."

"The worst . . . ?"

"You are quite right, Antonia," Miss Townsend said as she pressed a hand to her friend's wrist.

"Yes," Lady Wilma agreed. "Thank you for putting it so truthfully, Antonia." She turned her gaze back to Eva. "It is utterly deplorable, but the facts do speak for themselves, or the police would not have acted as they have."

Fury rendered Eva's fingers numb, and the scene before

her wavered in her vision. These women were so willing to condemn Lady Julia—and without a shred of proof other than what the law would consider circumstantial. She narrowed her gaze on Veronica Townsend, a woman who certainly had reasons to resent both her brother and Lady Julia, and who very well could have reason to hope Lady Julia took the blame for Lord Annondale's murder.

However, Lady Wilma's attitude made no sense to her. How could Lady Julia's aunt so readily believe the worst about her own niece?

"Well, unless you have anything to add," Miss Townsend said to her with a lift of her brows, "I believe you may be dismissed."

The Renshaw sisters never spoke to Eva that way. In fact, no one in the entire Renshaw household ever spoke that way to anyone. Even so, such a manner was nothing new to her, for she had encountered it at house parties and social events through the years. Thus, she flinched at neither the words nor Miss Townsend's haughty tone and stood her ground without blinking.

"Actually, Miss Townsend, I came out to offer my services to you. To any of you ladies, while you're staying here at the hotel. If I can be of any assistance to you at all, Lady Phoebe has instructed me to put myself at your disposal."

"Did she now?" The woman named Antonia sounded delighted. Although Eva had come specifically to make the offer to Miss Townsend, she wouldn't mind having an opportunity to speak with this woman privately, for she could be none other than the confidante Lady Phoebe had heard Miss Townsend speaking with on board the *Georgiana* yesterday.

"I have my own maid," Lady Wilma said dryly and turned her head away.

Too bad, Eva thought, for she would have liked the same opportunity to discover what, if anything, she had against Lady Julia.

She rejoiced inwardly when Miss Townsend's expression turned to one of interest. "My own maid didn't come. She suffers from dreadful seasickness, so I took pity on her and sent her home yesterday morning, before the wedding. I believe she went to Dorset to visit her family. I was going to call her back, but if you're willing . . ."

"I am. Very much so." Eva regretted those last words. She didn't wish to sound too eager. "You've been through a terrible ordeal losing your brother, and Lady Phoebe wishes to ease your burden as much as can be until we can all leave Cowes."

"Yes, Gil . . ." Miss Townsend sighed deeply. "My poor brother. All his wealth couldn't protect him." Then she brightened. "I should very much like to take you up on your offer. Can you be at my room by seven o'clock tonight, to help Mrs. Seward"—she gestured toward the woman named Antonia—"and myself dress for dinner? We are sharing a room."

"I'll be there, Miss Townsend."

"Good. It's Huntford, isn't it?"

"Yes, ma'am. I shall see you at seven."

"Yes. Please don't be late."

Phoebe stopped in her tracks when she reached the lobby. Mildred Blair had already disappeared through the street door, and even without a coat to protect her from the sea breezes, Phoebe longed to follow and see what the woman was up to. She hesitated before reaching a decision, thinking perhaps she should scurry after Miss Blair. But her conscience tugged her in the opposite direction, to the lifts, where Amelia and Fox had just ducked inside one of the cars. Phoebe hurried before the operator could close the door.

"Wait, please. I'm going up."

Inside, the evidence written on her siblings' faces convinced her she had done the right thing. The pallor she had noticed in Fox earlier not only lingered, but he looked even worse, his eyes red-rimmed and glassy and lips pinched and colorless. She cast a questioning glance at Amelia, who looked equally concerned about their younger brother. Phoebe wished to ask him if he was ill, but waited until the lift came to a stop and they exited the car.

"Fox, are you all right?"

"Let's go to his room first," Amelia said quietly and led the way down the corridor to the room adjacent to their grandparents' suite. Amelia put out her hand, and after a moment's hesitation, Fox dropped his key into it. In short order they entered the room, and Fox threw himself into an easy chair.

Phoebe went to stand in front of him. He didn't look at her but kept his gaze on his shoes. She repeated her question. "Are you ill?"

He shook his head. "Just miserable."

That simple phrase gripped Phoebe's heart. Not so much the words themselves, however, but the tone in which he said them. Gone was the bullying she had grown so accustomed to these past several years, and the manner he typically employed when ordering his sisters to find wealthy husbands. That Fox was full of bluster and arrogance. This one sounded forlorn and not at all sure of himself.

Phoebe crouched at his feet. A thump from the adjoining rooms made her lower her voice; she didn't want her grandparents overhearing this conversation through the walls. They had enough to worry about. "We're doing our best to help Julia."

He nodded but said nothing.

"He thinks it's all his fault," Amelia supplied. Phoebe pressed a finger to her lips and pointed to the wall that separated the room from her grandparents' suite. Amelia nodded, comprehending. She dragged an armchair closer and sat.

"Of course it's not your fault, Fox." Phoebe searched his features while he continued to avoid her gaze. "Someone murdered Gil, and right now Julia is being blamed, but she's innocent, and soon everyone will know it. That's a promise."

"You can make no such promise," Fox mumbled into his collar. "And it *is* my fault. I caused this."

She held out her hands. "How?"

When Fox remained mute, Amelia replied for him. "He thinks it's his fault Julia married Gil, and that if he hadn't pushed her to marry, none of this would have happened."

Phoebe's instincts nearly led her to blurt out the absurdity of that conclusion. She stopped herself just in time. The sorrow in Fox's features convinced her of the earnestness of his sentiments. This was no ploy for attention or bid for sympathy. That he snatched his hand away when she attempted to cover it with her own proved he wished for neither or perhaps didn't believe he deserved anyone's compassion.

Julia *did* marry at someone's insistence, but not Fox's. *Grams's.* Phoebe continued to ask herself if she blamed Grams. Guilt rose up again, and she simply shoved the question aside. She couldn't allow her brother to continue suffering under his mistaken impressions. Even if that meant a return to his habitual, insufferable self.

"Fox, you must believe me when I say you had nothing to do with Julia's decision to marry Gil—or anyone, for that matter. If that were the case, I'd be married now, too, and I promise you I have no intentions of marrying anyone anytime soon."

"Not even Owen?"

Amelia looked as eager as Fox for Phoebe's reply. "Not even Owen," she said clearly. "Quite simply, I'm not ready to marry, and I won't be pressured until I am. As for Julia, there were many reasons for her marrying Gil." She paused to consider her next words, hoping to find the right ones to set her brother's mind at ease. "Have you ever known her to do anything she didn't want to do?"

He shook his head.

"There, then."

"She could hang," he whispered.

"I won't let that happen."

The promise weighed heavily on Phoebe's shoulders when she left her youngest siblings and made her way back to the lift. Fulfilling that promise meant following every lead, yet she had let one slip away in choosing to comfort her brother. She might never know where Miss Blair had gone when she left the hotel, although she resolved to simply ask the woman when she returned. Mildred Blair might not be inclined to tell the truth, but Phoebe had learned in speaking with her earlier that upon occasion, her carefully sculpted façade showed a crack or two. Her *reaction* to Phoebe's inquiry could be as telling as the reply itself.

She would wait downstairs for her to return and then make a nuisance of herself.

The lift dinged as she reached it, and the man who stepped out wore an overcoat and carried a bowler. From his other hand dangled a black leather case that looked suspiciously like a physician's bag. Phoebe tensed. The lift operator inquired as to what floor she wished to go to. She ignored him, watching the man proceed down the corridor until he reached the door he sought. He knocked twice. Grams admitted the newcomer with a "Thank you for coming, Doctor."

"Grams, wait," Phoebe called out. She trotted down the hallway. Grams looked as though she would rather close the door without speaking to her, but she waited on the threshold.

"What is it?" Phoebe whispered upon reaching her. Just as she hadn't wanted her grandparents overhearing her conversation with Fox, she didn't want Fox and Amelia overhearing this latest development. She took Grams's hand and stepped into the suite with her. "Grampapa's unwell, isn't he?"

Grams nodded solemnly, her hand tightening around Phoebe's in a rare show of vulnerability. "You're not to say a word to the others. Especially not Julia."

"I promise I won't. Now please tell me about Grampapa."

"He was complaining of feeling dizzy, and when I caught him pressing a hand to his chest, I wasted no time in calling the doctor."

"Good. I suppose he said not to, that it was nothing."

"You know your grandfather well."

They sat together in the sitting room until the doctor came out from the bedroom. His eyes registered recognition when he saw Phoebe, and Grams introduced her. "You may speak freely in front of my granddaughter," she told him.

Phoebe couldn't help reflecting that only a year and a half ago, Grams would not have said such a thing. She would have insisted on shielding Phoebe from worrisome circumstances, as she continued to do for the rest of her siblings. It hadn't been easy for Grams to acknowledge that her middle granddaughter possessed an inner strength that rivaled her own; it had been a gradual process prompted by the startling events of the past year and a half. Yet Phoebe sensed Grams's great relief that she now had someone in whom she could confide. Someone to sit with and wait for the doctor's prognosis.

"He's resting now," Dr. Caines said. "I gave him a sedative, which will ensure he gets some sleep. I've also increased his nitroglycerin dosage, but he must see his regular physician as soon as he returns home. Now, when he wakes, he is not to be stressed. You must keep him calm and see he gets plenty of bed rest."

Though he spoke with authority, Phoebe also detected a note of apology. She believed he knew exactly what had caused Grampapa's anxiety, and she wondered how widespread that knowledge was. They would have to ensure no morning newspapers made their way onto Grampapa's breakfast trays.

Chapter 10

"I need to be at Miss Townsend's room by seven o'clock," Eva explained to Lady Phoebe when they met later in the hotel library. No one else occupied the room at the moment, so they needn't fear being overheard. "She's sharing with Antonia Seward. Isn't that the name of the woman you overheard Miss Townsend speaking to on board the *Georgiana* yesterday?"

"It *is*." Lady Phoebe looked pleased. "This is a stroke of luck. Do you think you'll be able to get them talking?"

"I believe so. They seemed ever so gratified that you sent me to attend them."

"That almost makes me wish it had been my idea." She gave a laugh. "But this also gives us some free time. Grams asked me to go out to the *Georgiana* again and retrieve more of Julia's things. Her jewelry, keepsakes, that sort of thing. This gives us a perfect opportunity."

Eva detected a certain designing tone she had come to recognize in recent months. "You want to have a look around. But can we do that, my lady? Won't the boat be off-limits as a crime scene?"

"I shouldn't think so. The police already gave the crew

permission to reboard. They believe they have their evidence and their culprit," she added dryly. She lifted her coat from the back of a chair.

Eva went into the dressing room and retrieved her own coat from the foot of her narrow bed. "What is it we'll be looking for?"

"I don't know. Anything. I just hope the crew doesn't interfere."

"At least Miss Blair herself won't be on board," Eva said. "She wouldn't leave us alone for a moment if she were."

"Yes, that's another bit of luck." Lady Phoebe shook her head. "If only I'd gone after her earlier. I'd give anything to know where she went in such a hurry. I don't trust her."

Lady Phoebe blamed herself for allowing Miss Blair to slip away. Eva didn't blame her one bit for placing her brother's needs above the secretary's activities, but Lady Phoebe saw it as placing Fox's needs above her sister's much greater concerns. A lump of admiration grew in Eva's throat at the thought of young Phoebe taking upon herself the responsibility of holding her family together. And now, with Lord Wroxly showing signs of infirmity . . . Eva sighed as she buttoned up her coat.

Near the Royal Yacht Squadron, they were able to hire a youth with a skiff, who rowed them out to the *Georgiana*. The weather had cleared, but temperatures continued to hover at chilly levels, not at all springlike. Eva turned her collar up, while Lady Phoebe sat with her chin tucked and brushed back stray hairs plucked loose by the racing winds.

A deck steward was ready to help them aboard when they reached the vessel. Even with the viscount gone, his crew continued to run a disciplined ship. "This is unexpected," the man said as he handed them onto the deck. "And a bit irregular. I don't know that—"

"It's quite all right," Lady Phoebe interrupted. "I'm here on behalf of my grandmother, the Countess of Wroxly, to gather up some things of my sister's. There's no point in leaving them here, is there?"

"No, I suppose not." The man frowned, as if he didn't quite agree, but couldn't think of a counterargument. He moved to open the door into the main saloon for them. When he started to follow them in, Lady Phoebe again spoke to him dismissively.

"We know our way to my sister's stateroom, thank you. If you'll excuse us. We shouldn't be long, although there is the matter of making sure everything is there. That nothing . . ." She cleared her throat. "Has been damaged or has gone missing."

Eva felt like applauding her mistress. The implication was clear. With the authority of the Countess of Wroxly, Phoebe had come to inspect her sister's belongings, and at the first sign of theft, the crew would be held responsible. After all, no one else had been on board since early this morning. The steward looked most unhappy as he nodded, took a couple of steps backward, then turned and strode back outside.

"Thought we'd never be rid of him," Lady Phoebe murmured. "Come along." They hurried below. There Lady Phoebe stopped and glanced at each closed door along the passageway. "Which do you suppose is Gil's office?"

"It's that one, there." Eva pointed.

"Ah." Phoebe strode to the door, tried the knob, and asked over her shoulder, "Have you got a hairpin handy?"

"Always, my lady." Eva plucked one from the simple coif she wore beneath her hat. Lady Phoebe moved aside to let Eva work. She crouched, bringing the lock to eye level, and inserted the hairpin.

"If there is anything worth finding, I expect it to be here."

"You're thinking about that conversation I overheard be-tween the viscount and Sir Hugh, aren't you?" Eva turned the hairpin with no results, so she removed it, widened the two ends, and reinserted it.

"I am. You said it didn't sound as if Gil was particularly surprised by what Sir Hugh was warning him about. That implies Gil already knew, and since Sir Hugh waved a wedding invitation under his nose, I'm hoping the same person sent a similar message to Gil."

Eva pushed the hairpin farther into the lock, twisted, and was rewarded with a click. She pushed to her feet and turned the knob. "There you are."

They hurried inside and closed the door behind them.

"I do wish I'd had the chance to speak with Sir Hugh today," Lady Phoebe said. "I might have asked him a few leading questions to see if he'd reveal anything about the matter, or at least to observe how he reacted. You know, Eva, I'm learning that sometimes what people don't say reveals more about the truth than what they do say. I believe that's definitely the case with Miss Blair."

"Very true." Eva looked about her, wondering where to start. The room held only a desk, a wall of bookshelves, and a built-in file cabinet. Lady Phoebe had already gone around the desk and begun opening drawers. Eva went to the file cabinet. She slid the top drawer open and then re-alized the scope of the endeavor. Folders and papers were packed tight, and she suspected she'd find similar disorder in the rest of the drawers. "This could take all day," she murmured.

Lady Phoebe didn't respond. She'd sunk into the desk chair, several envelopes in her hands, her head bowed over them.

Eva recognized the stationery. "Wedding invitations?"

"RSVPs. And they're addressed to Gil, not Grams and Grampapa, as the rest of them were. Odd." She slid the first card free from its envelope and frowned down at what she saw. She opened the next two, and her frown deepened.

"What is it, my lady?"

She had no chance to reply, for the door burst inward to reveal Miss Blair on the threshold, looking very stern indeed. "What, may I ask, are you doing in here?"

Startled, Lady Phoebe let the envelopes drop into her lap. Eva shut the file drawer rather more sedately.

"I'll thank you not to speak to Lady Phoebe in that tone, Miss Blair. We are here to collect some of Lady Annondale's things."

Miss Blair's gaze sparked with anger. "You'll not find them here."

"How do you know that?" Eva challenged, crossing her arms before her. "Lady Annondale had full access to this vessel, didn't she?"

The woman's nostrils flared. "I highly doubt that. Very few people were ever invited into Lord Annondale's private office."

"And I suppose you were one of those few," Eva surmised.

"Upon occasion, yes." She turned her attention to Lady Phoebe, looking past Eva, as if she no longer existed. "You might have supplied me with a list of the items Lady Annondale requires. I would be happy to gather them for you."

Yet Miss Blair sounded anything but happy. Eva's temper began a steady rise, and apparently, so did Lady Phoebe's. "My sister's requirements are my affair, Miss Blair. And since at present she owns the *Georgiana*, I see no reason why I should be banned from any particular area of it."

"Your sister does not . . ." Miss Blair let the thought go unfinished, but Eva easily guessed what she'd been about to say. That Lady Julia didn't own the *Georgiana*. But as the deceased's widow, not to mention his only living heir besides Ernest Shelton, Lady Julia had as much claim on the *Georgiana* as anyone, at least until she was formally charged and found guilty.

"Perhaps you'd like to tell us what you're doing here, Miss Blair?" Lady Phoebe asked sweetly. "Or are you also retrieving items you require at the hotel? If so, I doubt very much you'll find them here, either." When Miss Blair didn't say anything, Lady Phoebe gathered the envelopes from her lap and pushed to her feet. "My guess is you're looking for something Lord Annondale left behind."

The secretary's gaze dropped to the envelopes Lady Phoebe now held against her. She had the audacity to ask in turn, "As you and Miss Huntford are?"

Lady Phoebe shrugged and waved the envelopes in the air. "Just some leftover RSVPs to the wedding. My sister puts great store in such things. Sentimentality and all that."

Eva only just managed not to laugh. Lady Julia hadn't a sentimental bone in her body, at least not when it came to such matters. But it seemed that Lady Phoebe had hit just the right note, for the perplexity smoothed from Miss Blair's brow.

"Is that all?" she said with a poor effort to hide her relief. "You may have them. They're of no use to anyone else now."

"I'm still wondering why you've come," Lady Phoebe said, "and to this room in particular. What are *you* looking for, Miss Blair?"

The woman huffed. "I do not work for you, Lady Phoebe, nor for your sister. I am here on behalf of Lord Annondale's estate, on official business."

Eva had had more than enough. "You no longer work for Lord Annondale, either, do you? Now, is there something the Renshaws should know about Lord Annondale's estate? Some development you learned about before his death?"

Lady Phoebe looked eager for the answer to this question.

Miss Blair, however, shook her head. "No, not to my knowledge."

The truth or a lie? They were not to know, for she turned on her heel and exited the room.

Eva felt inclined to call her back but thought better of it. Miss Blair had enlightened them no more about her appearance here than they had enlightened her. They had reached an impasse, and perhaps for now, it was better that way. Eva turned to Lady Phoebe.

"Did you find something on those cards?"

Instead of answering, Lady Phoebe gazed down at them again. "A few are still sealed, as if Gil hadn't wanted to read them—or perhaps his time ran out before he had a chance to attend to them." She searched the desktop. "Where is the letter opener?"

Eva scanned the items on the desk. "I don't see one. Just rip them open."

"Not here." Lady Phoebe came around the desk and led the way to the main stateroom. She stopped short inside the door. "Look, Eva. The broken mirror."

On a dresser, the shards that had been gathered up from the floor had been placed within the frame of the piece. Eva went closer. One particularly nasty sliver showed a line of dried blood along one of its edges. Eva winced, imagining the pain of such a gash. Then her gaze fell to the floor, to the dark splatters on the rug.

"Blood, my lady."

"Yes. Julia's blood." Lady Phoebe sighed and opened the top dresser drawer. They began filling a valise with underclothes, nightclothes, and toiletries. While they worked,

Lady Phoebe explained what had so interested her in those cards.

"The first one said, 'I will be there.' "

"There is nothing unusual about that in an RSVP."

"The second one said, 'You left in too much of a hurry.' "

"That one is a bit odd, I'll give you that. Left where in a hurry?"

"And the third one said, 'It won't be long.' "

Eva stopped what she was doing. "That sounds vaguely threatening, or it could simply refer to Lord Annondale becoming a married man. Are the cards signed?"

"We should be so lucky, but no. What's more, they're typewritten, so there's no telling who might have sent them."

"Postmark?"

"London. Could be anyone."

"My lady, do you suppose Mildred Blair came here today to retrieve those cards?"

"I don't think so. She seemed relieved when she saw what I had."

"Maybe her relief was because you seemed to accept the cards at face value—as mere RSVPs and not subtly veiled threats."

"Does she think I'm that stupid?"

Eva smiled. "It's safe to say people of Miss Blair's ilk typically think their betters are stupid."

Lady Phoebe flashed her a disapproving look. "I do wish you wouldn't use that word, Eva. I'm no one's *better*."

Eva might have argued with that assessment, not because of Lady Phoebe's birth, but because of the woman she had become: kind, compassionate and, above all, intelligent. But she said only, "Yes, my lady."

Once they returned to Cowes, Phoebe and Eva went to the police station to deliver the provisions to Julia. Phoebe had hoped to see her again, but the officer managing the front desk informed her Julia had had enough visitors for one day.

"What does that mean? Who's been to see her besides me?"

"Can't say. It's the prisoner's business."

Phoebe winced to hear such a harsh term applied to her sister. Then she remembered the envelopes she had brought with her from the *Georgiana*. "If I can't see my sister, I need to speak to the inspector in charge of her case."

"The murder case, you mean," the insensitive man replied.

Phoebe tried not to scowl. "I've brought some new evidence." She reached into her handbag and drew out the cards. "These suggest someone had been threatening Lord Annondale before he and my sister were married. Someone who is *not* my sister, that is."

The man eyed the envelopes skeptically. Without much interest, he said, "You can leave them with me. I'll see they get to Detective Inspector Lewis."

Phoebe hesitated. She wanted to put these RSVPs directly into the detective inspector's hands herself and hear his opinion of them with her own ears. She feared if she merely left them, they'd be ignored or summarily discounted or, worse, lost.

She slid them back into her bag. "I'll come back."

The policeman leaned across his desk. "Now, see here, if you have evidence, you'd best turn it over. Otherwise you're interfering with police business."

"I'm doing no such thing. If I hadn't gone out to the *Georgiana* today, this evidence would never have been found. It certainly *should* have been, but for some reason, it appears to have been overlooked." She wanted to add that missing those envelopes was a sign of shoddy work on the part of the police, but she thought better of it. Instead, she insisted upon returning in the morning.

When the officer didn't question her further, she left the valise for Julia, knowing it would be thoroughly searched and any items the police deemed unsuitable would be removed. When she returned tomorrow, she would place the RSVPs in Detective Inspector Lewis's hands. Then she would see Julia and ask her if Theo had returned to Cowes—or perhaps had never left.

The thought that he hadn't raised a shiver.

"I cannot think of who else would have been here to visit her but Theo," she told Eva as they stepped back out onto Birmingham Road.

"Your grandparents, perhaps. And, of course, a solicitor."

"Yes, Grampapa's solicitor, though I doubt he managed to arrive this fast. But not my grandparents. Not with Grampapa on bed rest. And Grams wouldn't leave him to come alone. We've been gone a good while, and we'd best hurry back."

They walked north, toward the hotel, the cool sea breeze on her face helping Phoebe think. She hoped they would return to a telephone message from Eva's beau, Miles Brannock, with news that Theo Leighton had indeed returned to his estate in the Cotswolds. It was bad enough Phoebe had once suspected him of wrongdoing. She felt like a traitor, to both Theo and Julia, to entertain even a mild suspicion now.

"It wasn't Theo Leighton, my lady," Eva said, with her uncanny knack for reading Phoebe's mind.

She stopped in her tracks and turned. "How *do* you do that? Know what I'm thinking, I mean."

Eva smiled. "It isn't difficult. You think loving your sister gave him a reason to kill Lord Annondale."

"Didn't it?"

Eva shook her head, looking comfortable in her conviction. "I'd almost stake my life that he did not. And if he did, wouldn't he have turned himself in by now, rather than allow your sister to suffer another moment?"

"Eva, you're right! I hadn't considered that. Theo wouldn't let Julia spend a minute in a jail cell." She pressed a hand to her breastbone. "I'm so relieved. Come, let's hurry. If there's time before dinner, I should like to have a word with Ernie Shelton. And Sir Hugh. I do wonder where he's been hiding all day."

"Perhaps he's stayed in his room. He must be grieving his friend, after all."

"Perhaps, but he doesn't strike me as someone who likes to be alone, even in grief."

If she'd had any hopes of tracking down either man upon arriving at the hotel, her grandmother quickly quelled them when she met Phoebe and Eva in the corridor outside their rooms, as if she had been watching and waiting.

"Did you bring Julia her things?"

"We did, Grams."

"And how is she doing?"

Phoebe was glad Grams asked this question, for it allowed her to more easily ask one of her own. "They wouldn't let me see her this time. Did you by chance go down there earlier?"

"No, I didn't. And I'm afraid Julia will think we've abandoned her." Grams looked chastised, making Phoebe regret her question. "She doesn't know about your grandfather."

"Don't worry, Grams. Julia will understand."

Grams nodded, still looking sad. "I need you to look after Fox and Amelia tonight. Have dinner with them, and keep Fox out of trouble."

"Grams, really, Amelia and Fox are capable of looking after themselves. They hardly need me to play nanny these days."

Grams's expression turned stony. "Phoebe, please. I'm asking you to do this. Grampapa and I will have dinner in our suite, but I want you young people to eat together in the dining room. Fox and Amelia could use the distraction, a sense of things being . . . normal." Her voice caught ever so slightly on that last word, and Phoebe's heart turned over.

"Yes, Grams. We'll all have dinner together, and I'll make sure they're both occupied."

"Thank you, dear." Grams kissed her forehead. She quickly slipped back into her own suite, but not before Phoebe caught the glimmer of tears.

"Oh, Grams," she murmured.

Eva had kept going to their room, and now Phoebe joined her. Amelia was not there, giving them privacy to talk openly. Phoebe told her of her grandmother's request. "She rarely uses endearments with us. I've never seen her so vulnerable, Eva, and it frightens me. Grams has always been so formidable. The thought of her getting old, infirm . . ."

Eva touched her shoulder. "The countess is still formidable, my lady. She's going through a worrisome time right now, but she's strong."

"I hope you're right." She turned to read the clock on the bed table. "It's grown late, and you'll be expected at Miss Townsend's room in a little while. Amelia and I can tend to ourselves, so you won't have to worry about us. On second thought, I wonder where Hetta has gotten to."

"Did anyone think to reserve a room for her?"

"Good heavens, Eva, I don't know. I tend to think not, with so much happening all at once today. Poor Hetta. I'll see to it now." She started for the door, but Eva stopped her.

"Don't worry, my lady. I'll see to it before I go to Miss Townsend's room."

"Thank you, Eva. I'll clear it with my grandparents. I'm sure they won't mind the extra room."

"Before I leave, then, why don't we have another look at those RSVPs?"

Phoebe dug them out of her handbag and spread them out on her bed. There were five in all, and she had read only three on the *Georgiana*. She used her forefinger to break the seal on the remaining two.

"This one says, 'Don't bother guessing. You're not clever enough.' Good heavens. And this one . . . 'Your ignorance will be your undoing.' "

"That is certainly a threat, my lady."

Phoebe nodded. "They seem to be saying that because Gil wouldn't be able to guess who these notes came from, he would be unable to protect himself. They also imply Lord Annondale knew his murderer."

"Yes. The individual was toying with him, challenging him to guess."

"And Sir Hugh, as well, based on what you overheard yesterday. I do need to find him and have a little chat." She paused as a thought struck her. "Eva, do you suppose it's possible Sir Hugh was the person toying with Gil? Pretending to have received similar threatening messages would certainly have thrown Gil off from suspecting him."

"I was just having the same thought, my lady. 'Not clever enough,' the message says. It would take a clever man to suspect his best friend, even without Sir Hugh's claims of similar threats."

Phoebe thought a moment, then said, "They had been friends for decades, meaning they had many experiences in common. They fought in the Boer Wars together. They both served in Parliament, albeit Gil in the House of Lords and Sir Hugh in the Commons. And they served in the diplomatic corps in Ireland at the same time."

"Not in the Great War?"

"No, they were in Ireland for the duration. I wonder if something happened there . . ."

"You mean something to make someone seek revenge against them?"

"I do. But why now? Why not sooner?" She smiled rue-fully. "Rhetorical questions, both."

"We've been forgetting about something, my lady. The blood on the deck railing. Assuming it wasn't Lord An-nondale's, and the police found no evidence of that sort of wound on his body, then his killer must have been hurt somehow."

"Like Julia." Phoebe loathed thinking about this one detail that incriminated her sister more than anything else. If *only* Julia hadn't cut her hand last night, she might not be in this predicament now.

"No one else from the wedding has shown evidence of a recent wound. So far."

Phoebe gasped. "Perhaps that's why Sir Hugh has been keeping to himself all day." She frowned. "But like the rest of us, he *was* interviewed by the police. Wouldn't they have seen it?"

"That depends on where the culprit was hurt. Find the wound, my lady, and find the killer."

CHAPTER 11

In the lobby, Eva found Hetta sitting alone in an inconspicuous corner near the entrance to the library. Her overnight bag sat on the floor beside her, which, of course, indicated Hetta had no room to go to. She wore her overcoat, a dark, shapeless affair, while her equally nondescript felt hat sat on her lap. Eva wondered how long she had been there and if she'd eaten anything since leaving the *Georgiana* that morning.

"*Hallo*," the Swiss maid said without a hint of reproach, doubling rather than alleviating Eva's guilt.

"How long have you been here?"

Hetta frowned, and Eva berated herself for not having taken the time to learn a few basic German phrases. But then Hetta's brow smoothed. "Awhile. All right." She smiled and nodded. "I wait."

"Well, come with me, and I'll see about getting a room for you. Perhaps you and I can share. Right now I'm staying in Phoebe and Amelia's dressing room, but under the circumstances, it makes sense to put us together. The countess's lady's maid, Miss Shea, has her own room, but as the higher-ranking staff member, she can't be expected to double up."

Eva realized Hetta understood little of what she was saying, but she kept talking to fill the awkward silence until they reached the front desk. There she requested a small room suitable for the two of them and identified them as being in the employ of Lord and Lady Wroxly. The clerk consulted his ledger and announced that a room had been vacated only a few doors down from Phoebe and Amelia's.

"That's perfect. We'll take it." Eva turned to find Hetta frowning again. "What's wrong?" She couldn't imagine her fellow maid having qualms about sharing a room, if she had even understood that much. Thus far, Hetta had never exhibited self-seeking behavior of any sort. On the contrary, she typically went about her duties with a cheerful attitude and pitched in to help the other servants at home whenever she found a spare moment.

"Madame Julia . . . she doesn't come home. Hetta must go?"

"Oh . . . yes, I see." Of course, Hetta feared for her future. But how could Eva reassure her? If indeed—heaven forbid—Lady Julia wasn't exonerated, would the Renshaws continue to employ Hetta? With the estate fortunes dwindling, could they afford to keep a servant whose duties were no longer strictly necessary? Perhaps, Eva considered, she might serve Lady Amelia instead. Although Lady Amelia still had another year of school to complete, and she wouldn't be needing a full-time maid until she graduated . . .

Eva cut those thoughts short. She mustn't even entertain the notion that Lady Julia would be convicted, that she wouldn't shortly return to the family. Her mother had always told her that a positive frame of mind would see one through the worst of times, that one must have faith and work toward one's goal. She and Lady Phoebe were doing just that. They had been successful in the past, and she had no reason to believe this time would be any different. It was just that the stakes had never before been so high.

She placed her hand on Hetta's forearm and gave a gentle squeeze. "Don't worry about that now. The Renshaws will do everything they can for you. Besides, Lady Julia *will* be coming home. I'd stake my reputation on it."

After escorting Hetta up to their room, Eva made her way down two flights to Miss Townsend's room, which she shared with Antonia Seward. The two ladies immediately set her to work drawing baths, ironing and laying out clothes, polishing shoes, and helping them select jewelry from the cases each had brought. Most of Mrs. Seward's choices consisted of ropes of glass beads and smaller pieces set with paste gemstones. Miss Townsend's collection was rather more impressive. The pearls appeared genuine and of good quality; the semiprecious stones glittered with authenticity; the gold bracelets and rings warmed quickly to Eva's touch, as gold typically did.

After helping each woman select her dinner dress, she recommended for Mrs. Seward a necklace fashioned to look like green amber, with matching earrings; and for Miss Townsend a pearl necklace, with a braided gold cuff bracelet sporting tiny opals. Both seemed pleased with her choices.

Miss Townsend went in for her bath, and when she finished, she called for Eva to help her out. She stood waiting, wrapped in a towel. Eva carried her velvet wrapper to her and allowed Miss Townsend to lean on her arm as she stepped over the high rim of the tub. Then she swung the robe around the woman's bulky shoulders and closed it around her as the towel fell to the floor, thus preserving Miss Townsend's modesty.

"Thank you, Huntford. I cannot tell you how precarious it is for a woman of my age to step out of a bath without assistance. I don't know what I was thinking, letting my own maid go off to visit her family. A woman simply cannot get on without her maid."

Eva smiled and nodded, not showing a hint of her thoughts about this contrary notion. A woman certainly *could* get on without a maid; Eva did it every day.

"It was certainly kind of you, ma'am, to allow your maid the time off," she said politely.

"I've called her back, of course. No one could have foreseen how things would turn out." Miss Townsend went to study her reflection in the mirror above the sink. She ran a finger lightly beneath both eyes, where smudges tinged the excess pockets of flesh. "How are you with cosmetics, Huntford?"

"Quite adequate, ma'am, if you require it."

"Of course I require it," she murmured. "What woman of a certain age doesn't?"

Eva pulled the plug to drain the water. When the last of it spiraled away, she popped the plug back in and turned on the taps for Mrs. Seward's turn. Then she followed Miss Townsend into the bedroom.

The woman went behind the dressing screen to don her undergarments. She reappeared in a camisole, bloomers, and an old-style long corset with garters and sat for Eva to help her on with her stockings. *Fine silk*, Eva noted. Veronica Townsend and her brother might not have been on the best of terms, but he had apparently kept her in ladylike style.

After turning off the bath taps for Mrs. Seward, Eva

came back into the bedroom to find Miss Townsend waiting for her at the dressing table. Eva applied powder, rouge, and eye makeup. Miss Townsend smoothed on her own lipstick. That done, Eva helped her on with a crepe de chine undergarment that covered both the corset and legs, then slipped her dinner gown—black, in deference to her state of mourning, such as it was—carefully over her head.

It was as she did so that a raw streak on Miss Townsend's arm caught her eye. Eva's pulse jumped. A formidable scratch scored the underside of the woman's plump left forearm, from just below the elbow to a few inches above her wrist—a deep, wide abrasion with raw edges and surrounded by red, puffy flesh. She marveled that she hadn't noticed it previously. Had Miss Townsend been deliberately concealing it? Her speculations took off at a frantic pace. The blood on the deck rail had been especially incriminating for Lady Julia.

Eva tried to study the wound while she adjusted the dress and smoothed its folds. It didn't appear quite new, but then, she had no practical medical knowledge about such things, only experience from her own growing-up years and tending to the Renshaw sisters.

She decided she must risk being impertinent. After retrieving the string of pearls from Miss Townsend's dresser, she stepped behind the woman to secure it around her stout neck. "I couldn't help noticing, ma'am. That's a nasty cut you have there."

"What?" Miss Townsend all but snapped the question, then relaxed. "Oh, that. Yes. Gotten while tending my roses before we left home to come here. Serves me right for not simply letting the gardeners do the work."

"I suppose there is great satisfaction in growing one's own rose garden, ma'am."

She finished securing the necklace, and Miss Townsend turned around. "Yes, you're exactly right about that, Huntford. *Great* satisfaction. And for a woman of my age, that's certainly saying something." The sadness in her expression took Eva aback, and she sensed they were not discussing only roses. "It's worth a scratch or two."

"Still, have you had it looked at?"

"Ah, no." Her right hand went almost possessively to shield the left forearm. "It doesn't seem to warrant."

This at least gave Eva an excuse to look at the wound outright. She honestly couldn't tell if the abrasion was new or not. It certainly looked sore and tender, but then, some people healed slowly, especially people of a certain age, as Miss Townsend liked to put it. Lady Phoebe would be most interested to learn of this development, and Eva longed for the freedom to speak with her. It was not to be for some time, however, for now Antonia Seward called to her from the bathtub.

Something in Miss Townsend's square face made Eva pause. "Is there anything else I can do for you now, ma'am?"

"No . . . not at the moment, Huntford."

Eva repeated nearly the same routine with the other woman, but her mind remained on the angry slash on Miss Townsend's arm. So much so, Mrs. Seward scolded her for catching the hair at her nape on her necklace.

"Sorry, ma'am."

"I should think a lady's maid from such a noble house as the Renshaws' should go about her tasks with greater skill."

"Yes, ma'am."

"Well, that will be all, at least for me." Mrs. Seward sniffed. "Veronica? Do you require anything more, or shall we allow this creature to go about her evening?"

Eva stood with her chin level and her gaze straight ahead and, as earlier, gave no hint to her thoughts—which at the moment were not quite fit for polite society.

"That's all for now, I should think. Huntford, please thank your mistress for us. This is most appreciated."

Well, Eva had to give Miss Townsend credit for that much at least.

"Thank you, ma'am. Enjoy your dinner." She went to the door. With her hand on the knob, she turned back into the room. "Oh, and, Miss Townsend?"

"Yes?"

"My deepest sympathies on the loss of your brother."

She had purposely saved this for last, to put the woman entirely at her ease so she would not be expecting such a gesture. In the brief silence that descended, Mrs. Seward let out a huff, which she attempted to cover with a cough.

Miss Townsend's nose became pinched; her mouth, tight. Her eyes turned hard. "Yes. Well. Thank you, Huntford."

A subdued throng filled the dining room, and from the moment Phoebe stepped through the doorway, she felt the stares and heard the murmurs. As the maître d' led them to a table, she realized even some of the wedding guests who had remained at the hotel, including her aunt Wilma, cast judgmental glances in their direction. Phoebe wondered if Aunt Wilma had spoken to Grams about her and Amelia's interests in matters she deemed unfeminine, as she'd threatened to do yesterday on the *Georgiana*. Not that Phoebe cared a whit if she did, but she didn't want Grams any more upset than she already was.

She wished to ask the maître d' for a more secluded spot, perhaps a table in a corner, but a brief glance around the large room divested her of that hope. They should have waited before coming down, until the dinner crowd had thinned, but both Fox and Amelia had declared themselves famished, and Phoebe had had to admit to a growling stomach, as well. Funny, she thought, how such mundane needs continued in the face of the worst difficulties.

And yet when their food arrived, they all three fell to trailing their forks around on their plates, and when Phoebe did venture a bite or two, her vegetables tasted like sand and the medallions of beef like leather. However, she didn't think the hotel chef was to blame.

"I wish they'd all stop staring." Amelia lowered her face, as if her lamb kidneys held her fascination.

"They're technically not staring," Fox grumbled in return. "They're darting what they believe to be furtive glances in our direction. I feel like giving them all a good dressing-down."

"Please don't," Phoebe whispered somewhat more fiercely than she meant to.

Fox shot her an incredulous look, and she regretted snapping at him. She was still unused to *this* Fox—the chastened one who had lost the greater share of his former bravado. *That* Fox might not have stood up and confronted the whole of the dining room, but he very well might have made his sentiments clear in stage whispers that were meant to be overheard. This Fox, however, showed uncharacteristic restraint.

She offered an apologetic smile. "Sorry. This isn't easy. Let's just eat quickly and go. And don't give these people the benefit of seeing us look uncomfortable."

Her brother and sister nodded and from that moment focused entirely on their meals. Which accounted for Phoebe not noticing the man approaching them until his shadow, cast by the overhead chandeliers, fell across her plate.

"I—I wonder if I may? Er . . . if it wouldn't be an intrusion."

Startled, she snapped her head up, half expecting the voice to belong to a reporter hoping to collect sordid details about Gil's death and Julia's supposed part in it. The florid complexion and blue eyes magnified behind spectacles made her smile with relief. She gestured to the fourth, unoccupied seat at their table. "Mr. Shelton, please do join us."

Here were two fortunate opportunities in one. Phoebe had been hoping for a chance to speak with Mr. Shelton, and while she couldn't question him here in front of her siblings as she might have liked, she could further their acquaintance, which would make it easier to approach him again later tonight or tomorrow. His sudden appearance also helped take Amelia's and Fox's minds off the unpleasant sensation of being on display.

"Mr. Shelton, how nice." Amelia had brightened considerably. "I'm glad it's you," she added in an undertone. And then, her voice lower still, she said, "Are you sure you wish to be seen with us? We're attracting quite a lot of attention at present."

Fox nodded at that statement but also studied Ernest Shelton with blatant suspicion. He fell to practically seething when Mr. Shelton sat down and pushed a lock of mousy hair back from his forehead. Phoebe couldn't begin to understand why.

"Thank you so much." Mr. Shelton expelled an audible breath. "I do loathe dining alone, which I fear would have been the case had I not noticed you. I barely know another soul here."

Phoebe regarded Fox and said, "We're happy to have you, Mr. Shelton. I believe you met my brother yesterday."

Mr. Shelton gave a nod in Fox's direction. "Briefly. A pleasure to see you again, sir."

"And you," Fox murmured politely but also sat up straighter and stopped frowning. Phoebe supposed being called sir and not being spoken down to had elevated Mr. Shelton in Fox's estimate. "You're Gil's cousin," he said, as if only just remembering the fact. His skepticism showed once more on his young features.

"That's right. But what's this about attracting attention?" He directed his question to Amelia.

"Look around," she whispered, and Mr. Shelton accommodated her.

"I see. Hmm. Well, don't worry. Soon something new will happen to seize their interest. In the meantime, we'll pay them no mind." The waiter came then, and without having consulted a menu, Mr. Shelton ordered a rib eye steak. "If you wish," he said after the waiter had left them, "I could always knock over a table or two on our way out."

Phoebe and her siblings all regarded him in bewilderment, until he grinned and said, "It should do the trick and take some of the attention off you."

Fox sniggered, and Amelia broke into soft laughter, while Phoebe found herself admiring a man who could joke about something that had embarrassed him greatly only the day before. Especially when he did so to make them all feel better.

"Thank you, Mr. Shelton," Phoebe said, "but that won't be necessary."

"Please, call me Ernest. Or Ernie. We're practically family now, aren't we?"

"Are we?" Fox scooped braised vegetables onto his fork. "I mean, now that Gil is dead and my sister is accused of murdering him, are we still considered family?"

"Fox," Phoebe murmured. Her face prickled with heat.

"No, no, it's all right." Ernest paused while the waiter

returned with his steak. "Yes, Fox, I believe we are. Your sister is my cousin's widow, and that makes us related by marriage."

"She was only married to him for one day," Fox said bluntly. "Not even a full day."

"Be that as it may." Ernest cut into his rib eye, revealing a tender pink interior. The juices streamed onto his plate. "We have a connection now. I've lost my cousin, and you've lost your brother-in-law."

Fox set his fork down and pushed his plate slightly away. "Do you think my sister pushed him overboard?"

"Fox!" Here, at last, was the brother Phoebe recognized and often wished to throttle. She darted a glance at Amelia, who looked as if she might choke on the brussels sprout she had just put in her mouth.

"No, Fox," Ernest replied calmly, "I don't."

"Then . . . who *do* you think did it?" Amelia ventured, as if fearing the answer.

"I wish I knew," was Ernest's simple reply.

Fox studied him again, the speculation rampant in his gaze. "You're the Viscount Annondale now, aren't you?"

Ernest blinked, as if Fox had taken him by surprise. "I suppose I am. Yes."

He said it matter-of-factly, as if it meant nothing overly special, yet Phoebe had had this same thought when considering who stood to gain from Gil's death. She found herself liking Ernest Shelton. After his initial bumbling in the *Georgiana*'s dining room yesterday, he'd shown himself to be a thoughtful, kindly gentleman, and well spoken, despite his occasional tendency to stutter. And yet . . .

Amelia broke into Phoebe's thoughts with another question for Ernest. "Will you still be a veterinarian now that you're the viscount?"

"I haven't had time to give it any thought, really."

"But you must have considered it before Gil married Julia, when there seemed no prospect of his having a son of his own," Amelia persisted.

Fox's gaze narrowed on him as they awaited his reply.

"Ah, well...I...er...suppose I never stopped to contemplate the possibilities. I suppose the running of the estate might take up most of my time now, and—"

"But you *must* go on being a veterinarian," Amelia said with fervor. "The animals *need* you. You can hire someone else to run the estate, can't you?"

"Amelia," Phoebe snapped, suddenly feeling very much like the nanny she had told her grandmother Amelia and Fox no longer needed. "What Ernest does from now on is none of our business. It's for him to decide." And yet she found it nearly impossible to believe he'd never given a thought to how his life might change when and if he became Viscount Annondale.

Obviously, though, he hadn't given any thought to the possibility that he would *not* be inheriting the estate. It might be a slim chance, but the chance nonetheless existed that Julia might, at this moment, be carrying Gil's heir. It was a possibility Phoebe would keep to herself. She only hoped that Amelia would do the same, or that she had been too sleepy and too shocked when their sister pounded on their door last night to fully comprehend what Julia had told them.

Amelia, finished with her meal, played with the dessert fork waiting beside her plate. "If you don't remain a veterinarian, you'll have wasted your education."

"Amelia . . ." Phoebe had grown weary of trying to remind her younger siblings of their manners.

"I'll bear that in mind," Ernest assured her. "But what about you, Amelia? You expressed an interest in following the same profession."

"You should," Fox put in. "Then you won't have to marry. In fact, if you have a profession, you can't marry. Everyone knows a woman can't look after a household and a family if she's occupied elsewhere. You'll be better off."

Both Phoebe and Amelia stared at Fox in shocked disbelief. Never before had he expressed such an egalitarian sentiment. What was happening to this family?

CHAPTER 12

On their way back to their rooms after dinner, Phoebe sent Amelia on to the one they shared, and followed Fox to his. "Why were you rude to Ernest?" she wanted to know, placing herself inside his threshold and crossing her arms to let him know she wouldn't leave without an answer. She spoke quietly, however. Although the door to their grandparents' adjoining suite was closed, she wouldn't risk having them overhear.

He cast her an annoyed look, then shrugged. "I don't much like him."

"That's obvious. Why not?"

"I didn't like the way he was looking at Julia yesterday."

The disclosure took Phoebe by surprise. She murmured, "Him too?"

"What do you mean by that?"

She didn't feel like explaining to him about Curtis Mowbry and his photographs. Instead, she asked, "Looking at her how?"

"I don't know . . . in a way I didn't like."

"As though he liked her?" she suggested.

"No, as if he *didn't* like her."

"I never saw any such thing from him."

"Then you weren't looking closely enough. It wasn't all the time. Just when he thought no one would notice, especially Julia. And he hated Gil. Talk about something being obvious."

"*Hated* might be too strong a word." Phoebe sighed and crossed the room to sit in an armchair near the window. "I suppose he had lots of reasons to resent Gil. Gil wasn't very nice to him, if that incident in the dining room was any indication. But why should he resent Julia?"

"Because of what we talked about downstairs. Ernest becoming the viscount." Fox slid his arms out of his coat and tossed it over the foot of the bed and then worked his fingers into his necktie to loosen the knot. "I'm not a child, Phoebe. I understand that married women have babies, although I don't suppose after one day of marriage Julia is going to. So I suppose Ernest is satisfied that he'll be the new viscount."

Phoebe merely nodded and said nothing. She wasn't about to reveal any part of what had happened on Julia's wedding night.

"Which gave him the perfect reason to push his own cousin overboard," Fox continued. He perched at the edge of his bed, his expression challenging Phoebe to disagree.

"Why last night, though?" she reasoned aloud. "Why not sooner, when he and Julia first announced their engagement?"

"It might have been too obvious who did it if Ernest killed him on the estate. Besides, it's easier to make it look like an accident on a boat. Just one good shove and—"

"Yes, yes, you needn't be explicit."

He gave another shrug, then turned more serious than Phoebe had ever seen him—far beyond his years. "All the better for him that Julia is being blamed. He can't have foreseen that, but didn't you notice how much confidence he has now, in comparison to just a day ago?"

Fox was right. One might suppose his tyrant of a cousin's death had been the cause of Ernest's newfound assurance, but then again, so could having gotten away with murder. An unaccounted-for detail remained, however, and Phoebe decided she had nothing to lose discussing it with her brother.

"The blood on the railing is what convinced the police of Julia's guilt. Since there was no wound of that sort on Gil's body, they've deduced the source of the blood must have been his killer."

"Ernest might have just such a gash beneath his sleeve or somewhere."

"I don't like to think it."

"You like to think it was Julia, then?"

She raised her gaze to his to find it razor sharp with censure. "Of course I don't. But I also don't want to jump to conclusions in an effort to prove Julia's innocence, and neither should you. We're talking about lives here, Fox. Lives that can easily be destroyed. We can't sacrifice one for another."

"I can," he said so simply and readily Phoebe's blood turned cold.

She shook her head. "You only say that because you blame yourself for what's happened."

"Rightly so."

"No, Fox. It wasn't you. It was—" She stopped herself just in time from blaming their grandmother. Doing so wouldn't help Fox make peace with himself or the circumstances the family found themselves in. She said, truthfully, "No one is to blame. Julia did what she thought she must do for herself and for all of us. Now we must do what we can for her. That is all."

She waited for some indication that he believed her, but none came. He stared down at his feet, frowning, his thoughts hidden from her. She wanted to shake him, as she often wished to shake everyone in her family, though if she were truthful, she supposed they often wished to shake her, as well.

Nothing she could do or say would change his mind, for now. Fox must come to an understanding of these events on his own, and until then he would continue to blame and berate himself. That made her sad, while at the same time it strengthened her resolve to find the truth. Only one cure existed for this family's woes: having Julia back among them.

Eva dropped several coins, given to her by Lady Phoebe for this purpose, into the calloused palm of the boatman they'd found at the end of the pier. Phoebe seemed completely at ease as she settled into the small boat. Eva, on the other hand, entertained serious reservations about this man. Decades of salt and sea had scored his face, while his toil at the oars of his skiff had left his back hunched and his legs stiff, resulting in an unsteady wobble when he walked. Or was that the consequence of the sharp spirits she smelled on his breath?

Upon seeing the abrasion on Miss Townsend's arm, Eva had realized they must return to the *Georgiana* yet again—the third time today. Lady Phoebe had agreed when Eva had told her about it. They must search all the staterooms for signs of blood, including the main one where Lady Julia had cut her hand.

Of course, she hadn't meant that they should go now, in the near middle of the night, and a dark night at that. Heavy clouds blanketed the stars, with the moon merely a wisp of light peeping out at random intervals. At least the wind was down and the waves were subdued. Eva nonetheless clutched her stomach as the boatman pushed away from the pier, and breathed in deeply to offset the rolling of the little craft over the swells.

Lady Phoebe tapped the wooden seat beside her impatiently, a sound that grated on Eva's nerves no matter how she tried to ignore it. Really, she had meant for them to go in the morning, but as soon as she and her mistress had compared their evening experiences, Phoebe had insisted they go immediately.

Eva kept her eyes on the boatman, willing him to stay true to their course and not tip them into the next swell. A small reassurance came in the wavering reflections of the lights and the voices skittling over the water from other vessels. It might be late in her view, but vacationing yachters would be up for hours yet, enjoying their pâté and champagne and midnight suppers. She darted a gaze at the *Georgiana*, hoping its crew were not similarly engaged. It appeared not to be the case. But for the dim lanterns glowing every few yards along the main deck, all lay as dark as a ghost ship. The night deck steward would be making his rounds, and they hoped to avoid him. Hence traveling in a quiet rowboat and not a motor craft. If they did encounter him, they'd say they were once more there on behalf of Lady Julia, and Lady Phoebe would use her position to convince him to let them get on with their task.

The boatman drew them up alongside the ladder on the starboard side, and for a moment Eva was filled with indignation that her lady should have to climb aboard like a common sailor. But what else had she expected? If she had wanted ease of boarding, they should have wired ahead of their arrival.

Lady Phoebe showed no such qualms when it came to hitching her skirts and grabbing hold of the wooden rungs. Once assured of her lady's balance, Eva turned to the boatman.

"Wait here. Do not leave."

He stared blankly back at her.

"Do you understand?"

In lieu of a reply, he reached under the oilcloth heaped at his feet and drew out a bottle. With his thumb, he popped off the cork and settled back with a generous swig.

Eva heaved a frustrated sigh. "Don't get drunk and pass out, or you'll forfeit the rest of your payment."

He shrugged.

She turned away to climb the ladder, the drawstring bag she had brought thumping against her hip. Lady Phoebe had already reached the deck and now helped Eva over the side. They stood motionless and silent for a moment, listening for voices, footsteps, anything to alert them to the approach of the deck steward. Hearing nothing but the waves and the occasional burst of laughter from another boat, they headed inside, then made their way to the lower level.

"This way," Lady Phoebe said unnecessarily and entered the first stateroom they came to. Here Eva drew the electric torch out of her bag and switched it on.

"We would have been able to see better in the daylight, my lady," she couldn't help pointing out.

"We've already run the risk that these cabins have been scrubbed clean, in which case our coming will be of no help to Julia." Lady Phoebe took the torch from Eva and shined it all around the room and then moved into the bathroom. "This is obviously Veronica's room, and I detect no traces of blood anywhere."

They moved on, entering Sir Hugh's stateroom next and then what appeared to be Miss Blair's, with the same results. Lady Phoebe expressed her disappointment. "I had so hoped we might be able to shed doubt on Julia's guilt, but I see nothing here. And I realize I've no idea where Curtis Mowbry's berth might be."

"He mentioned it was a deck below the viscount's, which would place it among those of the crew."

"And we can't go down there, not now. All right, then, let's take another look at Gil and Julia's stateroom."

Once there, Lady Phoebe pointed the torch at the blood-stained area rug where the mirror had fallen and Lady Julia had cut her hand.

Eva crouched. "There's more blood there." She pointed to dried droplets making a thin trail to the dresser, where the mirror's frame and shards of glass rested.

Lady Phoebe crouched beside her, then sat back on her haunches. "It looks to me as though Julia did most of her bleeding right here. I doubt she was unable to staunch the flow when she bandaged her wrist. Whoever left that blood on the deck rail had been freshly wounded, probably by Gil during their struggle. The only question remains, What did Gil use?"

"If he had a weapon with him, it shows that he went outside knowing he would meet someone, rather than simply going for a walk, and that he felt the need to protect himself." Eva shined the torch around the room. "Your sister might know if Lord Annondale kept weapons on board."

They helped each other to their feet. Then Lady Phoebe went still, her eyes widening and her mouth slowly opening. "The letter opener."

"My lady?"

"Remember earlier, when we went through Gil's office and I found the sealed invitations?"

Eva nodded.

Lady Phoebe continued. "I looked for a letter opener, but there wasn't one. I wonder . . ."

"Would a letter opener be sharp enough to cut flesh?"

Lady Phoebe shrugged. "Possibly. Julia might know."

"Then I suggest we get back to Cowes, my lady, and go

and see your sister first thing in the morning. We can tell the police of our findings."

"Do you think they'll listen?" Lady Phoebe's tone implied this was not so much a question as a statement. If the police refused to take them seriously, what hope for Lady Julia?

"I cannot say. In the meantime, my lady, we should let the deck steward know we're here and instruct him not to let anyone clean this room. We must convince the police to come back."

Lady Phoebe nodded.

In the passageway, they didn't bother masking their footsteps or their voices, yet when they emerged onto the deck, they detected no sign of the steward.

"Let's walk around," Lady Phoebe suggested, indicating the port side. But they found no one there, either. "Do you suppose he retired for the night?"

"Highly unlikely. He'd be sacked should he be caught. Then again, with the viscount gone, protocol is sure to be lax. Perhaps we should go below again and wake someone. It's important the evidence we found not be disturbed."

"I only hope whomever we awaken doesn't take us for a pair of thieves or pirates." Lady Phoebe laughed nervously. They came around to the starboard side again, and she went to the railing and gazed down. "Eva, our boat is gone."

Eva hurried over and found herself gazing down into the black and quite empty waves. "Why on earth would he have left us, the fool? Oh, I knew going with him was a very bad idea, my lady. He was drunk and getting drunker."

"Perhaps he'll be back. Perhaps he remembered something he needed to do back onshore."

Eva didn't have the heart to express her thoughts about

that possibility. "I think we'd better wake a crew member and wire over to the island for another boat. Embarrassing as that will be."

Lady Phoebe murmured her agreement. They started to turn away, but Lady Phoebe looked out over the water again and clutched the rail. "Look, someone is coming this way. Is it him?"

Eva moved back beside her and attempted to make out the black outlines of the craft sliding noiselessly through the water. The type of craft was similar to theirs, but not quite. "I don't think so. But whoever it is does seem to be coming to the *Georgiana*." Her nape prickled a warning, and she grasped Lady Phoebe's arm. "I think we should not be here on deck when they arrive. Let's go back inside."

"And do what? Hide?"

"Exactly that, until we know who it is."

Phoebe refused to go farther than the main saloon, where she posted herself at a window. If someone climbed the ladder, she would see them before they saw her. But she wondered if they were being overcautious. "Perhaps one of the crew went ashore and is returning."

Eva shook her head. "I don't think so. Whoever is in that boat out there is being too quiet, just as we were, though, I doubt their intentions are as honorable as ours."

"I doubt it, too." A ripple of fear went through her, and she wished she had listened to Eva's suggestion that they wait till morning and come here openly—and perhaps with a policeman in tow.

"We should move elsewhere, my lady. We're too vulnerable here."

"We're fine," Phoebe whispered back. "If we need to, we can make our way from here through to the aft section and exit back out to the deck. But shush. Whoever has arrived should reach the top of the ladder any moment."

"I don't like this," Eva murmured back.

They waited for some minutes, and no one came scrambling over the side. They lingered another moment to be sure, but no one came.

"That's odd. I'm going for a look." She started to move to the door, but Eva seized her wrist ungently.

"I'll go. Please stay here."

"Eva—" Too late, Eva hurried out the saloon door. Phoebe was left alone for less than a minute before the door reopened quietly and Eva slipped back in.

"It's most strange. There is a rowboat quite like the one we came in, except it's not ours. There's a man on board, and he appears simply to be waiting."

"For who? You needn't answer that." A sense of alarm grew. "Eva, someone else must be here—someone who shouldn't be. I'll wager whoever it is was dropped off earlier, before we came, and is now preparing to leave."

"And might pass through this very room on their way out." Eva's face mirrored Phoebe's growing apprehension. They instinctively grasped hands. "We can't just stand here like sitting ducks."

"But where to go? Whoever it is could be anywhere on board, could come from any direction."

The sound of a door swinging open and closed came from inside the dining room, and Phoebe realized someone had come up the service stairs from the galley. Her heart thudding, she tugged Eva toward the passageway where the main stairs were located. In the dark, the toe of her boot slammed into the leg of a table secured to the floor, and pain surged through her foot and up into her leg. She only just stifled a yelp, but not the thud of her stumbling gait.

They pushed into the passageway, but they were not

safe. Footsteps advanced across the saloon in their direction. "The stairs," Eva hissed, and down they went again, releasing their grip on each other to use the hand railing to keep from falling. The footsteps continued their pursuit. Phoebe and Eva paused in the passageway at the bottom of the steps.

Phoebe pressed her hands to her thighs as she leaned over to catch her breath. "Perhaps it's merely the steward."

"The steward would have said something, demanded to know who we were."

"Right. Which way, then?" Phoebe made another snap decision. "Back into the stateroom."

They scrambled inside, but when Eva would have shut the door and flipped the lock, Phoebe shook her head. She went to the dresser and lifted the mirror's frame. She needed two hands to support its weight, especially when she raised it high above her head. She positioned herself beside the open door. Eva did likewise on the other side, holding her torch aloft. If someone tried to accost them, he or she would receive a double trouncing.

Phoebe sucked a breath into her lungs and held it. When a hulking shadow moved across the threshold, she steadied her trembling arms beneath the solid weight of the frame and prepared to thrust it downward onto the individual's head.

When she would have struck, a burst of light seared her eyes and rendered her blind. She stumbled beneath the weight of the frame, swung sightlessly downward, and then felt herself shoved backward, off her feet, and onto the floor on her back.

"Got you!" a man's gruff voice shouted.

The overhead lights flashed on, and Phoebe, blinking and still half blind, groaned as she rolled from her back onto her side, and pushed upright on her hands.

The voice spoke again, expressing no small amount of shock. "What the bloody blazes . . . ?"

The figure of a man in a dark blue uniform with nautical epaulets and insignia wavered in front of Phoebe as she continued to blink away her befuddlement. He held a kind of club or constable's nightstick, though his uniform and cap declared him part of the *Georgiana*'s crew and not of the Cowes police force. Behind him, Eva came forward, the torch raised. She swung it down on the man's shoulder with a sharp thwack, and he cried out in pain.

He spun around to confront his attacker, his own club raised to strike. Before he did, he must have made sense of the situation, for instead of striking, he let out a complaint. "What you'd go and do that for? And who the blazes are you?"

"I'm Eva Huntford, and that's what you get for knocking my lady off her feet, you swine."

"Well, what's your lady doing on my boat and in the middle of the night?"

Rather than answer, Eva pushed past him and helped Phoebe up. The man watched them with a perplexed expression that drew his snowy-white eyebrows together and caused his equally cottony mustache to twitch. His right hand rubbed at his left shoulder.

Phoebe established her balance and released her hold on Eva. "I'm sorry to give you such a fright, sir. Are you all right?"

Eva, she noticed, exhibited no such concern for the poor man but continued to stare him down with all the censure of a fiercely loyal lady's maid.

"I suppose I am," he replied grudgingly. "But you're not who I thought you'd be. I was following a man. How'd you two get here? Never mind. I might still get 'im."

He took off at a run, and Phoebe and Eva followed him up the main stairs and back to the saloon, and from there outside. He went to the railing and gazed out over the water. Phoebe and Eva flanked him.

"Blast. He's gotten away."

Phoebe curled her hands around the railing and craned her neck. "Eva, light the torch. Perhaps we can make out who it is."

Eva did as instructed, but the beam of light skimmed weakly across the tops of the waves and revealed nothing about the skiff or its occupants. Soon, they disappeared into the darkness, even as the splash and drip of their oars faded to silence.

The crewman—or deck steward, as Phoebe now identified him—pushed away from the railing and turned. "Blast and damn."

"Watch your language," Eva said sharply. She switched off the torch.

"Who was he?" Phoebe asked.

The steward shook his head. "Caught him prowling in the viscount's office. Pushed past me rough like, knocked me down, but I was up and after him in no time. Followed him through the galley and up to the dining room. The next thing I know, it's you two I'm after, and no sign of the bloke."

Phoebe exchanged a puzzled glance with Eva, then to the night steward said, "He must have come out through the saloon. That's when we ran to the main stairs and went below. We thought it was him chasing us."

The steward was still shaking his head. "I'd have caught him if not for you two lurking about. I recognize you now. You're Lady Phoebe Renshaw, aren't you? What on earth are you doing here?"

Phoebe raised her chin defensively. "My maid and I came out to collect more of my sister's things. We looked for you, as a matter of fact, but couldn't find you anywhere."

"That's because I was otherwise engaged chasing down an intruder. I'll wager he was collecting things, too—for himself. And I'd have had him if not for you," he lamented again.

Phoebe chose to ignore the accusation. "Did you happen to get a look at him?" She held her breath, then let it out in a whoosh at his reply.

"Too dark, and he was too fast."

"I'll wager you saw more than you think you did." When he scowled at Eva, she compressed her lips and looked contrite. "Sorry for that bash on the shoulder. I cannot abide anyone harming my ladies. However, think about the intruder. Did he have to duck through the doorways? Did his figure fit easily on the spiral stairs from the galley, or did his girth cause him to sidestep his way up? Was his hair darker than the shadows, or did a glimmer of moonlight catch it?"

The steward wrinkled his nose. "What are you doing? Writing a novel?"

"Don't be impertinent," Eva snapped back. "Think. Any detail that comes to mind might be of help."

"Help to who, miss?"

Eva, obviously losing her patience, drew herself up. "Just please think about what you saw. For instance, could you make out his hair color, if it was light or dark?"

The man made a show of scrunching up his features, as if deep in thought, and sighed dramatically a couple of times, but then his expression changed, and he blinked. "Now that you mention it, he was a good-sized bloke, and he might not have had hair at all."

"You mean he was bald?" Sir Hugh, perhaps, Phoebe thought.

The steward nodded slowly. "I remember the moonlight catching him as he raced across the dining room. I saw a flash of a light color—not hair, mind you, because it seemed

perfectly smooth. With a bit of a sheen. So now I'm thinking he was either bald or wore some kind of cap." He
paused, regarding the two of them. His gaze narrowed
speculatively. "If you don't mind my saying so, I hardly see
why I'm describing anything or anyone to you. The pair of
you don't exactly look like bobbies to me. And if you expect me to believe you were only here to collect some of
the viscountess's things, well . . ." He sniggered.

"I'll thank you to curb your rude insinuations." Eva
pointed her torch at him, and he lurched a step backward.
Phoebe knew Eva didn't mean to hit him again, not with
the initial fracas over, but apparently, the steward felt no
such assurance.

"See here," Phoebe broke in. "Let's go wherever it is
you have communications equipment and wire the Cowes
police. They need to know about this intruder, and other
things, as well. You'll probably want to wake the captain.
And I suggest the lot of you devise a more efficient means
of guarding the *Georgiana*."

Grumbling all the way, the steward led them below to
the wireless room. The captain, yawning and tousle-haired,
his hastily donned coat askew, joined them and ordered
his equally sleepy radio operator to contact the police.
That was how, some twenty minutes later, Phoebe and Eva
found themselves on a police cutter on their way back to
Cowes, with Detective Inspector Lewis standing over them,
looking none too pleased.

CHAPTER 13

"Detective, tell your pilot to stop." Eva pointed out over the water at another craft coming around the bow of the *Georgiana*. "That's our boatman."

"Where on earth has he been?" Lady Phoebe stood up in the police cutter and waved her arms in the air.

"Please sit down, Lady Phoebe," Detective Inspector Lewis said stiffly. "I take it that was the man who rowed you out." His mouth became a flat line, and he shook his head, demonstrating his disapproval, as he had done numerous times already.

Lady Phoebe sat back down with a huff. "He's coming this way. Please have your man slow down so he can catch up to us."

"Whatever you and that drunkard have to say to each other can be said tomorrow."

"Oh, then you know him," Eva couldn't help saying, for she had reached the same conclusion: a drunkard. Which probably explained why he had gone off and left them stranded.

The inspector scowled. "You're both lucky you're not under arrest or at the bottom of the Solent. That boatman is a menace, and no decent citizen should ever hire his services. The only reason we haven't arrested him or run him out of Cowes is that he hasn't killed anyone—yet."

"We only hired him because no one else was available," Eva told him, repeating Lady Phoebe's own justification for putting her trust in such a character.

"Exactly," the man shot back. "Everyone else of any repute was already engaged." He shook his head again. "What is Lord Wroxly thinking, allowing the pair of you to go running around at night?"

Lady Phoebe once more pushed to her feet. "Leave my grandfather out of this. He isn't well. We had good reason to row out to the *Georgiana*, and as it turns out, we were right. If you had only agreed to go aboard and view the evidence we found . . ."

"It's for the police to decide what constitutes evidence, Lady Phoebe."

"How can you decide if you don't see it?"

Seeing her lady about to lose her temper, Eva reached up to take her hand and gently tugged her back onto the bench seat behind the partially enclosed helm. She feared they had made a hash of things. Not that she regretted their actions, or at least their intentions, but had they paid closer attention to events on the yacht, perhaps the steward would have caught the intruder and they would right now know his identity, not to mention he'd have joined them on this boat ride back to the island. As it stood, Detective Inspector Lewis acted as if he didn't believe there had been anyone else on board tonight, and even managed to half convince the steward he had been chasing Eva and Lady Phoebe all along. Or if there had been someone, Mr. Lewis chalked it up to a common thief, taking advantage of the absence of the *Georgiana*'s owner.

It seemed the inspector was determined to ignore all evidence except that which incriminated Lady Julia.

A police car awaited them at the pier, and he herded them into it as if they were common criminals. She and Lady Phoebe slid into the backseat, while the inspector rode up front with the driver. A none too steady ride through the narrow streets and around sharp corners had Eva feeling queasy all over again, as if she still trod the *Georgiana*'s decks. She and Lady Phoebe traded only a few words, knowing everything they said would be overheard.

They were hustled into the police station and to a room that made Lady Phoebe shudder when the door closed upon them. For the moment they were alone, having been told by a uniformed bobby to make themselves comfortable while they waited for the detective inspector to return. The room held a table and a few inhospitable chairs. A gray linoleum floor and slightly lighter gray walls presented a bleak prospect for anyone having to spend more than a few minutes there. Eva hoped they wouldn't be there longer than that, and wondered if the police could stop them if they chose to simply walk out. They hadn't been charged with anything, so far.

"Are you cold, my lady?" Eva started to unbutton her coat, with the intention of throwing it over Lady Phoebe's shoulders. "You're shivering."

"I'm not cold. It's just that this was the room where Julia and I talked only this morning. And the thought that she's somewhere in this building, in a cell, behind bars . . ."

"Try not to think about it."

"Do you suppose they'll let us see her?"

"Considering the time, I doubt it very much. Perhaps we should consider how to get out of this pickle we've found ourselves in."

"They'll let us go. Detective Inspector Lewis brought us here to frighten us. But it hasn't worked. All I am is angry."

The door opened, and the detective inspector strode in. "Angry, are we?"

Lady Phoebe set her hands on her hips, but it was Eva who spoke. "Indeed we are, for the way we're being treated. We've done nothing wrong."

"I have a list of pending charges that say differently, including obstructing justice and interfering with a police investigation."

The man circled the table and sat in the single chair on the other side. He gestured for them to sit opposite him, like criminals about to be interrogated. Eva felt her gorge rise with indignation. Still, she held one of the chairs for Lady Phoebe and then lowered herself into the other one.

"Also, trespassing."

Eva folded her hands on the tabletop with a good deal more poise than she felt. "My lady, and any member of her family, for that matter, has every right to board the *Georgiana* at any time of day or night. The vessel *is* owned now by her sister, need I remind you?"

"Not if she murdered her husband, it isn't."

Lady Phoebe spoke from between gritted teeth. "She hasn't been found guilty."

"She hasn't been on trial yet," the man quipped.

Eva's queasiness returned. "Please," she said, making a great effort to appear meek. "Won't you at least listen to what we have to say? We might have simply waited for our boatman to return, or had one of the *Georgiana*'s crew row us back to town, but we didn't. We radioed the police to tell you of our findings."

"Your *findings*." The man sat back with a smirk.

"Yes, our findings." Lady Phoebe looked and sounded in danger of losing her temper again, so Eva spoke up before she could.

"The blood in the stateroom implies that Lady Annondale bled from cutting herself on the mirror, but it doesn't make any sense that she would leave without wrapping a bandage around the wound. And that would have staunched the blood had she then gone after Lord Annondale."

"She might not have wanted to take the time," the inspector said. "The viscount hobbled out on crutches, and she realized it was her chance to overpower him and push him overboard."

Lady Phoebe groaned.

"We discovered a letter opener missing from the viscount's desk," Eva countered. "Perhaps he used it to defend himself and slashed whoever murdered him."

Mr. Lewis looked less than convinced. "What does this letter opener look like?"

"We . . . uh . . . don't exactly know."

The inspector's jaw tightened. "What does that mean?"

"We've never exactly seen it," Lady Phoebe admitted in a small voice.

"Then how do you know there was one?" he demanded. "And what kind of letter opener could cut someone enough to make them bleed that much?"

"Wake my sister and we can ask her."

"You may visit her tomorrow, if you like," the man said blandly.

"And then there was the intruder on board tonight." Eva reached up to touch her hair. "A man who the steward said looked to be bald. Sir Hugh Fitzallen is bald."

The man leaned forward so suddenly that Eva, and Phoebe beside her, pulled back sharply. "You are not to go accusing a man like Hugh Fitzallen without proper evidence."

Lady Phoebe recovered her vehemence. "Why must we not suspect Sir Hugh, when you've slapped my sister in a jail cell?"

"That's different. Sir Hugh Fitzallen is a former war

hero and a diplomat. He's done this country good service."

"Implying what?" Lady Phoebe slapped both palms on the table for emphasis. "That my sister is guilty by default? Because a man who might have been prowling about the *Georgiana* tonight for who knows what reason is too virtuous to be considered a possible suspect?"

While Eva recognized the irony in Lady Phoebe's question, the detective inspector, apparently, did not. His eyebrows lifted. "That's exactly right."

Fearing Lady Phoebe might hyperventilate, Eva leaned to clutch both of her shoulders and gently massaged them. "Inspector, please allow us to see Lady Annondale."

"It's late. Tomorrow."

Implacable man. Isaac Perkins, the whiskey-tippling chief inspector at home, always grumbled at her and Lady Phoebe's unwanted assistance in cases like these, but he never threatened them with incarceration or spoke to them—leastwise not to Lady Phoebe—with such blatant disregard. She feared they might have met their match in Detective Inspector Lewis.

"All right, the two of you can go, for now. But this isn't over. And don't go meddling again, or your next visit to this police station will be an extended one." He came to his feet, signaling them to do the same.

Lady Phoebe remained seated. "Wait, there's something else. This morning we made another discovery on the *Georgiana*."

Eva cringed as Lady Phoebe prepared to reveal their earlier trip out to the yacht. Mr. Lewis's darkening expression didn't reassure her as he sank back into his seat.

"This was not the first time the pair of you snuck out there?"

"We didn't sneak anywhere," Eva replied rather hotly.

She didn't like anyone speaking that way about her lady. "We went out to gather some of Lady Annondale's things to bring to her here."

"Yes, and while we were there, we discovered a stack of RSVPs to the wedding," Lady Phoebe put in. "They contained threats, some subtle, others rather blatant."

"And you did what with them?"

"We brought them here and attempted to give them to you," Lady Phoebe said a bit self-righteously. "You weren't available, however, and I didn't like to leave them with just anyone, so they're in my hotel room."

"Lady Phoebe, the policeman manning our front desk isn't *just anyone.*" The inspector's patience was wearing thin, Eva could tell.

Lady Phoebe gave a slight shrug. "We'd have brought them tonight, but we never expected to end up here."

"Tell me what these notes said, if you can remember."

"Certainly, I can remember." Lady Phoebe recited the contents of the RSVPs, putting the most emphasis on the one that read, Your ignorance will be your undoing."

The man sat back, his hand moving back and forth across the underside of his chin. "Except for that last one, they're hardly even vaguely threatening, and none of them are what I would consider alarming." He shook his head. "I'd like to see these cards, but I've the feeling each one can be easily explained. Now . . ." He stood once more. "It's late, and I've had rather enough of the two of you. Don't let me catch you interfering with police business again. I don't care who your grandfather is."

He opened the door into the corridor and called out. "Hewitt, would you walk these two out, please? And see that they get into a taxicab." He turned back to Eva and Lady Phoebe. "You're to go straight back to your hotel. No more adventures tonight." With that, he left them.

A woman with thick brown hair that curled around the edges of her cap, a calf-length wool skirt, and a matching belted jacket filled the doorway in the detective inspector's place. The badge over her right breast pocket identified her as a member of the police force. "I'm Constable Hewitt. Come this way, please."

Lady Phoebe exchanged a surprised look with Eva and moved to follow. "You're a policewoman. That's splendid."

The woman replied without looking back, "I find it fulfilling."

Lady Phoebe hurried a little to match her pace. "Do you ever face dangerous criminals?"

Constable Hewitt shook her head. "Not as a matter of course. The rough ones are left to the men on the force. We women mostly enforce traffic laws, but any police work comes with its risks."

"That doesn't seem fair," Lady Phoebe mused. "I'd wager you're as capable as any of your male counterparts."

"Be that as it may, rules are rules."

They reached the street door, which Constable Hewitt held open for them. Despite the hour, motorcars and a few horse carriages traversed the street outside. On the pavement, Lady Phoebe turned to her.

"You must know my sister is here. Lady Annondale. I wonder if you might . . . check on her occasionally, just to see that she is all right. I'll return tomorrow to visit her, but the nights are long and . . ."

"It's my job to look in on the female prisoners. But don't worry. Your sister's being well treated."

Lady Phoebe's mouth slanted in disbelief. "If Mr. Lewis has his way, she'll be tried and convicted by tomorrow."

"My lady," Eva murmured, knowing alienating a member of the force wouldn't help Lady Julia. The constable's next words, however, surprised her.

"The detective inspector's a bit of a prig now, isn't he?" Lady Phoebe nodded, a slight smile curling her lips. "You noticed it, too?"

"There's a reason," the woman replied in a confidential tone. "He bumbled a case a while back—a big one. Listened to the wrong informant, got the wrong information. A killer went free. Lewis was with the Met back then. Got transferred down here because of it. Had to start all over again, a bobby on a beat. Ah, here comes a taxicab." She raised her arm high to signal the driver. The motorcar stopped, and Constable Hewitt opened the rear door for them.

"That certainly explains a lot," Lady Phoebe whispered to Eva as they approached the vehicle. "It must have been galling to have to leave the Metropolitan Police in London for a small-town operation here in Cowes."

"Yes," Eva agreed as they slid inside. "And unfortunately, it means no matter what we discover, Detective Inspector Lewis is highly unlikely to listen." Dismay forced a sigh from her. *He has his suspect, and he's going to do his best to hold on to her.*

Phoebe rose with a single intention the next morning: find Sir Hugh and ask him where he was last night. She wondered whether he—assuming it had been he—had been aware of Eva's and her presence on the *Georgiana* and had purposely used them to outwit the deck steward, or had the confusion been a happy accident for him?

Not that it mattered. If Sir Hugh had gone out to the *Georgiana* last night to search through Gil's office, it was an admission of guilt, as far as she was concerned. She could only surmise he'd gone looking for the threatening invitations, obviously not realizing Phoebe and Eva had already found them. Despite their anonymity, he must fear they might be traced back to him. He had sought to frighten Gil, had toyed with him, and then had struck a blow when Gil had been at his most vulnerable. The only question remaining was why. The two men shared so much personal history, Phoebe felt certain there must be something in the past, whether recent or remote, that had set Hugh on a path for revenge.

She nibbled on a slice of toast from the tray Eva had brought her, and washed it down with a swallow of tea. Amelia was already up and had gone down the corridor to their grandparents' suite.

Eva turned away from the armoire. "It's much warmer out today, my lady. Perhaps spring has finally come to Cowes."

She draped a flowing silk frock in deep royal blue with a matching hip-length jacket on the foot of the bed. Phoebe washed and dressed, and Eva helped her on with a pair of stylish but comfortable pumps.

"I'm off to find Sir Hugh," Phoebe announced when she was ready. "And you?"

"I'm heading back to Miss Townsend's room to see if I can learn anything about her brother's relationship to Sir Hugh."

"Good idea. Perhaps that Mrs. Seward might provide an insight or two. If she's spent any time as a guest in Gil's home, she might have overheard things." She adjusted the cuff of her jacket. "I'm going to check on my grandparents first. Assuming I can track down Sir Hugh this morning, I'd like to visit Julia directly after lunch."

"I'll accompany you."

"Good. See you later, then. Good luck!"

"Good luck to you, my lady."

Phoebe had proceeded a few yards down the corridor when the opening of a door stopped her. Her grandfather stood on the threshold, dressed, by the looks of him, for a trip into town. Phoebe glimpsed her grandmother's worried face over his shoulder.

"Archibald, please, come back inside. The doctor gave strict orders for you to rest."

Grampapa caught Phoebe's gaze with a grim expression and sighed. "I *shall* rest, Maude. In the taxicab on the way to the police station."

Oh, dear, Phoebe thought. She, too, remembered the doctor's recommendations. "Grampapa, please, at least wait until tomorrow."

"*Et tu, Brute?*" he murmured. Grams came up behind him.

"Archibald, you'll be taking a frightful risk with your health if you go out today. Please listen to reason."

Amelia appeared beside Grams. "Yes, Grampapa, you're not completely well, and you know it. Even I can see how tired you are, no matter how hard you might pretend." She paused, and Phoebe wondered how much her younger sister knew or had guessed. Their grandparents wished to spare both Amelia and Fox from further worries, but Amelia often proved herself to be much more astute than anyone guessed. She presently continued in a brighter tone. "And it's been so chilly outside. Do come back in and sit by the fireplace. We'll see Julia tomorrow."

He turned to face them both, his back stiffening with resolve. "I refuse to allow an entire day to go by without seeing my granddaughter. I will not have her think we don't care or, worse, that we believe her to be guilty."

"Grampapa, no! Julia would never think that." Phoebe placed a hand on his shoulder and attempted to nudge him back into the room. He didn't budge.

"Maude, you are welcome to come with me. In fact, I urge you to do so. But either way, I am going. I also wish to be there when our solicitor arrives."

"If you and Grams are going, I'll go, as well." Amelia sounded resigned.

Grampapa apparently had other ideas. "You will not, young lady."

"But, Grampapa, dearest, Julia is my sister. I wouldn't want her to think I don't care what happens to her."

"We'll convey your sentiments and your love, but you are staying here with Fox." His stance and his tone softened. "Please, my darling girl, for me. Jails are dreadful places, and I cannot abide the notion of you setting foot in one."

Amelia couldn't argue with that, not when remaining behind seemed to soothe their grandfather's anxiety. She went in search of Fox. Grams, seeing herself out-argued, relented and had her maid, the often dour-faced Miss Shea, bring her coat, hat, and handbag. While she was getting ready, Grampapa took Phoebe aside.

"Will you come with us? You and Eva?"

The request took Phoebe aback, but she nodded. "Of course, Grampapa." She didn't think it worth mentioning that she had been to the Cowes Police Station just last night, or that she had already intended returning there today.

"Thank you, my dear. I suspect there is much your sister won't wish to tell us. I know she confides in Eva, but I fear the police won't let anyone but a family member or our solicitor in to see her. Perhaps if you and Eva go in together, the police will allow it."

On the way to the police station, Phoebe clung to the hope that Grampapa's solicitor would find enough holes in the inspector's case that the charges would have to be dropped. But so many details worked against Julia: her own words about her marriage, her argument with Gil, the cut on her hand, her leaving the *Georgiana* to come into Cowes. . . .

As they were getting into the taxicab, Phoebe noticed

how pale Grams looked and how she stooped beneath her light spring coat. Grams, as a rule, never slouched, never stood any other way but straight and tall, despite her height often placing her an inch or two above most men. And dear Grampapa . . . As Amelia had said, he looked tired—tired and defeated. They both were showing their age, and a lump that could not be swallowed pressed against Phoebe's throat.

Despite being told yesterday that Julia could have only one visitor at a time, her grandparents were taken together down the corridor to the visiting room. Phoebe and Eva waited in the lobby for what seemed an eternity, but in reality was only about half an hour. When they returned, real fear clutched at Phoebe. Grams's eyes were puffy and red, and she walked more bent over than previously. And Grampapa—he looked as though he could hardly place one foot in front of the other, as if taking one more step would deplete his energy.

She exchanged alarmed glances with Eva, and they both came to their feet.

"It's dreadful, just so utterly ghastly, seeing our beautiful girl in this deplorable place." Tears trickled down Grams's papery white cheeks. Phoebe embraced her, and for a long, heartbreaking moment, Grams allowed herself to be held and supported before gently pushing away and attempting to square her slender shoulders.

Then Phoebe turned to Grampapa and realized he might indeed stumble and fall without someone to lean on. His breathing had become shallow, and he barely lifted his feet, as if he no longer had the strength to do so.

"Eva, I'm taking them back to the hotel," Phoebe said quietly. "See if you can get in to see Julia, please. Ask her . . ." She left off. Eva knew to ask Julia about the letter opener that should have been on Gil's desk. But would Julia give the matter any thought? Yesterday, she had practically blamed herself for Gil's death, if not directly, then indirectly, by marrying him for his money. Julia had to help herself—*had* to. Or what would happen to this family? "*Tell* her," she amended, "that she must believe in her own innocence and must fight to prove it—if not for her own sake, then for our grandparents. Remind her how much they love her, and how much they need her to come home."

Eva nodded a silent promise, and Phoebe walked her grandparents outside to their waiting taxicab.

CHAPTER 14

The taxicab stopped outside the hotel, and Eva paid the fare. Her talk with Lady Julia had not gone well, and she felt loath to report back to Lady Phoebe. As the motor pulled away, she took a moment to gaze out over the Solent, whose waves lapped the narrow beach on the other side of Queen's Road. The mainland was visible today, a strip of darker blue between the undulating water and the sky. When she turned back to enter the hotel lobby, the couple she saw exiting the building prompted her to make another sharp turn and pretend to head east along the pavement.

A glance over her shoulder revealed the pair, Ernest Shelton and Mildred Blair, had gone west, toward the Egypt Esplanade. Miss Blair had taken his arm and walked close at his side, lending them the look of a pair of young lovers. They seemed deep in discussion. Odd. Eva had never seen them together before, not in any capacity. Had not even seen them exchange so much as a word. Of course, they were acquainted, having both worked for the viscount, but being Lord Annondale's cousin and heir placed Mr. Shelton rather above Miss Blair's station. Eva's nape tingled with interest. She allowed them to proceed a dozen or so yards before following them. She tugged the light scarf she wore high beneath her chin and pulled the brim of her hat lower.

The shoreline changed, with the beach replaced by a seawall that held the Solent in check. To her left, a low stone wall bordered the grassy precincts of the Esplanade, where gypsies had camped long ago. The couple turned in at an entrance between two pillars, well before the land rose and became covered in tangles of ferns and grasses and creeping vines, dotted here and there with violets bursting from their buds.

Eva passed the entrance but peeked behind her to see where Miss Blair and Mr. Shelton had gone. They had seated themselves on a bench beneath the twisted, craggy branches of a windswept oak. They were not alone in the park. A father and three children took turns tossing a stick to a spotted, long-legged setter, who leapt and bounded in pursuit. Two women in nannies' uniforms occupied another bench, absently rocking prams as they chatted. Several others slowly strolled in pairs, threesomes, or alone, appearing to enjoy today's pleasant weather. A man with binoculars gazed up into the trees.

Eva turned into the park and took a circuitous route to a shady spot behind Miss Blair and Mr. Shelton's bench, where she pretended to be studying the roses surrounded by a carefully shaped boxwood border. Beyond them, purple alliums and blazing foxtail lilies waved gracefully in the breezes. Eva's quarry continued their close proximity, their heads nearly touching as they spoke. She strained her ears to listen, as she had done on the *Georgiana* when she'd come upon Sir Hugh and Lord Annondale arguing in the service pantry. Often in the past, she had good-naturedly chided Lady Phoebe for eavesdropping, but it seemed she had acquired the same habit.

"Julia . . ."

Eva's eyes widened. What *about* Lady Julia? It had been Mr. Shelton who spoke the name, and now she caught a few more words.

"Nearly ruined everything."

"Well, she hasn't." Miss Blair sounded impatient, waspish. "I do wish you'd stop whining about her. I'm so very weary of it."

Perhaps not lovers, then. Or, on second thought, perhaps so. Lady Julia believed Mildred Blair to have been Lord Annondale's mistress. Had she transferred her affections to the new heir? If so, it wouldn't be for his handsome looks or his sterling personality. Eva could hardly envision the two of them having a thing in common or Miss Blair enduring Mr. Shelton's insecurities with anything approaching patience. Yet, becoming his paramour would certainly be to her advantage. Considering his temperament, he'd be much easier to handle than Lord Annondale had been.

"How dare you accuse me of whining, with everything I've had to put up with all these years?" Mr. Shelton drew away from her, sitting angrily upright. "As if you're one to talk—"

"All right. Enough. Our worries will be over in the morning."

"You sound sure of yourself."

"I am. Darling Ernie, you mustn't worry so." Miss Blair adjusted the brim of her hat and sat back. "Everything will be resolved by luncheon tomorrow." Her head turned as she followed the setter's racing path across the grass. She continued watching him as he snuffled about the base of a tree, searching for his stick.

Miss Blair's profile was visible to Eva: the short, upturned length of her nose, the resolute angle of her chin.

Her ebony bangs stirred softly against her brow, and she gave her head a little shake, as if to keep them free of her eyes. Miss Blair seemed to her a study in confidence and poise, so much so Eva almost envied her. What she didn't envy, however, was the woman's coldness, and her apparent ability to switch her affections or allegiance or whatever it was from person to person with little or no to-do.

Miss Blair possessed a ruthless streak, make no mistake, and Eva didn't consider this an exaggeration. As the pair fell silent, Eva considered whether her opinion of Miss Blair was colored by the fact of her being female, whether she found Miss Blair altogether too assertive for a woman. Many people would, and they would judge a woman harshly for breaking with the conventions of femininity. But wasn't the behavior exhibited by Miss Blair—at least when it came to her intelligence and her proficiency at her job—similar to what Lady Phoebe aspired to? And didn't Eva encourage her lady in her aspirations?

Yes, but she also saw in Phoebe Renshaw a compassionate nature and an unwillingness to hurt others to achieve her goals. She didn't believe Miss Blair could make the same claims.

But what about Ernest Shelton? According to Phoebe and Amelia, he seemed a kindly man who devoted his life to animals. For that alone, he could be forgiven his timidity. Yet he had just accused Lady Julia of nearly ruining everything, and what else could he have been referring to but his chances of inheriting the Annondale title and fortune?

Perhaps the man didn't love working with animals as much as he professed, and was eager to leave his profession behind and live the life of a leisurely nobleman.

She waited until they exited the park, and then followed, but at a greater distance than previously, and she let them enter the hotel several minutes before she did. On the way in, she removed her scarf and hat lest they notice her and remember seeing the patterns and colors of the fabric. About her black worsted coat, she need not worry, since it blended with countless others to be seen on any public street. She saw no sign of them in the lobby, however, and rode the lift up to her floor.

She and Lady Phoebe found time to talk before dinner. First, Eva inquired after the earl and countess.

"They're resting and will take their dinner in their rooms again," Lady Phoebe told her. "I'm very worried about them. How I wish this were over and we could all go home."

While Eva helped her mistress into evening attire and did her hair, she told her what she had seen and overheard at the Esplanade. She hurried into the tale, putting off discussing her earlier visit with Lady Julia.

"I don't trust that woman, but Ernest . . ." Lady Phoebe plucked a hairpin from the dressing table and handed it to Eva, who pinned a curl in place. "Ernest has been lovely, or so he seems." She frowned at her reflection. "I can say this much. Fox doesn't trust him."

"He bears watching, as does Miss Blair. Something is going to happen tomorrow morning." Eva slid another hairpin into Lady Phoebe's coif, this one studded with glittering gemstones. "Miss Blair said their worries will be over in the morning. Tonight I'd like to go back to Miss Townsend's room and see if she might be anticipating the morning, as well. If it has anything to do with Lord Annondale's money, it will affect her, too."

Lady Phoebe nodded. "Now, tell me about Julia. Were you able to see her?"

Eva could postpone the inevitable no longer. With a sigh, she opened Lady Phoebe's jewelry cask and handed her a pair of ruby droplet earrings. "I was. Inspector Lewis hesitated at first but then relented. He decided it couldn't do any harm."

Lady Phoebe clipped on one of the earrings and turned on the bench seat to face her. "And?"

"She's not of a mind to cooperate, I'm afraid. She still blames herself for her husband's death. Even more so than previously, it seems, for she has little else to do but sit and ruminate. She's entirely guilt ridden."

"Oh, Eva, I'd hoped more time in that horrid place would cure her of that and make her see that she's no criminal. She didn't kill her husband any more than you or I did, and the notion of her doing penance in a jail cell is ludicrous. Why is she being so stubborn?"

"It's a Renshaw trait, I'm afraid."

Had she gone too far in voicing the observation? With any other member of the family, perhaps, but not so with Lady Phoebe, who nodded in rueful agreement.

"In all honesty, it's not stubbornness," Eva went on. "She's . . . *defeated* is the term for it. I've never seen her like this. Not since . . ." She compressed her lips, having been about to divulge a confidence, one she swore she would never speak of.

"Not since Papa died," Lady Phoebe guessed correctly. Their gazes met, and Eva looked quickly away before she silently confirmed what Lady Julia had never revealed to anyone else but her. Lady Phoebe was not to be fooled. "I know she's never been the same since Papa's death. For years I'd believed it hardened her. Made her stop caring about . . ." She sighed. "About so many things. I never saw her shed more than a few perfunctory tears over it, but you did, didn't you, Eva?"

She didn't answer. She didn't deny it but merely cast her gaze at the floor while visions of that dreadful day flashed in her mind and Lady Julia's sobs echoed in her heart.

Lady Julia had insisted upon a vow of secrecy, and Eva would never break that vow. Not even for her dearest Phoebe, who stared down at the ruby earring in her palm, which for an instant seemed to transform itself into a drop of blood.

"Did you at least ask her about the letter opener?"

Eva nodded, grateful for the change of subject. "I did. She insisted she didn't remember one in Lord Annondale's office."

Lady Phoebe continued studying the earring, then closed her fist around it. "I don't believe her. If only we could find it . . . But if it played a part in Gil's death, chances are it went overboard in the struggle and is at the bottom of the Solent. And all our hopes of freeing Julia along with it."

Phoebe rose especially early the next morning, dressed without waking Eva, and hurried down in the lift. She was determined to witness whatever Miss Blair and Ernie Shelton were expecting to happen this morning.

Her arrival in the dining room proved timely, for Sir Hugh Fitzallen was just being seated at a table by himself. She wondered if he, too, might be anticipating an important event in the next couple of hours. A bit of luck had him gazing up in her direction as he sat, and she used the opportunity to smile and wave. She knew exactly what the result would be.

He spoke to the waiter, who immediately came over to her. "The gentleman I just seated asked if you would join him for breakfast, my lady."

Yes, she had expected as much, for a gentleman could not do otherwise.

Mildred Blair and Ernest Shelton had acted suspiciously yesterday, and Veronica Townsend sported a wound that could have produced the blood found on the railing of the

Georgiana. But those particulars were far from conclusive, and questions remained about Sir Hugh.

She beamed at the waiter. "I'd be delighted."

Moments later, they gave their breakfast orders and were enjoying a pot of coffee. After trading the usual pleasantries, Sir Hugh turned somber.

"How are you holding up, with everything that has happened?"

"It's been a trial," she replied honestly, "but I have faith my sister will be exonerated."

"Of course she will," he was eager to agree.

"It's my grandparents I worry about most right now. This is taking a heavy toll on them. As you might be aware, my grandfather's health is precarious."

"I do wish him, and all of you, the very best." He sounded sincere, albeit his words were little more than correct, delivered with typical British reserve. Phoebe regarded him, from the top of his smooth, slightly shiny head to the wide span of his shoulders, to the breadth of his muscular chest. The deck steward had seen, as he put it, a good-sized bloke, who perhaps did not have hair.

"Thank you. But here we are discussing me, when you've lost a lifelong friend. How are you coping, Sir Hugh?"

"As you may well imagine, it's difficult. I keep thinking we'll meet for brandy in the evenings, or in the library to pore over maps and discuss past strategies and victories, as men who served together will do." He fell quiet, his gaze searching an invisible, faraway distance.

Phoebe seized the opportunity he had just provided her. "He saved your life, I understand."

He looked startled for a moment, then blinked. "He did at that. At Bergendal, in South Africa. Back in nineteen hundred."

"And you, in turn, saved his life, after his leg was destroyed."

His lips curled slightly, as if at a secret. "You've been checking up on me. My history."

"Isn't it common knowledge?" she asked innocently.

"Not for someone of your age," he replied with a chuckle.

"But why wouldn't I be interested in the man my sister was going to marry, and his closest friend? The individuals we choose to spend our time with say much about us, don't you think?"

"A shrewd observation, again, especially in one so young."

Phoebe shrugged and, not wishing to be sidetracked, plunged in again. "So you and Gil owed each other quite a lot, or did you consider your debts to each other settled after South Africa?"

"I don't know that we ever thought of our actions in terms of debt. We each acted upon instinct and afterward simply got on with it."

"That can't have been easy. I know how war changes people. I've seen the effects of the Great War firsthand. And Gil had to learn to walk again, with the aid of a prosthetic."

Sir Hugh nodded slowly, a frown scoring his brow. She weighed the wisdom of her next words. She risked bringing their conversation to an abrupt end, with Sir Hugh storming off, but she went on nonetheless.

"One can't help but wonder if Gil ever thought back to that moment he saved you from enemy fire, only to end up losing his leg. If he hadn't become distracted, would things have gone differently, with him escaping the machine-gun fire intact?"

His frown deepened. "What are you getting at?"

"I'm only speculating. It would be natural, wouldn't it, to consider what might have been if only . . . ?"

"You seem to be implying Gil blamed me for his leg. That he resented me."

"Did he?"

"Good heavens, no. We were in the middle of a battle. It easily could have been me seriously injured or dead. I can't believe for a moment Gil regretted saving my life. And to tell you honestly, I don't appreciate your implying it."

He pushed back in his chair, as if to come to his feet, but at that moment the waiter arrived with their food. To leave now would have created a scene, and Phoebe once again wagered on his being too much of a gentleman to do that—if not too much of a gentleman to have murdered his best friend.

"I'm frightfully sorry, Sir Hugh. I . . ." She drew in a purposely audible breath. "You're correct, and I don't know what has gotten into me. I do apologize."

He studied her a moment before reaching across the table and patting her hand. "It's quite all right. The strain of events . . . We're all a bit off our stride."

She latched onto another opportunity. "Very true. But strange things continue to happen. The night before last, my maid and I went out to the *Georgiana* to collect more of my sister's things and—"

He started, looking up sharply. "Did you? Was that a wise choice, going out there at night?"

"It *was* rather late, but I'd decided to go, anyway, rather than wait till morning." She sliced into her blood pudding. "I wished to collect more of Julia's things to bring to her first thing in the morning. It's so distressing, picturing her in that bleak cell. But do you know, we were not the only visitors to the ship? Someone else was there, not openly, but skulking about and even sneaking into Gil's office. I can't imagine what he was looking for, but Eva—my maid—and I were only a few cabins away, in the main stateroom. I shudder to think what might have happened if our paths had crossed."

"Did you see this individual?"

To lend credence to her story, she shuddered now. "Fortunately, we did not. The night steward did, however, though it was too dark to make out a great many details."

"A shame."

"Yes. Although, he did say the man—for a man he seemed sure it was—was bald."

Sir Hugh blanched. "Oh?"

Phoebe raised her eyebrows and, with a small smile to imply she might be jesting, asked, "It wasn't you, was it?"

He hesitated, then said, "I assure you, I am not the only bald man in the world."

"No, but you are the only completely bald man who attended Gil and Julia's wedding. And you are the only bald man who argued with Gil in the pantry off the dining room during the reception."

"How do you know about that?"

"Someone overheard you and told me about it. So please don't bother denying it."

His eyes narrowed; the frown lines across his forehead became sharper. "Friends sometimes argue. It doesn't mean anything."

"My source told me you seemed upset, even frightened. I wonder if it had anything to do with the threatening notes printed on wedding invitations in Gil's desk?"

The clatter of his fork and knife striking his plate startled her into silence. But only momentarily.

"Well?"

"I don't see why I should answer these questions. Who are you but an overimaginative, idle young chit?"

"True, but this idle young chit's sister has been wrongfully accused of murder. Where were you the night before last, Sir Hugh?"

"In my room."

"Can anyone attest to that?"

"As it happens, yes. I was in when the maid came to turn down the bedclothes."

"She came in the middle of the night? Doubtful. Here's what I think." She took a sip of coffee and set her cup decisively on its saucer. "I think you had yourself rowed out to the *Georgiana* in hopes of finding those invitations before someone else did. Unfortunately for you, I already had them. I'd found them that morning. What do they signify? Who was after Gil? Who is *still* after you, Sir Hugh? Or . . ." She paused to take his measure. "Or was it *you* threatening Gil all along and pretending to be threatened, as well, to throw him off?"

Sir Hugh threw his napkin onto the table and pushed to his feet. Without a word, he strode from the dining room. Far from deterred, Phoebe hurried after him, following him through the lobby and out to the terrace. He must have heard her footsteps, for he stopped short and turned. There were too many people about, however, for him to raise a vocal protest, at least across the distance between them. He waited for her to reach him.

"Are you intent on hounding me?" he demanded when she did.

"If it helps my sister, yes. At least tell me what those threats were about. Do they put my sister in danger, as well?"

Sir Hugh turned abruptly and kept walking, but at a slower pace, as if expecting her to fall in at his side, which she did. She grew puzzled when he descended the stairs and crossed the roadway to the strip of beach on the other side. The tide was high, and salty droplets, kicked up as the waves broke against the sand, pelted her arms and face.

Sunlight bounced off the water. Having come out without a hat, she shielded her eyes with her hand.

Sir Hugh let out a long sigh. "The truth is, I don't know the answers to your questions. I don't know who sent the threats. I received them, as well, except instead of being on wedding invitations, they came on blank stationery, without a hint as to who might have sent them."

"The messages I saw had a teasing tone," she said, "as though they were toying with Gil, trying to throw him off balance."

"It worked. Gil pretended not to take it seriously, but I know he did. That's why he insisted on having the reception on the *Georgiana*. He wanted to set sail immediately after and get away from England for a while."

"That's why you were to go along, isn't it? Because you were threatened, as well."

"Yes, and Veronica, too, though she knows nothing about it. Gil was afraid to leave her behind, fearing whoever this is might attempt to kidnap her, use her to get at him."

A gust of wind threatened to raise Phoebe's hems, and she pressed her hands against her thighs. Strands of hair whipped about her cheeks. She suddenly envied Sir Hugh's hairlessness and his attire. "Surely you must have some idea why someone would come after you in this way."

"No one has actually come after us. I feared there might be some attempt here in the hotel, or at least a continuation of the threats, but so far there's been nothing. And no, I cannot imagine who it could be. Perhaps it's all been a devilish prank."

"Perhaps, but Gil obviously didn't think so, or he wouldn't have arranged for all of you to sail away on the *Georgiana*. As for who is behind the threats . . . it seems to me there are only a few reasons to prompt someone to such behavior. Money tops the list. Do you owe anyone any great sums?"

He gave her a pained look. "Again, I feel no compunction to respond to your prying."

"Why didn't you go to the police?" she persisted.

He spun away, tramped several paces across the sand, and swung back around. "Because, my dear Lady Phoebe, I didn't dare."

CHAPTER 15

Eva and Hetta went down to the lobby together, planning to have a quick breakfast. Lady Phoebe was already up and had left her room, and Amelia was still sleeping, so neither of them needed Eva at present. Even at that early hour, the lobby buzzed with activity, with porters carrying luggage back and forth, and men and women in coats and hats stopping by the front desk. Eva took little interest in any of it, crossing the space without scrutinizing faces and wanting only a cup of coffee and a scone, with a side of fresh fruit.

Hetta, on the other hand, lingered near the desk. Eva couldn't begin to imagine why, and if she didn't know better, she'd have believed Hetta to be listening in on a conversation between the clerk and a gentleman in a calf-length tweed coat with a fur-trimmed collar.

After a few moments Hetta hurried over to Eva. She wore an urgent expression. "We wait. We watch."

"Watch whom?"

Hetta pointed at the man in the tweed-and-fur coat.

Eva's puzzlement grew when Miss Blair appeared from

the lift and approached the man. They exchanged a few words, and then Miss Blair returned to the lift.

When the gentleman in question turned away from the desk to find a seat along the wall, Hetta led Eva to seats of their own on the opposite side of the lobby. Eva estimated him to be in his midforties. He was clean shaven, his hairline was only just beginning to recede, and his eyes were sharp and darting, as if he was making a mental map of every detail in the lobby.

"Does that man have something to do with Lord Annondale?" she guessed, for why else would Hetta have pointed him out? Could he have anything to do with what Eva had overheard yesterday between Miss Blair and Mr. Shelton?

Hetta didn't answer her at first but stared down at her entwined fingers. Then she nodded almost imperceptibly.

"But how do you know that?"

"I follow Fräulein," she murmured.

"Fräulein . . ." Eva's puzzlement mounted. "You followed Miss Blair?"

Another nod confirmed this hunch. "No trust."

"When?"

"Yesterday."

Prying the information out of the other maid was proving a challenge to Eva's patience. She forced herself to breathe calmly. "Where did she go?"

"Uh . . . letters building."

"Letters . . . Do you mean the post office? Did she send a letter?"

"No." Hetta frowned in concentration. Then, "Tap-tap."

"Tap-tap? What is that? What does it mean?" Eva was about to throw up her hands in defeat, when the obvious occurred to her. "Do you mean a telegram?"

Nodding, Hetta opened her mouth to reply, then closed

it and pinched her lips. She pointed to one of the lifts. Miss Townsend and Mr. Shelton stepped out, followed by Miss Blair. She led them to the man in the fur-trimmed coat. He stood and shook hands with both of them. Eva came to her feet, but Hetta reached up, caught her hand, and pulled her back down.

"I tell you something. The Fräulein, she is on deck, says bad words."

"When? You mean when Lord Annondale died?"

Hetta nodded emphatically.

"Bad words . . . She was arguing with the viscount?"

Hetta shook her head and shrugged.

"Was she with a man or a woman?"

"Man."

Eva stood. "I need to find Lady Phoebe. Whatever is set to happen this morning is about to happen now. Hetta, keep an eye on them." Eva pointed first to her eye, then to the gathering across the lobby. "Find out where they go. Do you understand?"

"Watch. *Ja.*"

Eva hurried off, first to the dining room. Seeing no sign of Lady Phoebe, she tried the library, with the same result. Perhaps the terrace. She was practically running now, back through the lobby, where a glance revealed the group to still be there. Waiting for what?

She stepped out onto the terrace at the same moment she spied Lady Phoebe coming up the outside staircase. Phoebe saw her and gestured and quickened her steps until they stood together.

"Sir Hugh and I just had a little talk," she said breathlessly. She looked to be bursting with news, news Eva would have liked to hear, but there wasn't time.

"Never mind that for the moment, my lady. Something is happening in the lobby. A man I don't recognize just arrived, and Miss Blair, Miss Townsend, and Mr. Shelton appear to be meeting with him. There's more I have to tell you, but there isn't time now."

They hurried inside, to be greeted by something of a shock. From the street door, Lady Julia entered the lobby, immediately trailed by two uniformed bobbies. Miss Blair and the other three with her had disappeared somewhere. The pieces were beginning to fall into place. This man in the fur-trimmed coat could be none other than Lord Annondale's solicitor, and Lady Julia's presence must mean he had arrived to read the will. Which struck Eva as exceedingly odd, as wills were not typically read before the funeral, and Lord Annondale still lay in the morgue.

Lady Phoebe hurried to her sister, but Lady Julia walked by her with barely a glance. She made eye contact with no one but kept her gaze fixed on the front desk. The brows of the man behind it converged, and a corner of his lower lip slipped between his teeth in an aspect of apprehension or even fear, Eva thought. Foolish man. Did he believe Lady Julia to be a murderess? Did he think she'd make a scene?

The lift dinged, and the door opened, this time to reveal Lord and Lady Wroxly, who appeared as frail and wan as the last time Eva had seen them. The earl's nearly vacant expression brightened, however, when his gaze landed on his granddaughter. He spoke to the countess, and they made their way to her. The lift also deposited Lady Amelia, who appeared bemused and slightly wary as she moved toward her family.

And who could blame her? As when the police had first taken Lady Julia away yesterday, all commotion ceased, and a hush settled over the lobby. Eva wanted to chastise everyone present, tell them to go about their business and leave the Renshaws alone. How dare they seek entertainment from the misfortunes of others?

Lady Julia spared her grandparents a brief hug and a

few words. Amelia threw herself into her sister's arms and hung on to her even after Lady Julia released her. Eva saw Lady Julia nodding vigorously and holding up her bandaged hand, perhaps assuring them it was healing well. Eva took a moment now to puzzle over her attire, which she did not remember packing for her yesterday, when they brought her things to the jail. She searched the lobby, and her sights landed on Hetta. When their gazes met, Hetta stood and crossed the lobby to her.

"I see where they go," she whispered. "I lead you."

"I don't think it matters now. I believe I know why they've gathered this morning."

Hetta regarded her quizzically, but Eva didn't bother to explain. Her attention had been caught by the youngest Renshaw, just now coming in from the terrace. Had he been outside previously, when Eva went looking for his sister? If so, she had not noticed him. She wondered why he hadn't joined them, why he was appearing only now. She studied his young face and thought she detected a similar wariness to Amelia's, except that where she seemed overwhelmed and distraught, Fox seemed to be . . . well . . . skulking. Had he been following Lady Phoebe? Spying?

She regarded her mistress as she joined the rest of the family. The policemen who had brought Lady Julia stood at attention at a respectable distance. The family murmured quietly to each other, and Eva caught snippets that confirmed her suspicions about this morning's events. From the hallway that led to the rear of the building, Miss Blair came striding toward them. She spoke to Lady Julia, who nodded and turned back to her family.

"Well, it's time. I'll tell you what happens after." She nodded to the two bobbies, who came forward. "We'll go in now," she told them, then hesitated. "When it's done, might I have a few moments with my grandparents before we . . . we go?"

"Inspector Lewis said we were to return you immediately after, my lady," one said in a harsh official tone. He had a sharp nose and a jutting brow that spoke of an obstinate nature.

The other, whose portly physique strained the brass buttons of his uniform coat, made a face and rolled his eyes. "C'mon, Spence. A few minutes won't matter to anyone."

His mate scowled at him, but Lady Julia cast him a grateful expression. "Thank you." She glanced around her, and spotted Eva. She raised a beckoning hand. "I'd like Miss Huntford to accompany me."

A jolt of surprise went through Eva. Lady Phoebe, her mouth gaping, looked stricken, but only for an instant. She quickly gathered her composure and smoothed her features, and offered a nod of encouragement to Eva. For herself, Eva felt almost beholden to offer apologies to the rest of the Renshaws and wished Lady Julia had chosen her grandfather to accompany her.

Miss Blair was frowning and looked as though she wished to protest, though why the matter should concern her one way or the other eluded Eva. At any rate, she didn't have a chance to voice a complaint, for the stern policeman spoke up again.

"That's highly irregular. I . . . I don't think it should be allowed."

"Irregular? Why should it be, and why should you object if I desire my maid to attend me at this meeting?" Lady Julia's eyebrows went up in her haughtiest expression.

The man's brow jutted more heavily as he narrowed his eyes. "Is she your maid? Or is this one?" He pointed at Hetta, who stood uncomprehending yet still realizing she was somehow being singled out. The poor woman, with her Germanic complexion, blushed to the roots of her hair.

The policeman continued, "She claimed *she* was your maid when she showed up to see you yesterday."

This was news to Eva. A suspicion began to grow in her mind, but she stored it away as Lady Julia spoke again.

"That's true, but Miss Huntford *was* my maid until recently, and Hetta doesn't understand English. I want someone there to help me remember what is said."

The man echoed Eva's own thoughts. "Wouldn't your grandfather serve better in that capacity?"

Lady Julia raised her chin. "I hardly see why that should be of any concern to you." Then she turned to her grandparents. "Darling Grampapa, you'll understand why I want Eva, won't you? You needn't be upset by all of this. I merely want Eva there because she's so frightfully clever when it comes to remembering things."

He patted her cheek. "Whatever you wish, my dear." He looked up at Eva. "You know you have our trust." Eva nodded, bowing her head slightly. And to the policemen, he said, "I insist Miss Huntford attend the meeting with my granddaughter."

"Good. Then it's settled." Lady Julia walked briskly past the two policemen. "Eva, do come along."

"Where have you been this morning, Fox?" Grams asked in an offhand way as she perused the menu in front of her. Clearly, her mind was on other matters, namely, Julia. They had all decided to take tea in the dining room while they waited for the meeting with the solicitor to end. If they were the discreet and not so discreet center of attention among the other diners, so be it. Grampapa had declared himself unwilling to hide away any longer, especially when he felt quite certain no one in the Renshaw family had done anything wrong.

Phoebe glanced at the menu without registering any of its selections and set it aside. It shouldn't have surprised her that Julia had chosen Eva to attend the meeting. She shouldn't have been let down. But it hurt all the same, albeit she could not help admitting that, under similar circumstances, she likely would have chosen Eva, as well. She trusted Eva implicitly, as did Julia, apparently. Phoebe could not pretend she and her sister trusted each other in the same wholehearted manner. And while, again, this should not have surprised her given their history—and, if she were honest, it didn't really—the truth of it left her nonetheless dispirited.

And then there were matters with Sir Hugh Fitzallen. She hadn't been able to break through his reticence, but what he *had* been willing to reveal assured her he would not lift his smallest finger to help clear Julia's name. He feared endangering himself. He and Gil had become involved in some treachery, gotten mixed up with unsavory individuals. He believed those individuals had taken their revenge against Gil, and now he apparently hoped that by remaining silent, he would save his own life.

But no, there must be more to it than that. If it were only a matter of being pursued by criminals, why not go to the police and tell all? The answer struck her almost physically: Hugh couldn't go to the police, because then he, too, would find himself in prison.

Grams repeated her question to Fox, this time more testily, and Phoebe snapped out of her ponderings to realize he had never answered. In fact, he appeared not to have heard her, but Phoebe didn't believe that for a moment. Not when the tips of his ears were glowing red, always a telling sign. She caught the waiter's eye and signaled him over. At the same time, with false brightness she said, "Yes, Fox, tell us what you've been up to."

"Answer your grandmother when she speaks to you, Fox," Grampapa put in, not unkindly, but in a tone that insisted in no uncertain terms.

"Sorry, sir. Sorry, Grams. Er . . . nothing, really. Just hanging about." He caught Phoebe watching him and dismissed her with a terse turn of his head in their grandfather's direction. "So, they're reading the will now? But Gil hasn't been buried yet."

Grams flinched at the observation, but Grampapa remained calm. "Yes, it's not usual, that's for certain. I can only assume the solicitor came at Veronica's request. Or Ernest's perhaps, but I rather think it would have been Veronica being the impatient one."

"Why, Grampapa?" Amelia was playing with the edge of the table linen, until Grams reached over and stilled her hands. "What difference does a day or so make?"

Their grandfather appeared to consider. The waiter came, and Grams ordered a pot of tea and a tray of sandwiches.

When the man walked away, Grampapa leaned forward and lowered his voice. "It might be days yet before Gil is laid to rest." He had hesitated the tiniest bit before choosing those words, obviously searching for the most delicate means of expressing this. Dear Grampapa was always solicitous of his granddaughters' feelings, especially gentle Amelia's. It sometimes frustrated Phoebe to be treated as a child, but then she'd look into his earnest eyes and see the love he bore them, and she'd forgive him anything. "I suppose Veronica is feeling terribly at loose ends just now, without her brother to provide for her. One can't blame her for wanting matters settled, if at all possible."

That last, small addition to his statement caught Fox's attention. "Do you mean matters might not be settled with the reading of the will, sir?"

Grampapa frowned slightly, and Phoebe perceived his inner debate over whether to address that question. He and Grams exchanged glances. "We'll soon see, won't we?"

Were they wondering the same thing Phoebe was?

Whether Julia might be expecting? It would barely seem possible to the casual observer—there had hardly been time for Julia and Gil to be intimate. Yet Phoebe knew otherwise. She wondered if Julia would reveal the possibility to the solicitor, Veronica, and Ernest, then shook her head at the thought. She couldn't imagine her refined sister speaking such words to a group of people who were little more than strangers to her.

"What's on your mind, Phoebe?" Amelia reached out and touched her hand, and Phoebe glanced up with a start.

"I was just thinking about Julia." The truth, but with an omission. It wasn't her secret to tell. Besides, there might be nothing to reveal, and Ernest would inherit the title and estate, and Veronica would receive whatever her brother had left her, under the assumption that he had produced no heir of his body.

Her grandparents appeared to accept her reply without question. Fox, on the other hand, was studying her closely, until she met his gaze. Then he quickly looked away.

Their repast came, and they embarked upon a course of small talk that effectively skirted the only issue any of them truly cared about. They were just finishing when the waiter once more approached the table, this time with a message.

"Lady Annondale is waiting for you all in the hotel meeting room, my lord. I can direct you there, if you desire, sir."

The two policemen stood outside the meeting room, one on either side of the door. Julia waited for the family inside, sitting at a rectangular mahogany table. Eva sat beside her, and the two of them conversed in whispers. When Eva noticed the others, she hurriedly vacated her seat and found another at the far end of the table.

Grampapa replaced Eva at Julia's side faster than Phoebe had seen him do anything of late. Fox, in a rare moment of selfless consideration, followed him and held the chair for him. Grampapa sank heavily into it and covered Julia's hand with his own.

"You look troubled, my dear. Tell us what happened."

Phoebe and the rest of the family took seats around the table, all eyes on Julia.

"There was no reading. They brought me here for nothing."

"No reading?" Grams sounded outraged. "What sort of game are they playing?"

"I don't think it was meant to be a game." Julia fidgeted with the ends of her silk scarf. "There was meant to be a reading, but the solicitor, Mr. Walker, said Gil made a last-minute change, along with giving explicit instructions about when to reveal the contents of the will."

The answer didn't seem to satisfy Grams. "What on earth are they waiting for?"

"To see if I am . . ." Julia lowered her chin, then raised it with a gleam of defiance, though directed at whom, Phoebe couldn't say. "To see if I am expecting."

After a momentary silence, Grams raised a finger and pointed toward the door. "Fox, Amelia, go."

Neither made a move, not so much as the tiniest muscle. Grams seemed not to notice.

"Didn't you tell them it was impossible?" she asked.

"I did not. Because it isn't. And so now we'll see, first of all, if I'm let off, and, secondly, if I happen to produce a son. Gil's heir."

Phoebe flicked glances at her younger siblings, who were both wide-eyed with fascination.

Julia spoke again. "But that isn't all. We were told the general terms of the will. We learned that if I should produce an heir, the bulk of the estate will go to the child. Gil named me the child's trustee and guardian—"

"Thus putting the fortune at your disposal during the child's minority," Grampapa said, finishing for her.

"That can't have made Ernest happy," Phoebe murmured. She didn't think anyone heard her, but Julia turned in her direction.

"Not at all happy. He's to have no part in raising the child, not legally, anyway. Of course, if there is no child, Ernie inherits the title and the estate, as expected. Veronica will have an annuity and a certain property in Wiltshire with no entailment, and I'll have a modest stipend for the rest of my life or until I remarry."

"That all seems rather straightforward." Despite the observation, Grams wrung her hands, and Phoebe suspected she couldn't quite recover from the possibility of Julia carrying Gil's child.

"There was something else," Julia said. "Mildred Blair was here."

"For the meeting?" Grampapa gestured to Eva. "Do you mean in like capacity?"

"No. I mean as a beneficiary."

Grams pulled a face. "Of part of Gil's fortune?"

"Of course, Grams. What else?" Julia sat back. "She's to receive a lump sum. The amount depends on whether or not I produce an heir."

"That's the oddest thing I've ever heard," Grams declared. "Who determines the amount of a bequest to a servant based on who the heir is?" She looked to Grampapa for consensus, and it was then her gaze landed upon first Fox and then Amelia. "Are you two still here? Did I not tell you to go?"

"Oh, er . . . sorry, Grams." Amelia came slowly to her feet.

Fox hesitated another moment, then pushed to his. But they had already heard the pertinent details.

Or so Phoebe thought, until Julia pulled her aside a few minutes later while the others filed out of the room. "I had the distinct feeling it was Mildred who called this meeting," she said. "And she seemed most annoyed with the results."

"Mildred called the meeting?" Phoebe repeated somewhat inanely. "Why would she? Who is she to—"

"Exactly. Who is she?"

CHAPTER 16

Eva helped Lady Julia on with her coat, making a slow job of it to postpone for as long as possible her being returned to that hideous jailhouse. She didn't know what use she had actually served during the meeting, but at least Lady Julia hadn't had to face the others without an ally.

She had kept a close watch on everyone during the proceedings. Miss Blair, with her carefully applied cosmetics, had nevertheless betrayed her thoughts more than once. All three of them—Miss Blair, Miss Townsend, and Mr. Shelton—had displayed their frustrations, but Miss Blair in particular had revealed her resentment toward Lady Julia in her sour looks and pouting lips, especially when she had been made to sit off to the side.

Why should Miss Blair begrudge the family members their rightful places at the table? Why should she, an employee, think herself deserving of an equal seat beside them?

"It's time to go," one of the policemen said.

Eva didn't bother looking up to see which one had spoken. Her heart ached, and her throat grew pinched. After coming around to face Lady Julia, she made minor adjustments to her hat, her scarf, the placket of her coat.

Lady Julia stilled her ministrations with a hand on her wrist. "It's all right, Eva."

She nodded, unable to make eye contact, and stepped aside to let Lady Julia pass. But she followed, equally unable to allow her emotions to overcome her sense of duty. In the corridor, the family said their good-byes—briefly, briskly, for Lady Julia declared she would not linger and allow dignity to be lost. With the policemen trailing behind her, she set off with her chin high. Once again, Eva followed, not daring to look at the earl or countess for fear of seeing their tears and being unable to master her own.

In the corridor, she remembered to pose a question. Lady Julia had already given an answer once, but that answer hadn't satisfied Eva. "My lady, have you remembered anything about a letter opener in Lord Annondale's office?"

"Why do you keep asking me that?"

Eva trotted to keep up. "Because it could be important. What desk doesn't have a letter opener? Yet Lord Annondale's didn't when your sister and I were there."

"I asked my sister to keep out of this."

"She's not going to, my lady, and neither am I." Eva nearly tripped over the floor runner. "Please, if you could only . . ."

As they reached the lobby, Lady Julia's pace slowed, and she came to a sudden halt.

Eva moved to her side. "What is it? Have you forgotten something?"

"No . . . it isn't that." Her face tightened in concentration.

Eva tried to follow her line of sight, and her gaze landed on the photographer, Curtis Mowbry, coming in through the street door. He'd obviously had an errand in town, for he wore a topcoat and held his tan bowler. He also carried a leather portfolio under one arm.

"The photographer . . . I wish I could remember where I've seen him before. It's almost on the tip of my tongue . . ."

"Was he at an event you attended?"

"I don't know . . ." Lady Julia watched him turn into the conservatory. Then she pivoted to face Eva. "It's probably nothing. Never mind."

"Perhaps you should heed your instincts, my lady. It could be important. Give it more thought. If the answer comes to you, let someone know immediately." She sensed a presence at her shoulder.

"Whatever the pair of you are going on about, you can continue it later down at the station. We need to get our prisoner back."

Reluctantly, Eva let Lady Julia go. And then she cut a direct line to the conservatory.

Her grandparents having already gone upstairs, Phoebe caught up with Fox before he entered the lift. She stopped him with a grip on his shoulder. "You were out on the terrace earlier."

He flinched and turned. His face held all the indignation a fifteen-year-old could muster—which was considerable. "What of it?"

"I saw you at the top of the stairs leading down to the road. Were you following me?"

"Could you be any more swollen-headed? No, I wasn't following you."

"Then what were you doing on the stairs?"

"Enjoying the view."

"Which you can do perfectly well from the terrace. What you cannot see without going to the stairs is the beach, where Sir Hugh and I were talking."

He opened his mouth to reply, then shut it. His eyes

growing small and hard, he studied her, and she guessed he was weighing his odds of getting away with a lie. She smiled slightly—not a friendly smile but one that assured him she was more than used to his antics. He blew out a breath. "All right, yes. Someone has to look after you, don't they? What were you and Sir Hugh talking about?"

She decided not to dignify his first question with an answer and replied to the second. "Nothing that concerns you. If you follow me again, I'll go right to Grampapa. Do you understand me?"

She turned on her heel, but this time Fox reached out to stop her. "It does concern me, Phoebe. You know it does. You and Sir Hugh were deep in it—whatever *it* was. He's been up to something that involves Julia, and I've a right to know what."

"Actually, whatever he's been up to might have nothing at all to do with Julia." Did she believe that? She wasn't sure, but then again, anything that put Gil in danger also endangered her sister. She had wished to tell Eva about the conversation earlier, but there hadn't been time, and now she had disappeared somewhere.

Poor Fox was still blaming himself for Julia's predicament. It distressed her to see him this way: agitated, uncertain, desperate to do . . . something. Just as she felt, and certainly he was just as frustrated.

Tugging the lapel of his coat, she pulled him along into the nearby library. The reassuring scents of books and their leather bindings surrounded her, steadying her nerves. She took a good look around before she spoke, even leaning to see into the wingback chairs in the corners. "Good. It's empty. Yes, Hugh and Gil were up to something that involved them with the wrong sort of people. He didn't so much as tell me that, but I was able to surmise it for myself."

"Then go to the police."

"I can't. I've got no proof, and he won't talk to them."

"Not even to save Julia?" His voice rose nearly a full octave and cracked, something he had yet to outgrow, especially during times of stress.

"At this point, Sir Hugh seems interested only in saving himself."

"Then call Owen. If anyone can find out the information, he can." In his vehemence, he didn't seem to notice that he'd clutched her hand in a decidedly uncharacteristic gesture. Then their physical contact apparently dawned on him, and he released her, as though she were something slimy and cold.

Phoebe smiled, earnestly this time. "That's exactly what I intend to do if you'd let me get on with it. Not that Owen doesn't have his own concerns just now."

"Well . . . none of them can be as pressing as getting Julia out of jail. You'll keep me informed of what he finds out, won't you?"

"I shouldn't."

"Go on, Phoebe, don't be like that. You know I want Julia released."

"Yes, I know. But I don't want you involved."

"I can keep an eye on people." He grew visibly in height; Phoebe noticed he stood slightly on his toes. "On Sir Hugh. And Ernest. I don't trust him."

"You've made *that* perfectly clear."

Julia had said Miss Blair had called the meeting with the solicitor, but she might have done so at Ernest's urging. Was he impatient to speed along his inheritance? Of course he was not to be trusted, but then, neither were several others—like Sir Hugh. But at this precise moment, Phoebe's concern was for Fox and his obsession with blaming himself for Julia's arrest, and for the very real possibility he might take it into his daft adolescent head to personally do something to remedy the situation. She'd seen that spark in his eye before. Typically, it preceded some nasty prank he intended playing on her or her sisters, and right now she'd far rather that than have him go off half-cocked and get himself hurt.

If she couldn't dissuade him of his self-blame, then perhaps she had better give him some occupation to keep him busy but safe. Bad enough Julia languished in a jail cell, with a murder trial hanging over her head. She didn't think poor Grampapa could weather any further misfortune befalling his grandchildren, especially his heir.

She resisted the temptation to tousle his hair, which in the past year had darkened from wheat blond to a shade bordering on russet gold, rather like her own. To do so wouldn't please him one bit. She gave a decisive nod instead. "All right, Foxwood. Your job is to keep your eyes and ears open. But only inside this hotel. You are not to set foot outside to follow anyone, nor walk into a situation where you would be alone with them. Merely watch and listen. Make a note of who you see talking with whom. Anything beyond that, and I go straight to . . . to Grams." She had almost said Grampapa yet on second thought had decided Grams would pose the greater threat to keep Fox in line.

"I can go out to the terrace, can't I?"

She tried not to laugh but only just succeeded. How like him, always testing his boundaries. "Yes, I suppose the terrace can be allowed." A figure passing by the doorway of the library caught her eye. "And now I've got things to do," she said and hurried away.

"Hullo, Mr. Mowbry. How have you been keeping yourself occupied?" Eva stood behind the empty wicker chair opposite the one occupied by the photographer, and hoped he didn't notice her effort to catch her breath after hurrying after him. His long legs were pulled up in front of him, and a stack of papers sat on his lap. The portfolio she'd seen him carrying leaned on the floor beside him, propped against the leg of his chair. He'd thrown his topcoat over the arm of the chair beside him and balanced his bowler on top of it.

He looked up at her, at first blankly, then with a pleased expression. "Miss Huntford. Do sit." He gestured at the empty seat, as she had known he would. She came around and lowered herself into it and leaned slightly forward. The stack on his lap, she now saw, was not papers at all but photographs.

"What's that you've got there? Are they from the wedding?"

"Yes, as a matter of fact. I was able to use a darkroom at a local studio in town. I've been looking through them, searching for . . . Oh, I don't know. I had a silly notion I might find a clue that could help Lady Annondale."

"Is that where you were coming from when I saw you cross the lobby just now?"

He nodded absently, his gaze focused on the top photo. Then he turned the pile so the photographs faced her.

The topmost was of Lady Julia on the church grounds, standing alone against the backdrop of cherry blossoms and blooming white hawthorn. She wasn't looking at the camera but at some point beyond, into her future perhaps. She looked lovely and unaware that anything bad could happen to her. The angle of the lens spoke of a soft caress, renewing that sense in Eva that Mr. Mowbry's photographs had somehow crossed an intimate line.

He whisked the photo aside to reveal the next. This shot included Lord Annondale, yet all the focus again remained, inexplicably, on Julia. In a third picture, Phoebe and Amelia stood on either side of Julia, yet she might have been alone in the frame.

Could a total stranger have captured her so entirely, as

if he possessed her? Eva darted a glance up at him. He didn't meet her gaze and seemed unaware that her focus had shifted.

"I can't help but wonder, Mr. Mowbry, how you came to be a photographer."

He paused while lighting a cigarette and held out the case to her in offering. She shook her head. "I learned the trade from an uncle of mine. Then, when I joined up and they discovered I knew my way around a tripod, I was assigned as an official military photographer."

"I didn't know there was such a thing," she said in surprise.

"Oh, yes. Not that there weren't also journalists running about, but my job was to keep official visual records, not to mention taking propaganda photos meant to reassure those back home the allies were winning, and to inspire young men to enlist." He drew deeply on his cigarette. "The difference between the former and the latter is bloody chilling." With a wince, he gritted his teeth. "Sorry, Miss Huntford. Excuse my language."

"No matter. How long were you there? On the Continent, I mean?"

"I came home in early 'eighteen. The influenza, you know. And once I'd recovered, I was reassigned to a unit on home turf. Quite a relief it was, not having to go back."

"You were lucky." She reached for several more photos and pretended to scan through them. "You're very good at what you do, Mr. Mowbry. Why, it's almost as if you knew Lady Annondale previously, the way you instinctively find her best angles." She chose a photo randomly and held it up. "Or *have* you met previously?"

"Have we met?" he repeated.

Eva glanced at him over the photo and nodded.

He took a drag off the cigarette and released a long,

slow stream of smoke. "Well, not formally. I'm hired at the kinds of social events people like Lady Annondale attend. And, of course, I know *of* her—and the entire Renshaw family—by reputation."

"Yes, of course." He sounded perfectly reasonable, and this would explain Lady Julia's sense of recognition. "Odd thing, though. She feels almost certain she knows you."

"Does she?"

"She does."

"Well, as I said, it could have been at any number of social events."

"Hmm . . . So then, have you found anything?"

"Anything?"

"Yes, in your pictures. Any clue that might help Lady Annondale?"

"Er, no, not yet. Here." With one hand, he dug some photos out from the bottom of the pile and passed them to her. "These are from the *Georgiana*. One supposes if there is anything, it will show up in these photos."

She shuffled through them and sighed. "They seem straightforward enough, don't they?"

"I'm afraid so." He puffed on the cigarette and flicked the ash into the ashtray beside him.

"Might I borrow these for a little while?" she asked on impulse. "I'm a second pair of eyes, a fresh pair, and perhaps if I studied them closely, I might notice something you haven't. I promise I'll be very careful with them."

"Of course you may. And don't worry. They're just prints. I have the negatives safely tucked away." He leaned and tapped the portfolio beside him. When he straightened, he flinched slightly, just enough for Eva to notice.

"Are you hurt, Mr. Mowbry?"

"An old war wound," he said with a wry chuckle. "Unfortunately, being a military photographer doesn't exempt one from the occasional bullet or bit of shrapnel."

"I'm sorry to hear it." She knew better than to dwell on it or show him the slightest emotion that might be interpreted as pity. He wouldn't thank her for it; none of the men who'd come home permanently impaired welcomed anyone's pity. They wanted only to be treated like whole men.

She handed him back the photos from the church and then straightened the pile of those she intended to hold on to for the time being. She hadn't the faintest idea what she might be looking for, but if nothing else, if she had more questions for Mr. Mowbry, returning the photos to him would provide her with the opportunity. He had explained his familiarity with Lady Julia, and thus her sense of familiarity with him, easily enough. Still . . . something about it made her wary.

She gathered the photos to her bosom and stood. "Well, then, I'll return these to you later."

"Tomorrow will be fine." He slipped the remaining photographs into the portfolio and slid out a large envelope. Then he stood, as well. "Here. You can put them in this." He handed her the envelope. "Perhaps we might meet for lunch tomorrow, and you may return them to me then."

Startled by the suggestion, Eva stammered a moment before finding her tongue. "I'd be happy to lunch with you tomorrow. I'll be with Lady Annondale's maid, Hetta. Have you met her?" *Thank goodness for Hetta*, she thought, for she had no desire to share a meal privately with any man other than Miles Brannock. If only he were here . . .

"I believe I did. I'll walk with you, Miss Huntford. I'm going up for now, as well."

When they'd entered the lift, the operator, his hand on the control lever, started the ascent with a jolt that shook the car. Eva reached out for the wall to steady herself. Mr.

Mowbry stumbled, and when he righted himself, she glimpsed a trace of pain across his features. Her heart went out to him, as it did to so many veterans of the Great War whose injuries had yet to truly heal.

Phoebe used the hotel's public phone to put her telephone call through to Owen, then waited in the lobby for the operator to make the connections through the exchange. It took some twenty minutes, but finally, the concierge came to tell her the call had gone through.

She took a deep breath and lifted the earpiece. "Owen, I'm sorry to bother you."

"Phoebe, darling, it's no bother. I've tried calling there, but I haven't been able to get through. The exchanges have all been clogged. And no wonder."

"You've heard, then."

"Yes. Most of England has heard. I'm sorry to have to tell you that."

"Don't be." She switched the receiver to her other ear and leaned—or rather sagged—against the wall beside her. "I suppose I expected as much, but everything has happened so fast, it's all such a horrible blur."

"How is Julia?"

"Pretending to be strong. Terrified. And . . ."

"Yes? And what?"

"Owen, she's blaming herself for Gil's death. Not that she caused it directly, mind you, but she believes if she hadn't married him, none of this would have happened."

"What the devil put that notion into her head?" He sounded almost angry.

"Her guilt over marrying him. It was for his money— she admits as much. But, Owen, even that wasn't her fault. She thought she had to." Phoebe paused to steel herself for words of betrayal, but this was Owen, and if she couldn't speak the truth with him, then she had no business contemplating a future with this man. "Grams has drilled it into her for years that she must marry for the good of Foxwood Hall, and that's exactly what she did. Now she believes the fates or cosmic forces or what have you have conspired to serve up justice against her."

"Good God. Poor Julia. Look, I'll leave this afternoon. I can be there by tonight, probably."

"That's not why I rang you up. I need you to look into something. I had a chat with Sir Hugh earlier, and while he refused to offer any details, I'm fairly certain he and Gil had gotten mixed up with the wrong sort of people. They may have killed Gil and might still be after Hugh."

"Why doesn't he go to the police?"

She couldn't help a brief laugh at hearing this question yet again. "Because I think he's afraid of landing in prison himself."

"Ah. So he's no innocent."

"Nor was Gil. After Hugh said what he did, he seemed very sorry to have mentioned it."

"He'd let Julia . . ."

"Hang," she said, finishing for him, and he swore under his breath. "Owen, we need your help—"

"You needn't say another word, other than to tell me exactly what you and he discussed."

CHAPTER 17

Phoebe repeated the conversation she'd had with Hugh Fitzallen, including his denial that he had been on the *Georgiana* the night before last. When she had finished, Owen said, "Before the war, Gil's manufacturing plants were producing automobile engines exclusively. During the war, he diversified into aeroplane engines."

"Could the root of their trouble be connected to the war?"

"It wouldn't surprise me. Price manipulations, political favors, illegal business dealings. In supplying the military with much-needed resources, Gil would have had the upper hand in demanding just about anything he wanted. Not to mention, during the war, and even before, there were gangs popping up in every major city in England, especially the industrial ones. Gil could have gotten mixed up somehow with one of them."

"But the war is over. Why should any of that matter now?"

"Europe isn't settled, not by a long shot."

"What do you mean?"

He paused, and she could almost see him shaking his

head. "It isn't common knowledge, but no one particularly won this war. Yes, technically we did, along with our allies, and now we're sticking it to the Germans. What we're really doing is stomping them underfoot . . . and making them angry. The same imbalances that existed before the war still exist now, and they're festering . . ."

"You're frightening me, Owen."

"I'm sorry. I don't mean to. I'm simply being truthful. These gangs I spoke of, some of them are political, at least in the scope of their dealings, not that they care in the end who does what as long as they profit. We're talking about the nastiest sort of individuals. I really wish . . ."

"Yes, but you know I'm not going to stop."

"I know. I'll look into this and let you know what I find out, if anything. And don't be surprised if I show up on your doorstep. I should never have left you there alone."

"I'm not alone. I've got my family and Eva with me. But I've got to go now. Something odd happened this morning. Gil's solicitor arrived, supposedly for the reading of the will. Except there was no reading, because Gil made recent changes dependent upon whether or not Julia bears a child. An heir. The will is not to be read until we know for certain."

"Is it possible?"

"Yes."

He made a low whistle.

"And that sheds possible guilt on his sister, his cousin Ernest, and even his personal secretary, Mildred Blair. Seems Gil included her in his bequests, but her inheritance is dependent upon whether Julia produces a new heir, as is his sister, Veronica's. The question remains whether any or all of them knew about the changes."

"And I suppose it's your job to find out."

She recognized his tone of resigned acceptance and smiled,

though he couldn't see her. "That's right, and that's why I need to ring off. I have questions for the whole lot of them."

"Phoebe—"

"Yes, Owen, I'll be careful. I promise."

A deep, rumbling sigh came over the wire. "I suppose I shouldn't worry. If anyone can take care of herself, you can. With Eva's help, of course."

"Thank you, and yes, we've grown adept at watching each other's backs."

"But I don't have to like it."

"No, that's true."

"All right, but do know that if something *were* to happen to you . . . well." He rang off, leaving her smiling and feeling that he'd just wrapped his arms around her.

After parting with Curtis Mowbry, Eva decided to put herself at Veronica Townsend's disposal and see what else she could learn about her brother's will. Miss Townsend seemed all too happy to see her.

"You must be a mind reader, Huntford. I could very much use your help just now. Do come in."

The dresser drawers and armoire had been flung wide, and two portmanteaus sat upon the bed, waiting to be filled. Miss Townsend spoke as she proceeded into the bathroom. "I've decided I've had quite enough of this hotel. Stuffy room, substandard food . . . I'm sure even you must understand."

Eva found the food in the dining room quite good, actually, better than at some of the grand estates she'd visited with her ladies. She said nothing of that but wondered about Miss Townsend's intentions. The police had not yet given them permission to leave Cowes. She surveyed the room around her, deciding to start with the dresser.

"Antonia will be coming with me," the woman said as she reentered the bedroom, carrying an overnight case filled with toiletries. The sleeves of her shirtwaist were buttoned around her wrists, hiding the gash she had claimed resulted from working in her garden at home. "We're returning to the *Georgiana* tonight."

"Oh, I see, ma'am." Eva tried to keep her features even and not betray her skepticism.

"And, Huntford, not a word of this to Mildred."

"No, ma'am?" She hadn't meant it to sound like a question, but it came out that way all the same. What had this sudden decision to do with Miss Blair, and why should Miss Townsend need to keep secrets from an employee?

"Nor to Sir Hugh. Nor to anyone, for that matter. What I do is no one's concern but my own."

"I can see why you'd wish to keep your plans to yourself, ma'am. If you don't mind my saying, that was quite a mysterious business in the meeting room earlier."

"Indeed it was, Huntford." She studied Eva a moment, and Eva wondered if she had been too impertinent in her observation. She didn't wish to be told to leave, not yet. "It was rather irregular for you to be there, but I suppose I understand Julia's desire for it. Odd she didn't choose her sister, though. But perhaps having you rather than Phoebe ensured her privacy."

"Just so, ma'am. Lady Annondale is familiar with my talent for discretion."

"Yes . . ." Miss Townsend continued her scrutiny, while Eva pretended not to notice it. "*Are* you discreet, Huntford?"

"The very soul of discretion, ma'am. Always."

"Then I shall ask you a question. Do you think it's possible Julia is in a delicate condition?"

The question didn't surprise Eva. Though she knew what

her answer would be, she took a moment before speaking, as if weighing the wisdom of doing so. "It's highly doubtful, ma'am. Of course, I don't know for certain either way. About that, Lady Annondale has kept her own counsel."

"Do you think her sister would know? You and Phoebe are thick as thieves. Don't deny it. Have you asked her for her thoughts on the matter?"

Eva had leaned over the bed to place several shirtwaists into one of the portmanteaus. She straightened, assuming a thoughtful expression. "No, I haven't, ma'am. It wouldn't be proper."

"Perhaps not. But if you could . . . if you *would*, that is, I would make it worth your while."

Eva allowed her eyes to widen. She'd had experience only last summer with the sort of lady's maids who were all too eager to betray their mistresses for profit. Why not allow Miss Townsend to believe she might be one of them? "Is it very important, ma'am? Won't time tell all?"

Leaning against the tall bureau, the woman folded her arms. "But that will be weeks from now. Yes, it is important, Huntford, for those of us who wish to get on with our lives. What game my brother thought he was playing, I'll never know. It's one thing to make allowances for a new heir, but it's quite another to leave us all hanging, with nothing to live on, unable to plan for the future. It's insupportable, I tell you."

"I can understand that, ma'am."

There was a banging on the door, and a woman's voice called through the paneled oak, "Veronica, let me in. I forgot to take my key."

"It isn't locked, goose," Miss Townsend called back.

Mrs. Seward came into the room as breathless as if she'd run up the stairs rather than taken the lift. "Oh, good. The maid is here. We need help packing."

"Yes, I've already told her. Now, quickly, shut the door."

Eva continued filling Miss Townsend's portmanteaus while the two women discussed their plans.

"I asked the concierge to arrange our water transportation," Mrs. Seward said. She dabbed a handkerchief at her face and neck. "He'll also have a taxicab waiting for us in an hour. Will that be sufficient time?"

"It should be, now that Huntford is here." Another knock sounded at the door, and Miss Townsend frowned. "Who could that be? Huntford, would you please?"

Eva had barely turned the knob when the door burst open, pushed from the outside. She stepped out of the way as Miss Blair forced her way into the room.

"I'd like to know why the two of you need a boat. Where do you intend to go?"

Both Miss Townsend's and Mrs. Seward's mouths dropped open in expressions defined by indignation. Mrs. Seward spoke first.

"You were following me and eavesdropping on my business. How dare you?"

"I didn't follow anyone, and one can't call it eavesdropping if you spoke loud enough to be heard by everyone standing near the front desk."

Mrs. Seward's hands went to her hips. "I didn't see you there."

"Then you obviously didn't look very well. I'd gone down to report the water in my room not heating sufficiently in the mornings. And there you were, requesting boat transportation. I'll ask again. Where do you two intend going?"

"It's none of your business, Mildred." Miss Townsend crossed the room, stopping just short of trampling the younger woman's toes. "How dare you come barging in here like this?"

Miss Blair's reddened lips stretched into a smile. "If you're planning to return to the *Georgiana*, you can forget it this instant. You heard what Clarence Walker said. No one has any claim to that boat until the will is finally read. The same goes for the estate, though once the police release us, you may resume residence there—for the time being."

Eva hadn't heard the solicitor make that particular stipulation about the *Georgiana*. Had it happened before she and Lady Julia arrived in the meeting room? Taken aback, she had no wish to be asked to leave the room before she found out more. To that end, she eased backward into an inconspicuous corner, allowing the open door to partially shield her from view. A shame she hadn't worn green, which would have allowed her to blend in with the wallpaper.

"What's it to you what I or anyone else does, Mildred? You're not my brother's heir, for all he was good enough to name you in his will. A small bequeathal, is all. Nothing, certainly, to fill your head with such self-importance."

Miss Blair lifted her chin and leaned toward Miss Townsend, as if to meet her challenge. "I am still the estate secretary, until the new heir—or the new heir's guardian— dismisses me."

Through the gap between the door and the jamb, Eva watched as a newcomer entered the room. "W-what's going on in here?" Mr. Shelton stammered. "I can hear you all the w-way in m-my room."

"For goodness' sake." Miss Townsend hurried to close the door, but before she had quite shut it, a third visitor thrust his foot across the threshold. "Hugh, not now, please. We're discussing a family matter."

"Sounds more like a row than a discussion. Perhaps I can help." The baronet pushed his way into the room. "If Antonia can be here, I see no reason why I shouldn't be."

"Hugh, this has nothing to do with you," Miss Townsend said.

Miss Blair gave a mean little snigger. "Are you quite sure about that, Veronica? How do you know your brother didn't leave the *Georgiana* to Hugh?"

"To Hugh?" Ernest Shelton raised his voice, but no one paid him any attention.

"He's *Sir* Hugh to you, Mildred," said Miss Townsend, "and my brother would not have done any such thing." Yet she sounded less than confident. Her eyes narrowed on Miss Blair. "What do you know? Did my brother tell you what's in his will?"

Miss Blair laughed again. "If he did, it would have been in the strictest confidence, and I'm certainly not going to divulge a bit of it. You'll have to wait for the reading."

"The *Georgiana*, to me?" Sir Hugh looked positively gleeful. "Wouldn't that have been splendid of the old boy? After all, Veronica, you don't even like sailing. You've said as much."

"Then why was she planning to sneak out there this afternoon?" Miss Blair tilted her head in mock interest.

Miss Townsend reddened with anger. "The vessel is sitting out there empty. Why shouldn't I make use of it?"

"I'll tell you why you shouldn't," Miss Blair said sweetly. "Because it isn't yours, not yet at least, and your attempt to claim it for the purpose of selling it simply won't wash."

"Now, see here." Mr. Shelton moved forward, nearly stumbling over his own feet in the process. "No one is selling the *Georgiana*. If Gil left her to anyone, it's probably me. And besides . . ." He turned toward Miss Blair. "You have been wrong about everything so far, Mildred. Wrong about the reading solving all our problems, wrong about Gil coming to his senses about that little wife of his, wrong that he would ever see reason. And now he's dead, and we're left in this briny pickle. As I told you on the *Georgiana*—"

"I've heard enough—as much as I can bear." Miss Townsend flushed more violently still. "Get out, all of you."

Miss Blair shrugged and turned on her heel. Still smiling, no doubt contemplating his possible good fortune, Sir Hugh followed, his hands in his trouser pockets as he ambled along. As he passed through the doorway, he began whistling a tune.

Ernest Shelton stood his ground. "I'm telling you, Veronica, as Gil's heir, as I m-most certainly am, I will not stand for any chicanery on *your* part, just as I won't stand for Mildred's double-dealing."

"Get off your high horse, Ernie. Even if you are Gil's heir, the *Georgiana* isn't part of the entail. There's no reason to believe Gil left you anything he didn't have to." She scoffed, flicking a glance up and down Mr. Shelton's length. "He didn't even like you, and that's to put it mildly."

She couldn't see his expression, but Eva heard Mr. Shelton's sharp intake of breath. He turned about so suddenly, she started, and the animosity in his eyes struck her like daggers. He trudged away, and Eva came around the door.

"Huntford, are you still here?" Miss Townsend sounded weary. "Good. Please finish up with our things. As if I give a fig what that trollop says or thinks. I can very well do as I please. Isn't that right, Antonia?"

Mrs. Seward had retreated to the far side of the beds during the argument, looking on with saucer-shaped eyes. Now she came confidently forward. "Indeed, you shall not take orders from such a one as she, Veronica. Huntford, you heard Miss Townsend. Finish packing our things."

"I'm terribly sorry, ma'am, but I have to go." Eva bobbed a perfunctory curtsy.

Miss Townsend regarded her with mild amusement. "Don't be silly. We need you."

"Perhaps, but I just remembered something I must do for Lady Phoebe."

"But you can't just run off," Mrs. Seward declared indignantly. "There's work to be done."

"I'm sorry, ma'am," Eva repeated, "but I don't work for you."

"They're at each other's throats over the will, my lady. It isn't hard to imagine one of them having murdered Lord Annondale for what they would get in the bargain."

Eva's sardonic words had Phoebe picturing Gil's small group of family and friends nearly coming to blows in their greed. Following the example of Mildred Blair and Ernest Shelton, she and Eva walked arm in arm along the Esplanade to ensure their privacy as they discussed what each had recently learned. The rush of the waves hitting the beach, along with the occasional motorcar along the roadway, provided ample noise to drown out the details of their conversation from unwanted ears.

"And now we know what Miss Blair and Mr. Shelton were discussing when they walked this route," Eva continued "as well as the gist of their argument on the *Georgiana* before Lord Annondale died."

Surprised, Phoebe brought them to a halt. "Ernie and Miss Blair argued on the *Georgiana?*"

"Oh, yes. In all the hullabaloo, I'd forgotten. It's a long story, but Hetta overheard them having words."

"Hmm. Interesting." Phoebe pondered this information. "Do you think the pair were in on Gil's death together?"

"If they were, they're certainly not of a mind to cooperate with each other now."

"Nothing about this situation is straightforward. Ernie and Miss Blair have been behaving suspiciously, but they certainly aren't the only ones." Phoebe released a breath and shook her head. "Veronica, Miss Blair, and Ernie each had a motive because of the will. Each stands to gain much more if Julia doesn't have a child. Each of them might have gone to any length to try to prevent it."

Eva nodded. "Miss Blair's manner suggests she is more than a secretary. She is altogether too sure of herself."

The harbor was a deep sapphire blue today; the waves were crested with flecks of foam. White sails flashed in the sun. From this distance, the *Georgiana* appeared serene, regal. But she possessed neither of those attributes. She was a place of violence and deception.

Phoebe said, "We've suspected from the first Miss Blair was Gil's mistress."

"Yes, but she may be more than that. Would a mistress speak so brazenly once her paramour was no longer there to protect her? A mistress stands to lose everything. Even though she's named in the will, if the family put up enough of a legal fuss, they could block her inheriting. It seems to me a mistress would ingratiate herself as much as possible, rather than alienate everyone."

"She certainly has a knack for that," Phoebe agreed. "But what other role could she have played? Perhaps she knew something about Gil and held it over his head. Or perhaps she knows something about the family and can use it to get her way in the end. As Gil's secretary, she would have access to information no one else had. Except perhaps the solicitor."

"I've no doubt she believes she'll have the last laugh. Ah, I almost forgot. I've also discovered how Miss Blair sent for the solicitor without anyone knowing. Hetta followed her into town, where she sent a telegram." Eva's mouth slanted. "Apparently, Hetta has a greater mastery of English than any of us guessed."

"Does she?" Phoebe wondered what Julia would have to say about that. Then she turned her thoughts back to their suspects. "It would seem, then, that Miss Blair was eager to acquire whatever Gil left to her. Still, though, if she did have the means to blackmail him, why murder him? Why take the risk of being shut out from the money, not to mention losing her employment? It doesn't quite add up. Now, Ernie . . . or Sir Hugh . . ." She kicked at a pebble in her path. "Sir Hugh is frightened of something. Hunted, not the hunter."

"We seem to be back where we started, my lady. A handful of suspects, each with a motive, but also with something to lose with Lord Annondale's death."

"It seems to me Ernest Shelton had the most to lose if Gil *lived*. And as Veronica Townsend said, Gil didn't much like Ernie."

"Miss Blair mentioned the entail. We don't know what it's worth, do we? Lord Annondale's private assets might be more valuable than the estate. For instance, why were they fighting over who would take possession of the *Georgiana*? It could be that Lord Annondale's wealth doesn't lie so much with the hereditary estate, but with his business concerns."

"Good heavens, yes. Legal and perhaps *illegal* business concerns. But I still don't see how Ernie stood to lose anything with Gil's death."

"He might have hoped to eventually win over Lord Annondale's favor, and with it more of his assets, along with the entail."

"So then, your reasoning is that with Gil alive, Ernie had more time to change Gil's opinion of him." Phoebe considered. Given what she had witnessed on the *Georgiana*, it seemed unlikely Gil ever would have warmed toward his cousin, but Ernie might have taken a more optimistic outlook. The harbor once again drew her gaze, but this time she focused beyond it, on the blue-gray mainland to the north. "I can't see beyond a simple fact. If Gil and Julia had a child, Ernie stood—or rather stands—to lose everything. But perhaps I should have a word with Mildred Blair about the solvency of the entail."

They returned to the hotel soon after and parted ways. It took Phoebe some time to track down Mildred Blair, but eventually, she found the woman on the hotel's public telephone. She would have liked to know whom the woman was speaking to, but she spoke in such low murmurs that Phoebe couldn't make out the words without standing practically at Miss Blair's elbow. She retreated into the lobby to wait, knowing Miss Blair would have to pass through on her way to any other part of the hotel.

She sat near the entrance to the corridor and armed herself with a handkerchief. When Miss Blair appeared, striding at her usual brisk pace, Phoebe came to her feet, raised the handkerchief to her eyes, and stepped into the secretary's path.

"Oh! Look where you're going . . . Oh, it's you, Lady Phoebe."

Just prior to their collision, Phoebe had rubbed the handkerchief on the skin around her eyes to redden them. She looked up only briefly and pressed the linen back to her face. "Excuse me, Miss Blair. I didn't mean to . . . But today has been so stressful." Peeking out, she saw the impatience on Miss Blair's face. "Seeing my sister free, only to have her dragged back to that horrid place—it's too much. And all for nothing, since the solicitor came only to say he couldn't read the will. Why did he bother coming at all? Why would he toy with us so?"

She hadn't bothered to lower her voice, and now Miss Blair, looking alarmed, grasped her shoulder. "Do calm yourself, Lady Phoebe. Please."

"I've tried to remain calm, but how can I? My grandparents are at their wits' end. We all are." Phoebe slipped her arm through Miss Blair's, as if to lean on her for support, and started walking with her toward the library, which, as Phoebe well knew, tended to be empty this time of day. Not that it mattered, at least not to her. What she had to say to Miss Blair could be overheard, for all she cared. Miss Blair resisted for an instant, but as Phoebe continued her lament, the other woman seemed all too happy to leave the lobby and the inquisitive stares.

"It was cruel to release my sister, only to return her to the jail so soon after. A false promise of freedom. Do you know why the solicitor felt it necessary to come here, Miss Blair?"

"He was sent for, apparently."

"Yes, but by whom?" Phoebe lowered the handkerchief, no longer concerned whether Miss Blair perceived the false nature of her tears. "Was it Veronica? Or Ernest? Are they so eager to know what Gil left them?"

"One or perhaps both of them, yes."

A slight hesitation had preceded Miss Blair's answer. All pretense gone, Phoebe smiled knowingly. "You're named in the will, aren't you? Did you send for the solicitor?"

Miss Blair stepped back, as if struck. "You sent your maid to follow me."

"As a matter of fact, I didn't, and it wasn't Eva. But it doesn't matter who saw you at the post office. The fact remains, you sent for Mr. Walker. Why the hurry, Miss Blair? Poor Gil isn't even in his grave yet."

"Poor Gil." Her lips turned down in distaste. "Surely you don't believe that for a minute. If you do, you're a fool, Phoebe." Had Miss Blair meant to drop the *Lady* from her name? Or was she that flustered?

"I have no illusions when it comes to Gil," Phoebe said. "I believe he had secrets, and that one of those secrets might have caught up with him. The question is, How much do you know about Gil's background, and did you use the information to your advantage?" Phoebe stated rather than asked the question, hoping to put Miss Blair even more on the defensive.

The woman's composure surprised her. "What you really wish to ask is whether I killed him. The answer is no. I probably had more affection for him, despite his many faults, than everyone else put together. And yes, I telegrammed Clarence Walker. As I'm sure your maid has already reported, the stampede for his possessions has begun. I'd hoped to head it off before matters became a tangle. Unfortunately, that is not to be—not for several weeks. Our fates now lie with your sister."

"And the entail, Miss Blair? Is it worth as much as Gil's other assets?"

"Suffice it to say Gilbert Townsend was an exceedingly wealthy man." She started to walk away. Phoebe stopped her by once again moving in her way.

"I'm not finished."

"Oh, but I am." Miss Blair stepped around her and disappeared into the lobby.

CHAPTER 18

That night, when Eva returned to her room, she found Hetta in bed, turned toward the wall, the bedclothes pulled up to her ears. That didn't fool Eva in the slightest. After sharing a room with the woman at home, she'd become accustomed to Hetta's light snoring. She heard no such snoring now.

She switched on the lamp on the dresser. "I know you're awake. Please turn so I can speak with you."

Nothing happened for several seconds, and Eva began to think perhaps she'd been mistaken. Then Hetta rolled over. She peeked warily at Eva from behind a tangle of blond hair that had come loose from her braid.

Eva perched at the edge of her own bed. "Why have you pretended you cannot speak English?"

Hetta's blue eyes widened with alarm. "I speak the English not so well."

"But you do speak it. You've been deceiving us, Lady Julia most especially. It's a serious offense, Hetta."

"You tell Madame?"

"Someone must. I'd rather it were you. Why the pretense?"

Slowly, Hetta pushed up on her hands and sat up. She shoved the hair back from her face. "Something Madame Julia say when she meet me. She say to the countess, 'With her, I won't always have to watch my words.' I realize she like me for being Swiss, for speaking German."

Eva held Hetta in her gaze long enough for the woman to become uncomfortable. Her color rose, and she began to fidget with the coverlet. "I think you understand even better than you speak."

"*Ja*, this is true."

"So you've been listening to conversations that might not have been held in your hearing had we known the truth."

Hetta's head went down. "*Ja*. But I hear nothing bad."

"That is beside the point, and you know it." Eva folded her arms.

"*Ja*." She raised her face, and the lamplight caught the trickle of her tears. "I go in the morning?"

"No, Hetta."

Her face contorted. "I go now?"

"No, that's not what I meant. It'll be for Lady Julia to decide, once she is free. But you must be honest with her."

Hetta nodded eagerly and wiped her tears with the back of her hand. "*Ja*. I tell her." Her face fell again. "Do you think she is angry?"

"I don't know, really. She might be, at first. No one likes to be deceived. But you've given her good service so far. I know she adores the way you do her hair, and you're quick and clever when it comes to keeping her wardrobe in tip-top shape. Besides, I have a feeling Lady Julia will be so relieved once this is all over, she'll be inclined to forgive."

While a look of joyful relief filled Hetta's broad face, Eva felt a sinking in her stomach. Lady Julia's future depended on her and Lady Phoebe's ability to clear her name, and the odds against them doing so were beginning to seem insurmountable. They had determined Lord Annondale's circle of family and friends all had motives for wishing him ill, but until they could narrow their focus to a single individual, Detective Inspector Lewis would continue to dismiss the notion of Lady Julia's innocence.

Phoebe handed the porter a coin in exchange for the message he had delivered to her. Upon reading its contents, she drained her teacup and hurriedly finished dressing.

Amelia still wore her wrapper and was lounging on the settee, sipping her tea slowly. When she noticed Phoebe's urgency to ready herself for the day, she put her cup and saucer aside and sat up straighter. "What is it? Has something happened to Julia?"

"No. I have a visitor." After scooping the message off the table, she handed it to her sister on her way out the door. As it closed behind her, she heard Amelia's little cry of delight.

The lift seemed to take an eternity, but when the operator finally set the car down on the ground floor, Phoebe let him open the gate but pushed through the door on her own. A moment later a pair of arms closed around her.

"Owen. I didn't expect you this soon. Thank goodness you're here."

"There wasn't time to let you know. I drove through the night and caught the first ferry over this morning." He held her tightly for longer than was proper, but she didn't pull away. The sensation of his serge-clad shoulder against her cheek was too delicious to resist. As they parted, she studied his face, as he in turn studied hers.

"You must have discovered something important, to come all this way."

"I did." The second lift opened, and several people walked

off. He glanced into the main lobby. "Is there somewhere we can talk privately?"

"The library is usually empty during the day. It's become something of an office for me."

On the way there, Phoebe asked a porter to have tea and breakfast sent in. "You must be exhausted and famished," she said to Owen after closing the library's pocket doors behind them.

They selected a corner where, if someone were to venture in, they would still have a modicum of privacy. "Some good strong tea wouldn't be unwelcome right about now," he said.

"Tell me, how were you able to get away? I know there are problems at the mills. Your workers—"

"Are making demands, but not altogether unreasonable ones. The unions are not such a terrible thing, but sometimes what they perceive as being good for workers isn't actually to their benefit. The larger problem is that with the war over, the country is in debt, the value of the pound is down, and the prices of our exports are falling because of competition from countries able to produce the same goods at lower prices. The unions are resisting lower wages, but I'm afraid keeping things as they are might lead to industries cutting back and fewer people working."

"I thought with the war over, business would be booming all over the country."

He sighed. "I'm afraid that's not the case, and I worry it will lead to trouble in the coming years."

"What kind of trouble?"

The pocket doors opened, and a waiter wheeled in a cart holding a tea service and covered platters. He brought it over to them, asked them if they needed anything else, and left them alone.

"Never mind the fate of British business. We'll leave that for another time."

Owen poured tea into both of their cups, while Phoebe uncovered the platters to reveal sausages and eggs, kippers and toast. She spooned portions onto the plates and opened a pot of jam and another of marmalade.

Between mouthfuls Owen washed down with tea, he said, "I spoke to a friend who served in the war cabinet until recently, and he told me some rather interesting things that went on in Ireland during the last year of the war. Have you heard of the German Plot?"

"I do remember reading something in the newspaper about the possibility of the Germans helping Ireland gain her independence."

"That's right. Supposedly, Irish nationalists were encouraging the Germans to intervene and expel the British from the country, with promises of helping Germany win the war."

"The articles were vague, I remember, and then the stories disappeared altogether. It never actually happened, did it?"

"No." Owen cut into a sausage and speared a section with the tip of his knife. He held it up, waving it about, as he made his reply. "The Germans were rather busy with their own concerns at the time. The truth is, there never was a plot, and any such hopes in Ireland were shared by very few men. However, that didn't stop Dublin Castle from claiming that the plot was real and that it posed a danger. They used it as an excuse to arrest a slew of Sinn Féin members, well over a hundred men, and transport them to England for trial. It was a mess, and in the end, it allowed the much more extreme Irish Republican Brotherhood to gain a military foothold in the Irish opposition movement. It also greatly increased the popularity of Sinn Féin itself. Tensions have been rising ever since."

Phoebe knew the British government had established a royal constabulary to help fight the uprisings in Ireland. Because of their uniforms, they were called the Black and Tans. She said, "The Black and Tan War, which has been going on for the past year or so."

"Exactly."

"So, what does this have to do with Gil? Weren't they back in England before that began?" As soon as Phoebe asked the question, she remembered Gil's place—and Sir Hugh's—in the Dublin Castle administration, the British ruling body of Ireland. "Were he and Hugh somehow involved in the arrests after the German Plot?"

Owen nodded as he chewed. "They were among the loudest proponents of the measure, and according to my source, Gil personally ordered the arrest of a half dozen men. And here is where things get a bit foggy, because the truth was never supposed to come out. A consignment of weapons was stolen from an armory outside Dublin and simply disappeared. No trace of them anywhere, but a pair of brothers were arrested for being the masterminds of the theft. They confessed to shipping the guns off to England, where they were sold on the black market. Now, I'm getting this information thirdhand, or perhaps even fourth, but before the pair were executed for high treason, supposedly they claimed two English officials were their cohorts."

Phoebe nearly choked. "I can't believe it. Why would Gil and Hugh take such a risk? And if this is true, why weren't they arrested and tried?"

Owen held up a cautioning hand. "They were not named specifically, but almost immediately after the arrest, they were sent packing. To expose them would have opened up an investigation of all of Dublin Castle and brought too many men under scrutiny. With all the problems at the time, they didn't need one that threatened to bring British rule in Ireland to its knees. Things were covered up, and the identities of the perpetrators, presumably Hugh and Gil and probably several others, were protected."

"But why would they do such a thing?"

"Money. What else?"

"I can understand perhaps for Hugh, but Gil had scads of money."

Owen shrugged. "I suppose he thought he could use more. Or maybe the thrill and the risk appealed to him."

"Are you certain it was them?"

"Fairly certain, yes. This is more than hearsay. It's an unofficial, off-the-record report of what happened."

"And you trust your source?"

Owen nodded. Phoebe saw no trace of doubt in his countenance.

"No wonder Hugh refuses to speak to the police. Blast him, he'd let Julia take the blame for Gil's death rather than implicate himself." Phoebe put her plate onto the cart—barely resisting the urge to smash it down in her anger—and came to her feet. "We have to talk to him. He can't be allowed to get away with this."

Owen set his breakfast aside, as well. "That's why I'm here."

After discovering from Lady Amelia that Owen Seabright had arrived and Lady Phoebe had already gone down to meet him, Eva helped Amelia dress and then returned to her room. Hetta, too, had gone downstairs, leaving Eva with some time to herself. Finally, she had both the privacy and the daylight to peruse Mr. Mowbry's photos from the *Georgiana*. She drew the envelope from the top dresser drawer and spread the photographs out on her bed.

At first only the main focus of each one captured her attention. Lady Julia, the lines of her dress and veil, the po-

sitioning of her arms, the angle of her pose. Some included
Lord Annondale, looking proud and very much like someone who had just won a contest. Yes, and Lady Julia was
the prize. Not a woman, not a wife, but a kind of award or
accolade to the man's achievements. Other photographs
included Ladies Phoebe and Amelia, and the rest of the
family was featured in still others. Their expressions ranged
from jubilance (young Fox) to satisfaction (the countess),
to tender concern (the earl), to downright apprehension.

Not one of them could have conceived what the next
hours and days would bring. Not one could have pre-
dicted the disaster about to be visited upon the Renshaw
family. Lady Julia least of all. In her eyes, Eva saw the full
knowledge of the course she had set for herself, for good
or ill. It was not what one should see in a young bride's
face. Eva's throat constricted, and her heart broke yet
again.

She forced herself to concentrate on the smaller details
of the vessel itself. Some of the photographs had been
taken on the top deck. Those she set aside, being more interested in the ones taken along the main promenade deck,
along the railing. The designer of the *Georgiana* had done
a splendid job of seeing that essential equipment blended
with the general decor of polished oak, mahogany, and
teak. Coils of rope and life rings hung at intervals along
the outer walls of the main cabin and appeared more dec-
orative than functional. Even the hoists for the lifeboats
gleamed with fresh polish. Eva thought back and remembered them being of brass. Indeed, most of the outdoor fit-
tings were brass. She scanned several photos, then went
back to one of Lord and Lady Annondale that had been
taken in the shadow of one of the lifeboats.

The *Georgiana* carried two lifeboats, one port side and
the other on the starboard. Both were located near the

stern, where the blood had been found on the railing. The lifeboats, though not pictured, were suspended a good eight or nine feet above the deck, closer to the cabin than the railing. The mechanisms of the hoists were positioned directly below them, bolted to the deck, with lines that ran up along the walls of the cabin and were attached to the lifeboats from above.

Could something have become wedged within the workings of one of the hoists?

Eva's heart began to race. It was unlikely, to be sure. If the murderer and Lord Annondale had struggled over the missing letter opener, it would probably have ended up in the water. Still, it was worth a look. She pressed a hand over her pounding heart to attempt to calm it. She mustn't get her hopes up. Yet, for Lady Julia's sake, she couldn't help doing just that.

Phoebe positioned herself at a table on the veranda and held a newspaper up in front of her. She wore a hat and a light spring coat that matched her frock, and her leather pumps were made for comfortable walking. She kept her ears pricked while Owen moved past her to the man with the clean-shaven head, who was reading his own newspaper several tables away.

"Good morning, Hugh."

Phoebe peeked around the edge of her newspaper as Sir Hugh let his own fall to the table in front of him. He frowned a moment before recognition dawned. "Owen Seabright. I thought you left Cowes."

"I'm back. The sea air called to me."

"And a certain young lady, if my eyes didn't deceive me during the wedding."

"No, Hugh, your eyes didn't deceive you."

"Well, I haven't seen her yet this morning."

No, Phoebe thought. That was because she'd waited until Sir Hugh had become absorbed in some article or other before pulling her hat low and darting out to the table where she now sat.

Sir Hugh gestured to the seat across from him and bade Owen to join him.

Owen shook his head. "Not just now. There's something I'd like to discuss with you. Privately."

"Sounds serious. Something to do with . . . well . . . with what happened?"

"Not directly, no. Walk with me, Hugh."

Phoebe ducked behind her newspaper as Sir Hugh came uncertainly to his feet. She listened for their steps, which proceeded toward the stairway leading down to the roadway and the beach. Once she judged them to be near the bottom, she followed. On the pavement running parallel to the road, she fell into step beside them.

"Good morning, gentlemen."

Hugh turned toward her with a start. "Lady Phoebe, good morning. Er . . . not to be rude, but I believe there is something Owen would like to discuss with me."

"Indeed yes," she replied brightly. "We'd both like to speak with you. But not here. Let's keep going until we reach the green."

"What is this about? I don't appreciate being hoodwinked, you know. I've a mind to turn around and go back." Sir Hugh dragged his feet.

"I wouldn't do that if I were you," Owen told him. He continued strolling as though merely out for a pleasant morning walk along the seaside. "I'm prepared to help you if I can. However, if you won't cooperate with us, you'll sink on your own."

"You're not making any sense."

"Don't worry, Sir Hugh," Phoebe said. She slipped her arm through Owen's. "You'll understand everything presently." Along the Egypt Esplanade, they turned in at the park and tramped up the path to a secluded bench surrounded by trailing willows. "This will do."

"You two had better explain yourselves."

"Calm yourself, Hugh." With Phoebe sitting to Hugh's right, Owen flanked his other side. "And tell us what you know about the German Plot."

Hugh emitted a grunt and started to rise. Owen pressed him back down with a hand on his shoulder. "I don't know what you're talking about."

"Come, Sir Hugh, you can do better than that." Phoebe smiled sweetly. "Even I've heard of the German Plot. So don't pretend ignorance."

"What I meant," the man said after clearing his throat, "is I don't know any more than the average person. I was in Ireland at the time, yes, but that doesn't mean—"

"Again, you can do better than that." Owen took a stern tone. "I have it on good authority that you and Gil Townsend were very much in favor of punishing the so-called perpetrators."

"What of it? Traitors deserve to be punished."

"Very true." Owen paused, his eyes narrow and assessing. Phoebe saw the anger behind them, the growing storm Owen was keeping at bay. "When there *are* traitors. But there weren't, and I believe you were well aware of the fact. But you and the others used it to dispose of an inconvenience, namely, Irish opposition."

"That's not true. Those men were no innocents. They—"

"They might not have been innocent in the eyes of the British government, but they were *not* guilty of conspiring with the Germans, because no such plot ever existed.

Now, in the midst of all that trouble and deception, something else interesting happened. Something involving an arsenal outside of Dublin."

Sir Hugh fell to coughing, and after a moment Owen pounded on his back. That only seemed to make Sir Hugh sputter more violently. Phoebe reached over and stilled Owen's hand, and finally Sir Hugh's ragged breathing subsided.

"I'd say that struck a chord," Owen wryly observed.

"Why don't you tell us what happened?" Phoebe encouraged in a gentle voice meant to counter Owen's more severe manner.

Sir Hugh stared across the empty park and shook his head. "You've no idea what you're dealing with."

"I think we do," Owen assured him. "We believe whoever else was mixed up in the theft probably murdered Gil and will come for you next. Staying silent won't help you. Surely you must know that."

Still shaking his head, Sir Hugh released a long sigh. "You don't understand. We rerouted that consignment from the thugs it was originally intended for. If we hadn't, it might have been all-out war in Dublin, like the Easter Rising, but much, much worse."

"How selfless of you." Owen scoffed, his upper lip curling. "Here's what I believe happened. You double-crossed your Irish partners and then used the German Plot to get rid of them. That way you and Gil were able to keep all the profits for yourselves."

"That's not true."

Owen ignored the protest. "But perhaps you didn't get rid of everybody involved, and now one of them has popped up, intent on revenge. Or justice, from his perspective."

"You've no right making these accusations. You weren't there. You don't know." Sir Hugh's hands were shaking.

He looked and sounded like a man backed into a corner. "I tell you, things might have gone much worse."

"Where did you send the weapons?" Phoebe touched his forearm as she spoke. Hugh gazed down at her hand and patted it once in a gesture so much like her grandfather's she felt a tug at her heartstrings.

But Sir Hugh didn't deserve her sympathy, not for what he'd done in the past, nor for his determination now to allow Julia to pay for his misdeeds. Yet she saw beside her a broken man who finally perceived the end of the life he had been trying hard to preserve, for right or wrong. She knew something about that: she had seen it with her own grandparents, who had struggled every day since the war began to cling to the old ways—again, for right or wrong.

"You and Gil sent those weapons to England. That much we know," she said, while at the same time considering. "My guess is they went to one of Gil's engine factories. And then they were sold on the black market. Is that correct?"

"We did England a favor," he replied.

"In what way?" Owen demanded, his anger making itself heard. "Those guns weren't returned to the British government or used in the war effort. You and Gil merely traded one sort of thug for another. But the result was the same—guns in the hands of men with no respect for life or decency."

Phoebe reached around Sir Hugh again to touch Owen's wrist in warning. "That's not helping. The question is, Who wanted revenge enough to come after the two of you now?"

"I don't know, and that's the plain truth. If I had any inkling, don't you think I'd go to the police?"

"No, I don't think." Phoebe's own anger rose, despite her intentions of keeping her temper in check. Her hands balled into fists. "You're determined to save yourself while

letting my sister hang. Yes, hang. You've no more conscience now than you did a year ago. Well, Owen and I
aren't about to let you get away with it."

"What are you going to do?" He appealed to Owen.
"You said you were willing to help me."

"In so far as I can. But not at Julia Renshaw's expense.
Surely you can figure that out for yourself."

"Damned women," Sir Hugh muttered into his necktie.
"This all seemed to come about after the wedding an-
nouncement appeared in the society columns."

"So you're blaming my sister for you getting your come-
uppance."

Sir Hugh had no answer for that. He ruminated, his
nostrils flared and his breathing audible.

Owen slapped his thighs and pushed to his feet. With a
hand, he helped Phoebe to hers. "Hugh, I highly encourage you to think about who might have followed you from
Ireland. He somehow escaped being arrested at the time,
which suggests he—"

"Or she," Phoebe put in.

With a nod, Owen conceded her point. "Or she is able
to move about anonymously, with little to no fear of discovery by the authorities. And that puts you in a vulnerable position, because you'll never know from which quarter
the attack might come. Then again, maybe you pushed Gil
overboard and faked those threats sent to you. It's altogether possible he double-crossed you when it came to
those profits, and you decided to be rid of him."

"That's absurd. How dare you?"

"Oh, I dare. Think about it, Hugh. If you don't wish to
be implicated, then you'll need to be more forthcoming
about what happened in Ireland. But don't take too long,
because if you don't cooperate in trying to identify this individual, I'm going to the police with everything we know.
You'll stay alive, but you'll do so inside a prison cell."

With that, Owen offered Phoebe his arm. They started walking back toward the hotel, leaving Sir Hugh to follow or linger as he wished. The hurried footsteps behind them told her he had chosen the former, rather than be left behind on his own.

CHAPTER 19

Although Phoebe saw Sir Hugh several times throughout the rest of that day, he kept his distance. He seemed to be gathering people around him for the express purpose of avoiding another confrontation. If it wasn't Veronica Townsend and her friend, Mrs. Seward, it was Mildred Blair or Ernie Shelton. Funny, he had never shown more than a passing interest in any of them before. Owen agreed he was dodging them, but reminded Phoebe he wasn't going anywhere anytime soon. Perhaps Hugh would finally see the benefit of cooperating.

When the Renshaw and Townsend parties arrived in the dining room that evening, Sir Hugh was not among them. Although no open animosity had been expressed between them, the two groups traded only polite discourse and were seated on different sides of the room. After the meal, Phoebe's grandparents returned to their suite with Fox and Amelia, while she and Owen went out onto the terrace. About a dozen or so others sat scattered around the tables, enjoying the clear night. A few left their seats to descend the steps to the roadway and perhaps the beach. The temperature had risen during the day, and now a comfortable breeze skimmed off the Solent to stir Phoebe's hair and caress her cheeks.

"He's most certainly been avoiding us," she said as Owen held a chair for her at an occupied table.

"Foolish of him. It's to his benefit to speak with us."

"The same could be said for Julia." Phoebe leaned back in her chair and sighed. "She acts as though Eva and I are trying to hurt her rather than help her. She seems determined to punish herself for marrying Gil. Doesn't she realize what can happen to her?"

Owen's hand covered hers. "The truth might not have sunk in. It's too unthinkable."

"I just wish—" She broke off as a scream emerged from somewhere beyond the terrace. "What on earth was that?"

Owen's head turned toward the steps at the sound of another scream. They both surged to their feet, as did the others around them. At a third scream, several men ran toward the steps, followed by the women, who huddled together at the stone railing while the men ran down.

"What could that be?" one of the women cried.

"Tom, do be careful," another called down to her male companion. "Maybe you shouldn't . . ."

Owen shouldered his way through, with Phoebe at his heels. When they reached the steps, he turned, as if to speak, then shook his head and started down. Phoebe could only imagine he had been about to admonish her to remain with the other women, then realized the futility of such a suggestion.

The roadway was empty of vehicles, so they ran across. The other men from the terrace had already reached the beach. Above the lapping of the waves, Phoebe could hear a woman sobbing and a man attempting to soothe her. Owen took her hand as they stepped onto the sand. The woman's cries continued. Phoebe's apprehensions grew. A small group stood clustered on the sand, staring at something at their feet. A man crouched, reaching out. . . .

Another man broke away from the rest and staggered toward Phoebe and Owen, as if drunk. Sand was kicked up from his faltering strides. Phoebe half feared he would collapse on them. Then the street lamps from the road illuminated his face. She recognized Ernie Shelton.

He seemed not to see her and stumbled past. Phoebe turned about and reached out a hand to him. "Ernie. What's happened?"

"I . . . Phoebe? I d-don't know. I don't know." He spoke while continuing to pick his way across the roadway. When he reached the steps, he half ran, half stumbled his way up, disappearing into darkness until he reached the lanterns at the top.

Owen's hand tightened around hers. He had obviously dismissed Ernie, his attention once more on the sand. His jaw was clenched; his expression, what she could make out of it, grim. A gentleman in evening attire was helping the distressed woman off the beach. When they came within a few feet of Phoebe and Owen, she realized they were both young, no older than she. They walked with their arms around each other, she leaning heavily against his side.

"How could such a thing happen? Oh, Roger, it's so dreadful, so horribly violent and—"

"You mustn't think about it, darling," he soothed. "Let's find your parents and . . ." They went across the road, and Phoebe heard no more.

But their words echoed inside her. *Horribly violent.* Her stomach twisted. Her hand still in Owen's, she started forward. She felt his resistance for an instant, before his feet moved, as well, and together they joined the circle of onlookers.

A man whispered hoarsely, "Is he dead?"

The older man crouching on the sand pushed to his feet and nodded. Phoebe's breath hitched. Steeling herself, returning the fierce pressure of Owen's grip, she forced herself to meet Sir Hugh's empty stare.

"Stabbed," Detective Inspector Lewis pronounced to the group assembled in the hotel's meeting room. The main suspects were there: Veronica Townsend, Mildred Blair, and Ernie Shelton. Phoebe and Owen had also been asked—or rather ordered—to attend this meeting. Phoebe didn't yet understand why Grams and Grampapa were also present. Sir Hugh, of course, was missing, his absence a glaring reminder that this was no social occasion. "In the chest," the inspector went on relentlessly. "Through the heart. With this."

Mr. Lewis held up a knife some eight inches long, with a thick wooden handle. The double-edged tip identified the piece as a bowie knife.

Mildred Blair paled, her reddened lips standing out in gaudy relief against her blanched skin. Veronica Townsend's eyes opened wide. Amid the gasps from all around the table, Grams let out a muffled sound, not quite a cry but more than an audible breath. Ernie had been the first to find Sir Hugh's body, Phoebe had since learned. He sat hunched over the table, with his forehead braced on his fists. He glanced up once and then retreated into his huddle. The rest looked dazed, shocked . . . but were they truly?

Earlier, a host of policemen had swarmed the hotel and the beach, turning the headlamps of their vehicles onto the sand while they inspected the crime scene. In the glaring light the details had become stark and garish. Phoebe couldn't erase the vision of Sir Hugh lying faceup, as if stargazing. If only she and Owen had been more adamant about talking to him again, instead of allowing him to sidestep them all afternoon, would he be alive now?

"Can anyone identify this knife?" Mr. Lewis waved the blade in the air in an unnecessary gesture. He certainly had their attention.

Mildred Blair's mouth opened, but it was Veronica who spoke in a shaky voice. "It's Gil's. He brought it home from Pretoria."

"The Boer Wars, eh?" Mr. Lewis set the knife on the table before him. "We found no prints on it other than your brother's, Miss Townsend. Whoever killed Sir Hugh must have been wearing gloves, which suggests premeditation. Miss Townsend, can you tell me what your brother used this knife for?"

She shrugged. "It was a souvenir from his time in the army. He brought it with him everywhere. Tended to keep it on his desk, for some reason."

"The letter opener," Phoebe blurted. In answer to the others' puzzled expressions, she clarified, "There was no letter opener on Gil's desk in his office on the yacht. He must have used that knife. And I'll wager Gil had it with him when he went on deck that night. He must have expected some kind of confrontation and attempted to defend himself. And my guess is, he managed to wound his attacker before he was overcome and pushed overboard." She turned an admittedly angry gaze on the inspector. "That would account for the blood on the railing. Not the gash on Julia's hand, but the wound Gil inflicted before he died."

The door opened, and the photographer, Curtis Mowbry, shuffled in. Holding one of his cameras, he stopped short of the table, looking uncertain and ill at ease, his gaze darting from face to face, finally lighting on Mr. Lewis—and the knife, still held aloft. "I heard what happened. I was going down to the beach to see if my services might be needed, but I...er...received a message to come here instead..."

"Yes, Mr. Mowbry," the detective inspector said. "Do join us."

The photographer hesitated. "Was it as I heard? Is it Sir Hugh?"

Mr. Lewis gestured rather emphatically at an empty chair. "Have a seat."

"Do my grandparents need to be here?" Phoebe asked him. "Surely you don't think—"

"I need all of you to be here," the inspector snapped.

This earned him a reproving glance from Grams, who didn't suffer bad manners from anyone. But it was to Phoebe she spoke. "We wish to be here, Phoebe. Don't you know what this means?"

"That we're all suspects," Phoebe replied, half in sarcasm, half in fear of that being the truth.

"Exactly." Grams smiled triumphantly and said to Mr. Lewis, "And now you must release our granddaughter. It's obvious she's innocent. No one can commit murder from inside a jail cell."

"Not so fast," he said.

"Now, see here, young man." Grampapa rarely raised his voice to anyone, but he did so now as he came to his feet. "You are to release my granddaughter at once. She is innocent, and this vile act tonight proves it. I will not permit her to remain in a jail cell another hour. Telephone your people immediately and tell them to let her go." He turned to Grams. "You and I will go and collect her."

"Indeed, Archibald. I can hardly wait to have her in my arms again, our dear girl." As with Grampapa raising his voice, such avowals of affection on Grams's part were rare. After taking Grampapa's hand, she stood, her lips trembling and moisture gathering in her eyes.

"Wait one moment." Mr. Lewis came around the table,

as if to block their path to the door. "The Cowes Police Department has another murder to investigate, and that includes questioning all of you. Anyone who attempts to leave this room without permission will be charged with obstructing justice."

Grams pulled up to her full height, which made her taller than Grampapa. "Archibald, are you going to let him speak to us this way?"

Intending to intervene, Phoebe started to rise, but Owen moved quicker and was on his feet. "Maude, Archibald, perhaps it's best to let the man do his job. The sooner they conduct their investigation, the sooner this will be over and we can go home. Julia included."

After a hesitation during which she seethed with indignation, Grams conceded. "I suppose you're right." She turned again to Mr. Lewis. "But that doesn't give you an excuse to detain our granddaughter. Isn't that so, Archibald?"

"We insist she be released tonight." Grampapa helped Grams back into her chair and resumed his own. "If I have to call in every favor owed to me, I will, young man. Believe me when I tell you I can put a world of pressure on your entire police department."

"As can I," Owen said as he, too, sat back down.

With a grating sigh, the detective inspector returned to the table but remained standing. "I understand your sentiments, but I don't appreciate being threatened for doing my job. And just because Lady Annondale couldn't have committed this murder doesn't mean she didn't commit the first."

"That's ridiculous," Grams said with a sniff.

The inspector's expression was grim. "I've seen it before, Lady Wroxly. Two murders seemingly related, but with two different killers."

"Oh? And where might this have been?" Phoebe asked.

She remembered Constable Hewitt, at the Cowes Police Station, telling her about Mr. Lewis botching a case while he served with the Metropolitan Police. The constable said Mr. Lewis had listened to the wrong informant, and Phoebe wondered if he'd perhaps released a suspect when he shouldn't have.

He seemed taken aback by her question, then quickly regained his composure, along with his authoritarian manner. "That doesn't matter. But I might be willing to allow Lady Annondale to come to the hotel if you, Lord Wroxly, will assume full responsibility for her whereabouts at all times."

"Yes, yes, of course. Full responsibility, upon my word." The frown smoothed from Grampapa's brow for the first time in days. Weeks, even, for he had been wearing a grimace all during the wedding preparations.

"Excuse me, Inspector Lewis." Apparently recovered from the shock of seeing Gil's bowie knife, Mildred Blair drummed her fingernails on the tabletop. She made little effort to hide her impatience. "Now that you're quite through appeasing the Renshaws, may we please get on with this?"

"*Humph.* I'm glad somebody finally said it." Veronica Townsend offered Miss Blair a rare nod of approval.

Grams opened her mouth, surely to berate them both, but Grampapa laid his hand on hers, prompting her to pinch her lips together.

"Mr. Shelton," the detective inspector said so abruptly that Ernie winced. "You found the body. What were you doing on the beach at that time of night?"

"I . . . that is . . . What about that young couple who were there, as well?"

"They've been questioned," Mr. Lewis replied. "According to them, you were crouching near the body when they arrived on the beach. What were you doing there? When did you arrive? And did you murder Sir Hugh Fitzallen?"

Ernie shoved back his chair so violently, it fell over backward as he stood. "I don't have to answer that."

"Actually, you do. If you would care to have your solicitor present, that's your prerogative." The man calmly circled his own chair and sat, then slid his pencil and notebook closer to him. "Of course, doing so could be seen as a sign of guilt."

"That's not right, and you know it, sir." Owen thrust out a finger toward the policeman. "Asking for one's solicitor to be present isn't a sign of guilt. It isn't a sign of anything except not wishing the police to put words in one's mouth. Mr. Shelton, would you care to make a telephone call?"

"Ah . . . n-no. I'll answer the inspector's questions. I went down to the beach for some air."

"The terrace wasn't sufficient?"

"No, it wasn't. There were too many people about. I—I wished to be alone with my thoughts, and the Solent is peaceful tonight."

Mr. Lewis made some notes while nodding. "And how long were you on the beach before you noticed the body?"

"I—I'd walked a ways first. I didn't see him until I was on my way back. M-maybe he wasn't there when I f-first entered the beach."

"What did you do when you saw him?"

"I—I didn't know what to think. I didn't know it was Sir Hugh. I thought s-someone had fallen down drunk." He swallowed audibly. "I almost kept going, but s-something made me go closer. And then I saw his face and the b-blood and the dagger . . ." Ernie shuddered.

The inspector showed no emotion as he took notes. "And how long before the young couple arrived?"

"I don't know." Ernie gestured at the air. "I—I had no sense of time. I was too shocked. After I checked for a pulse, I simply remained crouched there, wondering what to do. And then I—I heard screaming."

"The woman," Mr. Lewis said with a nod and scribbled again on his notebook.

"Yes, and then e-everyone else appeared. And Lady Phoebe and *he* were there." Ernie pointed at Owen, as if he should be a focus of suspicion.

"Did you touch the knife?" Mr. Lewis asked Ernie bluntly.

"N-no, I didn't. You would have found my fingerprints on it if I had."

"Hmm." The inspector then turned his attention to each of the other occupants in the room. Where did they have dinner? Where did they go immediately afterward? Did they hear the screams . . . ? His questions seemed interminable to Phoebe.

Finally, he announced, "That will be all for the time being."

Before he could continue, Phoebe sprang up from her seat. She yanked her sleeves up to expose her forearms. "You arrested my sister based on her having cut her hand on the mirror in her stateroom. Now you've found the knife that most probably resulted in the blood on the railing. I think each one of us should show whether or not we bear a similar wound."

"Would you have us all strip naked, Lady Phoebe?" Mildred Blair raised an eyebrow in amusement.

Grams found nothing humorous in the question. "Miss Blair, *really*."

Phoebe faced Miss Blair. "No, I would not. However, if a struggle ensued over that knife, the most likely place for the killer to have been cut is on the hands or arms." She turned back to the detective inspector. "Well?"

"All right, yes." He nodded. "If you all please," he added to soften the request.

One by one, they shrugged out of coats, unbuttoned sleeves and pushed them up. Only Veronica Townsend's forearm revealed any form of gash. She immediately took the defensive.

"I told your maid the other day, Phoebe. I scratched myself while tending my roses before we left home to come here. Look." She held her arm out higher. "It's only a scratch. Not nearly deep enough to drip all that blood on the railing."

Mr. Lewis approached her and leaned to study the abrasion. "Hmm."

"Is that all you can say?" Veronica let her arm swing to her side.

He straightened and shrugged. "Inconclusive. However, I'm sure I don't have to tell you not to leave Cowes—any of you. And you, Mr. Shelton, are not to set foot beyond the boundaries of this hotel, or I'll have you brought in. Understood?"

Ernie didn't reply, but it was clear by his expression that the inspector had left no question in his mind.

Phoebe lingered as the others streamed out of the room, all except Owen. The time had come to speak up.

"Mr. Lewis," she began, and at his displeased look, she started again. "Detective Inspector Lewis, Owen Seabright and I have made something of a discovery that might help with determining who committed these murders."

"You, Lady Phoebe?" The man started to smirk, but after darting a look at Owen, he changed his mind. "What have you discovered?"

"Gilbert Townsend and Hugh Fitzallen had several things in common. They fought together in the Boer Wars. They also served together in Ireland, in the Dublin Castle administration. They were both there during the Easter Rising, and last year, during the German Plot deception."

"None of this is news." He tapped his foot impatiently. "What are you getting at?"

"That the killer might be someone connected to that last event."

Owen stood close at her side. "Hugh admitted to being involved, along with another matter involving stolen arms."

"Stolen arms?" The detective scowled. "Why didn't someone come to me sooner with this information?"

"Because it was our word against Sir Hugh's," Phoebe told him. "We'd hoped to persuade him to come to you himself. But he feared being arrested for his illegal activities while he was in Ireland. He also feared reprisals from others who were involved."

"It seems he was right," Owen murmured.

"This is the reason the wedding reception was a hurried affair on Lord Annondale's yacht," she went on, "and why he and my sister, along with Sir Hugh and Miss Townsend, were to set sail first thing in the morning. They'd received the threats and wished to leave England as soon as possible."

"Miss Townsend, you say?"

"Sir Hugh told me she knows nothing about the threats or anything else, but her brother insisted she come along on the voyage to keep her safe, and to prevent whoever was threatening them from harming her to get at him."

"I see." Mr. Lewis pinched the bridge of his nose between his thumb and forefinger. "I can't think of any irate Irish nationalists running around Cowes."

"Would they advertise?" Phoebe pointed out, earning another scowl from the inspector.

"Most of their identities are known to the British authorities." He let out a long sigh. "I'll take all this under consideration."

"In the meantime, you'll release my sister, yes?"

He compressed his lips, his nose flaring. "Yes. Tell your grandparents they may collect her within the hour."

Phoebe and Owen were in the corridor when Mr. Lewis called to her. "Lady Phoebe, bring me those RSVPs you told me about. I'd like to have a look at them now."

Chapter 20

Eva dabbed at her eyes as she let herself out of Lord and Lady Wroxly's suite. She had been present when Lady Julia arrived, and had been caught up in the joy and relief of the event. But it was time to give the family their privacy. Hetta followed her out, her eyes as red and teary as Eva's.

She and Lady Phoebe had had a chance to discuss the bowie knife used to murder Sir Hugh. Miss Townsend had confirmed that her brother kept the knife with him wherever he went as a kind of talisman, and that he typically kept it on his desk, whether that desk be at home, on his yacht, or in a hotel. It only made sense, then, that the killer had managed to wrench the weapon from Lord Annondale during their struggle and had been wounded by it. Lady Phoebe had surmised the most likely place would have been on the hands or arms, and Eva tended to agree with her. Yet no one but Miss Townsend bore any kind of cut or scrape, and hers could have been the result of a rose thorn, as she claimed.

Surely there had to be further clues on board the *Georgiana*. With Mr. Mowbry's photographs flashing in her brain, Eva had gone to bed exhausted that night but had slept fitfully, with disturbing dreams that woke her with a start more than once. When slivers of sun outlined the curtains, she had risen and dressed, while Hetta had slept on.

Now, at the end of the corridor, a man stood up from the small settee beside the lift. He faced her and waited. She recognized him immediately. Even at a distance, the scars that made the Marquess of Allerton impossible to confuse with any other man stood out. She hurried down the hall to him.

"My lord . . ." She found she didn't quite know what to say, except for the obvious. "Lady Julia is back with her family."

Theo Leighton nodded and let out a sigh laden with relief. "I thank God for that, Eva. I found out only yesterday what happened—Lord Annondale's death, Julia being accused . . ." His head went down, and his fingers raked through his hair. When he raised his face, his eyes were blazing. "If I had known, I'd never have stayed away."

"We tried to reach you at home. Miles tried." She didn't tell him the reason, that for a short time he had been something of a suspect.

"I didn't go home. After leaving the island, I simply chose a direction and drove. At night I stopped at whatever inn happened to be closest, ate a meal, retired, and started again in the morning. I was nearly to Devon when I picked up a newspaper. I don't have to tell you I turned my motorcar around immediately."

"My lord, I don't wish to ask you this, but I feel I must." She braced herself inwardly. "Can you prove where you were? Are there others who can vouch for you?"

"Eva, surely you can't mean to imply—"

"No. But with your . . . shall we say history . . . with Lady Julia, the police might ask."

He nodded. "Yes, yes, I see. I'm sure the innkeepers where I stayed would be more than happy to corroborate my whereabouts these past days. I paid them well enough for their hospitality." He paused, his head lowering again. When he looked up, she saw concern mingled with pain. "Eva, how is she?"

"She's held up remarkably well, my lord." No sense in mentioning how she had blamed herself for Lord Annondale's death. It was up to Lady Julia to tell him, if she chose.

"And now she's exonerated? That's what Owen Seabright told me when I saw him in the lobby last night. It was too late when I arrived to see her."

"I . . ." Detective Inspector Lewis had made it clear Lady Julia hadn't been fully vindicated, only that in light of Sir Hugh's murder, the police were willing to release her into her grandparents' recognizance—for now.

"Why are you hesitating?"

"The investigation isn't over," she told him. "The police admit they were perhaps hasty in arresting Lady Julia, but they haven't entirely ruled her out, either."

"Imbeciles." The war wounds that had left raw and pitted skin on Lord Allerton's face tugged at his mouth, lending him a sneer that would have been frightening on another man. Eva felt no fear, only sorrow, for him, for Lady Julia, and for a situation that might still prevent them from ever marrying.

She heard a door open behind her and turned to see Mr. Mowbry exit his room. He hesitated when he saw her, then continued his approach. He tipped his head to her. "Miss Huntford. That was some scene yesterday, wasn't it?" He pressed the button to summon the lift.

"Lord Allerton, may I present Mr. Mowbry," she said. "He was the photographer at Lord and Lady Annondale's wedding. Like the rest of us, he's been detained here by the police."

One of Theo Leighton's eyebrows went up. "Not as a suspect, I hope."

Mr. Mowbry gave a slight bob of his head, showing Lord Allerton the deference due his rank. "No, my lord, thank goodness. The police don't know who did the deed, but we're all relieved to see Lady Annondale released. The very idea that gracious lady could commit such a monstrous act is absurd."

The lift arrived, and the operator opened the door and inquired if they were going up or down. Mr. Mowbry hung back, allowing Lord Allerton to answer first.

"Neither." To Eva, he said, "I'm going to wait here until it's a decent enough hour to knock at Lord and Lady Wroxly's door. Owen told me Julia was staying in their suite."

"That's right." Eva noticed the lift operator beginning to tap his foot. She excused herself to Lord Allerton. "I'm going down," she told the operator and inquired of Mr. Mowbry.

"The same." He took his leave of Lord Allerton, and he and Eva rode downstairs together.

Phoebe and Amelia awoke that morning to a pounding at their door, which instantly alarmed them both. Phoebe sprang upright, her heart pounding, and Amelia shoved golden hair out of her eyes.

"What's happening?" Amelia murmured.

"It's all right. I'm here." Eva had already let herself into the room and was busy picking out clothes from the armoire. A tray of tea and toast awaited Phoebe and her sister on the table beneath the window. Eva went to open the door to reveal Fox on the other side.

"Your sisters aren't up yet," she told him.

"Theo's here," he blurted and poked his head around

her shoulder. "Amelia, Phoebe. Did you hear? Theo came last night, late. He's with Julia and the grandparents. Get *up*," he urged and took off down the corridor.

That day passed with the first semblance of normalcy Phoebe had enjoyed since before the wedding. The family, along with Owen and Theo, spent most of the day in her grandparents' suite, away from curious eyes. They avoided talking about Gil and Hugh, and the day felt rather like a holiday, an inclement one where no one felt like venturing outside and the hours were spent in conversation, cards, and simply enjoying one another's company. Owen and Fox spent a good hour or so in front of a chessboard. Julia and Theo bided most of their time side by side, joining in the general discussions but exchanging few words among themselves. Phoebe hadn't been present when they greeted each other for the first time earlier, and she burned to know how it went. She couldn't ask, of course. If Julia wished to share, she would.

They ordered breakfast and lunch brought up, but when it came time for dinner, Julia had had enough of the close quarters. "Let's all dress and go down," she said, brooking no debate from their grandparents.

Grams tried, anyway. "Are you sure you wouldn't rather stay here, where it's quiet and private? In the dining room, we'll be subjected to stares and whispers."

"Bother stares and whispers," Amelia said, with a fond look at her eldest sister. "I think we should go down. We've nothing to be ashamed of."

"Amelia's right." Julia shrugged one shoulder, as was her habit. But the bravado Phoebe expected didn't materialize. Julia sounded more resigned than brave. "The longer we put off going out in public, the harder it will be later."

"We'll face them together, a united front," Theo said and patted Julia's hand. Julia smiled at him, but the gesture quickly faded, like the bloom on a week-old rose.

Sitting at Julia's other side, Grams continued to look fretful, though she said nothing more on the subject. Phoebe wondered if part of her fretting might be due to Theo's reappearance in Julia's life. He had stayed away once the engagement to Gil had been announced, and though he had attended the wedding, he had left immediately afterward, without speaking to Julia.

Had he returned, hoping things would be different now? Julia's fading smile told a disappointing story. Phoebe suspected that her sister still blamed herself for Gil's death, that Sir Hugh's murder and its implications hadn't lifted that burden from Julia's shoulders. And blaming herself, she might go on punishing herself, denying any chance of happiness in the near future. Phoebe believed Julia would be happy with Theo. Perhaps not as wealthy as she'd like to be, but contented all the same.

Grampapa had been rather quiet. While that could be a result of his enormous relief that Julia had been released or simple fatigue, Phoebe noticed him studying the pair every so often, when he thought no one would notice. Rather than mirroring Grams's concerns, however, he looked thoughtful, as if only just realizing there might be something more than friendship between the pair. With a surge of hope, Phoebe thought perhaps Grampapa might become Theo's biggest proponent when it came to being a suitor for Julia.

Downstairs, Grams's fears came to fruition, but the family kept their chins high and ignored the stares. As they were led to a large table near the center of the room, however, Julia's pace slowed. For a moment Phoebe feared she might do an about-face, but instead Julia tightened her hold on Theo's arm and then allowed him to hold her seat for her.

When they ordered dessert, Veronica Townsend rose from a table across the room, along with her friend, Anto-

nia Seward, and Ernie Shelton. The three had apparently
formed an alliance, though Phoebe wondered how long it
would last once the will had been read. They advanced toward the Renshaws' table. Ernie and Mrs. Seward stopped
and hung back, while Veronica continued until she stood
beside Phoebe's chair.

"Might we have a quick word?" the woman said. "I've
been looking for you all day, or I'd not interrupt your dinner now."

Phoebe's puzzlement grew at those cryptic words. After
exchanging a brief glance with Owen, she excused herself
to her family and allowed Veronica to draw her away
from the table.

"I overheard something yesterday," the woman said.
"Something you were discussing with Inspector Lewis
after we were all dismissed. I couldn't help it. I paused outside the open door to the meeting room to adjust my ankle
strap, and I heard you talking. You mentioned Ireland."

"Yes, we did. It's something Gil and Sir Hugh had in
common recently, and it might have stirred up enough
controversy to cause what happened to them."

"I've debated whether or not to mention this. It might
have no bearing on anything. Then again, it could be the
key the police are searching for, now that it looks as
though your sister is innocent."

Phoebe didn't like Veronica's ambiguous choice of words
concerning Julia's innocence, but she let that pass.

The woman moved closer. Her gaze darted around the
dining room, and then her voice plunged to a whisper.
"Did you know Mildred Blair is half Irish? On her mother's
side."

Phoebe jolted with surprise. "Are you sure?"

"Oh, yes. She doesn't like talking about it much, but Gil
knew all about it. Seems her mother came to this country
to work as a domestic, married, and had Mildred."

"And her father?"

"Dead."

"Do you know if she still has family in Ireland?"

"I should say so. I understand her mother eventually went back. Mildred periodically receives post from County Clare, and I've a suspicion she sends money there. I tried asking her about it once, but she got a sour look on her face and walked away. She works hard at being a modern British woman. I suppose it hurts her pride, acknowledging her low origins."

Phoebe wanted to admonish Veronica for that last opinion, but another concern took precedence. "If you heard us talking with the inspector yesterday, why didn't you come in and tell us this?"

Veronica pulled up tall and sniffed. "I didn't like to. I don't wish to be involved. If you or the police question Mildred, she is not to know you learned of her Irish background from me. I'll deny having said a word."

"Why? What are you afraid of?"

"Mildred, of course," the woman replied, as if speaking to an idiot. "She's spiteful, and I've no doubt she'd devise some way to make my life difficult. You saw how she got Gil's solicitor to come all this way. With Gil gone, she should be out of my life by now, yet she's managed not only to hang on but also to continue to hold sway over Gil's estate. I don't know how she does it, but I tell you truly, I don't wish to have her for an enemy."

Mildred Blair—spiteful? Arrogant, icy, yes. Phoebe had seen that much for herself, as had Eva. Veronica's fear of her, and this new information, certainly shed new suspicion that Mildred Blair might have had reasons to want both Gil and Sir Hugh dead. But one question remained: Why now? Why not a year ago? Or two? Unless, Gil's marriage and his apparent happiness struck some violent chord in her and prompted her to violence.

"What was that all about?" Grams asked when Phoebe returned to her seat. Amelia leaned closer to hear her reply. Across the table, Julia watched her, her eyebrows drawn tightly inward.

"Just a bit of gossip," Phoebe said. "Nothing important, really."

Julia's gaze remained on her for several more seconds, her expression one of disbelief. Phoebe didn't wish to discuss the matter here, and both Grams and Julia seemed to be of the same mind, for they asked no further questions. Grampapa and Owen were engaged in conversation, but Owen's brief glance assured Phoebe he had been thoroughly aware of her exchange with Veronica.

"I thought I heard her say something about—"

Fox fell silent when Phoebe nudged his shinbone under the table. She shot him a warning glare for good measure.

"If you'll excuse me." Julia came to her feet. "I'll be back in a moment."

This got Grampapa's attention. "Anything wrong, my dear?"

"Yes, Julia, you're looking rather pale." Grams scrutinized her from across the table. "Are you feeling all right?"

"It's nothing. I'm quite fine, and I'll be right back."

"Shall I go with you?" Amelia offered, but Julia shook her head and left before anyone else could question her.

Her sudden departure filled Phoebe with unease. Had Julia overheard what Veronica had confided in her? Perhaps she'd gone to find Mildred Blair and confront her. But Julia hadn't yet learned about Gil's and Hugh's actions in Ireland, and how those actions might have brought someone to Cowes, seeking revenge.

One of Miss Blair's relatives? Possible. Miss Blair herself? She certainly would have had opportunity. Phoebe longed for the dessert course to end. She needed to contact

Detective Inspector Lewis and then make sure Mildred
Blair didn't suddenly disappear.

Eva had the evening hours after supper to herself. She
didn't wish to raise Lady Phoebe's hopes, but she left the
hotel with a particular goal in mind. After setting off east,
she passed the shops and hotels along Cowes Parade. At
the first of the piers, she turned in and stepped onto the
wooden planking, the vibration and slight swaying beneath her feet a familiar if still rather unwelcome sensation.

"I wish to hire your services again," she said to the griz-
zled, weathered boatman when she found him in his skiff.
Sounder-looking vessels lined the docks, but she had only
so much money to spare, so this man would have to do.
She only hoped he didn't wander off and leave her stranded
again.

"What happened to you the other night, by the way?"
she demanded of him. "Why did you leave us at the *Georgiana*?"

"There were a boat a-coming, miss. Knowing as how
you two were out there on the sly, I thought it best to row
away and come back for ye when the coast was clear."

Oddly, his explanation satisfied her, and Eva prepared
to step down into the rowboat. She didn't know what
made her glance landward at the roadway and then toward the Royal Yacht Squadron building beyond. Perhaps
the instinct for secrecy prompted her to ensure she was not
being watched. Not that she was doing anything wrong.
But in those quick glances, she spied something that made
her step away from the skiff.

"Ye change your mind, did ye?"

Eva gave a dismissive wave. By the time she reached the
walkway between piers, a sense of urgency gripped her.

Darkness had fallen, but there could be no mistake. Lady Julia had walked by, accompanied by a tall man who might have been mistaken for bald had he been glimpsed in the utter darkness of the *Georgiana*'s dining room in the middle of the night.

He wore a tan bowler. Eva had seen him with it before, but it simply hadn't occurred to her that this could be what the deck steward had seen that night.

The pair hurried along, stiffly, neither appearing to speak a word. Lady Julia was under strict orders from Detective Inspector Lewis to remain at the hotel under her grandparents' supervision. He would see this as a violation of her release agreement and, perhaps, an admission of guilt.

Eva dashed in pursuit but hung back far enough not to be noticed. The more she observed, the more a warning sounded inside her. The very fact that Lady Julia wasn't wearing a coat proved she hadn't left the hotel of her own will, and if Eva still had any doubts, the object being pressed to her side, barely visible unless one truly looked, convinced her.

They reached the long pier just beyond the Royal Yacht Squadron. A host of craft of all sorts and sizes lined the dock. Lady Julia's high-heeled pumps raised a clatter on the boards, and the bouncing of the structure nearly made Eva reach for the nearest piling as she followed them.

She darted behind one of those pilings when Curtis Mowbry glanced over his shoulder. Steadying herself with both hands, she peeked around the weathered beam. Mr. Mowbry was nudging Lady Julia along a ramp and then onto the stern of a launch, a smaller version of the one that had brought the wedding guests out to Lord Annondale's yacht.

Mr. Mowbry dragged the ramp onto the boat, and they disappeared into the cabin. Every instinct urged Eva to alert someone, and she stepped away from the piling with just that intention. But at the same moment Mr. Mowbry reappeared on deck and climbed into the wheelhouse.

He hadn't cast off the lines yet. Another instinct overrode all others—the instinct to protect. Eva ran on her toes to muffle her footsteps. As she reached the boat, she hesitated for one agonizing moment. Then, searching for any sign of Mr. Mowbry and seeing none, she leaped across the gap between the pier and the boat and ducked into the cabin. The effort left her doubled over and gasping for breath. Movement caught her eye, and through the port windows she spied his figure moving aft. Lines thudded as he dropped them onto the deck. A moment later, the vibration of the engine surged and the vessel lurched, nearly tossing Eva off her feet. Her stomach flipped and then flopped as the boat veered to the starboard, away from the pier.

Only now did she survey her surroundings, both dark and empty but for boating equipment, built-in seating, and cupboards. A companionway directly ahead of her appeared to lead downward. He would be kept busy, she reasoned, guiding the boat through the harbor. She went to the companionway and very carefully opened its door, knowing the wheelhouse was right above her head.

Six steps brought her to the lower level, where a tiny passageway revealed three doors, all closed. She tried the one nearest. The latch moved easily, and the door opened upon a marine head. Eva tried the next and found this one locked. The third door opened, and she discovered two berths inside, both empty. After returning to the locked door, she pressed up against it.

"Lady Julia?" She didn't dare speak in more than a whisper.

"Eva," came a hissing reply. "Goodness, is that you? I can't get out."

A locked door had never deterred Eva before, thanks to childhood lessons from her brother, Danny. Even that small reminiscence brought a pang to her heart, but she eased aside memories of him and reached up to slide a hairpin from her coif.

Within minutes the door opened, and a pair of arms nearly strangled her. "Eva, thank God. You've brought help, yes?" Lady Julia hugged Eva tightly once more before pulling away. "You did, didn't you?"

"There wasn't time. It was either jump aboard while Mr. Mowbry wasn't looking or risk losing you forever. We'll have to subdue him on our own."

"There's three of us, actually." Lady Julia stepped aside and gestured at the lower berth.

Eva gasped. Mildred Blair lay prone on her side, her eyes shut, her arms and legs bound with rope. A gag bit cruelly into the lower half of her face.

"She was already here when Curtis shoved me in," Lady Julia said. "I haven't had time yet to try to revive her."

Eva crouched beside the berth and worked at the knot holding the gag in place. "Set to work on her ankles, my lady." Within moments, Eva slid the gag free and dropped it to the deck. She tapped Miss Blair's cheeks, at the same time saying, "He held something to your side, my lady. Was it a gun?"

"Yes. He's armed. Only when we reached this boat did I realize how stupid I was to go with him. As if he would have fired on me in plain sight of everyone in the hotel lobby or along the parade."

"He's a vicious killer, my lady. You don't know what he would have done. You did the right thing."

"Let's hope so, Eva."

Miss Blair stirred, groaning.

"She's waking up," Eva said.

"Wh-what's happening?" Miss Blair tried to sit up, and

when she couldn't, she began to struggle. She wiggled her arms and legs, making Eva and Lady Julia's work all the more difficult.

"Miss Blair, we're trying to help you. Lie still and we'll untie you," Eva told her.

Eva's stomach hadn't stopped its pitching. She swallowed and bit her lower lip to give herself something else to focus on and worked the knots holding Miss Blair's wrists until her fingertips ached. A sense of panic began to set in. At any moment Mr. Mowbry could decide to check on his captives, and they would be defenseless to protect themselves. She could only hope navigating the harbor would keep him busy long enough. He must be heading out to open water, she surmised, and there would be a host of vessels in his way. But which way was he heading? East or west into the English Channel?

"There," Lady Julia declared, pulling the rope free of Miss Blair's ankles. "What happened, Mildred? How did Mr. Mowbry get you here?"

Miss Blair rubbed at her cheeks and chin and worked her mouth open and closed to ease the tension of the gag. Then she said, "He told me he had some new evidence to show me." She lowered her gaze and peeked sheepishly out from beneath her lashes. "He said it incriminated you, Julia, along with Ernie. I foolishly let him bring me here. The next thing I knew . . . Well, here you two are."

"We don't have time for explanations." Eva went to the door and listened for any sign of Mr. Mowbry approaching. A thought suddenly sent her pivoting to face the other women. She crossed the small space and gripped Miss Blair's shoulders. "How do we know you're not working with him? That you're being here, tied up, isn't a ploy to deceive us into trusting you?"

Miss Blair looked utterly taken aback. She rubbed at her wrists, and Eva saw they were bruised and raw. Miss

Blair then raised a hand to the crown of her head. She winced and let out a moan. "Feel this, Miss Huntford. It should convince you." Miss Blair took Eva's hand and guided it to a sizable lump beneath her hair. "If I were working with Curtis, would I have allowed him to do this to me?"

Eva shook her head. "No, I can't see you or anyone agreeing to that. My apologies. Now . . ." She moved back to the door. "We need to find some sort of weapons. One supposes on a boat, that could mean just about anything."

"Follow me." Miss Blair squeezed past Eva into the passageway, then led them up the few steps into the upper cabin. There she began opening cupboards, careful not to make a sound. Eva and Lady Julia watched her but remained alert for any movement outside the windows.

Eva's heart thudded in her throat. "Hurry," she urged in a whisper, still wondering what Miss Blair was searching for. Taking matters into her own hands, she went to a cupboard Miss Blair had already opened and took down a heavy steel wrench and a mallet. She handed the wrench to Lady Julia. "These will do."

"No they won't." Miss Blair opened another cupboard, and this time she pulled out a metal box with a handle and a flip latch. "Here. This should do the trick." She opened the box to reveal two pistols.

Eva's stomach turned leaden. "You're suggesting we kill him?"

"I don't think I could." Lady Julia backed away from Miss Blair. "No matter how much he may deserve it."

"This won't kill him unless you fire point-blank." Miss Blair reached into the box and lifted one of the pistols. She handed one to Eva. "Flare guns. They'll blind and confuse him, and possibly leave him with some burns. But unless we fire directly at him at close range, he'll live." She gestured with her chin at the wrench Lady Julia held. "You keep that. Once we've fired the flares, you knock him out. He certainly deserves *that*."

Eva expelled a breath of relief, then remembered Mr. Mowbry had a gun of his own—one quite capable of killing. "We won't have more than one chance to take him by surprise. My lady, you stay back until after we've fired." Not that she planned to allow Lady Julia to get anywhere near Mr. Mowbry. Instead, she would seize the wrench from her and use it on him herself if necessary, but she saw no reason to mention that now.

They crept to the outer door. Once again, Eva fought back the queasiness brought on by the swaying deck and envied the other two women, who seemed unaffected. She pushed the door open, and they stole outside. The roar of the engine filled her ears; its vibrations traveled through her legs and increased her sense of unsteadiness. The boat sped through the water, sending up a high, feathery spray behind them in the dark. The waves became choppier, and as they were making their way toward the wheelhouse ladder, a swell raised the boat and then dropped it into the hollow of a wave. They all stumbled, and Miss Blair's flare gun clattered to the deck.

"Who's out there?" Mr. Mowbry's head, minus his bowler, poked out from the wheelhouse. There was no time to hide. He saw them and ducked back into the wheelhouse. Before Eva could decipher his intentions and warn the other two to brace themselves, the boat took a sharp turn, then cut a wide arc. They were thrown to the rail, and the fallen flare gun skittered away into the darkness.

Pulling herself along the rail, Eva attempted to fire her flare gun into the wheelhouse, but the boat arced yet again, once more throwing them off balance. A scream pierced the roar of the engines, followed by a splash . . . and cries for help. Terror caught Eva in a stranglehold. In all the noise, she couldn't identify the voice. She looked all around her and spotted Lady Julia along the cabin's outside wall, attempting to tug a life ring from its hook.

Eva stumbled across the heaving deck to help her onehandedly, for in her other hand, she gripped the flare gun. Once the ring came loose, they returned to the rail.

"Where is she?" Lady Julia shoved windblown hair out of her face. "I can't see her."

"There!" Eva pointed at the water, where Miss Blair thrashed against the waves. She took the ring from Lady Julia and heaved it overboard, praying it would land close enough for Miss Blair to grasp it.

"Can you swim?" Lady Julia shouted down to her.

Eva didn't wait to hear the answer. The vibrations beneath her feet had lessened, and the motor quieted. A quick glance out over the water showed no lights, no signs of other boats nearby. They were alone, and Mr. Mowbry had cut the engine. The only movement came from the swells tipping the boat this way and that, and Eva's stomach with it. She wanted nothing more than to lean over the side and give in to the urgency of retching, of allowing spinning sensations to overwhelm her and swallow her whole. But if she did that . . .

They would all die. Lady Julia would die.

Mr. Mowbry swung out of the wheelhouse and onto the ladder. Eva wanted to yell to Lady Julia to run inside, to go where it was safe. But there was nowhere safe, and she didn't dare utter a word, not with the barrel of Mr. Mowbry's pistol staring straight into the heart of her most dire fears. She raised her flare gun, held her arm stiff, and braced it with her other hand. Though the engine had fallen silent, a roaring continued in her ears. Mr. Mowbry jumped down to the deck.

"You'll never fire on me, Miss Huntford. Not at this close range. You haven't the stomach for it. Or the nerve. Not even with a flare gun. Yes, I see what you've got there.

You might as well toss it away. I've no desire to hurt any of you. If you'd only minded your own business, none of us would be in this predicament right now."

"Lady Julia *is* my business, Mr. Mowbry. I wasn't about to simply let you kidnap her."

"I'd never hurt her," he said fiercely. "I'm no murderer, Miss Huntford, no matter what you may think. No matter what I've done. Gilbert Townsend and Hugh Fitzallen deserved what they got. It wasn't murder. It was justice. They were guilty, but because the law refused to prosecute them, I had no choice."

"No choice but to become their judge, jury, and executioner," Eva countered sharply.

He came several strides closer. Eva heard a noise behind her but didn't take her eyes off Mr. Mowbry long enough to find out what Lady Julia might be doing. She only hoped she was taking cover somewhere. That Mr. Mowbry still pointed his weapon at Eva brought her some measure of comfort. She didn't doubt he might try to defuse the situation by grabbing Lady Julia and training his pistol on her. He had to know Eva would cease all attempts to oppose him then.

"What is that compared to what they did?" he demanded. "I was away in France when it happened, serving men like them." His voice rose, and suddenly Eva heard it—the Irish rhythm in his speech. It was subtle, more so than Miles's, but there nonetheless. "My father and my younger brother remained at home, working the farm, trying to eke out enough to survive on what their English landlord allowed them to keep. They did nothing wrong. But when the arrests started happening, they were implicated. Tried, convicted, sent to England, to prison. Do you know what happened next, Miss Huntford?"

"I . . . don't know." Though Eva feared that, in truth, she did know.

"They died, both of them. Influenza. It raged through the prison. Do you know, Miss Huntford, who the landlord was that implicated them? That let them be dragged away with the others to eventually die? And do you know who ordered the transportation of those innocent men to England?"

"Are you talking about the German Plot?"

"Yes, indeed I am, Miss Huntford."

"Then the officials in the Dublin Castle administration were to blame."

"Hugh Fitzallen and Gilbert Townsend were to blame," he shouted, the sound echoing over the water. He lurched closer, stumbling almost blindly. Eva somehow doubted he still saw her; no, he saw Sir Hugh and Lord Annondale. He saw his father and brother, and other innocent men. He saw injustice and his inability to stop it. He saw his revenge about to take place. He raised his pistol.

Eva altered her aim. Trembling, tears blurring her vision, her blood traveling ice cold through her, she fired and was propelled backward from the thrust of the flare. Pops like drumbeats pierced her ears. Flames shot out, and smoke billowed. Through the haze, she saw Mr. Mowbry on the deck, rolling and screaming, his clothing on fire. She pushed onto her knees and attempted to stand. Behind her came running footsteps, and then Lady Julia rushed by her, holding something in her arms. What was it?

Foamy fluid shot out, dousing the flames and soaking Mr. Mowbry's clothes. They smoldered still, sending up wafts of steam and smoke. Soot and the sharp odor of gunpowder stung Eva's nose and throat. She coughed violently, and then Lady Julia was beside her, helping her to her feet.

"Eva, look!" She pointed out over the stern. A light shone on the water, cutting through the waves.

As Eva watched, it moved closer, and then she heard the rumble of the motor. A cry returned her attention to Mr. Mowbry. He squirmed and writhed, and deep remorse struck her for having fired—not directly at him, for she'd shifted her arm at the last minute, but near enough. She wished she hadn't had to. But when she kneeled beside him and attempted to assess his condition and offer words of comfort, she admitted to herself she would do exactly the same again.

CHAPTER 21

Phoebe stood at the bow of the police cutter and waved her arms wildly. She strained to see through the darkness and the smoke hovering over the smaller boat. Fear reduced her voice to raw shrieks. "Julia! Eva! We're coming."

Soon the pilot cut the engine and allowed the cutter to drift toward the launch. That was when she saw, through the haze, Julia leaning over the rail and shouting something at them. A frantic splashing off their starboard side caught her attention, and she understood.

"There's someone in the water," she called to Owen and Theo. A figure thrashed in the waves, though little but the surrounding white life ring was visible.

Detective Inspector Lewis ordered the searchlights switched on, and soon they were able to make out Mildred Blair bobbing in the water. She stopped thrashing and collapsed against the ring from obvious exhaustion. Mr. Lewis dispatched two uniformed officers in a life raft to retrieve her.

Within moments, the cutter had eased alongside the launch, and Detective Inspector Lewis instructed all on board to show themselves with their hands up. Phoebe saw only

Eva and Julia, with no sign of Curtis Mowbry. Yet unless Eva and Julia had managed to throw him over the side, he must still be on board.

"It could be a trap," Phoebe cautioned Mr. Lewis. "Curtis Mowbry might be waiting to spring out on you and your men."

"I'll handle this, Lady Phoebe. You and your friends are to stay back."

With her hands over her head, as instructed, Eva approached their port-side railing. "It's all right. Mr. Mowbry's been injured and is in no condition to cause any more mischief."

Mr. Lewis didn't at first respond, but instead scrutinized Eva and assessed the situation. "Where is he?"

"He's here." Eva lowered one hand to point. "He's lying on the deck. I . . . I don't think he'll be getting up anytime soon."

"For heaven's sake, Eva, put your hands down," Julia said as she went to Eva's side. She looked startled when she took in Phoebe and everyone else on board the police cutter.

The officers had secured lines between the two boats, and now Theo, ignoring Mr. Lewis's order to stay back, eagerly climbed over the two rails and onto the launch's deck. In an instant, his arms were around Julia.

"How on earth did you know where to find us?" Eva asked Phoebe some twenty minutes later, once the two boats were ready for the return trip to Cowes. She, Julia, Theo, and Miss Blair were now on the police cutter, while Curtis Mowbry and three of the police officers had remained on the launch.

"Fox," Phoebe replied succinctly. "He saw you leaving the hotel, and with Julia already missing, he decided to follow you. Once he saw what was happening, and with whom, he ran back to tell us. Inspector Lewis guessed Curtis Mowbry would choose this direction, heading into open waters sooner than if he had gone east. There would have been more boats off the coast of East Cowes that might have noticed something out of the ordinary."

Julia, listening in, raised her head from Theo's shoulder. "For once, I don't mind Fox being an annoying little nuisance."

"No, nor I," Eva agreed with a rueful chuckle. "Who knows what would have happened otherwise."

"The boy's a hero." Theo tightened his hold on Julia. "I suppose we'll have to be nicer to him from now on."

They shared quiet laughter over that and settled in for the trip back to Cowes. Phoebe snuggled against Owen's side for the first few minutes, but seeing Mildred Blair sitting alone, still dripping and wrapped in a blanket, she rose and went to sit beside her.

"Are you all right, Miss Blair?"

The woman shrugged a shoulder, for a moment reminding Phoebe of Julia. "Are any of us all right after what's happened?"

"No, I suppose not. But you've been through a harrowing time, and if there's anything I or my family can do for you, you must say so."

"That's frightfully generous of you, Lady Phoebe." An irony in Mildred Blair's voice belied the sentiment. She turned her face away.

Phoebe felt disregarded and dismissed, but she resisted the urge to walk off in a temper. "I do mean what I say." Miss Blair continued to ignore her, and Phoebe returned to Owen.

Detective Inspector Lewis seemed content to leave Eva, Julia, and Miss Blair alone during the return trip. But once they arrived in Cowes, he accompanied them back to the hotel and asked them to assemble once again in the meeting room. Before they did, however, he allowed Julia and

Phoebe to speak with their grandparents and their younger siblings and assure them they were all right. Eva went with them and explained how she had stowed away on the launch, freed Julia and Mildred Blair, and wounded Curtis Mowbry with a flare gun.

"Good heavens, Eva, we must never lose you," Grampapa fervently declared in a voice whose former booming resonance had suddenly been restored. He seized her hands and looked about to swing her in circles, though he stopped short of doing so. "Whatever you need, ask. It shall be yours. Do your parents need anything?"

"Thank you, Lord Wroxly. If there is ever anything, I'll be sure to ask," she said modestly.

"You must never hesitate, my dear."

Grams thanked her profusely, too, and then, with a nod at Phoebe, Eva excused herself to give the family some quiet minutes alone with Julia.

"We didn't know what to think when you didn't come back to the table," Grams said to her, blinking to combat the tears. "And then Fox came running in, all breathless, and told us that horrible Mr. Mowbry had taken you away. We were so frightened we'd never get you back . . ."

"I'm here now, Grams, and everything is all right."

Julia took the time to thank Fox, who blushed with pleasure and suffered her to embrace him. She did so quickly and with a minimum of fuss.

"It's my responsibility to see to my sisters' welfare, isn't it?" he said, with only the slightest display of self-importance.

Julia laughed, the most lighthearted sound Phoebe had heard from her in months. "We'll discuss that later," Julia told him and then turned her attention to Grampapa. His initial relief and excitement at seeing Julia safely returned having waned, he possessed a pallor that made him appear years older. Julia reached out to touch his cheek in a rare show of tenderness. "I'm really all right, you know. I don't think he ever had any intention of hurting me."

"Julia, I . . ." Their grandfather compressed his lips to contain the emotions he had rather not display. Phoebe understood, for to release those feelings would be to lose control of them, and he wished to be steadfast for them all, even now, when it was evident so much of his strength had left him. If he retained any vigor at all, it showed in the smile he summoned to put his grandchildren's worries to rest.

Amelia quietly waited her turn. Where Phoebe expected tears, Amelia showed a serene countenance. But she, too, had known danger in her young life. She understood, as did Phoebe and Eva, the fears and uncertainties Julia had faced. She hugged Julia tightly. "I'm so glad you're all right."

Miss Blair had also been permitted to run up to her room to change out of her damp clothes. Once they had all returned downstairs and assembled in the meeting room, Mr. Lewis had news to tell them. "I've had a communication from the police station. Curtis Mowbry has a laceration across his left thigh. It appears partially healed, but apparently it has started bleeding again."

Eva gasped. "I'd noticed a slight limp, and when I inquired, he told me it was a war wound. I took him at his word. If only I had said something . . ."

"These days there's no reason to suspect any man claiming to have been wounded in battle," the inspector assured her. "It appears Lord Annondale somehow managed to wound Mr. Mowbry before he died. Mr. Mowbry being so tall, it's only logical that as he leaned to throw Lord Annondale overboard, he bled on the railing."

"Only logical," Julia murmured and gave an ironic *humph.*

"I apologize, Lady Annondale," the inspector said somewhat ruefully, and she had the good grace to incline her head in acceptance. "Now then, tell me what happened out there. Miss Huntford, why don't you go first?"

Eva's case was the most straightforward of the three—she had boarded the launch voluntarily. But she related what Curtis Mowbry had revealed to her about his father and brother being caught up in the arrests surrounding the German Plot, and how he blamed Gil and Sir Hugh. Phoebe experienced growing sympathies for Mr. Mowbry—certainly for his family members—until she remembered nothing could possibly justify his heinous actions.

Julia's and Miss Blair's stories were rather more complicated.

"I was feeling rather peaky at dinner, as you might remember, Phoebe," Julia said.

Phoebe nodded, thinking her sister looked peaky now, as well. And then, with surprise, she noticed something else. Julia kept fussing with her left hand; she had put her wedding ring back on and was twisting it nervously round and round on her finger.

Julia continued, "As soon as I'd stepped into the lobby, Mr. Mowbry approached me. He was all smiles at first and offered to accompany me outside. I told him no thank you. Feeling as I did, I wished for fresh air and wasn't keen on having to make conversation. He wouldn't take no for an answer, and the next thing I knew, he'd gripped my arm, still smiling, and pressed something against my side that bit into my ribs."

She paused, and Theo leaned closer to her and covered her hand—the one bearing Gil's ring—with his own. Had he noticed she'd resumed wearing the piece? And what did it mean? Was it merely a formality that Julia, as a married woman—albeit widowed—felt obligated to uphold?

"After that," Julia said, "he walked me outside and hurried me to the pier and onto the boat he'd hired. Almost as revolting as being held at gunpoint was his declaration that he and I would be married as soon as we reached the Continent. He was in love with me, you see."

That revelation nearly knocked Phoebe out of her chair. "In love with you? How can that be?"

"Because he'd been obsessed with me since the summer of nineteen eighteen, when Henry paid him to follow me—"

"What is this?" the inspector interrupted.

"It's a long story," Julia said calmly. She exchanged a glance with Theo and gave a slight shrug. "Henry Leighton, Theo Leighton's brother, fancied he would be my husband someday. But that summer he grew suspicious that I was seeing another man—which I wasn't. As I said, it's a long story. But he hired Mr. Mowbry, apparently, to follow me about and take photographs in an attempt to catch me in the act. That's why he seemed so familiar to me," she said in an aside to Phoebe. "Ever since then, Mr. Mowbry has been monitoring my activities in the society columns. Once he saw I was to marry Gil—" Here she faltered slightly, frowning down at her ring, before she swallowed and went on. "Once he saw that, he realized he could have me and his revenge against Gil and Hugh at the same time."

"Oh, Julia, that's beastly," Phoebe blurted, aghast at how much forethought had gone into Mr. Mowbry's plans. "He's utterly insane."

"Insane, perhaps, but shrewd," Mr. Lewis commented. "Lady Annondale, how did he come to be the photographer at your wedding?"

"I can answer that," Mildred Blair said, speaking up for the first time. Wearing a smart outfit and with her hair back in place, she had regained her usual confidence and cool demeanor. "He answered the ad I placed on behalf of

Lord and Lady Annondale and came highly recommended. Though, in retrospect, one suspects those references were forged."

"And how did *you* come to be on the launch?" Mr. Lewis asked her.

"Quite by accident, I assure you. I had gotten a message from the Royal Yacht Squadron asking me to attend to some of my . . . some of Lord Annondale's affairs connected with the club. On my way there, I saw Curtis Mowbry at the pier, at the leasing office. I thought that rather odd, so when he exited the building, I followed him down the pier to the launch. He boarded and poked about, as one would do when preparing for a voyage. Why should a photographer need to lease a boat? It occurred to me, of course, that he wished to leave Cowes in the most efficient way possible. I asked him bluntly what he was doing. Before I could resist, he grabbed me, dragged me into the cabin, and forced me below, where he knocked me out, tied me up, and gagged me." Her eyes glittered with outrage.

Julia's eyes glittered, too, but with an altogether different sentiment. Phoebe had heard it, too, a tiny slip when Miss Blair had started to say *my*, but quickly amended it to *Lord Annondale*. What had she been about to say? My what? My employer? Then why not simply say it, rather than breaking off short and changing it?

My lover? Miss Blair certainly wouldn't wish to say *that* in mixed company.

But perhaps it was time she did.

"Miss Blair, just what was the nature of your—"

"No, Phoebe," Julia said briskly. "It's for me to ask, and it's high time I did. Miss Blair." She turned in her chair to face the other woman fully. "What were you to my husband? Were you his mistress?"

Miss Blair allowed the moment to stretch to the breaking point, before she blinked, seemed to grow taller, and calmly said, "I am his daughter."

"What?" Phoebe and Julia spoke at once.

The others in the room looked dumbfounded. Phoebe wanted to confront Miss Blair with a host of questions, but she stayed silent. As Julia had said, it was for her to ask.

But Julia, tight-lipped, her teeth clenched, merely said, "Explain."

Miss Blair drew a breath and expelled it slowly. "I am Gilbert Townsend's daughter. His illegitimate daughter, I should clarify. My mother was a housemaid on his estate, and he . . . well, he did as many men of his class will do. But he did at least have the decency to set her up comfortably for the rest of her life, and then he took an interest in me once I'd reached adulthood. I believe he even felt an affection for me, as far as Gil Townsend was capable of feeling affection—as you yourself will understand, Lady Annondale." She pronounced Julia's title with no small amount of sarcasm.

Phoebe expected Julia to bristle and was surprised when she instead let out a small laugh. "Indeed I do. But why the secrecy? Why pose as his secretary all this time?"

"I wasn't posing. I *was* his secretary, just as Ernest was his veterinarian. I might be his daughter, but he still expected me to be useful, to fulfill some function in this world. As I expected of myself, for that matter. For a woman such as me, it is either marriage or employment. I have no desire to be some merchant's or clerk's wife, which is the best someone like me could hope for. And as for why I didn't reveal my parentage earlier . . . well, I certainly don't have to tell you how people of your class look down upon people like me. Why should I wish to endure that kind of judgment?"

Again, Phoebe was surprised when Julia replied with a nod and a simple "I do see your point."

"All right, then," Detective Inspector Lewis said, so abruptly that everyone seemed startled out of their thoughts. "Anyone have anything more to add?"

None of them had anything to say, except for Julia, who had a question. "May we go home now, Inspector?"

He gave his wholehearted permission. They were not to leave until morning, however, as the last ferry of the night had already departed.

Phoebe enjoyed the first good night's sleep in days, as she suspected Julia did, as well. In the morning, she stood with Eva on the deck of the ferry, watching Cowes and the Isle of Wight recede into the distance behind them, while Portsmouth grew in size before them.

"I'll never be so glad to see Little Barlow," Phoebe said.

"Nor I," Eva agreed. "Please tell me there won't be any venturing away from home in the near future."

Phoebe knew better than to make any promises. "Why does trouble seem to find us no matter where we are?"

Eva turned to face her. "I think, my lady, because you don't hide from trouble. And where you are, I am, as well. There to help you face it."

"Poor Eva. Are you sure you wouldn't rather look for a new position in more predictable circumstances? Something safer? I don't know, lion tamer? Snake charmer? Perhaps something to do with dynamite? Any of those would be less dangerous than looking after me, I should think."

Eva laughed. "No, my lady, I'm afraid you can't be rid of me that easily. Now then, I see a certain gentleman who looks as though he'd like to have a word with you." She gestured, and Phoebe turned to see Owen standing just outside the deckhouse.

Their gazes connected, and she was struck with conflicting impulses. "I don't want to leave you alone."

"Then I'll make it easy for you. I'm going inside to check on the rest of the family." With a parting smile, Eva walked toward Owen. He opened the door for her, and she ducked inside. Then he came to stand beside Phoebe at the railing.

"How is Hetta doing?" Phoebe asked him. Julia and her maid had been reunited after Detective Inspector Lewis dismissed them last night, and poor Hetta had been pleading ever since, in her very broken English, for Julia to forgive her. No one was really quite sure what she felt guilty about, other than keeping her knowledge of English to herself these past months, but if anything, Julia thought it rather clever of her.

"Calming down. I believe your sister has finally convinced her she won't be sacked." He drew up closer beside her until their shoulders touched. In daylight, in a public place, it was the most he could offer without starting tongues wagging. Word of the Renshaw family boarding the ferry had spread with remarkable speed earlier, and it wouldn't do to court gossip. "And how are you?"

"You needn't worry about me. I've grown used to this sort of thing." They shared a wry chuckle before Phoebe turned serious. "I'm worried about Julia, though. About when it suddenly occurs to her what might have happened on that boat with Curtis Mowbry. And when it hits her— truly hits her—that she's a widow. I don't know what her feelings for Gil were, but I do know she didn't take their marriage lightly. There's bound to be remorse and grieving."

"Yes. But you'll be there for her when she needs you."

Phoebe sighed, the only reply she could make to this observation. She didn't know if Julia would ever need her, or admit to needing her. "And then there's the matter of the future. Whether Julia is . . ."

"With child," he murmured. "Poor Julia."

"Yes, for her this won't be over for weeks yet. And really, depending on how things turn out, it might never *be* over." She sighed. "I should go back inside. My family needs me."

As they turned away from the railing, Owen raised her hand to his lips, a proper gesture, should anyone be watching. No one but Phoebe would detect the prolonged contact of his kiss, or the lingering warmth that filled her as they made their way back inside to her family, or the sure message he'd conveyed to her that he, too, needed her.

As England recovers from its costly involvement in the Great War, Lady Phoebe Renshaw and her lady's maid, Eva Huntford, find the steady comforts of their lives unsettled by a local case of murder . . .

Eva is excited for a visit from her sister Alice, who lives in Suffolk with her husband and three children. But when Alice arrives alone, desiring a break from her family, Eva becomes concerned. Her dismay deepens as Alice starts spending time with a former beau, Keenan Ripley, who owns the nearby pear orchard. At the same time, Phoebe's sister Julia, now a widow and pregnant, is in a fretful state, and Phoebe struggles to be helpful to her.

When Keenan's brother Stephen, the new head gardener at the Renshaw estate, Foxwood Hall, is found impaled by a pair of hedge clippers, the police—including Eva's beau, Constable Miles Brannock—suspect his closest kin. Stephen had been eager to sell their orchard to an American developer, but Keenan had fiercely resisted. A table set with two teacups and scones suggests Keenan had company the morning of the murder—and Eva fears her sister was with him.

If Alice were to provide Keenan with an alibi, her reputation and marriage would be ruined. She denies being there but is clearly withholding secrets, much to Eva's consternation. Now, to protect her sister, Eva and Phoebe set off to expose the gardener's real killer, putting their own lives at risk.

Please turn the page for an exciting sneak peek of Alyssa Maxwell's next Lady and Lady's Maid mystery A SILENT STABBING coming soon wherever print and e-books are sold!

CHAPTER 1

The Cotswolds, September 1920

Her arms full of fresh-cut flowers, Eva Huntford entered her parents' kitchen and yet again caught her mother studying her reflection in the window above the cast-iron sink. Eva went to the scrubbed pine table and set down the bundle of feverfew, primroses, and violets she'd snipped from the front garden. Soon the flowers bordering the house would be gone as brisk fall winds chased the last of summer away.

"Do stop fussing, Mum," she said with a tolerant smile and a shake of her head. "You look lovely." She meant it. Her mother's health had taken a turn for the worse during the last year of the war and had remained a concern for Eva until recently. Now, the color had returned to her cheeks and she no longer huffed with every physical effort or wheezed to catch her breath. At fifty-four Betty Huntford might no longer be a young woman, but surely she still had many good years left, not to mention three grandchildren on whom she doted. "Besides, it's only Alice and the children coming."

"Just the children, you say." Her mother turned and leaned her back against the edge of the sink. "It's been months and months since they've seen me. What if they think their poor grandmum is getting old?"

Eva stifled a chuckle. "They're three, five, and seven." The oldest had been born right before the war; the other two, during, the result of Oliver's rare trips home on leave. "They think *I* look old. Besides, all they care about is getting a warm hug from their grandmum, being told how big they've gotten, and sitting down to an extralarge piece of your lardy cake."

She sniffed the warm, spicy scents rising from the oven. Her mum's lardy cake, made with freshly rendered lard, plenty of sugar, currants, and raisins, was the best Eva had ever tasted, and that included Mrs. Ellison's at Foxwood Hall. It was a trifle expensive, of course, and Mum only made it for special occasions. "Smells wonderful."

"To tell you truly, Evie, I didn't expect this visit, it came so out of the blue when Alice wrote to say they were coming. It's left me the tiniest bit addled, having to get the house ready for them on such short notice." Mum cast a nervous glance at the old coal-fired range, cast iron like the sink, but black rather than white. The house dated to the early decades of the last century, and the range had been set into the cavernous hearth that had once served for cooking meals. "They should be here any minute. Provided, that is, Old Bessie doesn't break down again. I do wish your father would spend the money on a new truck."

"Even if he had the money, he wouldn't spend it on a new truck, Mum. Not while Old Bessie still has a breath left in her."

"Yes, yes, that's true. I'll just . . . I'll set the table. Oh, and I'll put those flowers in a vase. You go keep watch for them."

Eva didn't argue. If setting the table and seeing that

every little detail was just so helped her mother expend some energy and feel less jittery, then Eva would leave her to it. In the parlor, she took up position by the front window that overlooked the road. Across the way, the poplar trees flanking the Pittmans' farmhouse were already glowing brightly gold, while the oak beside the Huntfords' barn retained most of its summer green, tipped only here and there in licks of flame.

The dry autumn air intensified the blue of the sky and the sharpness of the sunlight, making her squint a bit to see down the road. She did indeed hope Old Bessie, Dad's prewar motor wagon with its flatbed for hauling farm equipment, made it to the train depot and back. Poor Bessie had been making odd, grunting complaints lately that didn't bode well for her future.

"It was ever so good of Lady Phoebe to give you the day off," Mum called from the other room.

Eva nodded, though Mum couldn't see it. "It feels almost sinful not to be working on a Tuesday." Officially, she had time off only on Sunday afternoons, after church. But she happened to work as a lady's maid for a tolerant and thoughtful mistress, not to mention that Eva had helped Lady Phoebe's sister, Julia, now Lady Annondale, out of a particularly doleful situation earlier this year. Phoebe and the entire Renshaw family were only too happy to grant Eva the occasional favor, though she would never take advantage of their kindness.

Outside, movement caught her eye. There, down the road at the fork that led either west to the village of Little Barlow or north to the train depot, a little cloud of dust stirred in the air. A moment later Old Bessie's snub, rust-stained bonnet came into view. Soon, through the open windows, Eva could hear the truck's creaking and groaning and the *chug-chug* of her engine. "They're here, Mum!"

Although it must have been a tight squeeze to fit Dad, Alice, and three small children into the cab of the motor wagon, Eva was glad to see none of them rode in the bed. She always grimaced at the sight of local children riding in the back of open lorries. But then, Eva didn't believe any seat in a motorcar to be completely safe; they went too, too fast for her comfort, and all that jostling at high speeds couldn't possibly do a body any good.

Mum shuffled into the room, realized she held a dishrag in one hand and still wore her apron, and doubled back into the kitchen. When she appeared again she was smoothing her cotton frock—her second best—and patting stray brown hairs peppered with gray into place. Outside, Old Bessie puttered to a halt in front of the house and let out a hiss. Mum ran to open the front door, grabbing her shawl off the back of a chair on the way.

When Eva expected her to hurry across the threshold, her mother instead went still, rather like Old Bessie with her tires gone flat. Eva peered out the window to see into the truck; there, just inside the passenger door, was her sister's profile. Just then Alice turned, spotted Eva, and waved enthusiastically. She opened the door to hop out. Eva heard a sigh from her mother. "Mum, what's wrong?"

"Where are the children? Where are my Hannah, Lizzie, and Ollie Junior?"

Indeed. Three small children should have poured out the door after their mother, but there was no one left inside. Alice went round to the back of the wagon and slid out her overnight satchel. Dad joined her there and hefted her larger portmanteau. Together they came up the front path.

"Mum, Eva, it's so good to see you both," Alice cried. She smiled broadly. "It's so jolly to be home."

Before stepping outside, Mum cast Eva a look over her shoulder, and in that instant Eva saw her effort to bring her features under control, to hide her disappointment. Eva felt a sense of letdown, too. She had so looked forward to playing the indulgent auntie to her nephew and two little nieces. As her mother had said, it had been months and months since their visit at Christmas.

"Here she is, all safe and sound." Dad shifted the weight of the trunk in his arms, and Eva noticed that he, too, worked to keep his expression amiable.

"I didn't expect you to be here today, Eva," Alice said after Mum had embraced her, inspected her appearance from head to foot, and declared her "looking lovely though a smidgeon tired."

Alice and Eva hugged and then stepped back to admire each other. Alice, Eva's senior by three years, had their father's eyes and Mum's dark hair, as did Eva. And like Eva, Alice's features drew from both parents. People had always said the Huntford sisters looked very much alike, but Eva was taken slightly aback now to detect the beginnings of crow's-feet beside Alice's eyes and lines that spoke of weariness around her mouth. Those lines deepened to brackets as Alice grinned. "How spiffing of the Renshaws to let you out for the day. You must have them wrapped around your little finger. They say a good servant eventually becomes the master, and the master the servant."

"Do they? I've never heard that."

"Well, let's not all stand outside for the neighbors' entertainment." Their father led the way into the parlor. With a grunt, he set the suitcase down against the wall. Dad had trimmed his beard short for the summer and sported a bit more of a paunch between his suspenders than he had last winter, a result of Mum's talents as both a cook and a baker. He gave his stomach a pat now as he scented the aromas coming from the kitchen. With a sideways glance at his elder daughter, he said, "Little Ollie loves his lardy cake, doesn't he, Alice?"

When her sister didn't reply, Eva decided there was nothing for it but to ask the question quivering in the air between them. "Alice, why haven't you brought the children?"

"Yes, Alice." Mum closed the front door; turning, she clasped her hands at her waist. "Surely you didn't leave them in Suffolk with Oliver. How on earth is he to tend to them and the farm at the same time?"

"Don't be silly, Mum." Alice set down her overnight bag, collapsed on the sofa, and let out a weary sigh. "No, they're with their Ward grandparents, well looked after, I assure you."

Mum's frown etched deep lines across her brow. So much for concealing her true feelings. "You do realize they have grandparents right here who would have adored looking after them."

"Yes, but they have school now. Surely you didn't expect me to take them away from their lessons." Alice patted the cushion beside her, an invitation for Mum to join her. After bringing Alice's larger case into the room she and Eva had once shared, Dad lowered himself into his favorite easy chair. Eva crossed the room to lean against the mantel. "The truth is," her sister began, and sighed once more, "I needed a bit of a holiday. I've earned one. You remember how it can be sometimes, don't you, Mum?"

"I'm . . . not sure what you mean." Mum's forehead knotted more tightly. Dad tilted his head and narrowed his eyes as if perplexed by a difficult math problem.

"All the demands of children and husband and farm life." Alice held out her hands. "It's all so consuming sometimes. I just wanted . . . no, I *needed* some time to myself. And time with my family."

Mum's frown deepened still more. "How is Oliver? Is everything all right with . . . him?"

Eva guessed her mother's hesitation stemmed from her being about to ask if everything was all right with Alice *and* Oliver, meaning had they quarreled? Because that was exactly what Eva suspected.

"Oliver is just fine, Mum." Alice smoothed a nonexistent wrinkle from her skirt. "He's very busy now harvesting the wheat and barley."

"And he doesn't need your help?" Dad asked.

Alice looked up, her gaze shifting from parent to parent. "No. He's got day laborers."

"Oh. He can afford laborers? Isn't that a frightful strain on his profits?" Mum glanced over at Dad. "Why, your father almost never—"

"Do I smell lardy cake?" Alice made a show of lifting her nose into the air. She rose suddenly and hurried into the kitchen.

Her lips pursed, Mum gained her feet a good deal more slowly, with Dad rising and coming over to lend her a hand. "What in the world?" she whispered to him. Dad shrugged. "Time with her family? Her husband and children are her family. And she certainly didn't seem eager to answer our questions and put our minds at rest. Vincent, I'm worried about that girl. This isn't like her."

The oven door whined on its hinges. "Mmmm," Alice sang out with appreciation. "I'd say it's almost ready. Mum, have you any perry on hand?"

"In the pantry, luv," Mom called back, but her gaze never left her husband's.

"Is it Ripley's?" Alice's footsteps could be heard crossing the kitchen.

Her mother said impatiently, "Of course it is."

"Alice is no girl, that's certain," Dad murmured. "And

we've no cause to pry simply because she's come home for a visit. Maybe it's as she says—she needed a holiday."

"Yes, but *why?*" The conversation continued in hushed tones, giving Eva the impression her parents had forgotten she was still in the room. "I tell you, Vincent, there's something wrong. And I intend to find out what it is."

"Ah, here it is." Alice's muffled voice drifted from the pantry. "How has Keenan Ripley's yield been so far this year?"

No one answered the question about the local farmer whose family had long ago cultivated the species of pears that made Gloucestershire's unique cider, called perry. The Ripley perry was considered some of the Cotswolds' best. Even Eva, who only rarely drank spirits, was known to enjoy a pint on occasion.

"Would everyone like some?" Alice asked, her voice louder now as she apparently reentered the kitchen.

"Not for me, Alice," Mum said, her impatience once more conveyed by her rising voice, and Eva was certain her mother couldn't have cared less just then what she ate or drank. To her husband she whispered emphatically, "I'll soon know what's going on with that girl."

"Now, Betty . . ."

"No, I'm her mother, and I've a right to know when things aren't right with one of my children—" Mum's voice had begun to rise again, then suddenly choked off. A tide of red flooded her face, and her eyes filled, a sight that brought a sting to Eva's own eyes. Her mother's sudden wretchedness wasn't about Alice. It was about the one child she hadn't been able to help, to save. The child who had perhaps needed his mother, but he had been beyond her reach at the time. Eva's brother, Danny, who died in the war, whose body still lay in an unmarked grave in France . . .

The oven door again creaked open. "It looks ready," Alice called. "Shall I take it out?"

"I'm coming." With a last determined glance at Dad, Mum hurried into the other room. That left Eva and her father staring at each other. He looked apologetic and at a loss. Poor man, outnumbered by his womenfolk and often unable to puzzle out what were, for him, their mysterious ways. Eva blinked away the moisture in her eyes, went to him, and smiled up into his kindly face.

"Don't worry, Dad, I'm sure Alice is just fine. But if there *is* something wrong, I'll find out what it is, and I'll fix it."

The tables lining the stone walls of St. George's basement fairly groaned beneath their burdens, a circumstance that brought great satisfaction to Phoebe Renshaw. Her autumn charity drive for the Relief and Comfort of Veterans and Their Families, or the RCVF, had proved an unmitigated success, and by this time next week deliveries would be made to the wounded veterans of the Great War who resided in Gloucestershire, and to the families of those men who never returned.

"A job well done, my lady." Eva, Phoebe's personal maid, carried an armful of children's clothing, which she added to a pile on the nearest table. It was the fifth load she had carried down from the vestibule of the church above them in the past ten minutes. Eva had had the day off yesterday to welcome her sister, who was visiting their parents in Little Barlow, and it seemed she was determined to work twice as hard today to make up for it. Dearest Eva.

"The parish truly stepped forward this time, didn't they?" Phoebe continued scanning the goods piled high on each table. Besides clothing, there were linens and bedding, pots and pans, dishes and cutlery, tinned and jarred goods, sacks of flour, farming tools, and so much more. Toward the back of the room, two volunteers were sorting toiletries. Elaina Corbyn, the wife of a local sheep farmer, and Violet Hershel, the vicar's wife, spoke quietly together as they organized items and jotted down an inventory of goods.

Phoebe joined Eva at the children's clothing table and began separating boys' garments from girls'. "Now the real work begins," she said. "First the sorting and then the matching of donations to the requests we've received from the families who need our help."

"I'm happy to lend a hand, too, my lady." Eva's sister, Alice Ward, came down the steps from the sanctuary and set a box on the table marked *Cleaning Supplies*. A carton of Fels-Naptha soap peeped out over the edge of the corrugated cardboard container. Mrs. Ward so resembled Eva with her dark hair, trim figure, and small, even features, that often Phoebe had to look twice to know to whom she was speaking. Except that Eva, approaching thirty but not quite, still retained the bloom of youth, while time hung a bit more heavily on Alice Ward.

"I don't like to see you laboring during your holiday, Mrs. Ward," Phoebe told her with a laugh.

"This is pleasant work, Lady Phoebe. And with three children at home, I'm not used to sitting about all day."

Phoebe heard a little sigh from Eva. What was that about? Before she could ponder further, booted footsteps sounded on the stone stairs from outside. Two men made their way precariously down to the basement, one backward, the other facing front, carrying a large crate between them. A chilly draft from outside followed them down, prompting Phoebe to tighten her cardigan around her.

"Morning, Lady Phoebe," the one facing backward said.

"I've got pears for you. They're a little overripe for perry making, but perfectly edible, and there's no use in letting them rot. Make excellent pies and turnovers, I expect." Farmer and owner of a local brewery, Keenan Ripley continued taking small backward steps while his older brother, Stephen, guided him to a vacant spot on one of the tables. Unlike Eva and her sister, the brothers could not have looked more different. Keenan sported dusky red hair that curled over his collar, while Stephen's close-shorn locks were as pale and straight as straw. The brothers set down their load, and Keenan wiped a sleeve across his brow.

Phoebe went over to inspect the contents of the crate. An assortment of red, green, and gold pears met her gaze. "What do we have here?"

That they were pears was obvious, but Mr. Ripley knew her question involved specifics. "Some Barlands, Helen's Earlies, and Blakeney Reds, mostly."

"Are you sure you can spare all these, Mr. Ripley? There are a great many here." She couldn't help wondering if the fruit was truly unsuitable for brewing Gloucestershire's unique blend of pear cider, or if Keenan Ripley was in an exceedingly generous mood. She glanced up at both brothers and smiled. "Or should I say, Misters Ripley? I didn't know you'd returned to Little Barlow," she said to the elder brother, Stephen. Though she had been a young schoolgirl when he moved away from the village, Phoebe remembered him because he had worked at Foxwood Hall, assisting the head gardener, Alfred Peele. She remembered her grandfather once commenting that Stephen hadn't seemed at all interested in the family orchard, but would make a fine gardener someday. He had left a couple of years before the war started and hadn't been back since.

"Only just back, but you're right to address your concerns to my brother." Stephen Ripley shoved a pair of spectacles higher on his sunburned nose. "I've not joined him in the brewing business. In fact, Lady Phoebe, I'll be working at Foxwood Hall starting tomorrow."

"Will you? I didn't know." What came as a surprise wasn't so much the news that Stephen Ripley would be joining the staff at home, but that her grandfather hadn't informed her of the fact. With his heir, Phoebe's brother Fox, still a boy in his teen years, Grandfather had taken to confiding in Phoebe when it came to matters of estate business. He said she had a good head for figures and organization, and she considered it of no small consequence that he showed such confidence in her abilities. She couldn't help wondering why he had omitted to mention a new employee. But she carefully schooled her features not to show the slightest smidgeon of perplexity. "Will you be assisting Mr. Peele again?"

Stephen Ripley's self-satisfied grin revealed a row of well-formed if uneven teeth. "No, my lady. I'm going to be your new head gardener."

"Head gardener . . . ?" She trailed off, once again unwilling to reveal her thoughts. Alfred Peele had served in the capacity of head gardener at Foxwood Hall for nearly two decades. Yes, he was getting on, but the man still stood as straight as the hedges he kept trimmed to such perfection that, from a distance, they appeared to be solid walls of emerald and jade. Phoebe had heard no talk of him retiring—not so much as a wisp of a hint. And obviously Eva had heard nothing belowstairs, or she would have said something.

Then what had happened? She wouldn't ask Stephen Ripley. No, it wouldn't do to question the man directly, not when he had already reached an understanding with her grandfather. It wasn't her place. But she *would* ask Grampapa the moment she returned home.

From the corner of her eye she noticed Alice Ward hovering close by, and realized she might very well wish to chat with the brothers. Eva as well. All of them being of an age, they had grown up together, attended the village school right here in St. George's basement before the permanent school had been built next door, and before Eva had won her scholarship to attend the nearby Haverleigh School for Young Ladies.

But they would not exchange more than a few words until Phoebe moved away and busied herself elsewhere. For them to do otherwise would be considered impertinent. Oh, not to Phoebe—she never minded about such things. But the others had been raised to show deference to the Earl of Wroxly and his family, who had presided over the village and its surrounds these many generations.

"It's good to have you home, Mr. Ripley," she said to Stephen, and with a shift of her gaze, said to Keenan, "Thank you so much for the pears, Mr. Ripley. Your donation will bring a welcome as well as wholesome treat to many of our families who could not afford it otherwise."

She moved several tables away and began sorting kitchen gadgets: whisks, peelers, crimpers, mashers, et cetera. Meanwhile, the others did as she expected, with Mrs. Ward and Keenan Ripley appearing to become quickly reacquainted, and Eva and Stephen Ripley trading pleasantries. Mrs. Corbyn and Mrs. Hershel, older than the others, greeted the newcomers briefly but kept on working. Phoebe caught Eva's gaze and compressed her lips, and Eva nodded in the kind of comprehension they had become adept at over the past couple of years. With any luck, her lady's maid might unravel the mystery of Foxwood Hall's new head gardener.

Connect with Us

Visit us online at
KensingtonBooks.com
to read more from your favorite authors, see books
by series, view reading group guides, and more.

Join us on social media

for sneak peeks, chances to win books and prize packs,
and to share your thoughts with other readers.

facebook.com/kensingtonpublishing
twitter.com/kensingtonbooks

Tell us what you think!

To share your thoughts, submit a review,
or sign up for our eNewsletters, please visit:
KensingtonBooks.com/TellUs.